MURDER BOOK

MURDER BOOK

THOMAS PERRY

THE MYSTERIOUS PRESS
NEW YORK

MURDER BOOK

Mysterious Press
An Imprint of Penzler Publishers
58 Warren Street
New York, N.Y. 10007

Copyright © 2023 by Thomas Perry

First Mysterious Press edition

Interior design by Maria Fernandez

Library of Congress Control Number: 2022917394

ISBN: 978-1-61316-383-2
eBook ISBN: 978-1-61316-387-0

10 9 8 7 6 5 4 3 2 1

Printed in the United States of America
Distributed by W. W. Norton & Company

For Jo

1

Larson parked the car in the lot behind the Mini Market where there were no lights over the lot after closing, and he and Kirk got out and walked. The streets of Groomsburg were so quiet and deserted late on a weeknight that Larson thought he probably could have parked in the middle of the street and nobody would have noticed. That was an exaggeration, but the store windows along here had all been dark for hours. People in these old towns on the river all seemed to get up with the sun, and go to bed with it too. The stop light at the intersection ahead of them that blinked red in the daytime was blinking yellow now.

Their destination was just past the light, so it wouldn't be long. As they walked closer, he and Kirk scanned the area for signs of life, and saw nothing worth mentioning—no pedestrians, no headlights, nothing to worry about. They walked up to the electronics store, past the sign that said, "Computers, Phones, Warranty Repairs."

The big problem with electronics stores was that every last one of them had cameras recording everything that went on inside or outside. Larson and Kirk never paused or looked up, so there wouldn't be a recording of them peering into the shop or anything. They kept going past the window before they turned and went down the side of the building toward the back. They put on black face masks and Larson took out the roll of trash bags and peeled one off before they emerged and stepped toward the back door. Larson looked behind him and saw a car edged up to the rear of the building. What was that doing in the alley? But it wasn't a police car, it was empty, and not running, so he didn't let it distract him. He looked forward and saw Kirk standing under the first security camera pointing up at it.

Larson joined him, squatted and let Kirk, who was only about 160 pounds, climb up onto his shoulders. Larson stood and waited while Kirk slipped the trash bag over the camera and taped it closed with electrical tape. Then Larson carried Kirk to the next camera and stood still while Kirk put another bag over that camera and slid down to the pavement. Larson took out the crowbar, stuck the flat end into the space beside the metal door, and pried the door away from the jamb far enough to let Kirk push the blade of a screwdriver in to depress the lock's plunger and push the door inward.

As the door swung open, they were surprised to see lights on inside. They both slipped in and Larson quickly swung the door closed behind them, but it didn't seem to fit right anymore, probably because the door had gotten bent a little when he'd pried it aside. He saw a rubber doorstop on the floor, held the door shut, and jammed the doorstop under it with his foot.

He didn't expect to be in the store for long anyway. All they had been sent to accomplish was to smash the computers and phones that were there for repairs and mess the place up, and that wouldn't take much time. They were supposed to leave all the new computers and phones in the front alone. The bosses didn't want Donald Whelan to go bankrupt and stop earning money. They just wanted to show him who he was dealing with—people who could get to him, his store, his family anytime they wanted and make him hurt. Steel doors and locks wouldn't stop them.

Kirk was ahead of him, going through an open doorway into a larger space that was clearly a workshop. Larson followed him in, and then saw a spotless white table on each side of the next door, with a couple of stools under it. Above them and around the walls were sets of metal shelves with boxes that held cell phones, chargers, laptop computers, big-screen desk models, some with handwritten notes taped to them that looked like descriptions of computer problems, and bills that implied some of them were already fixed, waiting for somebody to pick them up and pay.

Kirk reached to the top shelf of the biggest set of metal shelves and stepped backward to pull it over. Boxes slid off shelves, dumping computers, phones, and parts onto the floor, and then the steel frame crashed down on top of them. Kirk looked back at Larson with a gleeful, delighted expression. Larson smiled too. Whelan would have to tell all those customers why he hadn't fixed their stuff. It would pass the fear to the others like an infection.

Suddenly the door between the two workbenches swung open, and an older man looked in, already staring in shock at the floor. Larson knew it had to be Donald Whelan confirming what he thought he'd heard. Whelan gaped when he saw Larson and Kirk, but he didn't shout or swear at them. He instantly pulled back and slammed the door behind him.

Kirk was after him in an instant like a dog after a squirrel, through the door and into the showroom. Larson was a few steps behind, and he saw Whelan crouch at the counter, reach under it, and pop back up to face Kirk holding a pistol. Kirk's eyes widened as he stopped short, but Larson kept coming. He swung the crowbar into Whelan's head, splitting his skull and sending a spray of blood across the counter and onto the white floor beyond.

⌐⊶

It was midafternoon and Harry Duncan was in the office in his apartment on Huron Street in North Center Chicago. From the window above his desk, he could look between two old gray stone buildings and see the North Branch of the Chicago River a bit over a block away. He was gathering the last notes and records of the investigation he had just finished and adding them to the case's fat loose-leaf notebook to be stored, when the desk phone rang. He picked it up. "Harry Duncan."

"Mr. Duncan, this is Lena Stratton in the office of Ellen Leicester. She asked me to call because she'd like to meet with you this week. Would you be available for that?"

It took Duncan enough time to consider it that he had to cover the delay by saying, "Let me just see when I'm free. When and where would she like to meet? Her office?"

"She'd like to meet you at the Atwood Restaurant on West Washington. If you could make it tomorrow after three, that would work."

Duncan realized his strongest response to the idea was curiosity, so he said, "I'm sorry, I'm busy tomorrow. Does she have any time today?"

"She could be available after six today, if that's better."

"I can do that. Let's say six-thirty. And you said the Atwood?"

"Yes. I'll make the reservation."

"Thank you," Duncan said, and hung up the phone. He couldn't help wondering if Lena Stratton knew who he was. Assistants eventually came to know just about everything about their bosses, which was one of the reasons why when his last one left he had never replaced her. He decided that this woman probably didn't know he and Ellen had once been married. To her Ellen was probably just US Attorney Ellen Leicester, and he was—what? Nobody. Ellen had been good at keeping a wall between what she knew and what others knew. He wondered what she wanted from him after all this time.

He finished the case record and stood the notebook upright on a shelf that held the last dozen, waiting for him to put them into storage when he got around to it. As he always did, he reminded himself to do it before the weight of them broke the shelf and dumped them on the floor. He had learned to call these notebooks "Murder Books" when he had worked Homicide. Too often these days that name wasn't inaccurate.

At six-thirty he walked up to the restaurant. It was all windows, right in the State Street shopping district, and he spotted her from a distance, sitting alone at a table for two, facing the back of the room. She had just turned forty-two on March 20th—there was no way he could erase his ex-wife's birthday and get that memory space back—and she still looked young. He stepped inside and she waved. As he walked toward her, he noted that she didn't smile.

He arrived and said, "Hello, Ellen. How are you?"

"Fine, Harry," she said. "Thank you for coming. She made a slight gesture to indicate the two coffee cups. "I assume you still take it with no sugar and a little bit of cream."

"Yes."

It was business. Her tone told him that, so he said, "What can I do for you?"

"Please sit down," she said. When he was seated across from her she said, "You know that I'm a US Attorney now, right?"

"Congratulations."

"Thank you. I'll try to give you the reason I called, as briefly as I can. Some disturbing trends have been emerging in the crime reports we've been getting lately. In the past year or so, there have been a number of career criminals showing up in unexpected places. The way this first came to me were reports that certain past offenders from this district began to disappear from here and turn up committing crimes in places like rural Indiana."

Duncan said, "What sorts of crimes?"

"Assaults and robberies by teams rather than individuals, extortion, and that sort of thing. There have been a few robberies that included murders. If it had been happening here, some of these crimes might not have made the TV news. It isn't that one crime is a big deal. But having a lot of them at once where there weren't any before might be. What we're noticing could be the very start of an organized crime syndicate."

"It's possible," Duncan said. "There's always somebody trying to be the next mafia."

"I've talked to a few colleagues inside Justice, trying to find people who might take something like this seriously. What I've found is that nobody else thinks it merits taking FBI agents away from espionage, homeland security, and financial crimes to look. Some people point out that we've got a huge backlog of criminal cases, as though I hadn't noticed. And so on. Everybody's got a reason not to do anything. And technically, most of this stuff should be the business of the state of Indiana, or at least the Indiana US Attorney's office."

"But you want to look into it."

"I can't see ignoring it," she said. "But I'll need more than a suspicion to launch a full-scale investigation, especially in another district. I think the solution is to have an outside expert take a look and either verify it or rule it out. It has to be done quietly. I looked at the private consultants and investigators who have been hired by the department in the past and kept on a short list. I saw your name."

"And you figured I must be on the skids by now and would be glad to take a job looking at muggings in East Jesus, Indiana."

"No. It's not like that at all. You should see the evaluations other prosecutors have given you." She lowered her voice. "The reason I'm asking you is that when I looked at the list of approved names, I saw yours. Our marriage didn't work, but it left me with all the knowledge I needed about you. I know you have the intelligence, the honesty, and the courage. I know from your record since those days that you have the experience. I don't really know those things about any of the others. This is also a job that's delicate. There are a lot of people who are very rigid about things like jurisdictions."

"I can imagine," he said.

"All I'm asking is that you go to some of the places where these things have been happening. It's a scouting mission by a well-respected consultant. You make your observations and write a report telling me it's something the government should investigate or it's not."

"I assume you know I get paid for this kind of thing."

"And you know the range of fees the Department pays," she said. "I've set your fee at the top level. It's not a gesture for old times' sake. I don't make any gifts of public funds. The record of your other services justifies it. And of course you can submit a claim for necessary expenses."

"Anybody know I'm your ex-husband?"

"I haven't mentioned to anyone I was doing this, let alone which consultant I want to contract. Ex-spouses are not relatives, you're not an employee, and I'm not your supervisor."

"True enough," he said.

"Look, Harry. I don't know what you feel about me after all these years, I suppose because you're too decent to say. If you don't want to help me with this, I'm in no position to blame you. But feelings aside, you also know me. I'm not lying to you about any of it."

"Fair enough," he said. "I'll take a look." He instantly felt a stab of regret. She'd had no right to bother him for any reason, let alone something like this. It wasn't even a smart plan. It was likely to alienate her colleagues and bosses and accomplish nothing. He considered saying, "On second thought, I take that back. This isn't for me." The words didn't come. Instead, he stood. "I've got to go. Email me the details and I'll start in a day or two."

⊙══╾⊙

A town slid into view as Harry Duncan drove around a curve in the road that ran beside the Ash River in Indiana. The river was a nearly opaque gray flow fifty to a hundred feet wide that meandered for eighty miles through flat farm country and second-growth woods. Duncan was fairly sure this town was the one that he had chosen as the place to start his assignment, but on maps these little towns were just dots along the water, and it was possible this one might be the wrong dot.

He had driven here from Chicago, which was the most recent of several cities where he had built his skills and reputation as a cop, and where he then became a private investigator and added to the number of people who would have liked to see him dead.

He was driving a boxy-shaped Toyota that he had bought in Illinois and driven straight from the dealer's lot to a custom shop, where they put in a bigger engine, and then removed every piece of shiny metal and all words, numbers, and logos, so the car would have been difficult to identify by name or to describe. His first act after heading into Indiana had been to install the set of Indiana license plates he had obtained through Ellen Leicester's office.

He wasn't exactly sure why he had agreed to take this assignment. His marriage to Ellen had lasted about three years. A divorce between two law students who had no children and virtually no money was quick and efficient, and then he'd left law school and driven to California. During the succeeding fifteen years they had never been in touch.

Since he had just finished a case, he'd had some time he hadn't yet agreed to devote to anything else, so he had given in to his curiosity about what she could want after all this time. He'd walked into the restaurant with the word "no" waiting on his tongue, but during the conversation he had delayed delivering it until he'd heard too much. He still wasn't sure why he had said he'd do it. She'd assured him this was going to be a simple, undemanding observation of a couple of small towns and a report. Maybe she was right.

Harry Duncan was exactly six feet tall with light brown hair and an athletic body that had sustained the sorts of scars incidental to a history of jobs that involved differences of opinion, but he could keep them unseen without much effort. Over the years he had become adept at making himself seem less formidable than he was so he could observe. The long drive had made him hungry, and he hoped the next town would have a good place to stop.

He drove the next two curves of the river and noticed a large one-story building with clapboard siding that identified it as antique situated in the middle of a vast parking lot with a tall lighted sign mounted above it that read, "The Elbow Room." It looked like a bar, and most bars served some kind of food.

There were a few cars parked around it, which he hoped meant it was open. He veered to the left and coasted across the lot into a parking space near the building, got out of his car, and walked inside the nearest entrance. He sat on a stool at the fifty-foot polished wooden bar and waited until the woman behind it came up to him and smiled. "What can I bring you, sir?" she said.

"Are you serving lunch?"

She smiled. "I'm sorry, sir. Lunch is eleven to one and it's now one-fifteen. You can have the same food, but we can't call it lunch." She reached under the bar and pushed a plastic-covered menu in front of him.

He looked at the menu. "Is the hamburger okay?"

"We've been assured that it's ground beef, made from an animal recently deceased. I'll be cooking it myself, so it will be safe to eat too."

"Then I'll chance it."

"I'll get it started. Before I come back you should think about what you want with it—lettuce, tomato, French fries, beer and what kind, onions and what kind." She went through a swinging door into the kitchen. About thirty seconds later she reappeared.

Harry Duncan confirmed his first impression, which was that he didn't want to stop talking to her, or even look away from her. She had long, straight, reddish-brown hair and green eyes that seemed constantly amused. Duncan had long ago become aware that the most beautiful sight on the planet was an adult female human being. This was a trait shared in some degree by every woman if she was watched by an astute observer, but this woman was striking. She was still smiling as she wrote down the rest of his order and offered him a local lager called "Ash River's Best." She set the brown bottle in front of him.

"I don't know," he said. "Have you seen the water in that river?"

"Drink a little of the beer. If you don't like it don't pay and I'll pretend to spill it." She took the bottle, twisted off the cap, and poured some into a tall pilsner glass.

He sipped it and admitted to himself it was very good, but to her he only held his right thumb up. She curtsied, as though accepting applause. Duncan ate his food while she opened a dishwasher under the bar, polished glasses with a clean white dish towel, and put them in an overhead rack. As he watched her work, he detected very small crow's feet at the corners of her eyes, and guessed she was probably just about his age. He would never see forty again, but his thirties were recent enough so he hadn't noticed any changes yet. She was better off, probably lied about her age and easily got away with it. He felt an urge to get her to talk so he could listen to her voice some more. "What's the name of this town?" he asked. "I didn't see a sign when I drove in."

"A guy clipped it on the turn one night and it flew into the river. We're all waiting for the new one to be delivered. The town is called Parkman's Elbow."

"Unusual."

"It's an old name. The first man here was named Lafayette Parkman. He built a thousand-acre farm along the water and named the river the Ash-Gray River. I guess it was because there was a Blue River and a White River already. Maybe Red was taken too. The name was gradually worn down to the Ash River. As you probably noticed, it meanders. Seventeen turns. People named the meander on Parkman's land Parkman's Elbow."

"I suppose that's why this bar is called The Elbow Room."

"Right."

"Is it a nice place to live?"

"That's probably one of those things we all ought to vote on. It's always been good enough for me." She looked at his empty plate. "Was the food all right?"

"It tasted very good, and I'm still healthy." He started to reach for his wallet.

"Don't get up. Finish your beer," she said. "I'll be back in a minute to give you your check. You can even have another beer if you don't get rowdy." She took his plates and disappeared into the kitchen again.

She was gone again for thirty seconds, and then came back in with her bill pad. She said, "Is your car the black one with no chrome on it?"

"Yes. Did I park in the wrong space?"

"There are two men outside checking out your car. I just thought you should know."

He said, "Thanks," and walked into the back hallway, past the men's room, and then out and around the back of the building. He looked in the parking lot and then up and down the nearby streets. There were no police cars parked on the lot, and no plain cars equipped with aftermarket devices like spotlights or extra electronics, so he knew the two men couldn't be cops.

He stepped to the corner of the building to look and saw a large man with a shaved head that was too small for his body so it seemed bullet-shaped. The man took a slim jim out of a small canvas tool bag, slipped it into the space between the driver's side door and the window, then gave it a tug to unlock his car door and swung it open. The man sat in the driver's seat, returned the slim jim to his tool bag, and brought his hand out holding a large screwdriver.

Duncan said, "I wouldn't pop the ignition lock if I were you."

The man looked up and a mischievous smile appeared on his face. He ducked his head to get out, stood up, and faced Duncan, now tapping the screwdriver on the palm of his other hand. "Why not?"

"It's my car, and I don't want it stolen."

"You've got that wrong. It's about to be towed by the transportation department. The plates are not new, but the car is, and the inspection sticker seems to be a fake. You can straighten it out at the department, pay the towing fee, and pick up your car after that. The fine for the fake sticker shouldn't be more than a thousand bucks, but you'll have to deal with the DMV to get a new registration."

"I'm guessing there's a way to get around all that?"

"Some people like to just pay their fines on the spot, if they have the cash with them. You could do that, but don't take time deciding. Once the car is up on the truck, they don't take it down."

"Since you're from the transportation department, I'd like to see your ID."

"It's in the tow truck. You can see it when they get here."

Duncan nodded. He took out his phone and took the man's picture, then pressed the video icon.

"Give me that phone," the man said, and started walking toward Duncan. He held the screwdriver low against the side of his leg, like a man in a knife fight.

The woman in the bar had said there were two men. As Duncan slipped his phone into his pants pocket he spun his head to look for the other man. The missing man was only a few steps away, walking quietly up behind him. The moment he saw Duncan's glance he started to reach behind his back, but then saw that the turn of Duncan's head had launched his friend toward Duncan, so he ran toward him too.

Duncan knew the one behind him was the more urgent danger, so he threw his left elbow back to catch the man between his nose and upper teeth, pulled him forward and jerked the man's shirt up to snatch the pistol out of the back of his belt, then brought it down hard on the back of its owner's head and then up again toward the chest of the man with the screwdriver.

The big man stopped short, put his hands in the air, and dropped the screwdriver.

Duncan said, "You are both under arrest on suspicion of impersonating a public official, attempted grand theft auto, soliciting a bribe, and assault with a deadly weapon. Get down on the pavement ten feet apart with your arms stretched out. If you don't comply, I'm perfectly happy to shoot you and then handcuff you so you I can keep track of you while you're bleeding out."

The two men obeyed.

"Bring your hands behind you and cross your wrists. I'm sure you know the position."

The two men followed his orders, and he took out of his jacket two sets of handcuffs and applied them to their wrists. "I'm going to search you. If there's something on you that can hurt me, tell me now."

The two men were silent.

He patted them down and found their wallets, glanced at their driver's licenses, and said, "Ray Barstow and Timothy Vance. Your licenses say you live in Chicago. Why would two guys like you turn up in another state shaking down people in a parking lot?"

They said nothing.

"It wouldn't be because there's a warrant for you in Illinois, would it?"

The big man said, "Are you even a cop? Let's see your badge."

"It's in the truck with your ID."

The other man said, "These cuffs are too tight."

Duncan said, "Be glad you have them. The cuffs mean I'll look bad if I shoot you. Get in the car. Remember to duck your head a little." He opened the back door of his car and held his hand on each man's head in turn to guide it in past the roof. Each of the rear doors had a ring welded to it, and a chain ran through them. He slipped it through both men's arms above the cuffs and secured it with a padlock. "One more word of advice," he said. "If you manage to kill me while I'm driving you in, make sure my body tips to the right so I don't drive into the river. You'll never get out in time."

Duncan started the car, drove out of the lot, and headed north along the river. "What are you two doing out here?" They said nothing. "You're both going to be charged with enough felonies just from the past fifteen minutes to put you away for years. I can make it worse, or I can forget a lot of things that make for longer sentences."

He took his phone out of his pants pocket, hid it under his road map on the passenger seat, and began recording. "We're going to know everything about you twenty minutes after the cell door closes on you, but I'd rather know what you're doing here. How did you even know about this town?"

"We heard there were jobs. We didn't have any."

"What was the job?" Duncan asked. "What do you do?"

"We were open."

"Who recruited you?"

"Where are you driving us?"

"100 North Senate Street, Indianapolis. That's the State Police."

"Jesus."

"It's for your own good. Would you rather be in a spotless first-rate place run by highly trained State Police officers or some remote village lockup that feeds you bologna sandwiches on white bread twice a day if they remember to? They know me in Indianapolis, and they'll take you off my hands without making you sit handcuffed to a bench for hours while they fill out forms."

2

It was four hours later when Duncan returned to the parking lot behind The Elbow Room. He walked in the rear door and went back to his seat at the bar. A minute later the woman who had been bartending when he had come in earlier walked up behind the bar and leaned back on her elbows on the narrow counter below the shelves of liquor bottles.

She said, "I saw you handcuffing those two guys who were checking out your car."

Duncan said, "Did you?"

"Yeah. It's not often I get to see one guy win a fight with two and then put handcuffs on them. How do you get to arrest people?"

"I was the one who ended up with the gun."

"Usually it takes a badge too. Where do you work? Are you a sheriff's deputy or state police?"

"I've been both of those. I'm working out of my car at the moment."

"Did you get fired or something?"

"A few times, but that isn't the reason why I'm working alone."

"What is?"

"Those two guys looking over my car wanted me to pay them a thousand dollars not to hot-wire it or tow it away. It turned out that they were wanted, and there were rewards for bringing them in adding up to thirty thousand dollars. Cops can't get reward money."

"You got thirty thousand?"

"So far. They might be wanted in other crimes that will come up when the report of their apprehension gets around to other states."

"Did you already get the check?"

"Yes. That was what took me so long to get back."

"Can I see it?"

"I deposited it as soon as I could. I don't like to have to hold on to a check for long, and it was an easy way to pick up some traveling cash."

"Good. You never did pay your lunch tab."

"That reminds me. You contributed to the detection and arrest of two dangerous felons. I think you should share part of the reward."

She laughed. "You can put my share in the jukebox if you'll pick a good song."

He took an envelope out of his inner coat pocket and placed it on the bar in front of her. "Three thousand dollars."

She looked shocked for a second and suspicious for another second, staring into his eyes. Then she put a fingernail in the opening of the envelope, lowered her head, and squinted into it. "Really? You're giving me that?"

"I'm just being fair."

"Did I forget to mention I wasn't stupid?"

"What's your name?"

"Renee."

"Okay, Renee. I swear to you I'm not trying to buy your affection or anything. Being a private investigator is a business, and when somebody helps me, I try to make sure that they know I'm grateful. If something else comes up I want them to consider doing it again."

"I'm sorry I insulted you. Just take the money back. Warning somebody shouldn't be something you take money for."

"Do you still have my bill for lunch?"

She turned toward the cash register and hit a key, and when the drawer opened, she took the little white slip out and set it in front of him. He took a twenty-dollar bill out of his pocket and handed it to her. She handed him his change, a dollar and thirty cents, and the envelope full of money.

"You know, when I went to turn those guys in to the state police, one of the cops mentioned that there seemed to have been a lot of other crimes happening around here. Is that true?"

"I can't say he was wrong," she said. "This area wasn't ever that way, but places change, sometimes not for the better. Lately there have been some worrisome things—tough-looking strangers coming around, some really nasty fights. There actually were a couple murders this year, one of them just about two weeks ago in Riverbend. You probably drove past the town to get here. There was another one a month or so before that in Groomsburg, in the other direction. Both were elderly men found in their businesses. It sounded like both times somebody broke in to rob the place, and they got in the way."

"Did the police arrest anybody yet?"

"Not that I know of. To tell you the truth, right now what I'm getting worried about is what happened to you this afternoon. Criminals in the parking lot trying to rob customers in midafternoon? That's a big deal for a bar."

"Yeah," he said. "It could be." He took a card out of his wallet and set it on the bar in front of her. "Please put this where you won't lose it. I'd appreciate a call if you notice anything else that worries you." He turned and walked toward the back door.

"Hey wait," she called. "You forgot your money."

"No I didn't." And then Duncan was out the door.

Duncan had been lying to Renee most of the time while they had been talking. He had never been fired from any of his law enforcement jobs. He had simply outgrown them, learned everything he could, and then left for a better one, usually in a different large city, where he might learn other things. The Indiana State Police had not said anything to him about an increase in crime in the Ash River area either. The suspicious rise in crime had been why he'd come here, the reason he'd been hired. He had not received a reward for bringing in the two shakedown artists. The money he'd given her had been part of the operating budget he'd taken from his bank when he'd left Chicago.

He had not anticipated that he would run into a pair of criminals within the first hour of his first day in sight of the Ash River. After he had captured them, the reason he'd taken them to the distant State Police headquarters was to avoid letting that obliterate his cover. The fact that Renee had seen the fight had presented a serious problem. He had told her he was a private investigator—and he was, with a real license—and handed her his business card, but he could just as easily have handed her one of the cards that said he was a furniture company executive or a personal trainer or a real estate salesman. He was aware that she may have been lying to him too. She wouldn't be the first woman to give a stranger a false name.

But Renee had been his first contact in Parkman's Elbow, and she had been observant and responsible enough to tell him about the men showing suspicious interest in his car. She seemed smart, and also worked in a perfect position to know about things going on in the town. During his career he had learned a lot from bartenders. They served people alcohol, a chemical that made them more talkative and less guarded, more willing to reveal personal information, and made the ones who had something to hide worse at it. The fact that she was physically attractive must add greatly to her appeal to both male and female guests. He had been lucky to find her, but he had to be careful with her.

For the next three days, Duncan drove from one small town along the river to the next, studying each one and searching for familiar signs of criminal activity. In many cities where he'd worked, houses that had been fitted with metal doors and bars on the windows were a sign of drug dealing. Adult women on the streets at night who weren't in a hurry to get somewhere were often working for traffickers. When more than one man rode in the same car on a route that seemed aimless, they might be casing buildings for burglary or armed robbery. Any building where there were lots of cars coming and going after midnight could be the scene of any combination of crimes.

He stayed in a Stop Inn chain hotel in Riverbend, which had a bar so he could watch and listen to people talking to the bartender, ate breakfast and lunch in diners up and down the river where he could overhear conversations at other tables, put on a friendly smile when he was in public, and talked to anyone who seemed receptive. Whenever he got into a friendly conversation that went past the weather and into the subject of the town and the region, he would try to get a sense of what people were feeling about crime, particularly the two recent murders. He drank in bars and restaurants in the evenings, but found no bar that seemed as promising as The Elbow Room. When he drove past in the evening, it had more cars parked in its big lot, and was livelier than the others. It seemed to be the place lots of locals preferred.

For a few evenings he drove by at different hours, sometimes parking down the road out of sight of the building but able to watch people coming and going at the lot's entrance. And then one afternoon, at about the time of day when he had first gone in, he pulled up to The Elbow Room, went inside, and sat at the bar.

After a minute Renee came out of the kitchen and saw him. "You fooled me. I thought you'd be back here sooner."

"Why? Did you miss me?"

"No. Actually, I just wanted my expectation confirmed. You're lucky. I haven't taken time out to spend your money yet. If you'll wait a few minutes, I'll get it out of the safe for you, and you can be on your way."

"No, thanks. It's yours."

She stopped and looked at him, her expression suspicious. "What are you doing here?"

"I came back for another hamburger."

She picked up a pad of order sheets, set it down in front of him, and wrote. "Rare? Medium rare? Medium?"

"Medium. Dill pickle slices, sauteed onion, lettuce, tomato. French fries. A salad. A bottle of Ash River's Best."

"Cheese on your burger?"

"No."

"Why not?"

"I have no objection to cheese, but not this time."

In a few minutes she was back with the plated food on a tray, set the tray down to unload it, and stood back against the counter beneath the wall of liquor bottles. "I've got to tell you, if I don't have any interest in you—and I don't—money doesn't change that at all."

"I understand," he said. "I don't have time for a girlfriend anyway. The hamburger is good." He took another bite.

She said, "Thank you." She began to wipe down the bar away from him with a cloth, walking along behind it and polishing it vigorously. Finally, after she reached the distant end, she walked casually in his direction, looked down at his plates as she passed, said "Everything still okay?" and when he nodded, continued to polish the other stretch of bar beyond him.

After he finished the food, she piled the plates on the tray and took it into the kitchen. She came back, opened the refrigerator under the bar, took out two bottles of Ash River's Best, and held up one of them toward him. "Want another one?"

He looked at the big mirror behind the liquor bottles to verify that the big room was empty except for a couple of busboys setting tables near the front, and said, "Sure."

She twisted off the tops of the two bottles, set one down beside his glass, and reached up to the rack above her, took a glass, poured the other bottle into it, and took a sip. "How long are you planning on staying around here?"

"Until my curiosity is satisfied, I suppose."

"Curiosity about what?"

"The town. The people. A person like you has probably got so much to tell me that it might be enough to get rid of me."

She gave a little laugh and took another sip from her glass. "I'll try. Parkman's Elbow kind of limits you. Not many people become geniuses because the school doesn't have the sort of faculty who can teach that. People don't have a lot of money because the only thing you can do to get big money is let a conglomerate buy your family's farm, and the last two generations sold about all of them already."

"Do the young people move away?"

"Not many. There's a kind of lethargy to some small towns. Parkman's Elbow is the kind of place where a lot of people who are born here never go anywhere else to live and never learn anything after age fifteen. The best-looking young women graduate and marry the boy in their high school class who's most conceited and assumes if he asks them to, they'll say yes. They do. After the woman realizes that wasn't a good idea, she divorces him and goes to live with the other classmate she cheated on him with. That's why there are twenty-three-year-old women with three kids by different men, and ones who have slept with everybody by age thirty-five."

"Is this you?"

"No, I'm just setting the scene for you. I could talk about my own marriage for longer than it lasted, but that would only make me depressed and you bored. Or I can say it didn't work out and be done with it."

"I'm okay with that," Duncan said. "I didn't mean to pry."

"Yes you did. You ever marry?"

"Yes. Not much joy left in that story either."

"I would like it if you would make an exception and tell me the truth about the money you gave me. You didn't get paid thirty thousand dollars for taking in those two guys, did you?"

"Yes and no. Governments don't cut a check instantly. The two guys will have to be charged and returned to other places. One of them disappeared near the end of his murder trial and the other will be put back in prison for a violation of his parole from an old sentence for armed robbery. The State Police will have to file to say I brought them in, and the state authorities in Illinois approve payment. It happens, but it all usually takes at least a year."

"So why did you give me that share?"

"Nobody wants to be thanked a year later."

"You have a point." She lifted her glass to him and took another sip, like a toast. "I'll try to spend it in one place. Thanks."

"You're welcome. You know, I've been thinking about that day. Those two guys couldn't have been waiting here for me. I'd never been in this area before, and stopped at this bar because I happened to see it when I was driving by. You might want to think about that, and watch for something else to come up."

"There hasn't been anything else at The Elbow Room. A few faces nobody had seen before, but none of them did anything except drink, like everybody else."

"Do you still have my card?"

"I don't remember throwing it out, so I must."

He set one on the bar. "Here's another one."

She picked it up. "Thanks." She looked at her watch. "Ooh. We've got to get ready for the after-work happy hour people. Thanks again for the money."

He said, "You know my name. It's on my card, but I only know your first name. What's your last name?"

"Parkman."

She took her glass to the sink and poured the beer out, and kept going past the end of the bar and turned right, where she disappeared. He left a twenty-dollar bill on the bar under his empty glass and went out the back door to his car.

3

The Elbow Room was a much livelier place in late afternoon than it had been during the after-lunch lull. He spotted Renee behind the bar wearing a long black apron with the belt pulled around her waist and tied in front in a bow. He watched her tip an aluminum beer keg onto its side, roll it along the floor to its spot with her foot, tip it back onto its end, insert the tap, pump the siphon's handle, feather the spigot to release excess gas and foam into a pitcher, then pour it down the sink and close the cabinet.

She looked up and saw Duncan staring at her.

He said, "Very impressive."

"I learned something in college after all," she said.

Duncan moved on and looked at the customers coming into the big room. There were small groups at about half the tables, and Duncan noted each of the people who caught Renee's eye or waved to her as they came in. If he saw them shake hands with or hug any of the waiters or waitresses, he noted that too. Something was going on around here. He hadn't forgotten that the two career crooks he had turned in to the state police had been loitering outside this building. If the bar heated up during the evening, he would not waste eye time on the people who were already on Renee's side.

Duncan began to survey the rest of the crowd, looking for people whose faces showed either strategic watchfulness or habitual expressions that made him suspicious. He noted a couple of those too, but drew no conclusions about them.

He had not yet decided what Renee was up to. She showed every sign of knowing quite a bit about the world. When he had been younger, he had assumed that women who were so physically attractive probably saw only the nice things the world offered, and not the cruel ones, but since he'd spent time as a cop it had seemed that something approaching the opposite was truer. The only advantage he had seen for them was that more men were interested in them. To a professional expert in human troubles, that didn't appear to be entirely an advantage.

Now that he had greater respect for her mental acuity, he knew he should beware. Very little human behavior, bad or good, was not premeditated, and he didn't know what she wanted, or who she really was.

He was as much a stranger here as the criminals were, but he believed he had accidentally made contact with a woman who was a popular, maybe even important, local native. He had instantly known he should try to strengthen their connection, but there was something in her personality that repelled him. Her casual air of superiority, her assumption that he, and probably every man, had a strong interest in seducing her were tiresome. He had ulterior motives for talking to her, and he assumed she had hidden motives also.

He watched her move along the bar and hug the woman she seemed to be replacing as bartender. He watched her interactions with people who stood at the bar to order drinks, and others who took to barstools and stayed. Duncan added a few people to his mental gallery of friendly regulars for the next hour so he could ignore them if the time came. Soon a man arrived to help tend bar and another woman arrived to wait on tables.

Duncan studied whatever he could—the flow of the crowd as the people who had a drink before or after having dinner at The Elbow Room were slowly replaced by the real drinkers.

After a few more minutes the young waitress taking drink orders came to his table. Her smile was friendly.

"I'm Madeleine. What are you drinking?"

"A glass of tonic with a slice of lemon."

"What alcohol?"

"None, please."

"You're not being scouted for the Olympics or on duty with the Secret Service, or about to fly an airliner to New York, are you?"

"Nope. I just don't want to be easy for women to tempt."

"That's smart. Even I can't be trusted, and I have to work for six more hours."

"Thanks."

When Duncan had his drink, he stood and walked out the door to the parking lot. He surveyed the lot, watching the cars coming in and their occupants walking to the entrance.

His eyes caught three men in their late thirties to late forties getting out of a pearlized white SUV in the lot. In a moment they were inside, striding single file up the aisle toward the bar. His eye was accustomed to settling on men like this as ones to watch. They were tall and had arms with the sort of knotty muscles a man acquired by doing pull-ups on a cell door rather than swimming and playing tennis. Two of the three had noses that had been broken at some point. Looking at them closely convinced Duncan that they were probably relatives. Their ages made them likely either cousins or brothers.

He estimated that given the number of people already waiting at the bar for drinks, he had time to take a quick look at their vehicle. He went to his own car, opened the trunk, and took out the slim jim he had taken from the man who had used it on his car, along with a large tube of epoxy cement he brought on car trips. He walked to the white SUV, looked around him to be sure nobody was watching, slid the slim jim between the driver's door and the side window, felt for the lock mechanism, tugged upward, and popped the lock. He opened the door and turned off the interior lights.

In a second, he was sitting in the car. He opened the console between the front seats and found a Sig Sauer 9 mm pistol. Under the driver's seat was a Kimber .45 pistol, and under the passenger seat a Glock 9 mm pistol. He reached to the dashboard and pressed the button to open the rear hatch, and hurried to look inside. Under a thick rubber mat he found three identical AR-15 style rifles in a row.

He took out his tube of cement and squeezed some into the three rifles' muzzles and some onto the upper receivers, and then pressed the mat down on them. Then he glued the Sig Sauer onto the side window beside the rear seat, and the .45 to the top of the dashboard. For the Glock pistol he ran a stripe along the top of the steering wheel on the side that faced the windshield, and pressed the pistol against it for thirty seconds to be sure the cement had set. As a last touch he switched off the dome lights, opened the four doors, and ran a stripe of cement along the place where each door lock would grasp the bar on the chassis. He left each of them open just enough so the two parts didn't touch.

Duncan returned the slim jim and epoxy cement to his car trunk and then walked back into The Elbow Room, already scanning to locate the three men. They were just behind three women sitting at the bar, and he could see that they were talking to them. After a moment the three women all got up and stepped away. Duncan could tell that whatever the men had said had upset them.

The three men sat in the women's seats at the bar, and Duncan watched Renee notice them and approach. "What can I get you, gentlemen?" she asked. The one who seemed to be the oldest and had led them in said, "We'll all have the free welcome introductory special."

She grinned. "I'm afraid there is no free special. This establishment strictly adheres to the rules of the world. The bar has to buy liquor and glasses, refrigeration, air conditioning in summer, and heat the rest of the time. We charge good prices, but we do charge. Knowing that, what would you like?"

"All right, three double shots of Laphroaig single malt scotch with a Budweiser chaser."

She beckoned to Mick, the tall curly-haired waiter, and repeated their order.

The same man said, "You're not going to make our drinks yourself?"

"Sorry," Renee said as Mick took the bottle off the upper shelf and reached up for the glasses. "I see some other customers who need my personal touch."

"We don't want the drinks if you don't make them."

"Anybody can pour a shot in a glass and set a beer beside it as well as anybody else."

The man leaned forward on his elbows, and his two companions seemed to crouch to get closer to hear. "Listen carefully, honey. We came here to have you buy us a drink so we can be comfortable and welcome while we explain to you the way this establishment is going to operate in the future."

She said, "Is this really going to be that kind of pitch?"

"It's not a pitch. It's an easy and simple business plan, both to understand and to operate. We will pay all necessary fees and provide one hundred percent of the services to keep this restaurant and tavern safe from fire, robbery, vandalism, and other contingencies. Your only contribution to overhead will be three hundred dollars per night and five percent of gross receipts. It could hardly be better."

"Did you tell me your name? I don't think I heard it."

"Clark," he said.

"Mr. Clark," Renee said. "I've listened carefully to your proposal. You were right that it's simple and easy to understand. In fact, it's very familiar. We will not be accepting your offer. It's extortion."

Duncan stepped forward so he was right behind the men. "Hi, Renee," he said. "Can you get me a draft beer, please?"

She smiled. "Sure, Harry." She walked down toward the taps, at least fifteen feet from the three men, where he wanted her.

One of the three men turned to look at Duncan. "Did she send you out to call the police?"

"Men's room. Why would I need police? I used to be in law enforcement myself."

"Get scared or get fired?"

"Neither. I just take breaks between careers now and then to study and explore."

"Study and explore what?"

"Lots of things," Duncan said. "Painting, music, foreign languages, photography—"

"Renee looks glad to see you. If you've got a thing going with her, tell her to pay right away or the prices all go up."

Duncan seemed not to hear him. "—piano, Brazilian Jiu-jitsu," he continued.

The older man took the last swig of his scotch, lifted the short, heavy glass, and pulled back preparing to hurl it at the shelves of liquor bottles.

Duncan's arm suddenly coiled around the man's head, dragged him off the barstool, and dropped him on his back.

One of the man's companions stepped toward Duncan, but Duncan seemed to have seen the next move forming in the man's mind. As the man threw a punch, Duncan grasped his wrist and redirected it into the wooden bar. The third man made it off his barstool and tried to throw his shoulder into Duncan to tackle him, but Duncan sidestepped, grasped the man's arm, and spun to the side, simply adding to his momentum so his head continued an extra six inches into the bar.

He said, "Gentlemen, don't try to leave. I lied about not calling the police. They'll be here in a few minutes, and they're going to want to talk with you when they arrive."

Duncan walked close to Mick and Renee by the taps and whispered, "Keep them in sight, but don't do anything to stop them unless they try to hurt somebody on their way out."

"What am I supposed to do then?" Mick asked.

He saw Renee's eyes move to watch something behind him. "Too late."

He turned in time to watch the three hurrying toward the front door. "A good start," he said, and took his time walking to the front window to watch them leave.

They were looking at him over their shoulders at that moment. Jerry Clark, the older man who had done the talking inside, reached his car. He flung the driver's side door open, and experienced a momentary disruption of his thoughts. The door hadn't been latched. But the interior lights weren't lit, and that man Harry was coming after them, maybe to get the license number and maybe for something worse, so he sat in the driver's seat, yelled "Get in!" to his brothers, and slammed his door shut.

Dennis, the middle brother, got into the passenger seat beside him and slammed his door. The third brother, Steve, did the same at the right rear door. Jerry made the engine roar into life and backed up all the way across the parking lot as fast as his car would go, then stopped at an aisle. As he looked ahead and shifted into Drive, he saw that the pistol he had left under the seat was now attached to the back of the steering wheel. He reached over the steering wheel to grasp it and found that it was firmly glued in place. If he drove straight, the pistol was aimed across his brother Dennis's chest, and if he turned the wheel to the right his pistol was aimed at his brother Dennis's legs. He began to zigzag the car in the parking lot toward the river road to see if a shot could hit Dennis if the gun went off.

Dennis was engaged in straining to pull his pistol, the Kimber .45, off the dashboard, and he was leaning forward to do it, so Jerry realized his steering wheel gun probably could hit Dennis. "What the hell is this?" Dennis shouted.

"It looks like somebody super-glued the guns to the car," Steve shouted. "Mine's glued in the middle of the back window. We'd better get home fast. If a cop sees us, he'll see the guns too and pull us over."

Just as Steve finished his announcement, Dennis's sweaty right hand slipped on the immovable pistol's oiled steel surface and his finger raked the trigger. The pistol gave a deafening discharge and punched a hole through the right side of the windshield.

Jerry roared, "Sweet Jesus!" and the car lurched forward, sending all three brothers backward against their seats. For a few breathless seconds the car rocked from side to side onto the river road while Jerry tried to restore control without touching the other pistol. At the same time all three joined in shouting a stream of blasphemous and obscene exclamations.

At last Jerry managed to apply the brake pedal effectively enough to bring the car to a stop just outside the edge of the pavement on the weedy left side of the road instead of the right, where it could have slid into the opaque waters of the Ash River.

Jerry was shaken, possessed by the urge to stand on solid earth, pumped his door handle, and realized it had no effect. "They glued the goddamned door shut too!" he shouted.

From the back seat, Steve said, "Come on, Jerry. Get us the hell out of here."

Jerry's rage grew. He yelled, "I am!" which was a lie, and tried to make it true.

As the car drove off, it was still distantly visible from the Elbow Room parking lot, because it had only begun one loop of the meandering river, so it disappeared and then reappeared. Harry Duncan watched it turn and disappear once more.

Renee said, "You should never have done that."

"Which?"

"Any of it," she said. "It's weird and crazy. Don't you own a gun?"

4

When Duncan got up in his hotel in Groomsburg the next morning, he showered, dressed, and considered which diner to select for breakfast. He chose Anna's Home Cookery in Parkman's Elbow in the hope that what had happened the previous night might spur some discussion he would like to overhear. The things going on seemed to be low-level criminality of a familiar type—shakedowns and selling protection. The three men had seemed to be trying to make themselves feared, so his response had been to make them look ridiculous and weak. He wanted to know how it was working.

He drove to the diner, ate, and listened. He heard a couple talking about the party they had gone to the previous night, when the hostess had "thrown herself at" the husband, this time more blatantly than ever. The husband seemed to be amused by the suggestion, which made the wife furious, and when he implied that she was imagining it, she made the suggestion that next time he should go alone. The other conversations were about the opening week of baseball season, the early clearing of ice in the river this year, somebody's kidney problems, and somebody else's leukemia diagnosis. Duncan's breakfast was a failure, but the food was good, so when Duncan left, he felt that his time hadn't been entirely wasted.

As he walked down the street toward his car, he saw that there was a police car parked behind it. Duncan was an expert on the ways crime groups operated and the ways they established themselves. He had noticed that wherever they appeared, it was essential that they find ways of corrupting the local police, so when he agreed to take on these preliminary scouting visits to infected areas, he usually stayed away from the police until he had made a decision about them.

Duncan stepped up to his car, pressed the fob in his pocket, and got in. The mirror showed him that a young cop was getting out of the police car and walking up to his window. Duncan rolled his window down and put his hands on the steering wheel, where they could be seen.

"Good morning," the cop said. He leaned down and smiled. "May I see your license, please?"

"Sure," Duncan said. "It's in my wallet. I'll get it out." He did, and handed it to the cop.

The cop looked at it, then looked at Duncan's face, then handed it back. "Mr. Duncan?"

"Yes."

"I thought that was who you must be, from the description we got of your car," he said. "If you have a few minutes, I'd like to talk to you."

Duncan read the name plate on his uniform. "All right, Officer Slater. Do you want to talk here, or at the station?"

"The station might be best," Officer Slater said. "You can follow me there."

Duncan's impression was inconclusive. It was possible Slater was trying to reassure him that the whole matter was minor, and then have him jumped at the station, beaten up, and locked in a cell, or see if Duncan would take a turn and try to escape, which was a crime; or he was just being friendly. Duncan followed the police cruiser to the police station, a red brick one-story building, and parked near Slater. Then he followed Officer Slater across a lobby that led to a blond wood counter with a gate in the center, then into an open bay with a few desks, and finally to a room with the number 1 on the door that Duncan knew was probably the only interrogation room. He waited while Slater went to another room for a moment, where Duncan knew he must be turning on the video recorder, then went inside with him and sat down across the table so he faced the camera mounted high in the upper corner of the room.

"You seem to know the routine. Have you been arrested a few times?"

"No," Duncan said. "I've done some police work over the years."

"Really? Whereabouts?"

"First six years in Los Angeles, five in Denver, a bit longer with the Illinois State Police."

Officer Slater said, "Since you're a retired law enforcement officer, maybe we can get right at this. Can you state your full name, please?"

Duncan did.

Slater looked at his watch. "And today is March twenty-third at eight-eleven. You were at The Elbow Room last evening. What time?"

"I got there around five. I hung around through the cocktail hour and then dinner. The diners gradually left, and they were replaced around nine by the drinkers."

"Did you meet these three men?" He laid out three photographs on the table.

"Yes, I did," Duncan said. "I'd say it was around ten, ten-thirty, but I'm sure the security cameras in the bar show them. They came in single file through the front door. I was curious, so I came closer when Renee the bartender came to serve them. I heard the oldest one—this one here—make a demand for free drinks. She said no. Then he announced to her that she was going to pay him for protection. It was three hundred dollars a night plus a percentage of the gross receipts of five percent. She said it was extortion and turned him down. One of them tried to throw his glass at the mirror. I dissuaded him, moved them away from Renee, and told them not to leave the bar."

"You told them not to leave?"

"Yes. I said the police were going to want to speak with them. Since they were there to show they were lawless and tough, I figured they would leave. And they did. I stayed at the bar until after midnight, and went to my hotel and slept."

Officer Slater studied Duncan, his face unreadable. "These three men are named Clark. This is Jerry, this is Dennis, and this is Steve. They live about thirty miles upriver in a town called Riverbend. They had a close call last night on their way home."

"Really?" Duncan said. "What kind?"

"They claim that you assaulted them in the bar and that after they got into their car and slammed the doors, they found they were super-glued shut. They also found that some unregistered firearms had been glued into their car—on the steering wheel, the dashboard, and the rear window.

"They were speeding on the river road when they passed Officer Damon's speed trap up near the billboard on the way out of town just past the railroad overpass. It looked to Officer Damon like the driver had a pistol gripped in his left hand while he was driving. The reason he was speeding was because he wanted to get home before somebody noticed the guns.

"Officer Damon noticed, turned on his lights and siren, and called for backup while he went after them. No intelligible response. If anything, the car went faster. After ten years on the force, it's still hard for me to imagine what a man thinks when he decides not to pull over for a law enforcement vehicle, particularly one obviously there to catch speeders. I still don't have a clue. Especially way out here he isn't going to outrun the police. His car isn't any faster or newer, he's not a better driver, he doesn't know the roads as well. The cop can drive all night and then call for a state police helicopter and a roadblock."

"It's still a mystery to me too," Duncan said. "Some people seem to have trouble thinking more than a minute or two ahead."

"This time they just had three patrol units wait for the car to go around the bend at the Florian Street loop. The car came around and stopped, pretty much blinded by headlights and spotlights while officers approached from both sides with guns drawn. It looked to most of the officers like the suspects were holding pistols, and when the officer told them to toss their guns out, they did not comply. At that moment they were about as near death as a healthy man can be. Fortunately, Officer Damon was still behind them, and he could see in his headlights that they didn't actually have hands on weapons anymore. He stepped right up, hammered out the side window, and asked them what was up."

"May I ask where these three men are now?"

"I expect they'll be released at around four-thirty after the court adjourns and the judge puts them on the schedule. There's the firearms issue, the speeding and reckless driving issue, the refusal to stop for Officer Damon, and probably some incidentals. They claim you assaulted all three of them, and you claim they tried to pull extortion on the owner of The Elbow Room. I don't know if you want to press charges."

"That would be up to Miss Parkman. She was the one they were asking for money and giving the ugly hints to. I can guarantee I'll testify that it happened if she wants to pursue it."

"I'll tell her that."

"Right now, you've got me thinking about her problems. Why is she the target of an extortion attempt? Does that happen to a lot of people around here?"

"So far I'd say that she would be a victim of good luck. It's a rarer kind of luck than the other kind, but it exists."

"Really?"

"Since you know her last name, you probably can guess. She's the current Parkman."

Duncan nodded. "That's the reason?"

"Correct me if I'm wrong," Slater said. "The average criminal is not usually a deep thinker. If he learns there's a person whose name alone tells him they own things, and if the person is a single woman, that person becomes a target. I can guess with some confidence that the Clark brothers were surprised there was somebody like you in the picture last night. Did you assault the three of them?"

"I'm sure the security cameras in the bar will show exactly what happened. I was about to usher them out of the bar when one tried to throw a glass, and two of them tried to attack me. If I'm charged with something, I'll plead not guilty. Anything else we should talk about?"

"No, I think that will do it. Thanks for taking the time to talk to me." He gathered the three mug shots and put them into a file folder.

5

The Riverbank Restaurant had twenty-five tables that were two inches thick and had been polished daily for so many years that at lunchtime when one section was not covered with white linen tablecloths it was possible to see the reflection of the front windows on them and read upside-down images of signs across the river. There were more tables on the deck extending over the water that had been made to look like a wharf with thick pilings and metal cleats and coiled ropes.

Harry Duncan walked into the interior and up to the lectern where a woman in her sixties verified his reservation in a leather notebook and took him to a table near the big windows overlooking the river. He sat in the seat that gave him the best view of the end of the restaurant that led to the hallway with the office, the kitchen, and the loading areas.

He made a mental note to see whether he could find out where this restaurant and the others rented their linens and who picked up their garbage, which had often been side businesses of organized crime crews. He also decided that he should try to find out whether any of them were supplementing their liquor supplies with cases that might have been taken from the back of a truck in another state.

He had only been seated for a minute when he looked up and saw something that made him curious. A blond woman in her thirties appeared from somewhere in the direction of the working spaces—the bar and the kitchen—talked with the older woman, and looked down at the reservation book, then scanned the dining room, as though she was looking for someone she knew. Then she was walking up the aisle toward him, making no attempt to hide the fact that she was looking at him.

She walked up to his table and stopped. "Hi, Mr. Duncan," she said. "I wanted to welcome you to our restaurant. You haven't been here before, and I hope you'll like your lunch. My name is Mona Durand." She set a menu on the table where he would be able to reach it.

"Thank you," he said. "You're the owner, aren't you?"

Mona smiled and shook her head. "Not exactly. It's a family business. My father keeps retiring and coming back two months later, like he forgot to stay home. My mother too, to handle the front of the house. It's always just to get us through the holidays, or the summer tourist season or something."

He said, "I read online that this was the best restaurant around here."

"That's nice," Mona said. "Renee Parkman is an old friend, and she told me a little bit about the bad experiences you had at The Elbow Room. I guess you made an impression on her guests, so when I saw your reservation, I thought I should say hello."

Since she was facing him, her back was to the restaurant entrance. Duncan could see a man about thirty-five years old, wearing blue jeans with a sport coat and black boots with the tops hidden by the jeans. He was standing near the corridor to the office with his arms folded, watching Mona and looking displeased.

Mona turned her head to see what Duncan was looking at, and her eyes widened and her back seemed to stiffen. "Well, I'd better get people seated for lunch or they'll go to the second-best place." She gave a little laugh and hurried away toward the front.

Duncan watched her go to the man, but she didn't hand him a menu or conduct him to a table. She simply paused in front of him and then walked with him into the corridor that Duncan judged must lead to the kitchen and whatever office there was. Duncan considered the possibilities and eliminated several. He was too young to be her father, too old to be her husband, and she hadn't been wearing a ring. She had implied he was a customer, but she hadn't been treating him like one. In fact, she had seemed startled to see him. She had gracefully covered it, but to Duncan she looked as though she was afraid.

Duncan ordered a salad and a lunch entrée of fresh trout with sautéed spinach, and dessert of mixed berries. His days of eavesdropping in diners and restaurants and evenings spent studying drinkers in bars had not been the healthiest diet, and this was a welcome change.

6

For thousands of years the meanders of the Ash River had kept extending wider and wider until they had formed places like Parkman's Elbow, where the river turned right around and came back within a few hundred feet of meeting itself.

Duncan sat in his car on the bank of the river a hundred yards from Renee Parkman's house just at sunset. He knew Renee would be at The Elbow Room getting into the last part of happy hour and making the nearly invisible transition to cocktails and the first phase of dinner. He was sure he could have sat on the broad front porch of her big old white house, and nobody would have noticed him until she closed the bar at 2:00 A.M. and came home.

He turned toward the river and looked across. The river at that point was deep and narrow, but there was a small, flat margin of mud along the far side with two great blue herons and three bitterns wading there and the flock of barn swallows Duncan had seen flitting overhead snatching bugs out of the air on the day he had arrived.

Today he'd seen that Mona Durand had a nice restaurant, with a substantial building on a waterside location, a surprisingly skilled chef, and enough customers, even at lunchtime, to keep it running. Renee Parkman had a hundred-and-twenty-year-old tavern that was still the popular bar. Even though they were ten miles apart it was not hard to see them as competitors. It was also pretty easy to see the two as great victims for extortion. The predators were circling The Elbow Room, and at lunch he'd seen signs that the crooks already had a foothold in the Riverbend Restaurant.

He waited until the sun was down and the light was fading, got into his car, drove it out onto the river road, waited there for a few seconds while some cars drove past, then swung the car around to face the other direction and pulled up just past a big old tree at the edge of Renee's large front yard. He got out, opened the trunk, and lifted out a thick, heavy chain and a canvas tool bag. He put them deep in the shrubbery near the tree, and covered them with leaves. Then he stood up, got back into his car, and drove to a grocery store in Parkman's Elbow to buy packaged snacks and coffee, and then to the hotel in Groomsburg where he had stayed the previous night, and set an alarm for 11:00 P.M.

Experience told him that the Clark brothers would be enraged at him and at Renee for their humiliation last night. The fact that neither he nor Renee had been afraid of them hurt their pride, and Duncan had pushed them around in front of a bar full of locals and glued them into their car. That had put them in danger of being shot for not surrendering to the cops. He believed they would come tonight, but not arrive at Renee's house until a bit after midnight. Twelve was the earliest starting time for sneak attacks, because that was the time when potential witnesses began disappearing into their homes and beds. The Clarks might strike much later, but they would not be there earlier.

They would want revenge, but they also had a practical motive, which was to terrify Renee into paying them a cut of her profits. It was either that or kill her. If they couldn't do that much, their extortion business around here would collapse. They could instead trash or burn The Elbow Room, but if they did, there wouldn't be profits for anyone.

He fell asleep, slept for almost four hours, and woke to the alarm on his cell phone at eleven.

He put on black pants, a dark long-sleeved shirt, and a dark baseball cap. He brought gloves and a black mask that he could pull up to his eyes if the time came, and a Glock 17 9 mm pistol, because it was the sidearm he had carried during a police career that had lasted enough years to make him an expert with it.

He drove back to Renee Parkman's house along the river, parked around the bend in the road in a grove of trees, took out of his trunk an old olive drab army blanket, covered the car with a dark gray protective cover designed for people who had no garages, and walked back until he was across the road from Renee's house, went down below the level of the road to the riverbank, lay on the blanket, and waited.

At a few minutes after three A.M. he saw two men walking toward the back of the Parkman house across what must once have been a cultivated field. They walked along at a steady pace, each using a flashlight to keep from stepping into an unseen hole or tripping over something. He watched their progress for a few minutes, as their lights came closer and closer to the big old white house. And then both lights went out.

It seemed to Duncan that the sudden darkness must mean they were close enough to be on more recently cultivated ground, where they could be fairly sure the way ahead was clear and level. But after a few seconds he heard the sound of an engine, and then the whisper of tires on pavement. Turning the lights off must have been a signal. After a moment, headlights illuminated the pavement and a car came around the bend along the river road. It was moving slowly, as though the driver was being careful not to attract attention.

Just before the car reached the border of the Parkman property the car's lights went black, and then the car stopped. It turned and pulled off the river road onto the edge of the grass of Renee's front yard.

Duncan crouched as he eased himself down close to the water where he was below ground level. He stood and moved along the edge of the water silently. When he had gone around the curve beyond the place where the newly arrived car had parked, he climbed up out of the riverbed. He listened, looked in both directions for the glow of headlights, saw none, and then stayed low, crossed the road, and stopped there.

Duncan made his way along the curve, staying close to the bushes and underbrush, moving in among them when he could. He was advancing toward the big old tree where he'd stopped before, and when he came to the curve he went to his belly. In a couple yards he felt the hard links of the chain under the leaves he had spread here. The canvas tool bag was just a foot inland from the chain. He reached inside and took out a couple thick, heavy padlocks, a shop rag, and a shackle. He wrapped the heavy chain around the tree's trunk twice and secured it with one of the padlocks.

Duncan cautiously stuck his head out from behind the tree and studied the dark silhouette of the man in the driver's seat. After a few seconds his eyes had separated the head from the headrest and verified that the man was looking at Renee's house, and not into his rearview mirror. Duncan slithered forward, dragging the chain behind him on the ground. It seemed to him to be taking too much time, but he forced himself to be patient, and then he was under the car. He wrapped the shop rag around the rear axle and then lifted the chain, gripping two links to place the chain over the axle gently and silently, and then wrapped it around without sliding it. He let it dangle and then put the shackle through two links, inserted the bolt to hold it there, and screwed the nut so it would be secure. He held it so the heavy lock hung free while he clicked it shut on two more of the chain's links.

He waited for half a minute and listened until he was sure he hadn't been heard. Then he slithered back the way he had come. As he went, he spread wet leaves from the big tree over the chain to hide it. He didn't rise to his feet until he was around the curve behind the car, so he could cross the road without being seen and go back down into the riverbed.

He walked along the river until he reached the place across from the Parkman house. He climbed up the bank and slipped under the army blanket to watch.

In a moment Duncan saw flashlight beams reappear, and the lawn behind the house was bathed in light. The two Clarks had arrived.

The driver of the car that had parked on the edge of the front lawn saw the lights also. Duncan heard him start his engine. The car sat in neutral, idling while the man waited.

The flashlights went out, and Duncan saw the dark silhouettes of the two men from the field reappear beside the house. They reached the front, and one of the men struck a windproof cigarette lighter. In the bright, flapping flame, Duncan could see the two men were each carrying a 1.75 liter liquor bottle with a handle and a white rag stuffed down through the neck into a liquid inside. The two men lit the rags.

That seemed to be the signal for the driver. He shifted the transmission of his car and stomped on the gas pedal, intending to drive up across the lawn to the front of the house as soon as it was ablaze and evacuate the two men who were lighting the rags. The car began to accelerate, dragging the heavy chain. As the car sped forward, the sixty feet of chain got used up. The chain straightened, rose up from the ground under the leaves, and became taut. The shackle and padlocks held and the car shot forward while the chain tore the rear axle off the car, bringing with it both wheels.

The car scraped along the lawn gouging a trench in it and then stopping short of the house when its momentum was used up. The next thing that happened was the first hint of something no human being knew—that the tree to which Duncan had attached the chain to had been invisibly weakened by a disease called Sudden Oak Death. It toppled toward the grounded car.

The crash of the heavy tree to the ground came at the moment when both of the arsonists who had been planning to firebomb the Parkman house's front porch with their Molotov cocktails had lit the gasoline-soaked rags.

The noise, light, and surprise of the car's destruction startled the two arsonists just as they were about to hurl their firebombs onto the wooden porch and against the front door. The two arsonists could see that their getaway car, a brand-new Cadillac SUV registered to their brother Dennis, was now an immovable wreck that, for the next few hours at least, would have the same address as the historic Parkman house.

To make things worse, each of the two men held an oversize liquor bottle filled with gasoline and a long but unpredictable wick which, at this moment, was flaming brightly an arm's length from his face. At any second this space was going to turn into hell.

Jerry, the oldest brother, had been thinking hard for more years than the others, so he made his decision first. He spun away from the Parkman house, took two running steps, and launched his Molotov cocktail in a high arc at his brother Dennis's wrecked car. Steve, the youngest brother, recognized Jerry's decision as the only possible way out. He was younger, faster, and stronger, but he had started his throw later, so the flame of his wick reached the inside of the bottle while it was in the air, ignited, and arrived on the hood of Dennis's Cadillac as a shower of broken glass and liquid fire.

Throwing the bottles at the car had ended the two brothers' concern that they were holding bottles of accelerants that were about to explode. The act also prevented some problems that would have been caused by throwing firebombs at a house inhabited by a woman who was charging them with extortion, and having no getaway vehicle for an escape. It might even give them a chance to hire an attorney who would contend that they had only come to a spot along the river to burn their brother's unsatisfactory new car as a protest. And if the fire managed to reach the gas tank, the car might be so wrapped in fire that it would take the police days to sort out what had happened. Jerry was actually smiling by now.

For Dennis, the owner and driver of the car, the decision of where to throw the firebombs was less satisfactory. At that moment, Dennis was sitting in a seat tilted about fifteen degrees and looking up into the dark sky while fire and glass rained down on the windshield of his recently purchased and newly wrecked car. He didn't understand it. The only thing that he thought could be happening was that his own brothers had been plotting to use this occasion to murder him and split his share of their criminal gains.

He felt the sting of hurt feelings burning hotter into rage. He pressed the buckle of his seatbelt, felt the strap across his chest go loose, flung open his car door, and dived over a stream of flaming gasoline that had sprayed past the car from the second bottle and was cooking the door. He rolled on the grass a few times to put out the flames that flapped from the sleeve of his sport coat.

As soon as his arm was safe, he used it to reach into his inner coat pocket to extract his old Smith & Wesson revolver, the only sidearm he had left that wasn't glued into his brother Jerry's car. Right now, that state of affairs seemed different from the way it had the night before. He suspected the one who had done the gluing was Jerry, trying to leave Dennis defenseless.

"You bastards!" he shouted, fired a shot in his brothers' direction, then another, and ran from the car into the dark shelter of the shrubs near the place where he had parked. It was a well-timed maneuver, because the dry branches of the tree that the car had toppled onto itself had just become part of the fire, and nothing good was going to occur after that.

7

The two police cars swerved to a stop at the Parkman house and Officer Slater and Sergeant Griggs got out and hurried up to the front porch. Griggs had his pistol in his hand, but he carried it pointed at the ground with his index finger outside the trigger guard. He was not an angry or violent man, but he could see something was up, and he knew it was something he wasn't going to tolerate. He raised his large left fist and pounded on the door, and then he sniffed his knuckles. "Gasoline. The whole place smells like gas." He put his pistol back in its holster.

He and Officer Slater heard the fire engines' sirens wailing along the darkened streets of Parkman's Elbow toward the river road. Even though the Parkman house was on the river on a large open plot of land that used to be a farm, it was in the central part of the town that locals called "the Elbow Proper," the part enclosed on two sides by the river's meander. The original house built by Lafayette Parkman had consisted of a smaller structure made of logs and mortar, last seen and photographed in 1891. The porch the two police officers were standing on had been built over and around the first one, when the house was enlarged and covered with clapboards early in the last century. Griggs was beginning to feel hopeful that he was not going to preside over the building's disappearance in a blaze tonight. The only things burning were a car and a fallen tree.

The door swung open and there stood Renee Parkman, alive and unhurt.

Griggs said, "Any criminals still around?"

"No," she said.

Griggs holstered his weapon. "Everybody here okay?"

"Yes, I am," she said. "Thanks for asking." At that moment Harry Duncan came up onto the porch.

"Who are you?" Griggs asked.

"I know him," Renee said. She caught something disturbing in Griggs's expression. "Not very well."

"His name is Harry Duncan," Slater said.

Griggs turned to Slater. "You might have mentioned him."

"He's the one the Clark brothers were complaining about."

"Pleased to meet you, Sergeant," said Duncan.

Renee looked past Griggs and stepped down the porch steps toward the burning car just as the pumper truck arrived with a half-dozen firefighters in helmets and turnout coats. Two of them ran from their perches on the side of the truck with a big hose and dragged it into the river. Two others unrolled a different hose with a heavy brass nozzle on it and the driver started the truck's water pump.

Another firefighter carried a large chemical extinguisher to the burning vehicle and shot white foam through a hose with a nozzle like a black horn, frosting the SUV like a cake to deprive the gasoline fire of oxygen. The men who had brought the water hose from the pumper truck directed a strong stream of water over the tree that had fallen on the burning car.

Renee, Duncan, Griggs, and Slater all stood and stared, wide-eyed as children. After a minute, Griggs said, "What the hell is that all about?"

Renee said, "I think they came to burn me up in my house, but it didn't work out for them."

Griggs accepted that for the moment and said to Slater, "Can you get pictures of the front and rear, and then if you can read the tag numbers, run them?"

Slater stepped down from the porch, walked to a few feet away from the now-smoking car, took a few pictures with his phone, and then turned on his hand radio and read his phone screen as he talked. Then he sent a photo to the police license plate reader system. After a few more seconds he walked to join Griggs. "Dennis Clark of Riverbend, Indiana."

"Familiar name."

"That's right," Slater said. "I believe he's the middle brother."

Griggs turned to Renee. "Can you tell us what his car is doing at your house?"

"Burning."

"I can see that."

Duncan said, "This visit was apparently part of the attempt to commit extortion against Ms. Parkman over The Elbow Room. They were angry when she refused to give them money and said no."

"Did you have anything to do with the anger?"

"I kept one of them from throwing a glass, and when the others tried to attack me, I discouraged them."

"I see. And now tonight. Can you explain any of this?"

"It occurred to me that Ms. Parkman was likely to be the object of their anger. The Clark brothers seemed to be the sort who didn't feel a discussion was over until the other person had surrendered or died. So I decided to come by her house and have a look."

"At what?"

"I saw two men with flashlights walking across the field to the back of the house, and then that SUV pulled up at the edge of the lawn. I went up behind it and chained it to a large tree so that it wouldn't be used as a getaway car if there was trouble."

"What happened?"

"I saw the two men who had walked to the house light a pair of Molotov cocktails. The driver started his engine and began to accelerate up the lawn toward the house so that he'd be there to pick them up and drive off."

"Okay," said Griggs. "I see the axle. And I see the tug didn't do the tree any good either. You have anything to do with the fire?"

"No. The two men at the house both had already lit the wicks of their Molotov cocktails before the axle went. They couldn't hold onto them. Their only getaway vehicle had just been destroyed. If they threw their firebombs at the house, they would probably get caught on foot and arrested for arson, and maybe attempted murder. The safest target to throw them at was their own disabled car—or their brother's. That was stupid and humiliating, but it was not a life-changing felony."

Griggs turned to Renee. "Does all that sound like what you saw?"

She shrugged. "I was asleep until the car-and-tree thing, but I don't know anything different. I didn't invite Mr. Duncan, and didn't ever ask him for help."

Duncan said, "She doesn't even like me very much. I just couldn't let those three kill her."

Griggs said, "You made a good guess. Where would you guess they are now?"

8

Duncan sat in his car on the dark street in Riverbend and watched the police climb the steps at Dennis Clark's house. They heard Griggs's voice. "Mr. Clark, this is Sergeant Griggs, Parkman's Elbow Police Department. You left a vehicle burning in my city this morning. I would like to speak with you about that. We are accompanied by officers of the Riverbend PD. In practical terms, if you turn the lights on, open the door, and come out, you will be happier than you will be if you don't."

The police waited and looked at each other for about twenty seconds. Then one of the Riverbend officers walked down the driveway, opened the trunk of his patrol car, and came back with a compact, heavy metal battering ram. As he reached the foot of the steps the door opened, but the man who came out onto the porch was Steve Clark, the youngest brother. Officer Slater asked him some questions, but it was impossible for Duncan to hear the conversation from so far away. He could see that while Slater was listening to the answers, he was reaching for the handcuffs on his belt with one hand and Steve's arm with the other.

Sergeant Griggs stepped inside and brought out Jerry Clark, handcuffing him as he came. Then one of the Riverbend cops went in and came out gripping the arm of Dennis Clark. Duncan could see that Dennis had a rope around his wrists, up behind his back, and around his neck, so he couldn't move much without choking himself. It looked to Duncan as though Dennis's brothers had needed to capture him to keep him from shooting them.

As soon as the three men were all in the back seats of police cars Duncan started his engine and drove. He turned the next corner, waited a minute, and then came back in the opposite direction toward his latest hotel.

When he was inside his room, he made sure the blackout curtains hadn't moved enough to let any annoying shafts of sunlight invade his long-delayed sleep, showered, and went to sleep. Six hours later he woke up and looked at his phone. There was a text message from Renee Parkman.

"I got your number from your business card. I didn't get a chance to thank you for saving my life. Thank you." The message was marked 4:57 A.M. It was now nearly one P.M.

He texted back, "You're welcome," and then shaved and dressed. He drove to a Target store he had seen in Riverbend and browsed in the stationery area. He bought a pack of five flash drives, four identical loose-leaf notebooks, high-quality printer paper, two cartridges for the small printer he had brought to Indiana in the trunk of his car, and a three-hole punch. While he was checking out at the register, the young male cashier said, "I see you have a kid in school."

Duncan said, "I don't have a kid. I'm going to try going back to learn all the things I missed."

He paid for his purchases and got out before he had to answer any more questions. That night he began building his murder book.

He already had names, photographs, and copies of the crime complaints for the two men he'd taken to the state police in Indianapolis, crime scene reports from the two killings of businessmen in the Ash River region that had helped cause his hiring, and notes and photographs he'd taken of the fire attack on the Parkman house. He began adding any information that he could find online—press reports of the recent series of crimes in the area.

He used public tax records and collected the names of owners of stores, restaurants, hotels, apartment buildings, car lots, insurance and real estate brokerages. He kept this kind of information filed in his laptop, using it to give him a sense of the place. His years of experience with organized crime groups had taught him to study the areas they hoped to control. What was there in the Ash River region to steal?

At eight P.M. he received a second text message from Renee Parkman. It was the one he had expected, but earlier than he had expected. It said, "I would like to talk. Can you come to the bar?"

He texted, "Yes."

At ten he drove to The Elbow Room, parked, and walked in the rear door, then came forward to the barroom. Renee saw him immediately, beckoned to one of the waiters, leaned over the bar, and said something to him. Then she lifted the hinged section up and held it so he could slip past her to get behind the bar and take her place.

She walked up to Duncan and said, "Do you want a drink to take with you while we talk?"

"No, thanks," he said. "I don't think I'll be here long enough to drink it."

She pivoted and led him along the bar to the corridor at the end of it, took out a set of keys, unlocked a door, stepped in, and switched on a light. Duncan saw they were in the bar's storeroom. There were metal beer kegs lined up along one wall, cases of liquor and wine stacked five-deep covering most of the floor, smaller cartons containing glass jars of olives or onions, small bottles of bitters, boxes of toothpicks and stirrers on wall shelves, a couple crates of lemons and oranges, a big double-door refrigerator, and a separate freezer.

Renee went to the liquor area, sat on a two-case stack, and pointed toward another stack a few feet away across an aisle. Duncan sat down and waited.

"Why are you watching me?" she said.

"I'm not surprised it seems that way. I happened to be in your bar when those two crooks decided I was their next victim. You warned me, so I came back to give you a share of my reward and see what you knew about what was going on here. The night when those three guys—the Clark brothers—hit you up for their protection racket, I decided the way to help was to make them look stupid in front of a lot of people. When I found out the next day from the local police that they were going to be released from custody, I knew they'd try to come after you. I decided not to let them hurt you."

"I was there to see all of this. Why me?"

"When I drove into town, I had no idea you or your bar existed."

"I can buy that. And you came back with your ridiculous reward story because you thought it would make me friendly.

Not flattering, but the impulse was familiar. I told you I'm not interested. So why did you protect me?"

"I told you the truth. I happened to figure out what they would be up to, so I prevented it—the only responsible thing to do. That's all. No ulterior motives."

"You seem to do a lot of things that are illegal. Are you a criminal?"

"No. I'm an extra-legal."

"Now we're getting somewhere—to another obfuscation."

"Before you get obsessed and start investigating me, I'll just tell you. I'm an outside consultant for nondelegated issues."

"Where did you get this nonsense?"

"I refer you to the Tenth Amendment of the Constitution of the United States. 'The powers not delegated to the United States, nor prohibited by it to the States, are reserved to the States respectively, or to the people.'"

"What's any of that got to do with you?"

"There are issues that the federal government needs to look into, but which were not delegated to it by the states. If a ranking official sent the FBI to look into it, that would be an obvious overstepping of the law, in addition to pissing off powerful people representing this state in Washington. I, as a special consultant for nondelegated issues, sometimes get hired to take a look around."

"It sounds crooked."

"Better than crooked. I'm an independent contractor, which means I'm not a payroll entry, I'm an operating expense, like pencils and paperclips. It's hard to find the cost I represent, so it can be taken from anywhere in the whole budget. It's not paid, it's spent."

"You want me to believe that you're here on behalf of our country, investigating for the government. What are you being paid to look into?"

"Recently, something has seemed to be happening in the middle of the country. For a long time, there was a fairly stable population of familiar criminals. No more. The Mafia has been on the skids for thirty years, since most of the leaders got sentenced to hundreds of years in prison. The current drug cartels deliver here through middlemen, so they can keep living on a beach somewhere warm. This is something else."

"What is it?"

"I don't know yet. The part I've seen is independent professional criminals leaving Chicago and appearing in places like this. Somebody seems to be recruiting them, and promising something better than what they have where they've been."

"And your assignment is to do what?"

"Just to observe and report. This job is really just a scouting mission."

"You said you're an independent contractor. How do you get hired?"

"I've had a few law enforcement jobs. There are still some people in government who know me. When one of these touchy problems pops up, I might get a call, or somebody else might. This time they want to know if we have a problem in Indiana. If so, what is it?"

"Why didn't they just send an FBI agent?"

"I'm deniable, an agent isn't. My being here is not going to be a bitter jurisdictional dispute. I don't have jurisdiction anywhere. I'm just a former cop with a private investigator's license, here to take a look."

"What's going to happen next?"

"The Clarks are going to be in jail until they get charged and bail is posted. I think they're done bothering you. The combination of extortion and attempted murder, arson, or whatever the DA decides to call it could mean a lot of jail time. And when the cops can search their house, there will probably be more charges."

"I meant are you through spying on me?"

"The simple answer is yes. What's next is nothing. You live your life, and I go on with what I came for and go away. You don't tell anybody anything about me."

"It's a deal," she said. "I'd better get back to work." She got up, unlocked the storeroom door, and held it open so he could leave, then turned off the light, stepped out, and locked the door. Once Duncan was out, he kept going and didn't look back.

9

Gerald Russell sat at a small round table in the office he'd rented in Indianapolis. He was fifty-six years old, with a tall, thin frame that he bent over in a slouch. At the moment, his long arms and legs were folded over each other, so he appeared to be clutching his torso.

The man on the phone call with him said, "The Clark brothers were arrested last night and they're all in jail. The middle one, Dennis, says the other two tried to kill him with Molotov cocktails, so they could blame his death on somebody else and then split his share of the money they've been saving."

Russell unfolded his long arms and legs, stood, stepped across his office, and slid the glass door closed. He was careful never to let himself speak freely when he might have a directional microphone pointed at him. He even pressed the sole of his shoe against the window to keep it from vibrating while he talked. He spent much of his energy keeping people from spying on him. He knew that the FBI's surveillance and wiretapping programs had helped to populate some prisons with people who had known enough to be quiet, but hadn't learned to keep up with technology. When this conversation was over, he would replace the phone.

He said, "This Renee Parkman who owns the bar, she did something to reduce them to this level of stupidity?"

"I don't think it was her. She's kind of a local character in the Ash River area, but it's not for anything like this. I'm sure you know the town is named after her family because one of them founded it. That's not power, and not much money."

"Then why is she a problem?"

"Looks, to start. From the time she was about ten, there were people laying bets on what year she would be Miss Indiana, I heard."

"What was the winning bet?"

"None. The family had pretensions, and wouldn't enter their daughter in a beauty contest any more than a mud-wrestling match. I heard she's a real bitch, she owns and runs the most popular bar in the area, and people like her. If she pays protection, a lot of the others will know there's no way to avoid it."

"Then we've got to fix this. What caused it?"

"Some things changed since we chose her. One thing is that she has a male friend."

"If people think she's the best-looking woman in the state, maybe somebody could have thought that might happen."

"Well, you know, a woman who could have any man but doesn't have one, some people assume is a lesbian. It doesn't seem to be true. The boyfriend is too much for the Clark brothers."

"What's his name?"

"He's told people it's Harry Duncan. There's no reason to assume that's true."

"Do you have some ideas about how to handle this?"

"I thought I'd call Rankin and ask him to put together a team."

"Hold off on that while I check with Chicago. I'll let you know what they say."

They both severed the phone connection and Russell sat at his desk. The Parkman project had been botched. The Clark brothers couldn't handle the work. There was no question that things had to change. He took the battery and SIM card out of his phone and stepped on it, turned on his new phone, and called the number he had been given.

When a male voice answered, he said, "Hi. It's me. The people who were supposed to bring in Renee Parkman need to be replaced. For the sake of security and secrecy I've decided to call in a professional specialist to remove and replace them." He added, "If there are no objections."

The voice on the other end said, "Go ahead," and then hung up.

Russell hung up and texted Mullins, "Make the call we discussed." Then he destroyed this telephone too, and activated the next one.

In a moment, he knew, Rankin would be getting his phone call. Russell couldn't help being excited. For Russell this was the gold rush phase. People were gathering now. The word had spread. The plan had been designed to leak, and bring people who wanted to be part of it.

Russell's power was mostly theoretical at this stage, but it could grow in minutes. Russell had instantly recognized the value of Mullins when he'd met him, and had made him his chief of staff and executive officer in the new organization, a permanent second-in-command in all that Russell intended to do. But he had to be careful. Russell had just called Chicago to take possession of Mullins's idea to call in Rankin to salvage the Elbow

Room situation, so if good things happened, the credit would go to Russell. Mullins had to be kept at the second-in-command position, and not allowed to grow too big. Talented underlings could grow into talented rivals.

⚬──╂──⚬

Judge Milliken authorized the release of the Clark brothers at the end of the day. Sergeant Griggs judged that the Clark brothers should not be released from the jail all at once, because they weren't getting along, and might murder each other. The first of the Clark brothers to be released would be the oldest, Jerry. He was the most vocal, and therefore the most annoying, and also the one most likely to irritate his brothers. The middle one, Dennis, was sullen and angry, so he had to be kept in a cell longest and given most time to cool off. That meant the youngest, Steve, would be let go second, between the others. If there was to be anyone to act as peacemaker, he would be the one, so his release would be timed so he could be a barrier between the others.

Since the Clark brothers' clothes had been bagged in plastic to prove they had been tainted by gasoline, Jerry was released wearing blue jeans and a sweatshirt from the Lost and Found box, both from a taller man with a bigger waist. He had to hold up the jeans with a length of shipping twine cinched and tied through the belt loops. Almost the moment Jerry made it from the steel door down the walk and reached the street he heard a car's tires hissing behind him. Then he heard the hum of a car window rolling down.

There was a musical voice, the voice of a woman who knew it would surprise him. "Hey, Cutie."

He looked at the car. It was a black Land Rover with tinted windows. The face of the attractive young woman in the driver's seat was turned in his direction with the window rolled down, and her big eyes were on him. He guessed that in the dim light she had mistaken him for someone much younger.

She said, "Aren't you Jerry Clark?"

"Yes, ma'am."

"I'm Jeanette. Chicago called and told me to come and pick you up."

Jerry Clark had a rare moment of wariness. "Why would Chicago do that?"

"The police drove you to the station, right?"

"Yes."

"Did they offer to drive you home?"

"No."

"Your brothers are both in cells. Do you have someone else on the way to pick you up?"

"No."

"Are you interested in a ten-mile walk?"

"No again."

"Then you should be nice to me. Do you have credit cards on you?"

"Yes."

"Then if you like, maybe we can stop at the Hilton at Pinetree Bend for a drink. I'll bet you can use one about now. I sure can, after waiting for them to let you out."

Jerry's legs took over and walked him right to the passenger side door. He opened it and climbed in.

"Seatbelts, please."

He pulled the belt across his chest and clicked it shut.

The cloth bag came down over his head and the strings tightened to close it. The needle slid into the vein of his neck. While Rankin was accomplishing that, Jeanette accelerated to make it through the first intersection before the light changed. No driver wanted to have to sit through a red light beside a dead passenger with a bag over his head.

When Steve Clark was released about two hours later Jeanette was waiting for him too. He was easier to attract to the Range Rover than Jerry had been, probably because Steve was still young enough not to be suspicious when an attractive woman wanted to get his attention. He was also young and strong enough to present a challenge to an attacker, so Jeanette made sure that by the time Rankin sneaked up to the Range Rover's window, Steve's Lost and Found Khaki pants were around his ankles and he was looking down, so he was easy to bludgeon with the tire iron before he knew it was coming.

Dennis was let go the next morning before the sun came up. Jeanette convinced him that Chicago had heard the way his brothers had treated him. When he got into Jeanette's car Rankin gave him a heroin overdose from the same batch of heroin as his brother Jerry. They drove Dennis's body to the same abandoned barn where they had left Jerry's. They left a cook spoon and disposable lighter between them. They left Steve's body on the riverbank three miles away. Rankin liked to have the evidence he left tell a story, and this time he had already accomplished it by leaving the bloody tire iron with Jerry's body in the barn. It wasn't likely someone would die by taking too much heroin and beating himself to death.

10

Monday morning was foggy, but it still began with the usual activity of the birds. While the dawn was barely replacing night in the sky, blue herons were already standing in the water at the edge of the Ash River hunting for smaller creatures, most often for tiny fish like the minnows that circled in swarms in the shallows, only visible in the cloudy water when they got too close to the surface. A few minutes later perching birds like the red-winged blackbirds were bobbing on cattail perches and there were flights of swallows swooping above the water to snap up the still-invisible winged insects. By the time the sun burned off the fog, Harry Duncan was walking along the river toward Tremmel's Deli, where he planned to have a long breakfast, watch, and listen to more conversations.

He had parked his car on one of the residential streets a block from the river that he had never been on before because the people he didn't want to become too good at spotting it probably didn't frequent that street. He had walked a half mile before his cell phone buzzed. He recognized the number so he pressed "Notes" to record the call.

"Hello?"

"Harry, it's me, Renee!" The voice was disconcerting, like the voice of a woman dying. "They have me!"

"Who has you?"

"When they came for me, I was waiting for them, but when I hesitated, they were already dragging me inside the car and driving off. One of them held his hand over my mouth and nose and was smothering me."

"What do they want?"

"They want money, and they said you have to be the one to bring it. They say they'll let us both live if you bring them ten thousand dollars in cash. They said that's to pay them for their trouble, and then they'll let me start paying protection."

"Where do I have to bring the money?"

"They'll call you at two A.M. You have until then to get the money ready and be waiting. You can't even think of telling the police or they'll know and kill me. Please, baby, just bring it, and this will all be over, at least for now."

"Tell them okay."

"I'm trying to stay calm, but if you don't, terrible things are going to happen to me and then I'll be dead." Her voice dropped to a whisper, and she said, "I'm pretty sure they plan to rape me, Harry, for a punishment. I can see the way they're looking at me."

"Give me that." There was a bang sound, as though the phone was wrenched away and hit something as a man pulled it too far from her hand. The call ended.

Harry Duncan looked at his phone to see if it had stopped recording and then tested to see if it had saved. He played back the recording. He could hear all of it clearly.

As he listened, he thought about the voice. It had a musical quality. The expressive parts of the conversation were very moving—the sound of a woman who knew she was in terrible danger. The voice told him she had already seen enough to be reluctant to make the call and drag him into the same danger, and yet, because she was a human being who wanted to go on living, uninjured, she was doing it. She sounded as though she couldn't help it, and was terribly eager to persuade him to follow the kidnappers' orders. It seemed to be the only way she knew to get this over with and spare herself torture and death. It was extremely moving.

Yet it was the quieter, less dramatic parts that he listened to most closely. She said, "They have me." The only information was that there were more than one, and they overpowered her, and they were male, or sexual assault would not have been an issue.

She was pretty specific about collecting and delivering the ransom money. She had advised him to get it now, early in the day, while the banks would be open and the delay would not get her killed. She wanted him to have the ten thousand dollars in his possession and be waiting for the call long before the bars closed. Then the mean-sounding man had come on. The phone call had contained everything that was needed. It was concise, and included nothing that didn't contribute to the kidnappers' plans.

He hurried back to his car and drove to the police station, and what he saw there surprised him. Several police cars were driving out of the lot fast, and at the other part of the lot cops in their personal cars were arriving. A few of them got out and ran into the station. It looked to Duncan as though they'd been called in early. He parked on the street and went inside by the front entrance. As he walked across the lobby toward the reception counter, he saw Sergeant Griggs near the back of the bay behind it. Griggs saw him and came to the counter. He said, "Hello, Mr. Duncan. How did you find out so early?"

Duncan said, "I just saw all the activity."

"The Clark brothers—all three of them—got murdered last night. Did you come to tell us something about that?"

"I didn't know until now."

"I'll bet you have an alibi, though."

"I was at The Elbow Room for a while, and then went to my hotel."

"What hotel?"

"The Hilton in Pine Bend. The security cameras will show me arriving after dinner at about seven and then show me leaving about six-thirty this morning, and nothing in between. There are cameras that should show the door of my room."

Griggs studied him for a moment, then said, "Thank you. We'll probably be in touch later."

"Okay." Duncan kept his facial expression unreadable. He turned and walked out the front entrance. The crooks had been busy. He wasn't sure why they had killed the Clark brothers. Maybe they had told the police something or their bosses suspected they would, but one part of the timing had to be to make the police distracted and busy. He had realized that telling the police about the kidnapping call and expecting their help would be foolish. He had handled kidnappings numerous times before. He would have loved to bring in the FBI, but a small, beleaguered local police force would only delay him and limit his options. It would be better to let them busy themselves hunting the killers of the Clark brothers.

As he got into his car he was already working. The woman who had made the phone call had done a skillful acting job, but she wasn't Renee Parkman. She had sounded about her age, or maybe a little younger. She had a good voice—perfectly controlled and expressive. But she had completely misinterpreted the relationship. Renee would never have called him "baby"; in fact, he would not have been the person she would call when she was in trouble.

He drove straight to the Parkman house. He knew that the woman had made the call using Renee Parkman's phone, and that his phone number was in its memory because Renee had texted him yesterday to get him to come to her bar. But did the crooks have Renee, or did they just have her phone? He parked around the bend where he had hidden his car the night of the fire, then walked into the field and came out behind her house.

It was now after seven, and people who worked in bars until closing time were usually in their beds at seven A.M. He went to the kitchen door and examined the lock. He took out his pocketknife, slipped it into the space beside the doorknob, opened the door, and entered the kitchen. The refrigerator was running. He stood still while he put away the knife, listening to the other sounds of the big old house. He heard an oil furnace in the basement begin to run. The house felt cool, so there was nothing odd about that. There were no dishes in the sink, crumbs on the counter, or any other signs of breakfast or last night's dinner. He heard no human sounds, so he went deeper into the building.

The stairs leading to the second floor were a risk, especially in an old house, but he had to take it. He held on to the railing and stepped only on the edges of the steps, where the nails held the boards down tight and they didn't creak. At the second floor landing he could see there were four bedrooms, all with the doors open. The second one in the side that overlooked the river had a number of bottles and boxes on the dresser and a couple of books on the nightstand, one of them with a bookmark in it. The bed was made, but this was definitely where she would have slept if she had been here. They had her.

But if they did, why had they had the other woman call him? Renee was a difficult woman. Maybe she had resisted and they'd killed her. Maybe they had kept her alive but suspected she would try to give him information if she was on the call. He couldn't assume she was beyond help. They didn't seem to have set this up to capture her, but also to get him to walk into an ambush. He went downstairs, pushed the button to lock the door, and left.

Duncan needed ten thousand dollars. He had an account with the Bank of America because it had branches everywhere. He kept it well stocked with money, and because of his profession he needed to use one branch for a week or a year, and then move on and have another waiting. He drove to the office in Parkman's Elbow and took out eleven thousand dollars in hundreds. He asked the teller to run the stack of bills through the counting machine a second time, because he expected the kidnappers would count the bills, and didn't want a discrepancy.

He bought a tin of cookies at the small market down the block, and inside his car he emptied the cookies and put ten thousand dollars of the money inside the inner bag with a layer of cookies on top, resealed it, then left it in the car trunk and got back in the driver's seat. The street was quiet, with little traffic, and the interior of his car provided additional insulation.

He listened to the recording of the woman's phone call, this time turning the volume up. He recognized a train whistle in the background. She didn't seem distracted by it, or even to hear it during her performance, but he heard it. The signal was a long whistle, then long again, then short, then long. He had timed the woman's call, so he found that the sound came at 7:27 A.M. The long, long, short, long was the warning that a train was coming to a level grade, and would be crossing a road.

Now he had the exact time when a train crossed a road and sounded that signal. He looked up the train companies that ran trains in the region of the Ash River. By far the biggest was CSX, which had about thirty thousand miles of track nationally. Some of the smaller companies had thirty miles. He learned there were apps for tracking trains. It took him an hour to collect the trains running in a fifty-mile radius of Parkman's Elbow that had gone over ground level road crossings during the period of 7:00 to 8:00 that morning. There were nineteen.

Duncan went through the list eliminating trains that were more than five minutes off the time of 7:27 A.M. and ended up with only eleven trains. He couldn't eliminate any more based on the information he had, but he could arrange the eleven in order of proximity to the towns in the Ash River area. A train whistle could often be heard for a mile or two, but it was unlikely to be heard for fifteen, or ten, even early in the morning. This left him with four trains—one crossing in Parkman's Elbow, two in Riverbend, and one in Groomsburg.

He still had another possible way to locate the place where the fake Renee had been calling him from. When she had been talking there was also a bird call. It had been unusual. It wasn't any of the calls Duncan had heard since he'd been in Parkman's

Elbow. He worked on his recording, rerecording only the part that held the bird call.

Duncan called four different science museums, two zoos, and six Audubon society numbers. Most of the places he called had nobody available who could answer technical questions like his. Some were selling tickets, some pushing memberships or special events. But five of them told him to call Cornell. When he opened Cornell University's website to find a phone number, he saw they had posted a page that allowed a visitor to hear some identified bird calls. He played a few. The problem was that there were several that sounded too similar to him.

He tried a few numbers that gave him the names of offices, and finally saw the words Ornithology Lab. He selected it, and in a few rings, someone picked up the phone on the other end. "Magnuson." It was a woman's voice. He estimated she was thirty to forty years old, and that gave him hope that she might be an expert.

He said, "Hello, ma'am. My name is Harry Duncan, and I'm calling you to ask for help with a question. I accidentally recorded a few bird calls this morning and I wondered if there was anyone at the Cornell Ornithology Lab who might be willing to help me by identifying the bird."

"I'm Ann Magnuson. I'm a researcher here. It sounds interesting. What's the bird call like?"

"It sounds to me like one of the calls that crows make. You know, it's something like this." He made an imitation of the sound, a series of clicks in the back of his throat—"Ah-ah-ah-ah-ah."

"Crows have over forty different calls in their language, but I think I know the call you mean. Want me to listen to your recording?"

"That would be great."

"Let me close the door so I can be sure to hear it." A moment later, she picked up the phone again. "Okay. I'm back."

Duncan played the sound. It was repeated, but less loudly. "Do you recognize it?"

She laughed. "Recognize it?" she said. "I was brought up on it. That call might be one of the five most famous in the world. It's the sandhill crane."

"Can you tell me anything about where it lives or anything?"

"I can tell you a lot. It's reputed to be one of the oldest bird species in the world—over two and a half million years without major changes. They're wading birds, and they're over three feet tall. The species also has a wild migration that tells me where you probably are. In the summer most of them live in northern Siberia or Canada. There are small year-round flocks in Louisiana and Texas, but every April the vast majority migrate. About six hundred thousand of them spend the month of April on the Platte River near Kearny, Nebraska. That's probably where you heard and recorded them. A few turn up in Idaho or Utah, and about twenty thousand in the San Luis Valley in Colorado."

"I'm in Indiana, along the Ash River."

"Oh, that explains your surprise, and why you don't recognize the call. It's quite a call, hard to forget. Indiana is on one of the migration paths, but they fly over at about twelve thousand feet, so you'd never hear them. This year a group of them have stopped in Indiana, a small group, but verified. The reason you've never heard that call or seen them is that this is the first time—at least since there were ornithologists to verify it—that they've stopped there. We don't know why yet. It could be pollution, climate change, disappearance of food supplies along their route, you name it."

"Do you know where they are, exactly?"

"I do, but it wouldn't be ethical to tell you. I would be sending a nonscientist to see them, which would risk affecting the studies that scientists are conducting with this group. I'm not saying you'd do harm, but each human being introduced to that space might accidentally change some variable that would alter what gets observed. The scientists might miss something that could save the flock, or even the species. It could be, frankly, a loss more valuable than my whole career of contributions. This is a short event, and they'll be gone in a month."

"Please," Duncan said. "I'll never go near them, but I really need to know where they are."

"I'm sorry. If it's really that important you could travel to Nebraska to see the main group. Imagine six hundred thousand. It's amazing and inspiring. Now, I should be going."

"Wait!" he said. "Please don't hang up yet. What I'm going to play is only a minute and a half long. It's the phone call that accidentally recorded the cranes."

Duncan played the phone call that the woman impersonating Renee had made.

He started it where the woman's voice said, "They have me."

Professor Magnuson was silent, listening to the melodious voice while it held back tears, trying not to beg, but sounding terrified. The bird calls came right after Duncan's voice said, "What do they want?" It was only about twenty seconds later that the recording reached the end, when the angry man wrenched the phone away.

There was a silence, and it lasted so long that Duncan said, "Dr. Magnuson? Are you still there?"

She spoke slowly and calmly. "I wrote down the name you gave me. Harry Duncan. Are you a police officer?"

"Six years in Los Angeles, a couple for the State of Indiana, eight years for the Chicago PD."

"If this turns out to be an elaborate deception to get access to the sandhill cranes, Cornell will ensure that the government sues you and anyone you may be working for. These birds are protected by several countries. Understand?"

"I do."

"The cranes are on the Ash River at the Groomsburg, Indiana, Veterans' Memorial Park. If you're for real, I wish you the very best. If you're not, then what I hope is best unsaid."

11

Duncan looked at the clock on his dashboard. It had taken him over three hours to get this far, and he had to move as quickly as he could. He knew the next thing he had to do was change cars. His wasn't exactly a distinctive vehicle. The style and paint job were intended to make it look like the second car somebody just drove to work and left parked in the lot. The modifications were all difficult to spot. The bigger engine and heavy-duty transmission, springs, and shocks were hidden. The most any casual observer could have noticed was that the tires were always new. But Duncan was sure that the people who had taken Renee would have studied his car.

He drove to Newmarket, a town twenty miles east of the river, rented a black pickup truck with tinted side windows, and paid the clerk to keep his own car in the back of the rental lot with its gray waterproof cover over it.

As soon as he had the pickup truck a mile from the lot he stopped and looked at Google Maps on his phone. He found several aerial photographs and street views of Groomsburg and used them to study the town and the land around it, including the Veterans' Memorial Park. A peninsula formed by one of the river's bends was cut across by a straight stretch of the river road. Most of the peninsula was a park that ran from the road to the river. It contained groves of tall trees, a picnic area, a baseball field, a few paths that were visible from the air, and a whole loop of the Ash River. He could see that along the shore of the park was a wide place in the river where the water was shallow enough to show stones and a few wisps of white water. He was fairly confident that this must be where the cranes had stopped. Groomsburg was also one of the four towns where there had been a train crossing a level grade around 7:27 A.M. He began to look for the railroad tracks.

Duncan widened the aerial field that he could get on his computer screen, and then found railroad tracks. What he needed to do was follow them to find the spot where a person could hear the cranes and also hear a train whistle, both in the proportions on the recording. A bird—even a big one—might be heard no more than a mile. The train whistle could be much farther away. What he needed was the building—maybe rustic, maybe industrial—where kidnappers could imprison a female hostage for a day and an evening without fear of being caught. He kept reminding himself that the building could be on either side of the river.

He devoted over an hour to going over large stretches of tracks in search of the building, but he hadn't found anything that looked probable, and he was aware of each minute as it passed. Time was everything now, and he had used over five hours. A lot could happen to a woman in five hours. The impostor had said they would call him for the exchange at 2:00 A.M., but in his experience with kidnappers they often gave a deadline and then called or showed up ahead of it to confuse and disconcert the counterforce, or to catch them while they were preparing a trap. He had to keep moving.

He started the engine and drove to Groomsburg in his rented pickup. The park's green and woodsy peninsula began only a few yards from the river road. The park entrance had a pair of brick stanchions with a thick chain connecting them and a sign hung from it with red letters that said PARK CLOSED. The entrance driveway beyond it was blocked by a truck parked across it.

The street-view photographs he had studied had shown him from a distance a permanent building with a peaked roof that was almost to the river. The municipal website had a shot of the building from the side. There had appeared to be public restrooms on the land side, and an office window on the river side. He assumed that the scientists had probably moved into the office, so after he spotted it he kept his speed constant and didn't look anymore.

Duncan was careful not to brake so he wouldn't alarm the cranes, the scientists, or the kidnappers. As soon as he was past the stand of tall old trees near the river road he opened his window and listened. He could hear a few birds in a ragged chorus of their now-familiar call. He closed his tinted window again and looked out across a section of bare grass at the river.

There was a boat. He coasted along the road, and then continued at the slower pace. The boat was an old-fashioned wooden cabin cruiser with the hull painted white and the cabin, foredeck, main deck, and gunwales varnished wood. The cabin was enclosed, with a broad windshield and small side windows, and a set of low ports on the hull below the deck that looked as though they probably served for light in the hold. There were numbers painted near the bow, so he used his phone to photograph it—FJ 4532-0.

As he passed downstream, he noticed that there was a varnished sliding door across the entrance to the cabin that was partially open, and that the stern had a ladder up from the water to the rear deck. He could also see that the boat not only had an anchor set at the bow, but also a second anchor lowered at the stern. They held the boat facing upstream and motionless in the current. He wondered if the boat was part of the ornithologists' expedition.

When he had passed the boat he slowed again and looked back in his rearview mirror. The boat was anchored over a quarter mile from the park, around a bend from it. He could not see the park, the birds, or the shallows from here. This had to be something else. Who could this be, and what were they doing? He had only been in the Ash River area for a few days, but he had not seen any boats on it. There probably were plenty in the summer, but it was only the beginning of April.

The boat was anchored in the center channel of the river, where the current was fast and the water narrow. Maybe it was here to keep it from scraping a bar, but its position would also keep anyone from approaching it on foot.

He drove on around the next two bends and then pulled over and stopped. The boat might have nothing to do with Renee's kidnapping, but he couldn't eliminate the possibility. The region was a string of small towns. If somebody disappeared from one of them, everybody would know the person. Every building was either occupied or known by everyone to be vacant. A boat anchored in the middle of the river was something else.

He used his phone to find that the Indiana Bureau of Motor Vehicles handled watercraft registrations. He found the number of the central office that handled the forms that had to be submitted and called it. He spent about ten minutes getting transferred to the office and getting to a person who answered the number for questions. When he got to the woman he said, "I'm negotiating to buy a boat, and I wondered if I could check to be sure it isn't stolen or anything. Its hull identification number is FJ 4532-0."

The woman waited for a moment and then said, "That's FJ 4532-0?"

"Yes."

"I can't tell you if it's stolen or not. A lot of boats disappear from storage and the owner doesn't know it until spring. But that's not its HIN. It's an invalid number."

"Thank you, ma'am," he said, and hung up. This might be some completely unrelated piece of dishonesty, but he knew he had to get a look in that boat.

The past few evenings had been cool, almost a return to early March. The river was still cold. The water was always nearly opaque, and there was sure to be little light along this stretch, because there were no streetlamps and few buildings. Getting near the boat would be very difficult and dangerous, and the chance she was there was slim, but so far this was the only idea he'd had that could be right. If he moved quickly and decisively, he might be able to find out before the kidnappers called him at two A.M. He had to try.

He had taken a small overnight bag from his car when he had rented the pickup truck, but it just contained a couple changes of clothes, a shaver, a toothbrush, and his Glock 17 pistol. It didn't contain any of the gear that he would need tonight, and he had a sense of time slipping by while he tried to think ahead so each of his moves would be efficient. He pulled back onto River Road and then turned east as soon as he could and headed away from Groomsburg, and then north again. He needed to be out of the Ash River area, and he needed a bigger town, so he headed for Bedford. On the way he divided his time between watching the road behind to be sure the kidnappers hadn't noticed his truck and followed, and using his phone to search for the right kind of store. The trip took him a precious hour, but it led him far enough away from the Ash River to make it unlikely anyone connected with the kidnapping would see him.

When he pulled into the lot of the large sporting goods store, he felt hope.

He parked in the middle of a few other cars, went in, and looked around him. It had been a cold winter in the upper Midwest, and there were still vestigial displays of heavy jackets and ski equipment, snowboards, and boots. There was a section for fishing gear that looked as though it was being expanded for spring, and there were hunting clothes from fall, some of them in Day-Glo orange and others in camouflage. He kept going past tents and sleeping bags, footwear, rain gear, and all kinds of supplies—bug sprays, powdered food, first aid items from Band-Aids to tourniquets, sunscreen, waterproof matches.

He entered the baseball section, which two young men were working to add to—more bats, helmets, shoes, gloves, balls, pitching practice nets, and shirts and jackets with the logos of every major league team. He walked up to one of the young men and said, "Do you have any water stuff, like scuba gear?"

"I don't think very much," the young man said. "Too early. Whatever we have would be over in that corner." He pointed.

"Thanks."

Duncan stepped to the corner and began to search. There were no wet suits, not even partial ones. He found a display that was apparently intended for competitive swimmers—Speedo nylon swimsuits, goggles, replacement straps and nosepieces, women's one-piece nylon suits. He took a set of goggles. There was another small area meant to appeal to people planning warm-destination vacations—shorts, golf shirts, a few sun-resistant foldable hats, sandals. But just beyond it he found a shelf of swim fins. Most were children's sizes, but he found three pairs in adult sizes, one big enough for him.

He felt the time slipping away, so he began making decisions. He kept the goggles and the swim fins. He picked out a black nylon swimsuit and a pair of black trunks. As he was stepping away, he saw a small pile of four plastic packages that said O'Neill over folded black synthetic cloth. He picked one up, and looked more closely. It was a Thermo-X rash guard. They had been stocked, apparently, to keep sun-starved Indianans from having the burn of their lives in some place closer to the equator. He found two in size large, took both, and held them tightly, almost superstitiously afraid he'd lose them.

On his way out, he picked up a military-style adjustable dark blue cloth belt for the shorts, and a Little-League-size baseball bat that was painted black. He picked up a set of leather shoe-laces, delivered everything to the register, paid with cash, and took it all away in two bags. As soon as he could, he removed everything from the bags and threw them and the receipt into the dumpster.

He drove toward the Interstate and then noticed a fast-food drive-through hamburger place coming up and remembered that he had not eaten anything all day. He pulled in and bought two hamburgers and a milkshake. He pushed the straw through the top of the milkshake and put it in the drink holder and unwrapped the first hamburger and set it on the passenger seat beside him before he pulled back onto the road leading to the interstate.

As he reached highway speed and took a first bite of the hamburger, he realized it was the first one he'd had since the one Renee had cooked for him the day he'd arrived in Parkman's Elbow. He couldn't help thinking about her now. He'd been part of kidnapping rescue teams—as SWAT team member, negotiator, undercover cop posing as civilian doing the ransom delivery—and what was disturbing him now was the memories of those cases in which the victim was dead, often before the police had even heard there was a case. In his career there had been three. Renee could easily be dead already, just like them. In his memory he had a clear image of her, and he couldn't help feeling the sense of futility and waste at the idea of a woman like her dying for nothing. The biggest indication that she was no longer alive was their having an imposter call him. The only indication that she might be alive was the far less certain notion that he might be right about the boat. If it was where she'd been placed, then why keep it in place if she was dead? In the next twenty minutes he finished his food, and congratulated himself for finding time for it. No matter what happened next, he knew he was going to need the calories.

He drove faster as the light began to fade. He knew that at about the time when he got close to the Ash River area, the small, narrow roads there would be slowed by people making their way home from work, so he tried to make up for it.

He raised his speed a little as soon as he reached any spot where he could see open space for any distance ahead. He needed to make good time, but getting pulled over for speeding would waste time that he couldn't make up.

When he got as far as Parkman's Elbow, he drove past Renee's house again to see whether anything had changed—if her car was out or a light had appeared behind a window—anything that showed the supposed kidnapping had been nothing but a scare tactic. Nothing had changed. He stayed on the river road to drive past The Elbow Room, and studied the lot to see if her white Volvo was there, but it wasn't.

He followed the river road nearly twenty-five miles until he reached the Veterans' Memorial Park on the outskirts of Grooms-burg. He slowed and darkened his headlights to go past the place, and then turned them off again to cross the open area where the boat was. He could see that the boat had still not moved. Fifteen minutes later, after his eyes had become accustomed to the darkness, he could see more.

Tonight the boat had the weak gleam of a small light visible in the below-deck porthole, and another one in the cabin, where the helm was. To him each one looked about as bright as a candle. It was only enough so that any occupants would see obstacles and openings. There had to be steps leading down from the upper cabin to the hold under it.

After Duncan had passed the boat, he went another hundred yards upstream before he slowly pulled the truck into a grove of trees and stopped the engine. He found that the low bushes and weeds were thinner inside the grove, where the trees got most of the sunlight. He removed his clothes and put on the Speedo swimsuit and the shorts over it, pulled on the rash guard, feeling the reassuring comfortable hug of the synthetic fabric, and then pulled on the second one over it. The label had said that the rash guard had an insulating quality, so maybe two would have more. He tried on the swim fins and the goggles to be sure they fit. Finally, he took the baseball bat he had bought, then attached the shoelaces to the handle with a slip knot, and tied them to the side of his belt, then removed the bat for the moment.

Duncan sat still for the next hour watching the boat, both shores of the river, and the roads above them. Nobody came near the boat. Nobody even seemed to see it. He knew that the only thing he could be sure the kidnappers would probably not be ready for was that he would arrive a few hours before they made their call. It was time. He reconnected the bat with his belt.

He went into the river slowly, feeling the icy water seep into his clothes and soak him. After a minute of pain, he wasn't sure whether his body was slowly warming the water trapped under his clothes, or if he was becoming numb to it. He slid the rest of the way into the dark river and began to kick his legs and let the flippers propel him. He felt the wooden baseball bat floating beside him on its tether bump against his kicking legs a few times, but he had started a distance above the boat and let the current carry him as he swam across the swift current. He didn't fight it much because it was taking him where he wanted to go.

When he reached the bow anchor chain he grasped it, clung to it, and stopped his motion. He pushed his goggles up onto his forehead, and listened, trying to hear any sounds from the boat's occupants.

The Renee impersonator had told him on the phone that the kidnappers would call him at 2:00 A.M. to tell him where to bring her ransom. That gave him four hours before they would summon him to his ambush. They would have to gather before then. Whatever he was going to do to save Renee and get out had to be done before they were ready.

He could hear no sounds coming from the boat. There were no voices, no footsteps of people walking on wooden surfaces, no mechanical noises. He saw no shadows that were shaped like a person or moved. He didn't know how much time he had before the cold made his body too numb to operate, but he knew that his time was getting shorter. He counted to two hundred while he waited for some sign that he wasn't alone, but it didn't come.

He had to make a move, and he decided it would be now. The rail on the bow end of the boat was at least five feet above the water. He let go of the bow anchor chain and let the current carry him along the side of the hull toward the stern. As he moved back, the height of the hull above the water decreased to about three feet. He stretched his arms above his head and kicked his flippers to raise himself above the water, grasped the gunwale above him, and held on. He used his hands to walk himself aft along the gunwale.

He kept going until he was below the place where there was a strip of glass to admit sunlight into the area below deck. Now, because he was hanging on the gunwale, he could reach high enough to pull himself close to it.

He pulled himself up until he could see through the glass into the forecastle. The light was dim, but he could see clearly that the space was divided into two sides with a two-level bunk bed on each. He was only a few inches above the top bunk on the port side. It was empty, but he could see beyond the edge of the top bunk, where a hand and arm protruded from the lower bunk.

The hand belonged to a woman. The woman's arm was wearing a navy-blue sweater. He didn't recognize it, but he'd seen Renee only about four times. She might have sweaters in fifty colors. He could not see this woman's head, which was hidden by the top bunk. The two bunks on the starboard side were empty, but the lower one was wrinkled, as though someone might have been lying there earlier.

He looked at the arm and hand, trying to see something that might prove to him it was Renee or wasn't. He couldn't tell. If this boat was connected to the kidnapping, the woman could easily be the woman who had imitated Renee. But this woman never moved, was not showing signs of consciousness, and never stirred. Wouldn't that straight arm sticking out be uncomfortable? Only if she was alive. This could be only Renee's body.

Duncan let the current pull him to the stern, and then grasped the short ladder to the side of the outdrive. He set his flippers onto the deck at the stern, disconnected the baseball bat from its tether, set it down, and climbed aboard. He knelt on the rear deck for a couple of minutes, listening. There were still no sounds.

He moved forward to the left of the cabin door and heel-and-toe walked along beside it until he reached the starboard side of the cabin. He bent down so he could get his face below the level of the deck and his eye to the glass where he could see inside the hull.

From this side he could see the woman lying on the lower bunk. She looked as though she could be dead—maybe strangled, or smothered, but he could see the chestnut hair, the nose and mouth in profile. She was Renee, or at least she had been Renee.

Duncan sidestepped forward to the corner of the windshield and looked into the cabin. He saw the wheel, a bit of dashboard, and then the arms and lap of a man sitting in the captain's high seat. The man was holding a computer tablet, and over his shoulder Duncan could see there was a map on the screen. Duncan pulled back without looking closely, but he didn't need to be close. He had already seen lots of green, a grid that had to be roads, and a long snaky white line that was the meandering river. The man had his jacket open, and he could see a large revolver, probably a .357 Magnum, in a shoulder holster.

Duncan made his way from the windshield to the rear of the cabin. He stood still at the cabin's varnished wood sliding door. He was aware that what the man must have been doing with the tablet was reviewing the tactics for luring Duncan into the ambush that would kill him. Duncan pushed the thought out of his mind. All he wanted to know was if Renee had been kept alive to pay the extortion payments, or killed so they could buy the bar cheap and forget her.

He knew that it was entirely possible he was about to die. He took two deep breaths, reached out to touch the sliding door, and suddenly slid it aside.

The man in the cabin looked up and said a single word. "You."

Duncan had guessed that the man would still have the tablet in his hands. He would lose part of a second, because his first impulse would be to put the tablet down before thought over-ruled habit and make him drop it to reach for the gun. Duncan didn't hesitate.

As the man's left hand opened his jacket and the right reached in for the gun, the man's chest had only the right hand to protect it, and Duncan jabbed the heavy end of the bat toward the man's chest. The force of the blow hit the fan of small bones in the back of the man's hand, and the hand jerked outward in pain. Duncan thrust the bat again, this time hitting the unprotected sternum, then spun the bat and swung it sideways against the man's skull, knocking him from the chair to the deck. Duncan could see from the bloody, open skull that the man was dead, but he reached into the man's jacket, tugged the pistol from its holster, and tossed it out the door onto the rear deck.

Duncan closed the door again and then went down the narrow steps to the hold, where the sleeping quarters were. He looked closely at Renee on the bunk, but saw nothing that indicated any awareness. She did not stir, and her eyelids revealed no eye movements. He grasped her shoulder, cradled her head, and pulled her toward him. He put his face close to hers so his ear was just under her nose. At first he couldn't detect any breathing, but then he thought he did.

He pressed his fingertips over her carotid artery and felt joy, then realized what he was feeling was his own pulse in his fingertips, strong because of the adrenaline and exertion. There was a terrible moment when he thought she had none, but then he felt something out of synch with his own pulse. It was slow and faint, but her heart was beating and her lungs were bringing her air.

He lay her back down and checked her for injuries. He found some minor bruises, a few scrapes, but no broken bones, cuts, or stabs. He tried to wake her by shaking her gently, rubbing her shoulders and arms, patting her cheeks, talking softly into her ear, rubbing her hands between his. He glanced at his watch and saw that it was past midnight.

He knew other kidnappers must be coming soon because it would take more than one man to move the unconscious Renee to bait his ambush, accept the ransom, and kill him too. He had to get her to shore before they showed up. He went back up to the cabin, where he found a chest that held life vests. He took the two of them that seemed newest and went back down to the bunks. He lay one of them flat on the bunk above Renee's pillow, pulled it down under her, threaded her arms through it, and tightened the straps. Then he placed the second life jacket beside her, rolled her onto it, pushed her arms through it, and tightened those straps behind her. He picked her up and climbed the stairs to the deck with her.

He looked carefully at the river and both shores. The current was strong on this stretch of river, but he had to get her across it. He set her on the deck, went back into the cabin, and retrieved his bat. He held it in the flowing water at the stern to wash the blood off, then slid the leather shoelaces around the handle again and tightened them, pulled on his swim fins, and lowered the unconscious Renee into the river. He kept a tight grip on the neck of the life preserver in front so it kept her face up, and slid into the river beside her. He held her head up, pushed off the boat, and began to kick furiously. He stroked with his free right arm and began to move. They were being swept downstream as he swam, but they were also moving away from the boat and closer to the opposite shore. Within ten minutes he had dragged her across to the shallows a distance downstream from the boat. He caught his breath, took off his flippers, slid his hand through the heel straps so they hung on his wrist, and then got a firm grip on Renee's life vests.

Duncan began to walk, dragging the life vests and Renee along in the shallow water. In a few more minutes he reached the wooded area where he had left his rented truck. He dragged Renee up onto the riverbank, put his flippers and baseball bat in the truck bed, and found the truck key where he'd left it. He opened the cab and started the engine. Then he knelt beside Renee and pulled her life vests off. As he was fiddling with the straps she began to stir. Her skin felt cold, and she was shivering now. He carried her to the truck, set her in the passenger seat, started the engine, and turned on the heater. He took off her wet clothes and scavenged his own dry clothes that he'd left in the cab. He put on her his boxer shorts, his T-shirt, his shirt, and his socks. The shirt came down to her knees and his socks up to her upper calves. The heater made the truck cab warm quickly.

He took a minute to peel off his wet clothes and replace them with his pants, jacket, and shoes, then went back to work on reviving Renee. He was massaging her back and shoulders, patting her hands, rubbing her feet. He talked constantly in a low voice, telling her it was time to open her eyes, time to answer.

He saw her moving a bit, and her breathing seemed to speed up. Then she opened her eyes. "Holy shit," she mumbled. "So hot." She strained to sit up, struggling against the seatbelt across her chest and waist.

He reached for the temperature control. "Sorry," he said. "I had to swim you across the river, and you were pretty cold."

Her eyes widened at the sight of him. "Oh, my God," she said. "Do you know what's happening? How did you get here?"

"Too long to tell now. Just sit tight." He got out of the cab and walked around the truck to the driver's seat. When he got there, she looked as though she was remembering everything at once. She began to cry. "Oh my God. That awful man." She sat there crying hysterically. He let her cry for a few seconds, then started the truck and began backing out of the grove of trees toward the road.

"What are you doing? Where are you going?" Her voice was angry and suspicious.

He said, "We've got to get out of here, right now." He reached the road and drove along with his headlights off until he turned the first bend, then switched them on and sped up. "Are you injured?"

"I got beaten up, and drugged with something that gave me a terrible headache. It's back now. I feel awful."

"Do you need to go to a hospital right now?"

"I don't think so." She ran her hands over her arms, then pulled at them and looked down. "What are these clothes?"

"They're mine. We were both on the edge of hypothermia from the river, so I shared the dry clothes I had with me."

"Great. I'll bet that was fun for you."

"It wasn't."

"Where are you going?"

"To your house."

"Shouldn't we go to the police station?"

"That's next after your house."

She was silent, as though the confusion, the drug hangover, the aches and pains were crowding her consciousness, and it was too much effort now to push through all of that just to ask questions she didn't care much about.

Her house was a distance away, and once she seemed to be recovering, she improved rapidly. When they reached her house, he jimmied open the door for her with his pocketknife and she went upstairs to put on some clothes that weren't his.

When she had changed, she noticed a flickering light on her bedroom curtain. She looked out the window and saw bright flames near the back of her house. She went downstairs to the backyard and stood near Duncan. He turned and saw she was carrying his shirt and shorts and socks in a bag.

She said, "Killed him, huh?"

"What makes you say that?"

"You're standing there burning a baseball bat in my charcoal grill in the middle of the night. Why else would that be, Duncan?"

12

As they drove toward the police station, he said, "Tell me whatever you can remember. There was a man, but there was a woman too, right?"

She said, "Yes. They came to my house just after dawn. I don't know the exact time. It was this guy about forty with short dark hair, kind of trim build, and a woman, a bit younger. She had deep blue eyes, and she was about my height and weight. They were both wearing suits, like cops wear. They said they were from the Riverbend Police and wanted to ask a few questions about the thing with the Clark brothers. The woman said they had all been murdered. As soon as I let them in the house, the man grabbed me, and I felt this sharp pain in my thigh, and realized she had stuck a needle in me."

"Anybody else?"

"I don't know. I was out a lot."

"Were you unconscious all day?"

"Not unconscious. I kind of woke up a couple times. I was in a big car, like a truck, but I was so weak. I tried to get up and couldn't, then realized I shouldn't. The woman was driving, and I heard the man say, 'She's coming out of it.' "

"Did they call each other by name?"

"Not that I heard."

"Did they put you on the boat or bring it to shore?"

"I don't know."

"What color was the woman's hair?"

"I don't know."

He looked at her, surprised.

"It was brown, but when she had just grabbed me and stuck me I tried to whirl around, and the hair looked like it had kind of moved to the side a little. I think it was a wig."

He kept asking questions all the way to the station. When they got there, they went in the front entrance and saw a lone police officer sitting at the counter doing work at a computer. Duncan said, "Hello. We need to see the watch commander as soon as possible."

The woman looked up. "Hi, Renee."

"Hi, Brenda."

The officer picked up a hand radio instead of a phone and said, "Sergeant, Renee Parkman is here."

A moment later Sergeant Griggs appeared from the open bay beyond the counter. He said, "Come in, both of you. I wanted to see you."

Duncan said, "She was kidnapped this morning and we just got her back."

As they walked into the bay, Griggs beckoned to Officer Slater, who got up from a desk and followed. He and Griggs pulled some chairs out and they all sat around another desk that Duncan assumed belonged to Griggs.

They began to ask Renee questions, and then the stream became a barrage. When they had exhausted what she knew about her experience, Griggs turned to Duncan.

"How did you find her?"

He played the recording of the ransom call, told them about hearing the train signal and the bird calls on the kidnapper's recording and his attempts to interpret and locate the sources of the sounds. He told them about finding the boat, about sneaking aboard and finding Renee apparently unconscious or dead. Finally, he said, "As you can see, she's alive, but the man keeping her drugged and held there is dead."

"What killed him?" asked Sergeant Griggs.

"A combination of poor character and bad luck. He tried pulling a gun to shoot me, and it didn't work out."

"So you're going to admit to killing him?"

"I'll let the coroner decide the cause of death."

Slater said, "Can you give us the exact location of the boat?"

Duncan said, "About a quarter mile downstream from the Groomsburg Veterans' Memorial Park. One more thing. Whoever goes out there would be doing the world a favor if one man boarded the boat, raised both anchors, and steered it downstream to a ramp so it could be transported to the police station on a trailer. Those sandhill cranes may not stop by here again for a long time."

Griggs said, "We'll do our best. We'll also call the professor at Cornell and tell her we appreciate her help. Write down her name and number." He pointed to his desk, where there were message slips and a pen. Duncan picked up the pen and wrote.

It was bright sunlight by the time Duncan and Renee walked out of the police station. She stopped, shading her eyes, but looking around her.

"Come on," he said.

She stood still. "I can't go home. They must know by now. What if they're waiting for me?"

"If you stay here, somebody is going to spot you. Get in the truck and we'll get you out of here."

Reluctantly, she stepped away from the station and got into the pickup truck. He started the engine, and then pulled forward to get out onto Main Street. "Where are you taking me?" she said.

"To return this car and pick up mine, then to Bloomington."

"Why Bloomington?"

"Because they're not there."

They drove to the rental lot, where Duncan returned the truck and picked up his black car, and then drove the rest of the way to Bloomington. As they drove, he kept looking in the rearview mirror to maintain a clear sense of all the cars behind him.

"Do you think they're following us?"

"I don't think they are."

"But they could be?"

"I don't know, so I look. Nothing suspicious so far. And the more distance we put behind us, the less likely one of them is going to just show up."

She said, "I feel bad that I didn't thank you for saving me. You had a horrible experience too. I didn't know how hard it was even to figure out where I was, and then swim in that cold water, and that guy tried to kill you. I'm so sorry."

"It's all part of my work," he said. "I'm being paid to find out everything I can about these people, and now I know a little more."

She said, "You're mad at me, aren't you?"

"No," he said. "Not at all."

"Because you have to take a person seriously to be angry."

"Do you like to argue?"

"No," she said. "I just wanted to find out about you, and now I know a little bit more."

They were silent until they got to the hotel in Bloomington that Duncan had picked out, the Cosmopolitan-Viceroyal. Duncan went to his car trunk and took out his overnight bag. They went into the lobby and he said, "You can have a seat and wait. I'll just get us checked in," and went to the front desk.

When the woman at the desk looked up, she said, "Are you two checking in?"

"Yes," he said.

He felt another presence close by, then heard Renee's voice. "Two rooms."

The woman said, "Yes, we can accommodate you. We've got two rooms that are already available right now." Duncan handed her a credit card, and she took an impression and handed it back. "Thank you, Mr. Bowles." She produced two little envelopes, wrote two numbers on them, put two key card blanks into the slot of a machine one after another, and said, "304 and 516. Have a nice day."

Duncan handed one to Renee and kept the other. They stepped into the same elevator. Duncan pressed the 3 and the 5 buttons. When the elevator stopped at the third floor Renee got out, and Duncan rode the elevator to the fifth, went to his room, showered, closed the curtains to achieve near-perfect darkness, and went to sleep.

At six the hotel phone in his room rang. He picked it up and said, "Hello."

Renee said, "Hi. I'm really hungry. Want to have dinner downstairs with me?"

"Are you calling from down there?"

"No. From my room. That horrible woman took my phone, remember?"

"I've got a couple of burner phones. I'll give you one to hold you until you get a new one. I'll bring it. Fifteen minutes?"

"Okay."

When he arrived in the restaurant downstairs, Renee was nearby in the lobby watching the elevator. She was wearing the gray sweater and blue jeans she'd put on to go to the police station, but her hair was washed and shiny. She must have gotten makeup in the hotel's shop, because it was fresh and expertly done. She looked beautiful. If there was anything left of the drugged and manhandled kidnap victim, it was now completely internalized.

The restaurant was a good one, and they were both very hungry, so the interest they showed in their menus was partially sincere. When they had ordered, Duncan produced the throwaway phone, got it working, and gave it to her. She said, "Thank you. The first thing I'm going to do is call the phone company and deactivate the other one."

"Don't do it," Duncan said. "The police might be able to find that woman who injected you and called me. She might be foolish enough to leave it working."

Renee's cheeks flushed. "You mean she might be stupid like me, the one who was going to have the phone company freeze it."

"I don't think I have a problem saying what I mean, and I didn't mean that," he said. "We both know you're smart. And nobody expects you to predict everything the cops are going to want."

After that, they spoke mostly in quiet monosyllables, and avoided looking at each other much until the meal was over. When the waitress brought the check in a leather folder Renee started to reach for it, but sensed it was a bad idea and watched him take the check and write in the signature "Jason Bowles."

They walked out and got into the elevator. She pressed the numbers 3 and 5. When the doors opened on the third floor she said, "Thanks for dinner," and stepped out.

Duncan managed to say, "Good night," just in time before the doors slid shut.

He went back to his room and spent some time using stationery and a pen from the room writing a first draft report to be added to his murder book. He retold the story of the phone call from the woman kidnapper to demand ransom, his verification of the kidnapping, his steps in finding where Renee was being kept, and the rescue.

When he had finished, he began a separate report of the deaths of the three Clark brothers. He had already written about the events leading to their arrest after the car fire, and he was aware that the little he knew so far about their deaths was only going to be an introduction to whatever the police investigation revealed.

When he had come to Indiana he had started to document what he learned in his scouting mission in the way he had learned to document murder investigations. His murder book had started, as his investigation had, with the public information about the two murders that had occurred just before he'd come, and now there had been three more and a kidnapping resulting in the death of one kidnapper. His murder book had already evolved into something much bigger.

He worked until he was tired enough to sleep again, put the pages into his overnight bag, and went to sleep.

This time when the phone by the bed rang, he could see that the clock by the bed's red display read 1:58. He said, "Hello."

"It's me again," Renee said, "I'm sorry to bother you."

"It's okay. What's up?"

"I'm scared. I'm not crazy or anything, and I don't usually feel this way. But I'm scared."

"Have you heard or seen something?"

"No. I just—I can't sleep. Every time I close my eyes, I start remembering, and then I'm afraid."

"It sounds like a delayed reaction, perfectly normal. I'll come down to your room. We can talk. Keep the door locked until—"

"No. I'll come there. I'm ready to go."

"Okay. Do you know the room number?"

"I just dialed it. I'm leaving now." She hung up.

Duncan went to the closet and found an extra blanket, and then put on a pair of pants. There were two pillows on the bed, so he took the one he'd been using and set it on the blanket, then heard the knock at the door. He looked out the fisheye lens set into the door and saw her, then swung the door open.

She came in and he turned on the overhead light. "No," she said. "I don't need to talk. I just want to sleep where there's somebody I know who won't let those people take me again. You have a gun, right?"

"Yes," he said.

He went to get the blanket and pillow from the closet shelf, then tossed the two couch cushions onto the floor. "You take the bed."

"No," she said. "Not good enough. I want to be next to you. Is that your side? I'll take this side."

He took his pillow with him and lay down where he had been.

She went to the other side of the bed, lay down, and pulled up the covers. He lay still and began to relax. After a few minutes he felt the bed move and then saw her silhouette in the dim light of the clock. She pulled her sweater up over her head and off, then stepped out of her jeans, then lay back down in her bra and underpants.

"What are you doing?"

"Getting comfortable. We're adults, right?"

"Yes," he said.

"Besides, you probably got an eyeful when you took my wet clothes off last night."

"No," he said. "I kept it dark so they wouldn't see the truck. Good night."

13

Early the next morning Renee was dressed and seated on the couch when Duncan became conscious. When he opened his eyes she said, "Hi. Good morning."

He glanced at the clock. "Sorry to keep you waiting. We had a busy day yesterday. Did you sleep okay?"

"Great. Thank you for taking me so far from town, and for letting me sleep here. I was so scared, but after I came up here I realized I should feel safe. We're going to have another busy day today."

"Doing what?"

"Breakfast first, and then driving me back to Parkman's Elbow in time to get some things done before the beginning of the evening shift. It's got to happen."

At 4:00 p.m. Renee was waiting at the head of the big table in front of the bar, sometimes called the birthday table because it was long enough for twelve on a side. Waiting with her were Victor

MacDonough, the most experienced bartender of the late shift, a big man about fifty years old; Madeleine Foster, a dinner shift waitress; Rice and Stallings, the waiters; Jimmy and Mike, the busmen and dishwashers; and Patsy and Tanya Moss, the sisters who tended bar during early evening and dinner. They came in and sat down last because they'd had to eat dinner before their shift.

Renee had put up signs on the front and back doors that said "Closed. Will reopen at 5:00 P.M." and then locked both doors. Harry Duncan sat on a chair near the front door and watched.

When everyone had settled at the table and their pleasure in talking to each other was overtaken by their curiosity about why Renee would call a meeting they began to look at her expectantly. She picked up a spoon and hit a glass to make it ring once. At that point Danny Flaherty, the chief cook, came through the swinging doors wiping his hands on a white towel and sat among the others.

When everyone was silent, Renee said, "Yesterday morning I got kidnapped. It was kind of an escalation of the bullshit that was going on with the three men named Clark who came in here trying to sell us protection three or four nights ago. That guy sitting over there—his name is Harry—figured out that the kidnappers had drugged me and were holding me in a boat anchored in the middle of the river, and dragged me across to shore."

There were murmurs of shock and sympathy, and more than a few looked at Duncan a second time.

Renee continued. "I don't know much about why this kind of thing has been happening. The people doing it are all new to me. But we're under attack."

She paused and looked at each of them for a few seconds. "Because all of you have worked so hard, and in spite of that, have been nice to everybody who came in here, The Elbow Room has made a lot of money—almost all of it for me. It's not worth risking anybody's life so I can make more money, so I won't. Tonight is the final night of business as usual. At closing time we'll all meet here again at the birthday table and split whatever cash we have at that time—the night's cash intake and the money that's in the safe at this moment. This Friday, as always, you'll get your paycheck deposited directly to your bank account. This will go on every two weeks until the first of the year. That's eight months. At that time, I'll decide what happens next."

"What do you mean by that?" Madeleine asked.

"I grew up in this place, and I really want to save it. If I'm sure the danger to all of us is back down to normal levels, we order a truckload of liquor and go right back to our old bad ways. But if things have gotten worse, I may drive a bulldozer through the front door and out the back and go do something else with my life. I don't know which it will be. In the meantime, you all have my gratitude and respect. As of lockup tonight we're all fired. We will still get our Elbow Room pay until January first. Any questions?"

"I know I speak for everyone when I—"

"That's not a question," Renee said. "Meeting adjourned." She stood, walked, and shouted, "Let's have a great last night. Nothing left but empty bottles." She waved her right arm in a circular motion and the workers got up. Some went to their jobs and buttoned vests and tied aprons while a couple went to unlock the doors and take down the signs.

Harry Duncan sat back and watched the bar's workers go back to their jobs. Renee walked up and sat across from him at his table.

"I assume you were listening."

"I was. I know it must be hard to do, but you weren't wrong. Money isn't a good thing to get people killed for."

She had tears forming in her eyes, and she sniffed and shook her head to stop them. "What I hate most is giving up. It took those people about a week to make me give up what generations of my family struggled to make."

"You're not giving it up. You just said you'll hold on to the place and reopen when it's safer."

"I'm not naive enough to really think those crooks are going to go away and leave me alone. But it's fine. I'm not a trained restaurateur or the jolly local publican. I'm a spoiled college girl who had learned how to throw a good party, so I kept doing it. I'm not putting my friends in danger just so I can keep making more money than I need."

"Good for you," he said.

"Are you leaving now?"

"If you want me to, I will. Otherwise, I thought I'd stay around and see what the last night is like."

"Fine," she said. "Then let me buy you a drink."

"Buy me a tonic with a lime in it."

"No alcohol?"

"It's my last vice, and I want to be perfect."

She went behind the bar, drew him the tonic, dropped the sliced lime in it, and held it out for him to take. Then she moved along the bar to the next man, who said, "Two single malt scotches on the rocks."

"What label?"

"Balvenie."

"Coming up."

Duncan watched her pour the amber liquid from the fat bottle over the ice in the crystal glasses and slide them gently to their new possessor, and then he moved and kept walking.

He had learned when he was a cop that it was best to look at any building from as many angles as possible. He kept going out the front door and began to walk the perimeter of the parking lot, sipping his tonic. He looked at the colors of the cars and trucks and where they were parked before the light faded and they would become harder to differentiate. Parking lots of bars and restaurants tended to fill up from the building outward and from the lit-up areas to the darkness, but there were some exceptions that it was useful to remember.

People who didn't want to be visible would park at the edges of the lot even if they arrived early. Darkness and distance weren't always about guilt, but they were a good place to look for it.

He was trying to get a good sense of the people he might meet later in the evening after the alcohol had been flowing for a few hours and the word that tonight was the final night had seeped outward into the general consciousness. He had noted earlier that the people who worked for Renee were all parked close to the building, but in the back of it. He had seen on his other nights observing the place that they usually stayed until the bar was closed and the place had been cleaned and locked, and then left in a group. That provided safety for the vulnerable and a sense of purpose for the more intimidating among them. He approved.

As the light retreated from the Ash River flood plain so did the business-hours traffic of delivery trucks and mail vans and flatbeds carrying construction equipment and dump trucks taking last loads. It was replaced by a mild rush hour, a steady stream of commuter cars, and after a brief pause, the evening traffic that came from the houses in the outlying areas and farms, toward the parking lots of places like The Elbow Room.

Duncan studied the lot to gauge the rates and the fill levels as he walked. Judging from the other nights of observation, things were happening more quickly than usual for a weeknight. He knew that The Elbow Room was a venerable landmark. It was probably the place where the majority of the local people had been on the night when they'd had their first legal drink.

He walked the circuit of the lot and then went in the back door of the kitchen and headed to the back hallway. By then people of both sexes were edged up against the two walls in line for the restrooms.

As he came forward toward the open barroom he could hear and feel the presence of a much larger crowd than the other nights—their voices, the sound and vibration of their many more feet, and for all he knew, the air pressure and faint hiss of their breath made the old building seem alive. As soon as he stepped into the barroom he saw Renee's eyes flick to focus on his, and she beckoned, ignoring the crowd while the other three bartenders kept pouring and serving.

When he reached her, they leaned toward each other over the bar's wet surface. "Everybody is working as fast as we can, but we're falling behind. I owe you a lot," she said. "I'll owe you more if you bring me a case each of whiskey, gin, vodka, and tequila from the storeroom."

He was surprised at first that she would ask, but it occurred to him that if there was anybody in the bar tonight sent to cause trouble, pretending to be a harmless bar employee wasn't bad cover for him. "Fancy brands?"

"Anything you can reach." She handed him the key to the storeroom. "The dolly is in there with the liquor."

He pivoted and headed back out the way he had come, past the people waiting their turns at the bathrooms, unlocked the door, and went inside and closed the door behind him. He built a five-high stack of liquor cases, tipped his stack so one side of it lifted a little, slid the foot of the dolly under the bottom one, and tilted the stack back so it rested securely against the two bars. He opened the door, pushed the dolly out, followed it, and stopped to relock the door. The people in the hallway could see he was on a mission to extend and feed the party, so they stepped apart in the hall to let him pass. When he reached the barroom and made the turn, Renee was already at the hinge on the bar's surface to lift the top and let him behind the bar.

He unloaded the five cases from the dolly, and Renee put her mouth beside his ear to say loudly, "Now we need three cases of reds, two white. They're drinking everything up as fast as we can open it."

Duncan took the dolly and turned back into the hall toward the storeroom. He made a stack of wine cases and wheeled them out of the room and up the hallway. The bar seemed full of people who were, or considered themselves, regulars. They had been drinking for hours, and by now some of them were laughter-prone and others getting nostalgic and weepy.

He delivered the wine and made two more trips to the storeroom before he set the dolly against the storeroom wall, went to the kitchen, and took a dish cart out among the tables. The busboys weren't able to keep up with the movement of glass. He cleared empty glasses from tables until the cart was too full of them to hold more, and then delivered them to the kitchen, helped the dishwashers get them loaded and a wash cycle started, and then went out for another load.

When the continuous supply was restored, he took a trip up the back hallway to get another look outside. As he got near the door, he felt a hand touch his arm and half-turned to see whose hand it was. It was a young woman with big blue eyes and copper-colored hair. She looked distressed as she said, "You work here, right? I saw you with the liquor cases." The voice was beautiful, almost musical.

Duncan felt sweat forming at his hairline. He knew the voice. This was the woman who had impersonated Renee on the phone call. "How can I help you?" he said.

She said, "My car is in the lot, out there." She pointed. "I was going to move it closer to the door, so when it's really late I won't have to walk way out there in the dark by myself. Now it won't start. It's a practically new Range Rover. I'm wondering if you could just go back there with me and take a look."

"I'm not a mechanic."

"Maybe not, but is your car stalled somewhere?"

"No, but—"

"Then you're an automotive engineer compared to me. Please. It's almost new. What I'm really afraid of is that some creep saw me leave it and then did something to it so when I go back there alone, what happens is up to him."

Duncan suspected that if he refused, she would try to kill him right away or she would say something nasty and leave to call the other kidnappers. Either way, she would disappear. If he pretended he was fooled, he could at least take a picture of her car's tag number. He said, "I'll walk back there with you, but I don't know what use I'll be."

She clung to his arm. "I'll think of something you can do."

She pulled him out away from the bar toward the outer reaches of the lot. He kept his demeanor cheerful and self-effacing, and his eyes off her face so she wouldn't wonder if he had made her. She kept her hands on his arm and pulled him, probably to get him away from the bar faster. It occurred to him, as it had many times in his career, how easy it was to separate a victim from anyone who would even notice he was gone. He formed the theory that she might have had a romantic relationship with the bearded man in the boat. Her mission might be to get Duncan out of the way of someone intending to harm Renee tonight, or she might simply want to kill the one who had killed her lover.

They were far out on the lot now, walking among the rows of cars in little more than the light of the stars. She reached into her purse and pressed her key fob, so her car yelped twice.

This made Duncan jerk his head toward it involuntarily. He realized instantly that he had let her manipulate his attention, and he compensated by stepping back to keep her from getting behind him. He saw that her left hand held both the purse and the fob, and now the right was in it and coming out with—what?

He caught sight of a glass tube in her hand, and at once disparate things became a picture. She wouldn't use a gun because it was too loud, and he could probably wrench a knife away from someone so much smaller before she made a fatal cut. Renee had been injected with something, and no wounds had been found on two of the Clark brothers. While he was reaching for her purse, she was raising what was in her right hand to her mouth to grip the cap with her teeth. She was about to bare the needle.

Duncan snatched her right wrist and held it, and then swung her in a circle, making her accelerate as she went in an arc. Her body swung against the nearest car, hit hard, and fell. He stepped forward to force her to drop the needle, but instantly changed direction because as he bent over she pushed off and lunged toward him, the hypodermic needle in her hand.

He knew that the doors of her car were unlocked because he had heard her press the key fob twice. He was close to the passenger door, and he took a step backward along the side as though retreating. As she charged toward him, he grasped the door handle and yanked the door open, sidestepping behind it and giving it a hard push toward her.

The needle was the first thing to reach the car door, and the speed and force Duncan had added to the collision broke the needle off the glass tube. He gave the door a second push, and the window's surface hit the woman's shoulder and the door propelled her backward. Duncan went to one knee to pick up the needle, but he didn't see it. He sprung up to fend off the woman, but she wasn't coming at him. She was gone.

He dropped to his belly to see if she had slithered under the Range Rover, but she hadn't. He moved to see if she was under any nearby car, but couldn't see her. He turned on his phone to produce light, but saw no sign of a human shape, either in motion or hiding. Duncan ran to one side of the Range Rover and sighted along the aisle of cars, and then moved to the next aisle, and then the next two perpendicular aisles.

He stopped at the tailgate of the Range Rover and took a picture of the plate. Then he used the phone to send it to Officer Slater's phone, and then called him. He said, "Hi, Officer Slater. This is Harry Duncan. I just got attacked by the woman who made the kidnapping call pretending to be Renee Parkman."

"How do you know it's her?"

"Her voice. She also tried to stab me with a hypodermic needle."

"Do you need an ambulance?"

"No. Not yet, anyway. I'm in The Elbow Room lot by her car, but she got away on foot. She's five-five, bright red hair, like copper. Blue eyes. I sent you her license number so maybe you can get her name. Now I'm heading back into the bar."

"We'll be there in a few minutes."

He punched in Renee's number and then realized she'd never hear a call over the noise in the bar. He texted her, "The woman kidnapper, 5 ft 5, blue eyes, has bright red hair tonight, could be coming after you. Stay with the big guys."

He opened the driver's door of the Range Rover, popped the hood, tore out the wire bundle running along the side, then ran for the bar. He reached the front door and walked quickly through the place, his eyes scanning for anything that reminded him of the red-haired woman who had attacked him—any woman who was wearing any headgear that could hide the red hair, one who was her height and shape but may have put on or removed a wig, one with the light-leather purse he'd seen her reach into for the needle.

Duncan made it to the bar, ducked under the hinged break in the top, and stepped to Renee. He came up from behind while she filled a pitcher of beer. She half-turned and spoke over her shoulder. "How did you find her?"

"She found me," he said. "She just tried to inject me with a needle. She was the woman who called me up pretending to be you."

She put the pitcher on the bar so the man standing there could take it away.

"What do we do?" she said.

"I called the cops and they're on the way. For now, we watch out."

Duncan noticed Vic MacDonough had been watching without seeming to. Duncan said, "The woman involved in Renee's kidnapping was here and tried to stab me with a needle. She has red hair and blue eyes. She looks twenty-five to thirty, five foot five."

MacDonough said, "Does she still have the needle?"

"That one's broken, but they're small. She could have twenty more in her purse."

"Or something bigger and badder."

"I didn't see a gun."

Duncan sidestepped from one worker to another, warning each of them individually.

A few minutes later he saw the flashes of red and blue lights move across the windows and knew that the police had arrived. Slater came inside while the other cops stayed in their cars and cruised up and down the aisles in the parking lot.

Duncan and Slater met near the end of the room, where they had the widest and most inclusive view of the crowd. Slater said, "Have you seen her again?"

"No. I'm thinking she realized she was lucky to get away alive."

"Not you, though, huh?"

"I would have liked to turn her over to you guys, but I'm still feeling lucky that I could find Renee alive and get her back. There's a long shot chance that the Range Rover in the lot can lead you to the identity she's using, if not to a real name."

"Other officers will be taking a look at the car about now. The plates you took pictures of are stolen from a 2019 Chevrolet originally sold in Arkansas and reregistered in Gary. The vehicle identification number may lead to her, but when I see some hocus pocus in a car's history, there's usually more to come."

"Yeah, the stolen plates are usually the sign it's going to be a waste of time. Sorry."

A few minutes later, after he had made the rounds of The Elbow Room, Slater went off. Two other police officers stayed for the next hour, watching the area to spot the red-haired woman or some indication that the bar's adversaries were about to cause more violence. To Duncan it seemed likely that their presence helped keep the evening calmer, and may even have reminded some people that accepting a ride home was not an admission of weakness. They also helped the crowd get over their reluctance to let The Elbow Room close on time.

At two A.M. Madeleine said to Renee, "You don't have to, you know. What are they going to do to you, shut the bar down?"

"Pull my liquor license," Renee said. "We could never open again. As soon as the cops are out the doors, lock them and turn off the signs."

The bartenders, waiters, dishwashers, and busboys were already helping the last customers keep going until they were on the outside in the lot. It was only a few minutes before the Elbow Room staff were the only ones left. They all went into their nightly routines of vacuuming and mopping, picking up the used glasses and loading them into the dishwashers, wiping tables, and inverting chairs on them so the floor polisher could move freely.

Duncan helped MacDonough take the cases of empty bottles and unopened liquor back to the storeroom. When they were inside, MacDonough bent over, moved a crate aside, and opened a trapdoor. The two men went down the steps into the cellar carrying the cases of unopened liquor and stacking them. The ones they left in the storeroom on the ground floor were cases of empties. As soon as the two men were up in the storeroom again they closed the trapdoor and pushed the crate over it.

They went to the office, where Renee had opened the safe. She handed each of them some canvas bank deposit bags full of cash. She left the safe open. MacDonough looked at her. "No point in locking it right now, is there?" she said. "It's empty."

As they went out and up the hall to the bar, they saw that the staff had moved the big party table to the spot in front of the bar again. Renee said, "If anybody wants a free drink before we get to the end of this, go make it for yourself. Just don't drive drunk."

A few people went behind the bar while others moved chairs and settled. Renee, Duncan, and MacDonough set the canvas bags on the table. Renee said, "During our break a few hours ago, Madeleine and I opened the safe and split some of the cash we had on hand into equal packets. Somebody can start handing them out." Several people carried bags to the foot of the table and began walking back to the head handing each person a banded stack of bills. Another group worked the opposite way. When they met, Renee called out, "Did everybody get one?"

Lots of people answered "Yes," and nobody said "No."

"Then put it away now. You're going to need both hands for this. Now let's split tonight's cash. Pull all the cash drawers and dump them on the table. Really empty them. Look under the bill slots for the big bills. Spread it all out so people will be able to reach it."

The table was covered with green bills. "Next, everybody start by taking five hundred dollars. Take five hundreds or five hundred ones, it doesn't matter except to you." When the process was completed, she said "Okay. I think we can safely do that a second time. Everybody take another five hundred."

She repeated the five-hundred-dollar order five more times before Rice, the waiter, stood and said, "Thank you, Renee. I'm done. Split the rest without me. I assume I'll see you all around town. Maybe we'll go fishing when it gets warmer."

Within a minute or two the idea had caught on, and all the others had done the same. Renee said, "All right. I propose that we put the leftovers in a fund for when we reopen. I hate washing the windows in this place. We can use it to pay a window-cleaning service to make them perfectly clean before we open up. Is everyone okay with that?"

There was a round of applause, and then two of the waiters scraped the remaining cash into a bag while Madeleine held it open and then handed it to Renee, who carried it to the office and locked it in the safe. When she came out, she hurried through the crowd of employees, shaking hands, but ducking the kisses. "Come on, stop it. Everybody go home and wake up the one you really want to kiss. Get out of here. If your regular paycheck isn't in your account next Friday, call your bank. If they don't fix it call me."

When the final stragglers were out, Duncan said, "You're not going back to your house, are you?"

"Nope. Madeleine said I could spend the night at her place. And I'm going to ride with her. Thanks for asking. In fact, we're going now. You can go out with us."

He walked to his car and got in, then watched her lock the front door and then walk a few paces in the lot to Madeleine's car. He started his engine and drove around the building. The only car left was the black Land Rover that belonged to the woman with the needles, disabled when he'd yanked some of the wiring out. He kept going around the building and saw Madeleine's car turning to leave the lot to take the river road toward the town center, gave it a few seconds to move out of sight, and then followed at a distance. At first he kept his lights off, not turning them on until he was in the main part of the downtown section.

He followed until he saw the car make a turn, and then drove one block farther to turn up the first parallel street, then sped to the first corner. He waited at the first corner watching for Madeleine's car to pass on the parallel street, and then started again and waited at the next corner. Her car stopped and turned into a driveway in the middle of the third block, so he waited a few minutes for the women to go inside and then noted which house's driveway it had been and drove on.

Duncan had been set off-balance by the evening, and as he drove, he had no trouble identifying what was bothering him. The violence this group were bringing into this string of small towns seemed wildly out of proportion. The money they could hope to squeeze out of this region wasn't enough to make this effort pay off. There must be something else.

Much of what they had done could have been part of an attempt to simply terrify the local people at the outset. People who were afraid enough would tolerate a lot. But paying some thug a thousand bucks not to tow your car wasn't going to even keep the thug fed for long. Getting even the best local bar to pay for protection couldn't be enough to bankrupt the bar, or the money would stop coming. The terms the Clark brothers had demanded would have left the bar intact, but it wasn't enough to keep three Clark brothers going, and it would have been even less after the bosses had taken their cut.

He had been studying the behavior of career crooks like these for most of his working life. This time of night was when many of them were likely to be out, and not many other people were. After the bars closed in most cities the world seemed to be deserted except for cops and criminals. Before he went to sleep, he would take a last look at the town.

14

Gerald Russell sat in the passenger seat of the Lexus IS 350 F Sport. He liked the interior and he liked the 311 horsepower engine that could propel it along a road at one hundred forty miles an hour. He liked even better that it looked like nothing special. Every Lexus for the past couple years seemed to have that ugly front end, a screen like the front of a fencer's mask. He had made sure that this one would be the color of dusty asphalt, so it would be hard to see on a road. He was almost a quarter mile from The Elbow Room, sitting at the edge of the empty parking lot of a supermarket that had been closed since midnight. It was almost 3:00 A.M., nobody had seen Renee Parkman leave the bar when her employees did, and she wasn't at her house. There had been some talk about her closing down the bar, so maybe she had been clearing out her desk or something, but it shouldn't take this long.

His lieutenant, Mullins, had found him a driver named Gil Banks, a genuine pro. He had done more than a few getaways, including a couple in which the troubles he was taking his passenger away from were killings. Russell respected Mullins because Mullins didn't need to have every damned thing explained to him. He had known that finding and hiring the right people was the most crucial way to achieve success. Mullins had outdone himself by hiring Banks. He was a terrific driver—able to go race-car fast, but also tireless, patient, and above all, silent. He even shared one important quality with Russell. Neither of them had ever been arrested, let alone charged with anything. A routine police stop would turn up nothing.

Russell took out his phone and touched the line that didn't say Mullins but had his phone number. He heard Mullins answer, "Mullins." Russell said, "What's happening?"

"The customers went home, the cops went toward their station, and the staff seem to be all gone too. We haven't seen Renee Parkman or her boyfriend yet."

"Then you'd better move in before she disappears too."

Mullins left his phone line open while he spoke into a handheld radio. "Time to go get her, guys," he said. Along the river road south of The Elbow Room, three cars that had been parked off the road swung out and coasted down onto the road again. None of them had their lights on. They all turned in the direction of The Elbow Room, gliding along the dark highway, sticking to the middle, straddling the center line to keep from going off the unlit pavement.

The cars were all moving about twenty-five miles an hour, each following the occasional flashes of red brake lights of the car in front of it. Mullins's car reached the entrance to The Elbow Room's parking lot, and the other two pulled in past it. One drove to the back door and the other to the front, and both stopped. Mullins used the handheld radio to say, "Hold where you are until the truck gets finished." Then he switched to his phone and pressed a number. "Bring the truck in now."

A moment later a flatbed tow truck pulled onto the lot. It went to the spot away from The Elbow Room near the edge of the lot, pulled around the disabled Range Rover stranded in the lot earlier in the evening, and backed up to its front end. The driver jumped out, tilted the flatbed so it touched the ground, took the end of the cable from the winch, attached its hook to the ring under the front end of the Range Rover, activated the winch to drag the Range Rover up onto the flatbed, connected the safety chains to it, and raised the bed to level it. He threw a strap over the vehicle and buckled it, gave everything one hard tug, got into the cab of his truck, and drove out of The Elbow Room's lot.

Mullins called Russell. "The Range Rover is on the truck and gone."

"Thanks," Russell said. He disconnected and then pressed another line. "Hello, Jeanette. Do you know who this is?"

"Yes," she said. "I'm really sorry. It was a stupid mistake."

"I wanted you to know that the Range Rover is on the tow truck. It will be cut up for parts by dinnertime tomorrow."

"Oh, man," she said. "That's good news. Thank you. I owe you."

"We still need to have a talk about that, but at least this much is done. Don't come back to Parkman's Elbow unless I tell you to."

"I won't."

He ended this conversation too. He said to Banks the driver, "Take me up near the bar now."

The Lexus moved, its lights off like the other cars. When it had come within about two hundred feet from the building, beside Mullins's car, Banks stopped. Russell called Mullins. "Send them in."

A moment later car doors began to open and eight men in dark clothes got out. They closed the doors of their cars but left the engines running and converged on the bar. Two of the men carried a crowbar and a flashlight, and a couple of others had wire cutters and screwdrivers. Russell watched, and in a few seconds the men were disconnecting wires along the eaves and on the back of the building, and then a man inserted his crowbar and popped the door open. Four men went in through the front entrance with guns drawn. Russell heard no alarm sound—no tone, bell, siren, anything. He knew the ones at the back door were doing the same. He was pleased.

Inside the bar, the men of the attack squad went about sorting themselves out. They were all experienced users of force, but most of them had never worked with any of the others before. As they came into the bar, they eyed each other to memorize faces so they didn't make a fatal mistake later. Mullins came in through the front door and walked among them.

"They're probably hiding somewhere," he said. "You've got to go room to room and flush them out."

As Mullins headed back out the front entrance he thought about the room he had just seen. The floors had been mopped and polished, the tables wiped, the chairs inverted on the tables. In the counters along the back wall there were piles of napkins, crates of clean glasses, flatware holders with separate spaces for knives, forks, and spoons, salt and pepper shakers, piles of clean plates. The place looked as though they were ready to open up in the morning.

It was going smoothly. Four men went down the hallway on the right side of the bar that led to the restrooms, and four went down the left side of the bar that led to the storeroom, pantry, and kitchen. There was no jostling or hesitation. Mullins lingered for a minute in front, then returned to his car to wait.

Nearly two hundred feet away, Mullins's employer, Russell, surveyed The Elbow Room and the surrounding lots, and felt pleased. The men were doing this right. No lights had been visible on cars, and no light had escaped the building yet. All the cars were now parked near the building with their engines running, so if anything went wrong, it would be easy to get everyone out in seconds. Sometimes in operations like this, there were well-hidden alarms that went off, even fire alarms, but nothing like that had occurred so far.

Russell listened to the radio transmissions and what he heard felt to him like congratulations. "The barroom is clear." "The restrooms are both clear." Russell heard a toilet flushing in the background, and smiled. It was like evidence that there was no resistance. But it didn't mean the visit was accomplishing anything.

He said into his hand radio, "You are looking for Renee Parkman. She's the whole reason for this. She's the one we need." He liked to give instructions to his guys. He believed that it gave them the illusion that he was right there with them facing risks and making decisions. The truth this time was that he'd misjudged Renee Parkman. He'd thought that since nobody had seen her leave, she'd be here.

The men inside the building had finished their search for Renee Parkman and Harry Duncan. They went back over the areas they had searched, this time looking for things to steal. They had not been given permission to steal anything, but they knew that stealing things would contribute to the ruin of Renee Parkman, and was therefore in general consistency with the mission. The safe bolted into the wall in the tiny office had been left locked. It was probably empty anyway, if the bar was shutting down.

The cash registers were worth a lot of money, but they weren't something these men could use. They had all been emptied of money and the cash drawers put back. This pushed them into the category of loot that was effectively worthless but got a man a much longer sentence. There was a lot of liquor on the shelves behind the bar, but it all seemed to be one bottle of this and one bottle of that, most of the bottles opened, with silver pour spouts in place of the caps and stoppers.

Some of the men had noticed that there was a storeroom full of liquor cases on their first incursion into the building to find Renee Parkman. Now a couple of them returned to the storeroom to look more closely. The first two dozen cases were full of empty bottles, but farther into the room, they began to find whole cases of pristine stock. A case of twelve bottles of seventy-five-dollar scotch or two-hundred-dollar champagne seemed like a treasure at this hour of the night. The other six men were drawn by the light, and a few cases had begun to migrate out of the storeroom when one of the men froze. "You hear something?" Another man held up his hand and put his index finger to his lips. The room fell into a profound silence. Then he began to tiptoe, listening.

Whether they had heard something or not, the idea caught on. If someone else had heard it, then it must exist. If it existed, it didn't matter who hadn't heard it. The man credited with hearing it pointed down at the floor. Another man whispered, "We know they aren't anywhere else."

Two of them went straight to the largest and heaviest item they could see. It was the wooden crate that Duncan and MacDonough had pushed there. The two men who thought they'd heard something pushed the crate aside and revealed a section of the wooden floor with a ring set into it that could be pulled up from its recessed spot and used as a handle.

As the men converged on the trapdoor, there were probably many theories, but the most prominent was that the basement was a hiding place for Renee Parkman and her boyfriend, and the noise had been caused by one of them tripping over something.

Time began to be important as soon as the trapdoor was open. Moving in fast was essential. The first man went down the narrow steps quickly, turning on his flashlight and holding his gun ahead of him, and as the next one came down after him, he saw the old porcelain socket fixture on the ceiling had a bulb in it, but he didn't see a light switch at first, so he stuck with his flashlight, sweeping the basement with its beam to detect anyone hiding, and moved sideways to get out of the way of the ones coming down the steps.

The psychology and social issues among the men during the raid had been complex. This was their first attack together, so none of them wanted to be seen as men who hung back or ran slower when things got dangerous. They wanted to be leaders, so at any moment many were trying to lead, and were feeling irritated at anyone else who was doing the same.

The three flashlights sweeping in three patterns across the space while the men were moving caused moving shadows on the walls behind the cases, and one of the men seemed to think he'd seen an enemy ducking down to open fire. He fired three rapid shots at the imagined man, and one of his companions fired a round through each of the cardboard cases in the hope that he was crouching there. The three holding flashlights realized the lights made them targets and quickly turned them off.

One of them yelled, "Stop firing!" but two others began issuing their calls to "Get down!" and "Spread out!" at the same time. This seemed to trigger a shouting match that made them all incomprehensible. There was another shot.

The report was followed by a grunt, and the plea, "Don't shoot. It was an accident." Someone replied, "Then drop your gun!" and another said, "Turn on a light."

If anyone had noticed the sound of the trap slamming shut during the deafening claps of the pistols firing in the enclosed space, they had not grasped its significance. Instead, the related matter of the darkness seemed most urgent. No fewer than four men repeated the yell, "Turn on a light!" but none of them felt safe enough to be the one to do it at first. The room was silent for a few seconds.

One man shouted as loudly as he could, "I'm turning on a light."

The beam was bright enough light to show two men lying on the stone floor wounded or dead. The man with the flashlight stepped behind the row of liquor cases and aimed its beam on the two figures lying on the floor. "It's not them. They're both our guys."

This time the comments from his peers were different. "Oh, God. Are you all right?" Another said, "Probably not. Can't you see the guy got hit in the head?" There were a few more communications to God and Jesus, a couple in which aspiring leaders ordered strangers to apply a bandage or a tourniquet to other strangers, and even a few assurances of "You're going to be all right" to the dead.

Someone said, "Can you get a signal on your phone?"

"I got nothing."

"We're underground and surrounded by stone and mortar."

Outside the building Harry Duncan was heading for the place a few hundred yards away where he had left his car. Going inside the bar to close the trap and roll the refrigerator over it had been risky, but he couldn't go in and arrest two carloads of armed men, and he'd had to do something. He moved along the riverbank as quickly as he could. As soon as he was in his car pulling away, he called the police.

Russell was getting impatient. How long did it take to drag one woman out of an empty bar? He pushed the button to lower his window. Sitting here getting more and more irritated had caused him to feel a wave of nausea, and he hoped the fresh air would help. He leaned partway out the window. He heard a faint sound that he had not heard before because the windows had been closed. It was a "Bup bup bup bubbup" that sounded as though it were coming from a distance.

"Jesus," said Russell. "Gunfire. Get me out of here."

As he said it, his right-hand man, Mullins, stepped quickly from his car to Russell's and said, "Something's wrong. We should get out."

"Not you," said Russell. "You've still got a job to do. If the guys come out and see we're both gone, they'll lose respect for us. They'll think we're cowards, running away."

"What do you expect me to do here?"

"Supervise. Get them out of here. Show them we don't leave a man behind." Russell nodded to Banks, and the Lexus swung in a tight arc to get out onto the river road and head southward away from the town of Parkman's Elbow.

15

Harry Duncan parked a few blocks from Renee Parkman's friend Madeleine's house, then walked the rest of the way in the blue-gray light of the predawn. He went up on the porch and knocked. He heard no response, so he knocked again. This time he felt a vibration of the floorboards under his feet. He watched the curtain of the front window to his right. It twitched aside as someone looked. He waved, and a moment later the door opened.

Renee said, "What's up?"

"Eight or ten guys went to The Elbow Room and broke in."

"Is it still there?"

"It was when I left about fifteen minutes ago."

"What time is it now?"

"About five."

"Was it necessary to tell me now?"

"They went there looking for you."

She turned and walked back into Madeleine's living room, and then stepped into a pair of sneakers and tied them. She hurried into the kitchen, took the pen off a pad, and scribbled something.

"Just thanking my hostess." She turned and stepped to the door and went out with him.

Duncan said, "I left my car a couple blocks down this way."

"Where are we going?"

"Your house."

"Is that a good idea? They must know where I live."

"I'll check it out before you go in."

When they reached his car, he said, "Don't get in just yet." He stared at the nearby houses, up and down the street at cars parked there, got down on his hands and knees and used his phone as a flashlight to look underneath the car, then got up and opened the hood and examined the engine compartment.

Renee said, "No nukes?"

"Not this time." He opened her door, then his door, and gave the interior a careful look. He sat in the driver's seat and started the engine. She got in beside him.

As he moved the car away from the curb, he said, "You've closed The Elbow Room. Do you have some additional strategy you're planning to try?"

"I just didn't think that my friends deserved to be in danger so I could buy more stuff next year. Now I'm asking your advice. You're the Whatever-the-hell-you-are."

"True. I am. I think it's time to run away for a week or two. Start thinking about what's at your house you need."

"Not much. Papers and jewelry are in my safe deposit box at the bank, and I've got a lot of credit cards. I'd like to make sure things are turned off, locked up, and so on."

"Credit cards make you easy to trace. For now, it's safer to use cash as long as you can. We can stop at a bank and get you some." He drove through the predawn town seeing only a few other cars. When they reached her house he pulled up to the front steps. "Give me your house key and sit tight." He took her key ring, got out of his car, unlocked the front door, and pulled out his pistol and a flashlight and went inside. After a few minutes he came to the door and beckoned. As she walked in past him he said, "It's clear."

She went inside and upstairs, packed a soft bag with wheels but carried it downstairs on a shoulder strap, and went from window to window making sure each was latched, made sure the deadbolt on the back door was locked, and finally turned down the thermostat. On the front porch she took out her keys and pressed the fob, listened to her car give the beep that meant it was locked through the garage door, then went down the stairs and stood at the trunk of his car.

He put her bag in the trunk, they both got in, and he drove off. She said, "Where next?"

"An airport some distance from here. Maybe Indianapolis. Have you thought about where you want to spend some time?"

"No."

"I'm going to get you to an airport, buy you a plane ticket, and get you on the plane. If you don't have anybody you can stay with, I've got some friends in Los Angeles."

Gerald Russell was back in his office in Indianapolis. He had not slept. On the drive from Parkman's Elbow he had barely blinked. Now he was simultaneously waiting for enough time to pass so he could call Chicago and desperately trying to think of a way to report that would maintain Chicago's trust in him.

As the time got used up, he drank coffee to stay alert and fully awake, but slowly the black liquid became a poisonous acid that sat inside him and felt to him as though it was etching the lining of his stomach. His phone rang, and he looked at the number on the screen.

Them. It was them. He felt an impulse to duck down, as though they were watching him. He knew they would never make a FaceTime call, and that gave him the courage to answer. He lifted the phone. "Russell."

"Good morning." It was the voice he found the least intimidating, the man with the cultivated accent. "Do you have an update for me?"

"Yes, of course," Russell said. "Things have been moving along in the right direction, although I never let that satisfy me because I know the pace of this project matters too." He waited a tiny fraction of a second for some kind of human response like encouragement, but none was coming, so he kept talking.

"Renee Parkman, the woman who owns The Elbow Room, closed it down last night. I had hoped to get the formalities begun right after closing time, so I was there with a crew of eight men, but apparently she was so terrified and broken that she and her current boyfriend vanished. Since she seems to have left town for good, it's possible I can take ownership through a tax sale or a loan repurchase. It won't cost much."

"What else?"

"We're moving ahead in all areas at once," he said. "We've got another seventeen businesses paying for protection since last week."

"We're not interested in any of this," the man said.

Russell's heart pounded with joy. Now he could say he had tried to be open and report on everything, but Chicago had not been interested. "I'm sorry to bore you with details," Russell said. "It's just another way to get the properties, by raising the vig until they fall behind and have to make me a partner and eventually let us buy them out for almost nothing."

"We know," the man said. "Remember the reason you're good at the details. You're a realtor, not a gangster. When I hear you use slang like you were a mafia boss from yesteryear, I only feel weary despair. Remember what you're there for and get on with it."

"Yes," Randall said. "I'll have my guys step it up."

"Do that."

Russell heard nothing, so he looked at the phone again. Chicago was gone. Russell closed his eyes, partly in relief, and partly because closing his eyes felt so good after being up all night and all morning. He opened his eyes, blinked a few times, and then turned off the office light. He went to the couch, lay down, and let his eyes shut. His stomach hurt, but he knew his exhaustion would overwhelm and defeat the discomfort.

⌁

After they had stopped at a branch of Renee's bank so she could get cash, Duncan drove toward the Illinois border, but stopped at Terre Haute, Indiana, instead of going on, and pulled up in the short-term lot at the airport. She looked at him. "This is it—Terre Haute?"

"This is it. Anybody looking for you at an airport will think you either left from Indianapolis or drove on to O'Hare or Midway."

"I guess that makes sense," she said.

"Have you decided where you'd like to go?"

"I think so. I have relatives in a couple places, but if these people want to find me badly enough, they could ask around and find out who they are. So I've decided to visit an old friend in Denver. I met her in college, and nobody but me really knows her."

"That sounds like a good choice," he said. "I'll go in with you and buy your ticket."

"Why? I have money."

"Because I have a credit card in the name Mike Carmody. It won't show up when somebody starts running credit checks on you. Keep the cash for Denver."

There was a flight that would stop in Denver in three hours, so after he bought her ticket he sat with her for a while in a Starbucks near the airline ticket counters. While they were having their coffee she said, "Do you see any?"

"Any what?"

"Whatever you're scanning the crowd for."

"People who are scanning the crowd for us. I haven't seen any yet."

"Then you're free to go. Thank you for doing so much to help me and make me safe. If I go the rest of the way in, past the security area, nobody with a weapon can get anywhere near me. If I see anybody scary I'll hide in the ladies' restroom and call the cops."

Duncan stood. "Okay. When you get where you're going, maybe you can give me a call and let me know."

"First thing," she said. "At least one of the first five things."

"Good enough." He stood, took his coffee cup, turned, and walked out the door of the terminal toward the short-term parking lot.

16

Duncan drove into Terre Haute and rented a room at a La Quinta Inn for two days. He used his company credit card for Polestripe Tonsorial Supply. On this one the name was Roger Collins. He preferred commercial account names, commercial addresses, and businessmen's names so common they were hard to remember. The country was being crossed and recrossed every day by sales, advertising, manufacturing, importing, and distributing specialists buying and selling such a variety of products that nobody remembered them all.

He parked in the lot and opened his trunk, and then his suitcase. He repacked his wallet with the right cards and license, then hesitated for a moment, thinking he might leave his gun in the locked case attached to the car under the floor where it would be very hard to find and nearly impossible to steal, then took it with him.

His feelings about guns were complicated. When he was in the Los Angeles Police Academy, the instructors trained cadets hard. They taught him everything about his weapon including when he'd need it and when he wouldn't. They had him fire thousands of rounds through targets hung at various distances. There were lots of practice sessions made to train his reflexes to shoot accurately and his judgment when not to shoot at all. As long as he had stayed with the department, he had retested every month and gotten a small bump in pay for maintaining high scores. In a very short time he had become so comfortable carrying the pistol that he felt uncomfortable without it.

Early on, he had noticed something odd. He had learned a lot of methods, techniques, procedures, and options. But if a person was carrying a gun, the biggest option was the gun. All those other methods were fine, but the gun kept reminding him that it was there, tempting him to use it. This time, he kept it in his suitcase and brought the suitcase inside.

He had not slept since the last night of The Elbow Room, and now he was exhausted. He went to his room and slept until six the next morning. When he woke he went to work on his murder book, and kept at it for most of the next day.

On the evening of the third day in Terre Haute, Duncan used his burner cell phone to call Officer Slater at the Parkman's Elbow Police Department a few minutes after the night watch had begun.

"Hello, Officer Slater," he said.

"Jesus, Duncan," Slater said. "I thought you were dead. The state police are getting ready to list you."

"If you could head that off, I'd appreciate it," Duncan said.

"I'll try." He paused. "Do you happen to know the whereabouts of Miss Parkman?"

"Yes, I do," he said. "I drove her to the airport in Terre Haute and bought her a plane ticket to Denver. She was going to stay with a friend of hers from college for a while to let herself cool down. That was my idea."

"Good idea," Slater said. "She seems to have been the main object of the new extortion racket."

"Do you have any information you can tell me about what's going on there now?"

"The big stuff happened a few hours after I talked to you the night the bar closed. We had a couple of calls from people who had driven past The Elbow Room and said it didn't look right, like it was vandalized. When we went into The Elbow Room it was after six A.M. The basement under the storeroom had two male fatalities from gunshot wounds. If you know anything about that, we should set up an interview as soon as possible."

"I do," Duncan said. "I was out in the lot and saw a few guys had broken in. I closed the trapdoor, but I didn't see anything that happened in the basement."

"Too bad," Officer Slater said. "Both men had fired weapons. Hard to tell whether they shot each other, or somebody else shot them or what."

"I couldn't think of anything they could be after except Renee, so I left to pick her up and get her out of town to let things cool off."

"I'd say from outcomes you did the right thing," Slater said.

"Thanks. Have you figured out who the dead guys were yet?"

"I just heard from the sergeant that we already got some print matches in during day watch. The names meant zero to anybody here, but we're getting more information."

"Great. If their prints are on record there will be something on them. How about the first one—the kidnapper from the boat?"

"That one I know about. His name was Rankin, Paul R. He was forty-two, and had a record for a range of violent infractions and crimes in Illinois."

"Do you have an address for him?"

"I remember it was in the Chicago area, but I'll look it up for you when you come in. When can we expect you?"

"Tonight or early tomorrow. I'm still in Terre Haute, so I've got a long drive, and you might be off duty before I get there."

"Good enough. Don't come in telling everybody we're sharing information. Whatever I have time to copy I'll leave in the top of my locker so somebody can get it to you if it's after my shift. I can't leave it lying around."

"Are you sure you want to do that?"

"Yes. We're not set up to handle this. They brought twice as many men to raid that empty bar as we had on duty that night. So far, you're the only one who's given us any actual help. If I don't see you when you get here, I'll see you tomorrow night."

Duncan had made the drive only two days earlier to get Renee Parkman to an airport that enemies would not anticipate she would use. The trip had taken about four hours and forty minutes, but it had been on interstate highways occupied by hundreds of long-distance trucks and a dense stream of sedans, SUVs, and pickups. When he packed his suitcase in his hotel room, he took special care to save the information he had added to his murder book file, sent it to his office computer, and put his laptop on top so he could hide it in the deepest part of his false floor in the trunk. This had become a case that merited extra precautions. He was checked out of his hotel and on the road again just after midnight.

At a few minutes before three A.M. Officer Glen Slater finished making the copy of the information that the state police had sent on the two dead men and the destruction at The Elbow Room. He put the zip drive in an envelope and set it above his locker, where it would be easy to find. His turn to take a shift patrolling the town was due to start in five minutes, so he put two protein bars in his pocket, took a bottled water from the refrigerator, and stopped in the men's room for a piss before he headed out the back.

He started the engine of the black-and-white with the giant number 826 painted on its roof. To him the numbers were kind of funny, because there were only seven cars in the PEPD fleet. The numbers were for identifying who was on a radio call, but seeing one did seem to imply a bigger force. He pulled out onto Main Street and headed up the empty pavement, looking for anything different—a broken window, an old person walking along the street looking lost, or a person not standing up at all.

The night wasn't as cold as they had been lately, so he rolled down his window. Being exposed to the night air added another dimension to his patrols, because it let him hear things. A dog barking in the night or a car alarm were sometimes as revealing as a phone call. He took the usual routes—coasting quietly along the alley behind the stores along Jefferson Street shining his flashlight on loading doors, then turning at the end of the block of stores and going up Constitution Avenue. He drifted into the intersection with each residential street for a moment to scan for anything new. He took his time at the places that were perennial trouble spots—around restaurants where liquor was served, and along the riverbanks inside the town.

After about an hour he heard a call from Rhonda, the dispatcher on duty tonight. "1-826, request location."

"Heading north River Road coming up on Grand Avenue."

"We have a call of a domestic, four four two Washington."

He pushed down on the gas pedal. "Show me en route."

"Roger 826."

He sped through the center of the city, his lights on but no siren, staying on the major streets to get close faster. Like every cop, he dreaded domestics. The danger was always exaggerated when the two were in love, or had been, especially to the cop. He didn't know who lived at 442, but he was fairly likely to recognize them when he got there.

On the radio Rhonda said, "The caller was the female. No indication of any weapons or hostages."

"This is 826. Show me on scene." He put his microphone in its holder, got out of the car, and made quick strides to the door and knocked. There were lights on behind the window, but no sounds. He listened and knocked again, more loudly. "Police," he said. "Open up."

The door opened. The one in front of him was male, about thirty-five and wearing a sport coat, as though it were five in the afternoon. He looked at Slater's nameplate and said, "Good evening, Officer Slater." He was smiling. "Come in."

Slater stepped inside. "Thank you. We received a call from this address—"

Slater was suddenly aware that someone was behind him. He half-turned and realized there was another man in the room.

"Don't get nervous, it's okay," the man said. "No danger. We just wanted to talk to you alone for a few minutes. Afterward, you can just tell them this was a false alarm or a prank call, or whatever."

"What do you want?"

The man smiled. "We want a friend on the police force." He slowly lifted his left hand and grasped his lapel between his thumb and forefinger and pulled it away from his chest so he could reach into the inner pocket to pull out the white business envelope sticking up, then held it out to Slater.

Slater reached out and took it. He could feel that what it held was money. "Who are you?"

"My name is Mullins. That envelope is two thousand five hundred dollars. If you're our friend, then once a month there will be another one. It goes on forever."

"And what do you want for it?"

"Friendship, nothing beyond that. Like any other friendship. Maybe an introduction to another friend of yours. If you hear something bad is coming our way, you'd warn us like you'd warn any other friend. You can put that money away. Even if you don't want to be friends, you can say no and keep it. What do you say?"

Slater quickly pulled his gun. "I say you're under arrest."

He heard something behind him, and realized that there must be another man he hadn't seen stepping inside and closing the door, but before he could turn to face him the bullet was penetrating his skull.

A half hour later, Harry Duncan drove into Parkman's Elbow and called Officer Glen Slater's cell phone. The phone rang eight times, its screen lighting inside his shirt pocket and showing through the fabric of Slater's shirt, but he had been strapped with the seat belt into the passenger seat of car 826, and there was nobody alive nearby to hear it.

17

Duncan went to Slater's funeral three days later. The family had been surprised that Slater's body had been released for burial so soon. They had been a police family for the past three generations, and more than once a funeral had been held up for an autopsy and some other forensic work. All homicides were serious, but the murder of a police officer didn't happen often or get treated as routine.

This time the medical examiner had found that other than taking photographs, testing the blood for drugs and alcohol, and drawing the pictures of the wound on the human male template on the form, not much needed to be done. He had been shot from behind at close range with a 9 mm round. His own 9 mm weapon had not been fired. The body had stopped bleeding before it had been transported.

The funeral was held at the Presbyterian church and the burial at the Protestant cemetery off the northeast corner of the Parkman land. As in many old towns, there were more bodies in the cemeteries than there were walking around. The Protestants probably still held an edge, but the Catholic cemetery had been gaining on them for over a century.

There were small contingents of police officers from nearby towns and another from the State Police. There was a solitary bagpiper who apparently had needed to be brought from India-napolis. After the saying of the appropriate words and the burial, Duncan stayed to observe the civilian mourners. He had seen a few funerals in which the people responsible for the death had shown up to watch from a distance, but this time he couldn't pick out anybody watching from a safe distance.

A woman who was almost certainly Slater's mother was given the folded flag from the coffin, but Duncan didn't speak to her. She thanked the police chief, a white-haired man with a limp, for the glowing words he had said about her son, who had been actively engaged in at least four important investigations to pro-tect the people of the town.

Duncan heard her say, "I just couldn't stand the thought that he might have died for nothing, like most people do." The chief's face fell, and shortly after that he managed to slip away to speak to someone else.

Duncan waited until the night shift had begun and then drove to the police station. When he walked to Sergeant Griggs's office door, Griggs looked up at him without surprise. He said, "Come in." He got up and shut the door behind them, then waved at the empty chair in front of his desk. "You can sit if you want." Then he returned to his desk chair. He looked tired.

Duncan said, "Sergeant, I'm terribly sorry about Officer Slater."

"You didn't come here for that, but thank you. I saw you at the funeral. I didn't see Renee Parkman."

"She doesn't know."

"Why didn't you tell her?"

"I don't actually know where she is. She flew to Denver to stay with an old friend from college while things cooled down. She said she'd call me, but hasn't yet."

Griggs opened a desk drawer and placed a business envelope on the blotter. "What can you tell me about this? Slater wrote your name on it."

"I asked him if anything had come in from the State Police about the outsiders that he could share with me," said Duncan. "He didn't say anything about keeping it from you, so I'm pretty sure he would have told you he was leaving it for me. That night he got killed, so he may not have had the chance."

Griggs said, "You were a cop. You know this isn't done. Police reports and evidence stay put."

"I know. But this isn't a normal case."

"You're right." The sergeant looked at Duncan. "Did Renee tell you that Glen was a cousin of mine?"

"She didn't tell me things like that."

"Glen's Slaters are cousins of my mother's Slaters, not siblings, so we're third cousins or something. We always got invited to the Slater picnic on Memorial Day."

"That's the test," Duncan said.

"I guess so," Griggs said. He lifted the envelope and held it out to Duncan.

Duncan accepted the envelope, and then the sergeant reached into the drawer again and took out a second envelope, this one a thick manila one, which he held out. "These came in after Glen died."

Duncan accepted them, and then asked, "You're letting me have these? Why?"

"I'm sorry, Duncan. We just don't have enough people to do this. The outsiders have us outnumbered. I can't solve this problem. The state police have been working hard to get us information and do the forensic work, but so far, I haven't got a commitment that they'll take over. Keep that. I hope it's what you need."

⊶

The files that the State Police had sent the Parkman's Elbow Police Department electronically included many sorts of information about the two men who had been found dead in the basement of The Elbow Room. There were photographs of the basement storage area taken before the bodies were moved. There was an after-death photograph of each man taken from above, showing the face, neck, and chest, and another which included the fatal wound. There was the medical examiner's diagram and a summary report. There were the two rap sheets for the dead men, since both had been arrested often and convicted at least a few times.

Duncan noted the most obvious facts. Darren Spanszic, 38, had been shot through the side of the head. Like the other man, Telinski, he was a victim of an accidental homicide, a bullet fired in a dark, windowless cellar by a man who either thought he was already under fire or was outsmarting an enemy who was about to fire. Some of the bullets might have been ricochets, but those were not distinguished in the report.

Darren Spanszic had carried an Illinois driver's license that said he lived at 5648 Rilling Street in Chicago, and had a date of birth in 1984. He'd had a juvenile record that had been sealed when he reached eighteen, and then an escalating series of infractions that began with petty theft and ended with armed robbery. He had served sentences in the Kewanee Life Skills Re-Entry Center, Decatur Correctional Center, and Menard Correctional Center. Duncan noted the incarceration dates. His next step was to begin looking for men who had served time with Spanszic. He had the record of Telinski, the man killed with Spanszic, he had the record of Rankin, the man who had kidnapped Renee Parkman, and the records of Vance and Barstow, the two men he'd caught breaking into his car and turned in to the police on the day when he'd arrived in town.

Duncan read the police records of the other men. He didn't find anyone who was in the same prison at the same time as Spanszic, but he did find out that Ray Barstow and Timothy Vance had been at Stateville Correctional Center during 2018, and that Peter Telinski and Jerry Clark had been in Centralia Correctional Center together from 2010 until 2014 and that Telinski had also been in East Moline Correctional Center with Steve Clark in 2020. They might have known each other, and might not, but Duncan found connections among the men quickly.

Duncan went back to check the address on the license of Spanszic against the addresses of the others. At the time their licenses were issued, they had all, with the exception of Rankin, lived in the Beverly neighborhood in the southwest part of Chicago. He knew the section, which was a part of town where there were cheaper rents than in some other areas. He kept searching for connections. Somebody, or some small clique of people, must have hired all these men, and at least a few others.

The two men he had taken in on his first day in Parkman's Elbow had been from the same part of Chicago, and they had said they'd heard from Mickey Rafferty that there was work for men like them in the area along the Ash River. He had not put too much faith in that at the time, but since then a lot had happened to make him reconsider the conversation. They had been standing in the parking lot of the exact establishment that the Clark brothers had intended to extort two nights later.

For a moment he wished he hadn't sent Renee Parkman into hiding. He would have used her to look for things specific to the Ash River area—Parkman's Elbow, Riverbend, Riverbank, Pine Bend, Groomsburg, all the small towns. He would have asked her to look in the police reports for anybody with a name she had heard before. Somebody involved in this bunch of criminals was likely to have a local connection.

She had not given him a call, as she had promised, so he had no simple way to find her in Denver, and that led him to the other problem—she wasn't easy to work with. This was his job, and she wasn't especially inclined to do any of it for him.

He wasn't a cop anymore, but he was accustomed to the laborious, concentrated way that cops carried out investigations. The next step was to collect all the new evidence and incorporate it into the murder book so it had an objective, verifiable existence. If something happened to him, then somebody—the next consultant that Ellen or her successor hired, some Indiana State Police detective, an FBI investigator—would know everything he'd worked hard to find out.

The last set of records and reports in the packet referred to the man Duncan had killed with the baseball bat on the boat. His name was Paul Rankin. He had a record, but everything he'd been convicted of was old. He appeared to have gotten smarter before he'd become a kidnapper and killer. His face and head had suffered some damage from the bat, but his Illinois driver's license picture was the way Duncan remembered him. The license said he lived in an upper-middle-class neighborhood in the northern Chicago suburb of Highland Park. The building had an apartment number. As he looked at the photograph, he imagined Rankin posing as a lawyer. He had the right sort of eyes for that sort of identity. They looked sharp and intelligent. It was interesting to Duncan how many people who had those kind of eyes were dead or in prison.

Gerald Russell heard the electronic signal that told him someone had come in the lobby entrance to his main real estate office in Evanston, Illinois. He looked at the nearest monitor, which showed him that a young woman—young-looking, anyway—was standing in front of the elevator down there. He hoped it wasn't another one of those people who had seen one of his signs and thought anybody in the real estate development business must want to build a crappy little house for them or remodel their garage. He stared at her image on the screen, but she was silhouetted in the late afternoon sun, and he couldn't see her well. Time was going by, and he needed to know if she had actual business or should be sent away.

He turned the elevator on, and it went down to the first floor. When the door rolled open the bright light in the elevator shone on her, and he could see her clearly and in color. He let the door roll shut behind her, but he didn't let the elevator rise. He turned on the intercom. "Hello, Jeanette. Didn't I tell you to stay away from me until I got in touch?"

She said, "I thought you just meant stay out of Parkman's Elbow. That's the town we were in at the time. I went home to Chicago. To the apartment where Rankin and I lived. It's lonely there now."

"I suppose it must be."

"Paul had a lot of faults, but I met him when I was very young. We were used to each other is the way I think of it."

"Are you here to tell me you're quitting?"

"Could I do that?"

"You could disappear and hope they don't care that some things didn't go right with you."

"We were hired to kill the Clark brothers. Are they not dead enough?"

"You also were supposed to kidnap Renee Parkman."

"We got her."

"And you made the ransom call to her boyfriend. You were supposed to get him to bring the money and get killed. He didn't. You didn't fool him. And somehow, he knew where to find her."

"I didn't tell him."

"And then you went to the bar the next night and tried to kill him, without telling anybody, much less asking somebody."

"That, I see now, was wrong."

"It made Chicago think you have no discipline."

"What does Chicago want for that? Will it be cutting off a finger, like the yakuza?"

"They expect people to select their own punishment. If it's not good enough, they'll do something more."

"Will you let me come up?"

"I don't see much point in that."

"When you told me that you had my car towed from the parking lot and saved me from the cops you said you and I still had to talk. I want my talk."

She heard him sigh, but the elevator began to rise. After a few seconds the elevator stopped. "What are you doing?"

"What does it look like?"

"I didn't tell you to take off any clothes."

"I'm asking for a big favor. I don't want to get cut or burned. I need you to feel the same way about me, that disfiguring me would be a terrible shame and a waste."

The elevator began to rise again.

18

The Riverbank Restaurant had been open at five-thirty every night for more than eighty years. There was a display of antique menus in a glass case on the wall of the bar, and one from 1939 had the same hours printed on it. On this night, Mona Durand's mother Amelia was back at her old station behind the hostess's lectern welcoming diners.

Nearly the first were a group of several men who arrived at once. They looked to Amelia Durand like a rugby team. Four of them had shaved heads, and they all seemed to be tattooed. A couple of them had ink designs that showed on their necks above their collars. A man Amelia had never seen before, spoke for the others. "There are eight of us," he said. "We'll push two tables together."

Amelia bristled, but refrained from saying anything about the impertinence. Even fine restaurants made more money on alcohol than food. Men in their thirties drank the most and tipped the most, particularly when there were several of them together bragging and showing off.

She let them make their own double table and seat themselves, gave them menus, and returned to her post while Sandor, an experienced waiter who had come to the Ash River region many years ago from Budapest, moved around the table writing down drink orders. Sandor's competence was soothing for Amelia's nerves. Her daughter Mona was the owner of the restaurant now, and every one of the old stalwarts was helping her learn to be a better restaurateur. That was the way she thought of herself and her husband too. They were two more old timers teaching Mona to be a better businesswoman.

She ignored the eight men except when she heard occasional brays of loud laughter and glared to convey her displeasure. She seated diners at other tables, filling in from the periphery first before seating anyone toward the center, where the eight had settled in. She observed that they were enormous eaters and drinkers. She had worked in this and other restaurants most of her life, and was used to the various trade-offs. Often the most obnoxious people were the most profitable, and if she wanted to make her daughter's reign at the Riverbank as successful as her own generation's, then she would have to tolerate some of them and remind her daughter to do the same.

But these men were staying too long. They kept ordering things, but Amelia had regular customers with reservations coming in and she didn't have tables for them. She created a waiting list, put some of them in the small barroom, talked a few of them into the idea that sitting at an outdoor table on the decorative wharf beside the building was a springtime treat, and even offered a complimentary glass of wine.

The eight men stayed. The sky was getting dark and the air was cold on the deck outside, so people began to show signs that their growing impatience was reaching the point when they would get into their cars and leave.

Amelia Durand went to the large double table wearing her professional hostess's smile. "Gentlemen," she said, "if there's anything more we can offer you, I'll be happy to send Sandor, your waiter. We can also arrange for a takeout order, if you like." She looked at the men around the table, saw no requests. "Then I can have Sandor bring you your check? We can also do separate checks."

Mullins stood, his hands held open with the palms upward. "Oh, no need for that. I'll just go with you and take care of all the charges."

He smiled at his seven companions, some of whom clapped and others called, "Hear hear," or pumped their fists in the air, which made them seem to Amelia even more like an athletic team.

Mullins followed Amelia Durand toward the front of the restaurant to the cash registers where the waiters usually stood to run credit cards and print checks and receipts. She said, "How would you like to take care of the charges? Credit card, debit, or cash?" She was trying to avoid being offered a personal check, which she didn't want from a set of tough-looking drunken strangers.

Mullins smiled warmly. "Oh, I have an arrangement with your daughter Mona."

Amelia scowled. "What kind of arrangement?"

Mullins's smile grew as he savored her disapproval. "Don't worry. I'm not a boyfriend. It's purely business." He seemed even more pleased by something he saw behind her.

Mrs. Durand looked. It was her daughter Mona.

Mona stepped up. "Mother," she said. "What's going on? We've got like five parties with reservations standing in the bar or outside." She glanced at Mullins.

He said, "I'm Dan Mullins. I work for Mr. Russell's company."

She studied him for a full second. "Mom, could you please get the waiters to add up the tabs for Mr. Mullins?"

Her mother looked at Mullins, then her daughter, obviously reluctant.

Mona said, "Go on, please. I'd like to move out the people who have finished and get the next serving started."

Her mother hurried away. Mona said to Mullins, "Why did you bring those men here?"

"You're late on your payments."

"I don't even know you."

"Part of what you've been paying Darren Spanszic for was not having to meet me or the others."

"He hasn't come by in almost two weeks."

"Darren was the victim of an accident."

Mona began to feel frightened. She hadn't wanted to find herself in a conversation about people having accidents. Her face must have shown it.

"Darren is dead. Your deal wasn't with Darren. It was with the company, and the company isn't dead." He paused. "I know that you were a friend of Renee Parkman. You probably know that she didn't want to pay either."

"I heard that."

"I'd tell you to ask her, but I don't know where she is anymore. Her bar is closed down, and she's nowhere to be seen."

"Is Renee dead too?"

"I have no idea about her, or her boyfriend either. But I have another idea. I'll give you my credit card. Charge it for the dinner cost for me and my friends. Tips too. Let your mother see the charge. When she goes home, issue a refund for that amount."

He watched Mona's face go through a sequence of unpleasant expressions. He got tired of waiting. "Okay?"

She said in a monotone, "Okay."

"And I don't want to seem impatient, but I'd like you to deliver this week's payment to the address on this card by Friday." He handed her a business card.

She clutched it in her hand but didn't read it. "Okay."

19

This week Duncan moved outward from the dead men. The six subjects were all from Chicago, but they all had come to Ash River country to get money. Why? It wasn't close or convenient to Chicago. Did one or more of the men have some direct connection to the Ash River region? Were one or more men born in the area, or had they gone to school in the area and moved away? Somebody seemed to know a lot about these communities and the businesses in them.

He checked the criminal records for any old addresses, but found none in the towns along the river. It was time to go to Chicago, but first he had to make a phone call.

Duncan sat in the chair near the window and poked some numbers into his phone. His call was answered by a female voice. "United States District Court, Northern District of Illinois. If you know the extension, please dial it now." Duncan dialed a five-digit extension.

Another female voice said, "Yes?"

Duncan said, "It's Harry Duncan."

"Oh, you just caught me. I was on my way out."

"Do you want to talk another time?"

"No, this is probably good. Have you got something for us?"

"You asked me to figure out whether somebody is putting together a new organized crime syndicate to operate in the rural Midwest. Everything I've seen says this group is trying to do exactly that. They've started with extortion, but it's just a way to get fully entrenched and feared before they get into other things."

"Who are these people? Have you got names?"

"I've got a surprising number of dead names. I already told you about the three Clark brothers. They seem to have been assigned a protection franchise that was to include the most successful bar in the area, The Elbow Room. They approached the owner and I think a couple other owners, but failed to sign them up as extortion victims. When they failed the Clark brothers became homicide victims themselves. I think that was probably a punishment and a demonstration so the others would know that failure wasn't an option.

"After the Clarks were dead, the owner of The Elbow Room, Renee Parkman, was kidnapped, drugged, and held unconscious on a boat anchored in the Ash River. They demanded a ransom and prepared to kill the one who delivered it. Fortunately, I was able to step into that job, so the male kidnapper was killed instead. His name was Paul Rankin."

"Male kidnapper?" the woman said. "Was there a female?"

"Yes, there was. She made the ransom call pretending to be Ms. Parkman, and I believe she also handled the drugs."

"What makes you think that?"

"When I got to the boat, the victim was drugged, but the only kidnapper there was Rankin, and there were no drugs on board. Two of the Clark brothers had been killed by injection a couple days before. And a couple days later, just after I recognized the woman's voice as the one on the kidnapping call, she tried to stab me with a hypodermic needle in the Elbow Room parking lot."

"That probably won't convict her," Ellen said. "You know how that goes. It's hard to sell a woman as the dangerous suspect in a trial, and you probably won't even be able to testify. What else have you got?"

"After the kidnapping, Ms. Parkman announced she was closing the bar until at least January of next year. It was getting too dangerous to operate. Late that night after the closing, a group of about eight men arrived, apparently to capture her while she was packing up. Instead, while most of that crew were inside the building, one of them searching the basement storeroom apparently got startled and opened fire, and others responded. Two of the intruders were found dead the next morning, having shot each other in the liquor cellar."

"You make it sound like that whole region is completely out of their minds."

"A good police officer named Glen Slater was shot by one of these people the next night. The kidnapper Rankin is dead. These two men found at the bar are dead. The three Clark brothers are dead. That's seven fatalities over a period of a month in a town that hasn't had that many in its whole history," Duncan said. "You asked me to find out whether a crime organization is taking root. Your answer is yes."

Ellen said, "I believe that's what we've got. But we can't do anything about this without more evidence. I need names, actual proof that this is what's causing the problems in that area. I need to have people who can testify in a hearing and answer questions that come out of nowhere. I need more victims who are alive, and witnesses to everything."

"And what I need is to have some help available for the next phase of this. I went into it posing as a good-natured guy who was just wandering around exploring, but within an hour of crossing into Ash County I ran into a pair of armed ex-cons who tried to hold my car for ransom. The ants were at the picnic before I got there. Since then, I've stopped the people who came after me, and when I could, I slowed the rest down. But now we're up to seven dead and counting. This stopped being a one-man job a while ago."

"I can't just assign federal officers to do this investigation on my own gut feeling, Harry," Ellen said. "I need a pile of evidence. I need to seem a little reluctant, or this will be dismissed as just an ambitious US Attorney trying to get noticed. There are sure to be local authorities who feel stepped on. There could be senators—full-fledged United States senators—who say, 'What made you think you needed to spend federal money to hound the people of my state?' You've got to get me the answer before we do this."

"That wasn't our agreement," said Duncan.

"This isn't about some deal between you and me, Harry. You just said seven people have been killed. It's about restoring order and justice in the middle of the country. Lives are at stake. Have you changed so much that you don't care about that?"

"I'll get back to you when I can." He ended the call before he could say anything he would regret, then sat with his forehead resting on the palm of his hand for a few seconds. Then he went to bed.

⚬—⚬

Duncan's alarm woke him in the early morning. He stood up and began to do things—start the coffee, make a trip to the bathroom, lift his suitcase onto the bed, brush his teeth, shave, shower, get dressed.

He went to his car, opened the trunk, and stowed the bag in the back, drove up to the electronic gate, stuck his parking ticket into the slot, and watched the gate rise so he could drive up the ramp toward the opening to the street.

Duncan reached the street and turned right to drive up the right lane beside the hotel. He glanced at the rearview mirror for a second, then sped up, looking behind him in the mirrors as he crossed the next two intersections. It took him a moment to confirm the bad news.

Duncan took a fast left turn, then a right, and added speed for the next right, turned left into a narrow alley, and then stopped and stared into the mirror again. He muttered to himself, "Wait for him, wait for him. Here. He. Is."

A car made the last right turn fast, came to a stop at the entrance to the alley, and then kept going without turning in behind Duncan, then accelerated again and drove on up the street. Duncan was sure that the driver was planning to set up a surprise for him at the far end of the alley.

Duncan backed out and went off in the opposite direction. He made a couple turns and got onto the ramp at the entrance to Interstate 70 East. As he drove, he took out his cell phone, tapped the call record, and then the federal extension he had called last night. When the call connected and went to its voicemail he said, "Hi, it's me. I thought you should know that this phone extension has probably been compromised, and maybe your whole system. There are some gentlemen who were just following me, although I've managed to stay invisible for the past two weeks. In the hours since I called you, they've apparently picked up my number. I'll wait a couple days for your people to sweep your lines before I call from a new number."

He put the phone in his pocket and concentrated on his driving on the long, nearly empty interstate highway. When he reached the first rest area, he pulled off the highway and parked not far from the service building.

He took the battery out of his phone and began to search the underside of the car and engine compartment. He found two tracking devices made by Spytec stuck magnetically to steel surfaces. He looked up that model on the internet and found the lithium batteries held a two-month charge and the device was designed to send alerts to its owner if the car started moving or stopped. He didn't like it. Whoever was assigned to follow him was smarter and more professional than any of the previous ones. He took the two devices with him as he walked toward the service building. On his way he stuck them to the underside of a randomly selected car that would be driving eastward as soon as its owners returned.

He drove out of the lot to the first exit, and then north to Interstate 80 and entered on the westbound side. What had just happened was disturbing. When he'd first gone into police work, people capable of tapping a government phone line used to have real jobs.

After three hours Duncan stopped the car at a giant electronics store and bought four new burner phones and five hours of phone time, and put them into his bag in the trunk and headed for Chicago. He decided that when he got there he would stay away from his apartment and check into a hotel. He had no idea whether the Chicago contingent of the gang in Indiana had found his apartment yet, but it was something he didn't want to explore right now.

20

The start had been the dead men. He needed to do more foot-work now, and look more deeply into who they had been and the connections they'd had. It would not be the dead criminals that mattered. It would be the lines he drew between them and out from them that would get him what he needed. He decided to begin with Darren Spanszic. He rechecked his murder book for the address. Darren Spanszic had lived at 5648 Rilling Street in Chicago.

Duncan drove there after midnight. People who didn't have an honest reason to get up during the day often didn't. They came home just before dawn, when the energy and possibility of the night had been exhausted. They flopped onto their beds, their perceptions often blunted by whatever they'd been drinking, injecting, or swallowing. The daytime was sleep interrupted by the body's need to get up and urinate or the eye's need to seek more darkness, and then more sleep. They came out at the same time as coyotes, prowled all night looking for easy prey, and dis-appeared again when the coyotes did. Men like Darren Spanszic sometimes had lucky streaks, and when they did, were able to live that way for long periods between convictions.

Duncan went up to the front of 5648 Rilling Street. It was an old clapboard rowhouse divided into four sections, each with its own steps and a door with the letter A, B, C, or D and a flat black mailbox that had a paper tag with a name on it. He found the one with the name Spanszic, stuck his tension wrench into the lock, inserted the pick of his snap gun with it, and pulled the trigger. The snap gun poked the pins over and the tension wrench held them out of the way long enough for him to open the lock. Duncan went inside, closed the door quietly, and stood with his back to it while he put away the pick gun and listened while his eyes got used to the darkness. He smelled the air, taking advantage of the time while his nostrils were still used to the fresh night air and would be sensitive to anything else. He nosed the air for floral smells that would indicate that a woman lived here now or had recently, and for dog smells that would warn him he might get attacked. He waited until he could discern shapes in the dim light and he was confident that nobody was about to ambush him.

He moved inward across the small living room. There was a framed picture on the wall ahead, and when he reached it, he saw it was an enlarged snapshot of a family. There was a father in a suit, his starched white collar over a tie that was too short and wide for any recent decade. The man's hair was combed straight back with something the consistency of motor oil. The woman's hair was like a cap, short and permanent-waved. She appeared to have no makeup on, and her face looked worn. There were five kids, all with dark hair and hollow eyes. There was no way to tell for sure whether these were ancestors of Spanszic's, but he doubted it, because few people who were frequently arrested or evicted could be bothered to hold on to things like family photographs. The picture had probably been on the wall when Spanszic moved in.

Duncan moved to the kitchen and opened the refrigerator. This confirmed his impression that no woman had lived here with Spanszic. The refrigerator was bare except for canned beer and a small block of cheese that must have been missed when he'd thrown out everything perishable. Duncan closed the door to snuff the light, and ventured deeper into the apartment.

In the bedroom there was a queen-size bed, covered by a blanket and sheets that smelled like a gym locker. He opened the dresser and found a couple of pairs of white socks that had lost their shapes, and some white briefs that had stretched so the elastic in the waist was useless. He opened the closet and found by touch that there were only eight hangers with anything on them. It seemed that Spanszic had taken his better clothes with him to Indiana and left the rest.

A police search was usually carried out by several officers and technicians in bright light and might take days. What Duncan could do right now was try to understand what living here must have been like. It didn't look as though Spanszic had much money. He also didn't have a girlfriend. When somebody asked if he was interested in going to Indiana to help start an organized crime gang, it must have seemed promising.

His presence in Indiana also made it seem likely that he had a phone and was on good terms with at least one person who knew him. The two thugs Ray and Tim that Duncan had arrested at The Elbow Room had said Mickey Rafferty had told them there were jobs there. It was possible Rafferty had just been repeating a rumor, but also possible that he had been the one who had recruited Spanszic. Somewhere in the apartment there must be some paper, and that might tell Duncan more. He knew that the apartment had electricity for the moment, because the refrigerator was working.

He stepped into the closet and closed the door, then tugged the string that extended the chain that worked the light, and the bare bulb came on. He looked down and saw that there were two cardboard boxes on the floor below the clothes. One held three pairs of shoes that showed scuffing and heel-wear, a couple of baseball caps with whitish sweat stains, a knit cap with a moth hole. The other was stuffed with paper—receipts, business envelopes with address windows, some of which looked like bills that hadn't even been opened. He turned off the light again and went out to bring the single chair back into the closet with him. He set it down, closed the door, and tugged the string to turn on the light again.

He sat on the chair and looked at the bills. The newest one he could find was from January. After that the collection stopped. Spanszic didn't seem to have given up the apartment, but after that the bills must have been collecting somewhere else, probably in Indiana.

He felt around deeper in the box, and found a small spiral notebook. He opened it and looked. There were ragged strips of paper with holes along the edge stuck inside the spiral. Pages had been torn out. He looked at the ones that were left. There were shopping lists with three to five items on them, addresses and phone numbers that had been scribbled at odd angles as though he'd had a phone in one hand and a pen in the other and nothing to hold the notebook still. Then Duncan found something intriguing. "List of guys—Mullins." For numerous pages among the jottings, names and numbers kept appearing.

On some pages Spanszic might write several names along the top or in the margin. Other times he seemed to be in the middle of something and put a note down—"J. Kirk knew Larson in Missouri. Call J." Duncan needed no more proof that the notebook was promising. He put it in his coat pocket and went on looking in the box. There were old phone bills. The local calls were not listed, but the US Attorney's office could probably get them if necessary. He took a credit card bill, a car insurance bill with a card at the bottom to be kept in the car as proof of insurance, and a pay stub. Some entity called Russell Inc. had actually paid Spanszic some money. He pocketed that stub too.

He heard a thump. It had sounded as though it had come from outside the building, but his main impression was that he hadn't heard it before, and now he had. He reached up and pulled the string that turned off the lightbulb in the closet, then resumed his seat on the chair.

Duncan listened for more sounds. After a minute or two of silence he decided that he had better move to a place where he could see a threat coming and retreat if necessary. He felt his pockets to be sure he had secured his finds and then opened the door. He bent low and crept across the room to the bedroom doorway, where he stopped. He went down to his belly and extended his neck just far enough to look up the hallway toward the front of the apartment. He was looking for movement, or even dark shapes where there had been none before, and listening.

After a long wait he had heard nothing, and seen nothing. This would almost certainly be his last chance to visit Spanszic's apartment. Had he looked everywhere? No, but he had found a few things that might lead him beyond Spanszic to living men. That was enough to be worth preserving, and it was best done by getting out now. He stood and prepared to move toward the front door where he had entered, when he saw a dark shape appear outside the front window.

The shadow moved from left to right along the curtain, and then ducked, placing the man down beside the front door. The man had crouched, waiting for someone to emerge.

Duncan backed into the bedroom he'd just left, then turned and went to the only window. He turned the latch, slowly lifted the lower half of the window, and climbed out, listening for the sound of the man approaching from the front door of the house until he believed the man hadn't heard. He took one more chance by closing the window in case the man looked along the outer side of the house. He could head around the back of the building and reach his car, but he reconsidered.

What he wanted now was to learn the identity of the man waiting at the front door. He hadn't come here to evade criminals. He had come to learn about them. He moved quietly toward the front corner of the house, so he would be behind the back of the man at the door. He got there and stopped. He looked to be sure his idea of the man's location had been accurate. As he did, he saw that a car was turning onto the street perpendicular to Rilling Street, coming toward him. The night was dark and there had been little traffic for hours, so the car's headlights seemed blinding.

Duncan knew instantly what this development meant, and he knew that he had to decide whether to try to use it or not. If he did, it would have to be right now. He took his cell phone out, selected the camera, set it to video and held it up to his right ear, so the lens would be facing the man. He watched the approach of the vehicle toward Rilling Street. When the moment came, he stepped out into the bright beam of the car's headlights, coming around the corner of the house and walking a course that was taking him right past Spanszic's front door.

He let the man hear his footsteps on the sidewalk, and as he had expected, the man was made anxious by the brightening headlights, and the sound of Duncan's footsteps coming up behind him startled him. He spun his whole body around to face Duncan. The phone's camera was aimed directly at him for the time while the headlights were bright and close. Then the car reached Rilling Street, turned left onto it, and kept going.

The man seemed intensely aware of Duncan, so as Duncan continued up Rilling Street he hit the icon on his phone to switch to selfie mode. Now he could see his own face on the screen or maneuver the phone to see what was behind him. He spoke into his phone as he walked. "I know how late it is. I just don't care how late it is. If you don't open the door for me when I get there, then don't come knocking at my door the next time you need something." He could see the dark silhouette come away from the front of Spanszic's apartment, turn toward him, push off, and follow. It had taken the man at least ten seconds to form a theory about what had just happened, but it was the correct one. Now he was picking up speed, thinking he was about to solve his problem.

Duncan fed more nonsense into the phone. "If you don't answer, then I'm going to assume you get the point, and I'm going to be there in a few minutes." He did it to cover the fact that he was studying the man who was coming up behind him. He wanted to be sure if the man produced a gun, he saw it in time, and he was judging the man's speed and distance. The man had built up surprising momentum with very little noise. Duncan dropped the phone into his coat pocket, sidestepped the man's lunge and gripped the man's coat in two places to alter his trajectory so it would intersect with the telephone pole two steps beyond them.

The man hit the pole with his shoulder, dropped to the pavement beside it, and reached to grasp a space by his neck, grimacing in pain.

Duncan knelt beside the man. "Broken collarbone, huh? Bad luck. That hurts like hell." As he spoke, he patted the man down. The only weapon he found was a folding knife with a spring-assisted blade, which told him the man had not come to kill anybody. He opened the blade and then reached for the other possession he'd found in the pat-down, the man's wallet. The man started to roll over onto that pocket, but the attempt instantly brought pain from his injury that made him forget the wallet.

Duncan kept the knife in his hand and looked in the wallet. He pulled the driver's license out. "You're Mickey Rafferty?"

"Yeah."

Duncan took out his phone and turned on the flashlight app. "No, you're not. I've met Mickey Rafferty. Did you kill him, or just steal his wallet?"

"Look at the picture."

Duncan looked at the picture on the license. It was the man lying on the sidewalk, not Mickey Rafferty. He examined the blade of the knife, then examined the wallet. He found a spot in the wallet where he would have expected a compartment. It felt as though it had been glued shut. He sliced it open and pulled out a second Illinois license. "Charles Alan Dennison," said Duncan. "I think we need to have a longer talk. It's a shame, because you're going to feel worse and worse until somebody gives you a shot. I'll make it as quick as I can. Tell me how you fit into what's going on in Indiana."

Dennison's eyes assumed the look of concentrated focus that Duncan had seen in people wearing earphones. The eyes were open, but looking at something that wasn't there.

Duncan stood over him and stared into his eyes, waiting. "You know, I've got a little video of you crouching in front of Spanszic's apartment to ambush somebody in the street, and another one of you running up behind me to attack me. Anything I do to you will look like self-defense."

"I'm helping them find people who have experience and balls so they can build crews."

"Just like the Mafia, huh?"

Dennison tried to shrug, but gave a groan of pain.

"Who's paying you to do it?"

"People who will kill me if I tell you."

"I could kill you if I want."

"I know they will. I don't know if you will."

As Duncan stood there, he tried to blame Dennison, but he had made the right choice. As Duncan considered what to say next, he still had the wallet in his hand, and absentmindedly bent the one credit card through the soft leather. It felt odd. There was something that felt like a lump. He stuck his finger into the wallet and felt for it. The lump felt like folded paper, so he pulled it out, unfolded it, and saw it was a check. The name printed in the upper left corner was "Russell Inc."

He said, "Who is Russell?"

"I don't know him."

Duncan held up the check. "He knows you. Seems to like you too. Four thousand bucks." He put the check back in the wallet and the wallet into his inner jacket pocket. "I don't suppose it would be worth the risk to ask him to write you another one to replace the one I've got."

"He's the guy. He does the up-front stuff in Indiana, but he's representing somebody bigger who is based here."

"Who?"

"I don't know."

"Have you talked to him?"

"I'm not at the level to have anything to say to him."

"If you wanted to, how would you get in touch with him?"

"I never even thought about it. There's a lot of risk to putting yourself up and forward like that. You better have something to say that the big guy wants to hear. The people just above you would think you were going around them to try to replace them." He squinted at some invisible cue from his body. "Look, I told you what I know. I'm in pain."

"You're right. I'll take you to the hospital now. I'll let you off at the emergency room and leave, so you don't have to make up a story that includes me. Can you walk?"

"Not much."

"Then I'll go get my car and pull up here to get you." What he hadn't told Dennison was that he would probably get in touch with him in the future and ask him more questions. Now that he had something to hold over him, he had an informant. He trotted to the side street where he had parked his car. He got into the car, started it, but kept his headlights off. He made a U-turn so when he turned onto Rilling Street he would be on the side of the street where Charles Dennison was lying. He could pull up to the curb beside him and help him in.

As he approached the corner he looked to his right, and what he saw startled him. A car had parked beside the telephone pole where Dennison had been hurt, and two men were out lifting him into the back seat. They set him on the empty seat and then both climbed back in.

Duncan realized that he had been fooled. He had seen that the man waiting to attack him outside Spanszic's door was alone. Before Dennison had taken that position, he must have called for his friends to join him because there was a man in the apartment. All this time, Dennison must have been waiting for them to arrive.

Duncan glanced at the clock on his dashboard, and saw that only about ten minutes had passed since he'd seen Dennison's shadow through the curtain. He backed up the side street, completed another U-turn to head away from Rilling Street, and made the first right turn to get out of sight before the men in the car with Dennison decided that their best priority was chasing Duncan down and killing him.

He had learned this part of town years ago when he had been a Chicago police officer. Much of his work had taken place in a few neighborhoods like this one, because it was one of the places where people lived who committed crimes. He strung together a series of back streets and alleys for a couple of miles before he emerged onto Michigan Avenue and the hotel where he had checked in when he'd arrived.

He left his car with the lone sleepy parking attendant and took the elevator to the room. He used his key card and opened the door of his hotel room only an inch to give anyone waiting for him a chance to make a move prematurely, then switched on the light.

He felt relief as he came in, closed the door, and locked it. This hadn't been a bad night for the cause. He had found Spanszic's notebook. He had found Charles Alan Dennison, somebody he might find useful later. And most intriguing, he had a check written by the man who had been building this new organized crime ring. His name was Russell.

21

Russell had a company. Duncan didn't know if it was a real company with offices or trucks or machines, but it had employees of a sort, and it had a checking account. He began looking for Russell Inc. online, starting with the ones the search algorithm listed first, and then noticed the identifier: "page 2 of 414,000." He looked at the check he had taken from Spanszic's apartment. There was no address on it. The check had an account number, and it was drawn on one of the biggest banks in the country, so he scanned the check with that information and kept it in his murder book. He did the same with the check he'd taken from Charles Dennison's wallet. Maybe he would learn something else today that would at least narrow the search, so he moved on.

Duncan began to work on Spanszic's notebook. There were reminders and shopping lists, drawings and doodles and diagrams that meant nothing to him. In various places there were also the names and addresses he had noticed as soon as he'd found the notebook. Scribbled among the pages were the names and telephone numbers of thirty-two men.

One of the names belonged to Telinski, the man who had been killed with Spanszic in the basement of The Elbow Room. He was aware that Telinski's inclusion would mean nothing to a jury, which meant it would mean nothing to Ellen Leicester. To Duncan it was an indication that Spanszic had been making money by suggesting men as possible recruits for the criminal organization that had been troubling the towns along the Ash River.

Charles Dennison had shown up at Spanszic's door in the middle of the night. Maybe he had only come because he had found out that Spanszic was dead and decided to scavenge his possessions, but maybe he had come for the notebook.

Dennison's reason for coming could be one of the easy questions Duncan would need for the start of his next conversation with Dennison. When he was a cop Duncan had learned to open with easy questions that the suspect could answer without making his incrimination grow, and then slowly lead him into other areas, asking him to clarify a statement or explain something. Sometimes if the questions kept coming the suspect would let slip details that led somewhere.

He had to study each page to decipher the eccentric handwriting, some of which was big and crude, other times small and shaky, as though one had been written at night under the influence and the other during the midday hangover.

Duncan stopped often to research details with his laptop. Mickey Rafferty was dead. His death had been reported in the Chicago Tribune last August, when he was first taken for a drowning victim because he was found in Lake Michigan, but later identified as an overdose victim because his autopsy revealed he had a lethal dose of heroin in him. This information was valuable to Duncan, because it made the fact that Dennison had been in possession of Rafferty's driver's license incriminating, and might make him willing to share more details about the criminal enterprise.

The fact that Rafferty, whom he'd known, had died of a heroin injection, though he had never been a heroin addict, had instantly made Duncan think of the red-haired woman who had tried to stick him with a needle in The Elbow Room's parking lot on the bar's final evening. Maybe he could get Dennison to talk about her, since he and she were likely to end up being the only suspects in Mickey Rafferty's death. It wasn't evidence, but it was enough for conversational purposes when he next saw Dennison.

Duncan followed these tenuous threads for hours, making surmises based not only on the new evidence, but also on his experience with men who lived by practicing the many methods of taking other people's money. He made a new entry for each name in Spanszic's notebook, writing down everything he could find out about each man.

He wanted to end this job. He knew he should never have accepted it in the first place. Even if his connection to the US Attorney never came up and destroyed them both, it existed. And even though she now had fifteen more years of experience, and her sharp mind and sharper tongue had become much more formidable, she was still Ellen. She had been good at manipulating him when they were in their twenties. Now that she had him working a case that had already revealed about three dozen men who wanted to kill him, she wanted him to take on more risk without any hope of backup.

He had been trying to put together all the information he could get and make it into a document to pass on to her. She wanted names of people involved, and now he had a lot of them. He had found connections between some of them. He had the name of one of the high-ranking people, and he might even have a potential informant. There were a few other things he needed to do before he finished, and some of them were urgent, opportunities that would disappear if he waited.

The state police had sent the police in Parkman's Elbow the record for Rankin, the man who had kidnapped Renee Parkman. It was in the Chicago area, but it was in a very different neighborhood from the one where Spanszic had lived.

Highland Park was twenty-seven miles north of Chicago, and it was a suburb that had more rich people than poor people. The vehicles on the streets were mostly foreign-made sedans. There seemed to be no pickup trucks or vans, but Duncan knew that in the daytime there would be some that belonged to tradesmen or landscapers. Paul Rankin had lived in a modern development called The Dwellings at Highland Park, which consisted of two long, low buildings that held condominiums.

Duncan stopped his car just after midnight on the street about twenty-five yards from the front entrance, at an angle that he judged would be out of the field of vision of the security cameras he could see mounted on the buildings. He opened his window and sat there appearing to look at his phone, but kept his eyes above it.

He was looking to see which windows had lights on, waiting to see if there was a security guard in a car cruising around the grounds, watching the sidewalk to see if there were people coming home late, listening for sounds of music or voices, and trying to detect any people already there waiting for someone like him to show up. The place could easily be under surveillance by either the police or the organization that had hired Rankin.

He put away his telephone, patted his coat pockets to verify that he had with him the items he had intended, and then got out of his car and locked it. He began to drift toward the building, looking around him for signs of any human presence.

He saw a car pull up in front of the building, spotted the windshield signs for both Lyft and Uber, and watched a couple get out of the back seat and begin to walk toward the front steps of the building. He timed his strides so he would reach the entrance just after they did.

When the man unlocked the door, which seemed to require both a key and a numerical code on a keypad, the woman pivoted inside quickly, and the man was starting to do the same so he could close the door and let it lock, when Duncan began to limp awkwardly. He held his left leg straight as though the knee was stiff or destroyed. In order to swing the leg forward with each step he developed a painful-looking move in which his left shoulder had to flex upward.

The man saw it and hesitated, then pushed the door open wide. He spoke to reassure Duncan. "Don't hurry. I'll hold the door."

"Thank you," Duncan said, and smiled in gratitude. "I didn't mean to hold you up."

"Not at all," the man said. "We're not in any rush."

But his wife apparently disagreed. She was already fifteen feet ahead of him and gaining speed, holding her body rigid as though she was slightly irritated. She strode past the elevator and went up the stairway. Duncan suspected that she had anticipated that this new man wouldn't try the stairs, and she wasn't in the mood for an awkward elevator ride with him. As the front door clicked shut and relocked, her husband hurried up the stairs after her.

Duncan stood at the bottom of the stairs, listening for them to get to their condo and close the door before he did anything. Elevators made noise—bells ringing and doors opening and closing. Any number of people could hear it at this time of night and get curious.

There was a sound from far up the stairway that Duncan interpreted as the closing of a door, and he started up the stairway, taking quiet steps. He climbed to the top floor and then walked down the hall and stopped at number 410.

The lock was one of the electronic ones used on hotel doors, but he had come prepared for this. Among the photographs in the state police file concerning Rankin's death had been one showing the contents of his pockets. There had been a fob for operating a car, a plastic card with a pair of small arrows on one side, but no logo on it. There had been no house key. The fob had reminded Duncan that there were many kinds of keys.

He knelt in front of the lock and took from his coat pocket a box a half inch thick and two and a half inches square, with a set of insulated wires a foot long and a smaller box at the other end. He held the larger box up to the front of the door. There was a card the size of a credit card attached to the box. A couple of tiny red lights on the smaller box lit up and stayed lit for about ten seconds. Duncan detached the card from the box and stuck it in the slot on the lock. A tiny green light on the lock lit up and Duncan opened the door, went in, and closed it behind him.

He was pleased with the way the RFID device had worked for him. This was the third time he had used it in cases, and it had worked every time. An RFID lock had a transponder for magnetic recognition of a key card. If the lock recognized a card it unlocked. This device sent a signal that got the magnetic signature from the transponder and programmed a new key card. It had only cost him three hundred dollars, but each use had been worth much more to him than that. He pocketed it, stood still, and listened for a minute before he moved again.

He produced a small Maglite and moved silently from room to room. There was a huge kitchen, three bathrooms, formal dining room, living room, and three bedrooms, but only the largest had been furnished as one.

The master bedroom was the last room in the condominium. He ran his flashlight's beam over it. Duncan had searched thousands of rooms in his career. He'd noticed that people who didn't obey laws liked to keep their secret possessions where they could get to them quickly in the middle of the night. As he looked, he realized that the reason there had been no police seal on the door prohibiting entry was not that they'd finished searching it, but they hadn't been here yet. Everything was where it should be, and nothing was tipped over or appeared to be missing.

He took a pair of surgical gloves from his pockets and pulled them on. He looked at the king bed against the wall. The covers had been pulled up, but it hadn't been made. He went to the side of the bed away from the door, bent over to sniff, and thought, "This is her pillow." He sniffed the other. "This is his. They haven't been washed since they last slept here."

He moved to the doorway of the master bath and swept it with his flashlight beam. She was definitely a permanent party, not a one-night visitor. The bathrobe was ambiguous, but the bottles and jars weren't. There seemed to be a hundred of them—hair products, skin lotions, bath gels, makeup, and on and on.

Duncan turned back to the bedroom and realized that the number of incriminating things in the master suite was large, and none of them were really hidden, just stored. Rankin had apparently been confident that his condo would never be searched. In a tall built-in cabinet, there were firearms—a dozen pistols of that many makes and models, from a compact Kahr CW380 semiautomatic to a Ruger Super Redhawk .44 Magnum revolver that weighed over three pounds and was thirteen inches long. Rankin also had rifles. There were three variations on the AR15, each with different scopes and configurations, and a big Barrett .50 caliber M82 long-range sniper rifle that could take apart a brick wall over a mile away.

Duncan considered disabling the weapons, but since the Chicago police hadn't gotten to the condo yet, he hoped to persuade federal investigators to see it as it was. The cabinet also held a supply of ammunition of two dozen types, at least three cleaning kits, and a collection of scopes, including night vision scopes. In the next cabinet there hung a couple of bulletproof vests, one smaller than the other that was clearly intended for a woman.

He closed both cabinets and went to the large built-in dresser drawers and pulled open the bottom one. It looked like a teller's drawer in a bank, there were so many banded stacks of bills. He wasn't especially surprised. Rankin had been a killer and a kidnapper. Such people generally didn't accept checks, so the money to pay them tended to come from somebody else's bank, sometimes electronically, and sometimes in banded stacks of cash. A killer might let it stay that way so they could avoid drawing attention to themselves by depositing it in their own accounts. For a long time now, banks had not only been reporting cash transactions over $10,000, but also deposits clearly made in smaller chunks to avoid the reporting requirement.

The next drawer down was more surprising. This one held Canadian and Australian dollars, British pounds, euros, and other currencies. There was also a passport that had a photograph of Rankin, but the name Calvin Ray Hampton. To Duncan it appeared to be real. The pages even had stamps showing he had traveled on it a few times. There was no other passport in the drawer with Rankin's name. That meant that either Rankin was the alias, or Rankin had never had a reason to travel anywhere other than for business, and had used the name Calvin Ray Hampton for years.

Duncan found a small box of other items in the name Hampton. There was a birth certificate from Louisiana, a Social Security card, some credit cards, and what seemed to be a deed to the condo. Duncan reminded himself that he was here to collect evidence, and that he had to use this time as efficiently as he could. He used his phone's camera to take pictures of the guns, ammunition, vests, money, passports, and other identification, then returned them to their places.

He still wanted something that would prove who had hired Rankin for the crimes in Indiana, and any other contacts he had made, either before or since. He still hadn't found any papers that told him anything about these matters. He remembered seeing a desk in one of the rooms when he was clearing the condo, so he left the bedroom and walked toward the next room.

He had been at the doorway of this room when he was clearing the condo, but he'd only been looking for enemies. It had been designed as another bedroom, but there was no bed. There were large full-length mirrors on the walls and four long movable racks like the ones in stores that held women's clothes on hangers. Some were in garment bags, and others protected by the clear plastic covers from dry cleaners.

He wondered if all these clothes were part of some theft operation, but when he looked at the sizes on the labels, he found they were all in the same size except an occasional garment that was one size up or down. Unless there were five or six sisters who wore exactly the same size in everything, this was one woman's wardrobe. He moved the beam of his light and saw there was also a door to a closet that seemed to be full too. He moved in that direction, but on the way he noticed a large framed certificate on the wall.

He stepped close to it and read. "North Louisiana State School of Nursing certifies that Jeanette Gay Walrath has satisfactorily completed all requirements and hereby grants her the degree of Registered Nurse." He used his phone to take a picture of it.

The diploma made him move to the closet door to test a theory. He stepped inside and found himself in a long, narrow walk-in space with wooden poles on both sides, some just beneath the high closet shelf, and a second just above waist height. Each pole was about six feet long, going from one sectional divider to the next, and followed by the next set of poles. He didn't look too closely, because he had already spotted what he'd been looking for. At the end of the walk-in closet was a horizontal board that held a row of coat hooks with about thirty purses hanging on them.

He stepped close and began at the left end, pushing each one aside as he rejected it, and concentrating on his memory of the one he was looking for. The purse had been tan leather with a shoulder strap. There was a latch like a gold strip about four inches long and one wide, and she had just flipped it and the purse dropped open like a mouth.

He saw a glimpse of textured leather that seemed right, reached for it, and pulled it out from the tangle of others. He didn't remove it from the hook, just put his thumb under the latch and released it. Gravity made the purse drop open. There were about thirty hypodermic needles with the steel tips protected by plastic caps.

Rankin's girlfriend was the red-haired woman from the last night of the bar. He closed the purse and came out of the closet. What he needed now was a photograph of her. If she carried her weapons in the purse, maybe that was where her driver's license was too. He took the purse off the hook, opened it again, and cautiously put his hand inside to open the zippered compartments, but he found nothing like a license or a wallet. He hung the purse on the doorknob and widened his search.

He ran his flashlight along the walls, but there were no photographs. Of course there weren't. This was her stuff, and most women didn't hang pictures of themselves. He had already looked fairly thoroughly in Rankin's area and hadn't seen any.

He remembered a room like a den or office farther along the hall near the living room. They might have photographs there.

As Duncan started along the hall toward the den, he heard the hum of the elevator in the hallway. He listened carefully. If it stopped at the second or third floors, the motor would stop. He might even hear a distant bell. The hum didn't stop, and then he heard "ding" and the doors rolling open. Duncan had to get out of sight. He hurried out of the hall and into the dark living room, rushing along the wall toward the dining room.

As Duncan reached the rounded arch leading into the dining room, he heard the sound of heavy footsteps in the hallway just outside the entrance door. He stepped across the dining room, through the swinging door into the kitchen, and paused to keep the spring-mounted kitchen door from swinging back. He turned on his flashlight and quickly swept the room with it, then turned it off again.

The kitchen was ostentatiously large, with cabinets and sinks beneath the counter space on three sides and a Sub-Zero refrigerator and two built-in double ovens on the fourth. There was an island in the center of the floor with an eight-burner stove and a giant hood above it. Duncan stepped to the pantry door, but realized it was no hiding place. The shelves had been devoted to bottles of liquor and wine racks, and the floor to cases of beer, wine, and soft drinks. He closed the door and stepped to the cupboard doors below the long granite counter.

He swung open the nearest two doors, and felt his guess confirmed. They were empty—no hand-held appliances, not even any bowls, pots, or pans. Why would a pair of killers with drawers full of cash cook?

Duncan heard sounds coming from the outer door, and then felt what seemed to be a subtle change in the air pressure as the door to the living room swung open. Duncan quickly pushed his feet into the cabinet, hand-walked himself the rest of the way in, and pulled the cabinet door shut after him.

Duncan shifted onto his stomach in the tight space, then heard the sound of the swinging door as someone entered the kitchen. The light came on. Duncan turned on his phone and began to record.

The voice was female. "Who wants what?" she called.

Duncan recognized the voice instantly. It was clear and melodious, as though she were singing. He began the thought, "redhead," but now he knew her name was Jeanette, so that replaced the description.

A man came in. "Gil has got to drive, so water for him. Mr. Russell wants a gin and tonic, and both of us want bourbon over some ice."

Duncan heard the scrape of the bottom of a bottle being pulled from a top shelf in the pantry, and then another. He decided it must be Jeanette because the top shelf would be well above her head and the bottles would tend to drag.

"Sounds easy enough," she said. Duncan heard the clinks of the bottles on the counter near the sink, and then heard a cabinet above the counter open. He heard clinks of four glasses.

The refrigerator opened and closed, and the man said, "Here's the tonic. Is there a bowl or something I can put the ice in?"

Another overhead cabinet opened and closed. "Here you go." A second later an icemaker began spitting ice cubes into the bowl.

Jeanette said, "Paul always made the drinks, so I don't really know how much to put in. I never learned."

"Do you have a jigger?"

"You mean like a shot glass?"

The man's heavy footsteps moved to the pantry. "Here's one," he said. "The bigger side is a jigger. If you order a drink in a bar or a restaurant this is the measure of liquor the bartender puts in it. It's an ounce and a half."

"Is that enough?"

"If they want more they'll say so."

"Okay."

There was the sound of bottle tops being unscrewed and set on the counter, then ice being dropped into glasses, and then liquids being poured. Finally, the tonic was poured in, fizzing. The two picked up glasses and went out, pushing the kitchen door and then letting it swing back and forth.

Duncan opened the cabinet door a crack and listened, then pulled himself out onto the kitchen floor. He moved to the kitchen door and heard, "I'll just throw some clothes in a suitcase, and then you can take it to Mr. Russell's."

Duncan understood. Her killer boyfriend Rankin was dead, so she'd decided to hit on the most powerful replacement she could find. He remembered seeing a couple of suitcases in the room and wondering whether Jeanette, who had lived with Rankin, was preparing to move out, now that he was dead. His train of thought stopped.

She had told someone that she was going to fill a suitcase to take to Russell's, so she was going into that room. She would see that her purse—that purse—had been moved from its hiding place among the others. He briefly tested the idea that, surrounded by women's clothing, she might not notice the change, but that was fantasy. She would walk into the room, see the purse instantly, lift it from the doorknob, and then get the men. Then the search would begin.

He had to prevent that from happening. He tried to imagine a way he could sneak from the kitchen to the dining room, across the living room that seemed to be where Jeanette and her male friends were sitting and drinking, to the hallway and the woman's wardrobe room. If he could find the circuit breaker panel, maybe he could flip the main switch and plunge the condo into darkness. A kitchen might be where the panel was, since there were so many electric appliances there. He took the chance of turning on his flashlight again to sweep the walls, but they were bare.

He saw the pantry door and knew the pantry was his last hope of a breaker panel. He stepped inside, closed the door, and swept the tiny room. There was no panel, but set into the ceiling was a rectangular wooden frame. He tried to shake the shelves on the walls and found they were firmly attached. He piled cases of beverages on the floor until they were about four feet high. Then he used the shelves to steady himself as he climbed up on the cases. He reached up and pushed on the two-by-three-foot wooden rectangle covering the access hatch, lifted it up, and set it aside so he could pull himself up through the hatch and into the attic. He hoisted himself up and then closed the hatch.

He used his flashlight to confirm his first impression. This wasn't like the attics in houses. It was a cavernous space that seemed to stretch over all the condominiums for the length of the building. Along the attic floor he could see wiring for overhead lights, sheet metal conduits for the ventilation hoods in the kitchens, assorted pipes that stuck up toward the flat roof. And at set intervals there were other access panels exactly like the one he had just used.

It occurred to him that he would need to come back this way, so he took one of the spare gloves he had brought and set it on the hatch cover. He sighted along one end of his hatch to the next one, which was about fifty feet away and in line. He knew that one would open in some other unobtrusive place at the other end of the condominium, probably another closet.

He was aware that if he walked straight to it, he would be walking right above the heads of Jeanette and her friends. They would hear noises coming from the ceiling. He looked at the hatch he had just left, and judged that the pantry must be about fifteen feet out from the entrance door to the condo. He also guessed that the next access hatch in that direction would be above the pantry of the condominium across the hall from

Rankin's. He realized that if he moved in that direction half the distance to the next hatch, he would be above the building's common hallway, which at this hour was uninhabited space.

Duncan walked quietly to the spot above the common hallway, turned right and walked until the other hatch above Rankin's condo was to his right, turned right again and walked to this second hatch. When he reached it, he lifted the cover off and set it aside. He used his flashlight and confirmed his expectation. Below him was a closet, the one in Rankin's master bedroom. For the first time since he'd heard Jeanette and her friends arriving, he felt a bit of hope mixing in with his intense concentration. He lowered himself until his arms were straight and he could reach out with his right hand and touch the pole where Rankin's clothes hung. He grasped it, then let go of the hatch frame with his left so both hands could clutch the pole and lower him to the floor.

He knew that every second he had taken getting here had made it less likely he would survive, and that his best hope was to move deliberately and efficiently. He stepped from the closet to Rankin's dresser, opened the bottom drawer, reached in and felt his hand touch the bare wood where the banded stacks of money had been. She must have loaded all of it into some kind of bag. Had she already been in the wardrobe room to get the bag?

He moved to the bedroom door. He believed she wouldn't leave the condominium without her purse full of hypodermic needles. He heard nothing in the hallway, so he stuck his head out to look in that direction. There was no light streaming from any of the bedrooms.

Duncan moved along the hallway as quickly as he could without making noise, and sidestepped into the wardrobe room. He lit his flashlight, found the purse hanging on the door-knob where he'd left it, took it, pivoted, and moved toward the doorway, when the sound of footsteps reached him. They were light and sharp, high-heeled shoes on the hardwood floor. "Just a couple more things," Jeanette called to the men waiting for her. "I'll be ready as soon as I've got them."

Duncan's decision had to come now. He wasn't a cop any-more, and he was not going to be able to make a citizen's arrest of a homicidal woman and three male criminals without shooting somebody. He was the one who had entered the condo illegally. He had nowhere to go but the place where Jeanette was going to go, the walk-in closet. This outer room had dresses and long coats hanging on steel racks, but they wouldn't hide him. He headed for the closet and hurried into the closet to the board of hooks on the end wall. As he hung the purse on one of the hooks on the board, he simultaneously hoped that it was the right hook so she wouldn't notice it had been touched, and felt terrible that he was giving a killer back her favorite murder weapon.

The closet was tightly packed with clothes on hangers. There were two poles on each side of the long, narrow space, the upper pole for blouses and jackets, and the lower pole for skirts and pants. On the floor beneath the lower level of clothing was a row of shoe boxes. Duncan ducked between clothes on the lower rack to his right, moved behind the row of shoe boxes, stood, and made himself still just as Jeanette flipped the light switch in the outer room.

He heard the two spring-loaded latches of a suitcase snap open. A wooden drawer rolled open on its metal track, and then minutes passed. He imagined her putting things in the suitcase.

He knew that the moment of greatest danger was coming, and he listened for it as he stood behind the flimsy wall of clothes and shoe boxes. He knew he would need to crouch down slightly so his head would not show over the upper pole. He practiced the move to be sure he would be low enough. It was awkward and required tensing the muscles of his thighs and back and staying that way.

He heard the footsteps again and knew that she was coming to get her hypodermic needles, so he crouched down and held himself there as she reached the doorway. She turned on the closet switch and the space was bathed in white light.

She was feet from him, and if she was going to see him it would happen now. He couldn't look and study her facial expression or the movement of her eyes, because if he could see her, she would see him.

Her heard her walk straight past him to the back of the closet where the purses hung. He heard her moving, and assumed she was pushing purses aside to find the right one, and then she walked back toward him. He knew that if she'd seen him, she would jab a needle into him and try to get its contents pumped into him before he could react. He concentrated on remaining perfectly still and listening.

"Jeanette?" It was a male voice, coming from the hallway. Was it the same voice as he'd heard in the kitchen?

"I'm in here."

Duncan heard heavier steps and the man's voice, now from the entrance to the closet. "Can I take this suitcase out? He's getting impatient."

"Just let me put one more thing in first." She hurried past Duncan and turned off the light. "I'll just be a couple more minutes."

He heard one click of a suitcase latch, then the other, and the suitcase's wheels rolling on the hardwood floor down the hallway toward the living room. Duncan waited, then heard her footsteps going toward the hallway, and the light went off.

Duncan came out of the closet to the doorway, and realized that she was not heading to the living room, but in the opposite direction, toward the master bedroom. He had to get there before she went into Rankin's closet, or she would see the open hatch and start screaming. He looked toward the living room to be sure the man with the suitcase was gone, then went toward the master bedroom, moving as quietly as he could.

When he reached the master suite, he saw something he had not anticipated. There was light visible beneath the closed door of the bathroom. He passed it and went into Rankin's closet. He closed the closet door, turned on his Maglite, and used a coat hanger to extend his reach to lift the edge of the hatch cover to close it.

She was in the bathroom attached to the master suite, barely five paces from where he stood. He heard the flush of the toilet and then the water running in the sink.

He waited to hear her open the door. He ran through his options if she chose to open the closet. He could crouch and hope she didn't see him. He could try to get behind her and choke her out before she could scream. The choke hold had been outlawed in almost every police department, but he wasn't a cop anymore. If he failed to prevent her scream, the three criminals down the hall would come running with guns drawn. Some people would die, and he would likely be one of them.

As he waited, he heard another set of male footsteps, this time coming up the hallway with heels hitting the floor like a man marching. There was a loud knock on the bathroom door, and then a new voice. "Jeanette, it's three-thirty. What the hell is the holdup?"

Duncan heard the door to the hall opening. "I was just fixing my makeup. Don't you want me to be beautiful for you?" This time the melodious voice was soft and seductive. It made Duncan think of a snake.

The man said, "There's nothing to fix. You look like a movie star, but don't start acting like one. Come on."

Both sets of footsteps went down the hall, this time at the speed the man had gone when he'd arrived, so Duncan pictured him gripping her arm and pulling her along.

Duncan came out of Rankin's closet, took one of the two chairs from the table in the corner of the room, set it under the hatch he had just closed, stepped onto it, and used it to reach the hatch cover, push it up and out of the way, and then climb up into the attic again.

He closed the hatch cover, turned on his flashlight, walked straight to the space he had judged to be above the fourth-floor hallway, and spotted the hatch where he had left a spare rubber glove. He went to it, opened the hatch, and descended into the pantry, first using the shelves on each side as rungs in a ladder, and then settling some of his weight on the top case of liquor. He reached up and closed the hatch, and then lowered himself to the floor.

There was no light coming from under the closed pantry door, so he came out, stepped to the kitchen door, and saw no light leaking from there either. He slowly pushed open the door to the dining room, and saw no light in the living room. He went into the dining room and made his way to a spot where he would be able to see the living room and down the hall to the bedrooms. He knelt on the floor, took out his pistol, held his Maglite as far from his body as possible, and turned it on. Nobody jumped out of a hiding place to fire at him, and the condominium was still. He put the flashlight away.

He stood by the dining room table, staying far back from the window, and looked through it at the street. He took out his phone and selected the camera, raised it high above his head, and took several pictures. He brought the phone down, looked at the first one, and enlarged the image with his fingers. The car was a Cadillac Escalade, a gray color that was almost black.

Duncan started for the door, but then changed his course. He ran down the hall to the master bedroom, opened the closet door, picked up the chair he'd left under the hatch, and set it in the spot where he had found it, closed the closet door, and ran back to the living room.

He opened the door to the fourth-floor hallway, stepped to the elevator, and hit the button. He needed the speed more than he needed the quiet now. It took a few seconds for the elevator to rise to him. It arrived with a "ding," the door opened, and he slipped in and selected the lobby.

When the elevator door opened on the ground floor Duncan stepped to the entrance and looked out. They hadn't left yet. The Escalade's engine was running and he could see steamy exhaust coming from the tailpipes, illuminated by the overhead lights of the building.

Duncan watched the Escalade pull away and make a turn at the first corner. In a second he was out the door, running for his car. As he started the engine, the first tiny droplets of rain appeared on the windshield. He pulled out into the street without turning on his headlights, and made the turn the Escalade had made. He could see the car's red taillights at least two blocks ahead, but he kept going without trying to narrow the distance.

He felt good about the extra work he'd had done on his car, and especially the black matte finish with no reflective chrome. He had considered doing it for years, but it didn't seem practical until enough other people were buying cars with this kind of paint job so it wouldn't seem unusual.

The rain droplets were appearing on the windshield more frequently now, and a few bigger drops hit among them and caused small rivulets to slide downward. He turned on the windshield wipers and maintained his speed. A moment later, as though he had summoned it, a curtain of strong rain came along the street and swept over the car.

It was nearly four now, and the streets of this part of the city were almost empty. The heavy rain must be making this unlighted black car nearly invisible from a distance. As he drove, he was careful to look both ways before entering any intersection. If his car was hard for gangsters to see, it would also be hard for the driver of a fire truck or ambulance.

The Escalade made another turn, and then a third one onto a strip of commercial buildings in Washington Heights. Duncan drove at a reduced speed to the intersection and then inched forward. He could see that the Escalade had stopped. A door opened and then another, and a tall, thin man opened an umbrella as he ducked out onto the street and scurried into a two-story brick building. A second man, this one not as tall, but muscular, came to the open door and held an umbrella. The passenger who emerged was Jeanette, and the man walked with her, holding the umbrella for her. The driver pulled away from the curb and turned into the ground level parking lot beside the building and out of sight.

Duncan drove on. After he cleared the intersection and was out of sight of the building they had entered he turned on his headlights. He drove a few more blocks, then turned right, and took a long route to come back around to approach the building from the other side. He opened his side window a few inches and took a series of pictures with his phone as he drove by the building, and then two shots of the street signs, before he turned left to head back the way he had come. It had been a tense night, but he had collected some surprisingly good information for his murder book.

22

Duncan used a new burner phone to make the call at three in the afternoon. He dialed, listened to the female-sounding machine voice, and then punched in the five-digit extension and waited. He knew that the wait at this hour might be a long time, because it was the part of the afternoon when important people had meetings or worked at things that required intense concentration.

He set the phone on speaker, plugged in the charger, set it down on the hotel room's table, and then returned his attention to the pictures and notations he had printed in the business center downstairs. He had already copied the photographs and videos he had taken on his phones to the laptop and then thumb drives, so the US Attorney could send them to whomever she pleased, but the paper copies of things were what he was counting on. She, or her deputies, wouldn't be going to court with any of this stuff. Probably all of it would have to be verified, and much of it duplicated, by the FBI investigation before charges were filed. But the text and pictures he had produced, together with the reports of the Indiana State Police and the Parkman's Elbow PD, made an impressive display. The physical murder book would be much harder to ignore than the digital version.

The phone on the table said, "You've reached me. Identify yourself."

"Hello," Duncan said. "It's me."

"I'm surprised to hear from you during business hours."

"Sorry. I know how busy you must be, but I need to give you the information I've got. I'll hand it over any time that's convenient for you. I'm in Chicago right now, and I can be at your office in fifteen minutes."

"I've told you what I'll need. If you've got it, send it to me. I'll have my assistant give you an email address that was set up just for this purpose, and she'll shut it down afterward."

"Some of it is in digital form, but much of it isn't. I'll need to deliver it in person. You can do what you want with it after you've seen it. I think you're going to want to hand it over to the FBI to get them going, but that's your decision."

"Yes, it is. You sound as though you feel your investigation is finished, and you've reached a conclusion."

"My conclusion is still what I told you before. Yes, there is a group, made up mostly of small-time professional criminals, recruited and hired to move into the small towns along the Ash River in Indiana and try to build themselves into a crime syndicate. They've started with extortion because it brings in steady money and gives them a chance to scare the populace."

"And you have enough evidence and enough information so I could go into a courtroom and convict some people."

"In my opinion, you will when you have what I'm going to give you. I have names and photographs of both living members and dead ones. I've traced and documented their recruiting operation, learned the way members are selected and paid, and I've even got two paychecks—not copies, originals—so the accounts can be identified and studied. I know where the highest-level man operates when he's in Chicago."

"It sounds as though I'd better take it."

"Yes. I can bring it to your office, or I'll meet you anywhere you want, at any time."

"I need to do this someplace where we won't be under the eye of thirty surveillance and security cameras, and this isn't it. I don't want to have to explain in a courtroom who the man with the papers is, and what was on the papers he was giving me."

"No cameras means in the outdoors, either in the country or a residential neighborhood where people don't have a lot of money for security cameras."

"You were the cop. Which is better?"

"Open spaces, where you can see everybody who sees you."

"How about Foster Beach?"

"That would be good. After dark would be best, to avoid the joggers and dog walkers."

"Nine-fifteen? I'll follow you to a parking spot and you put your bag or whatever you're bringing in my trunk, and then we go."

"Done. See you at nine-fifteen."

⚬━⚬

At six-fifteen, Duncan went down to the underground parking lot to examine his car for transponders, listening devices, or other electronic gear intended to track, spy, record, or sabotage. Weeks ago, he had warned Ellen that he believed her secure phone line had been tapped. He knew that the regional federal office would certainly have fixed the intrusion by now, and he had just heard her say some things that showed she was confident that it had. That didn't mean that her faith wasn't misplaced. If the person who had created a breach hadn't been caught and locked up, it was always possible he could find a way to do it again.

There were at least twenty-five miles of beaches along the Chicago shore of Lake Michigan, and Shoreline Drive was a road where he was confident that he could spot any followers. The sun was not going to set for another hour at 7:32 P.M., so he had plenty of time before the road behind him would become a lot of indistinguishable headlights.

He drove to the northernmost end of the string of beaches and watched the behavior of the cars in his rearview mirror. He watched for cars that stayed behind him, adjusting their speed to his so that they didn't come too close or drop back too far. He watched for drivers who changed their appearance as they drove, taking off or putting on a hat, taking jackets off or putting them on, turning low-beam headlights or fog lights on for a while and then off. He tried to spot cars that worked in pairs, one pulling up while the other dropped back, or passed him to dispel the thought that they might be following, but kept track of him by remaining on a cell phone call with the car watching from behind.

Duncan used the crude but effective method of pulling off the main road and then back on, seeing if anyone followed him through both maneuvers. He also slowed down abruptly at a turnoff to force a follower to go past and then pump its brakes while the driver watched him in his mirrors to see where he was heading. None of the drivers made those mistakes.

He approached the entrance to Foster Beach at 7:38, just after sundown, and decided to go past it and keep going as long as the waning light lasted. He kept going, trying variations of his feints without spotting anyone falling for them, and then took a sudden turn and drove up a parallel street going north until he reached Foster Street, turned, and drove to the beach's parking lot.

It was April, so the lot and the beach looked deserted. He drove the area slowly to be sure that neither his enemies nor any enemies of the US Attorney's office might have come early to set up an observation post in advance. He paid particular attention to the food stands, bike shop, and boat rental. They were closed and supposed to be locked up at this hour. He got out of his car at each one to make sure that they really were locked. He even went to the doors of the restroom building and found them locked too.

He drove away from the buildings to a distant part of the lot where the pavement met the sand, keeping his lights off, waited, and watched. At 9:14 he returned to the Foster Street entrance and stopped there.

The black sedan arrived at exactly 9:15, so he drove to the spot where he had parked before, turned around, and backed in between a pair of white lines. Ellen was alone. She imitated the move and backed into the space beside his.

Duncan got out of his car, opened his trunk, and carried a large plastic cooler to the back of her car. She popped the trunk open with a button on her dash. He set the cooler in her trunk and closed the lid.

Her driver's side window slid down. "Good evening, Harry."

He stepped to her window. "Hi, Ellen."

She smiled. "We had planned to get out of here right away. No chat."

"Right," he said. "I'll be watching for the news story of the official investigation." He turned toward his car.

She said, "Are you saying you're giving up?"

"I think I already said on the phone that I've finished the scouting—all a single investigator can do. It's time for the next stage, when a few dozen FBI agents take over."

"I know you're probably right," she said. "When we were in law school, I always felt you were better at it than I was. You picked things up quicker, and you were more cunning."

"But look at us now, huh?"

"You know I wasn't thinking anything so mean-spirited. I've always wished you had stuck with it. I think I wanted to marry you in the first place because of that talent, and I've always been afraid that getting the divorce made you quit."

"You had very little to do with it. I had already stayed long enough to see what spending a whole career in law would take. The divorce set us both free."

She stared hard at him. "You never married again after that."

"Well, I guess we've caught up now."

"I apologize for calling you in on this case. It was questionable ethically. I just saw the names on the list of retired agents and cops who were freelancing, and you were the only one I knew who I was sure was up to this."

"I think you're probably in the clear ethically. I'm done, and I didn't disgrace either of us." It occurred to him as he was saying it that he had killed a man with a baseball bat, committed a few burglaries and assaults, and more. He had never lied to her when they were married.

"I'll have your fee transferred to your bank. Take care, Harry."

"You too." He buckled his seat belt and closed his door, then started his engine and looked up to see if she was going to pull out first. She was still looking at him, as though she wanted to say something else, but he looked down at his dashboard. In a couple seconds, he heard her pull out, then looked up and watched her drive toward the exit.

It occurred to him that this was probably the last time he was going to see his ex-wife. He had a passing, pale memory of the Saturday morning years ago when she had suddenly said, "I'd like it if you could go out today and give me some time alone." He thought she needed to study. When he came home, she had cleared out all her clothes and her books for law school. The note she had left was no longer clear in his memory. It was something about how the marriage had been a mistake. She had called a couple times after that to set up appointments to come and get things she hadn't taken the first time. She had taken the dishes and silverware that had been wedding presents, and things like the pots and pans and bath towels. They had not talked much. He had not gone to law classes after that. He had withdrawn after a couple weeks and driven his car toward California. In two months he had been accepted into the Los Angeles Police Academy. He had found it challenging and distracting. It had occurred to him years later that it might have saved his life.

He waited for Ellen to get out of the parking lot and head north on Lake Shore Drive. He watched her black sedan reach the speed limit with the smooth, powerful acceleration characteristic of the cars people like her drove.

He wondered whether the reason she had chosen him for the Ash River investigation was because she was curious about what had become of him over the years. What was going on in the Ash River towns was big, and it had become extremely violent very quickly, but US Attorneys were always being made aware of things that were big and violent.

There was a bang like a hammer blow to the right side of his car, and a shower of tiny cubes of shattered safety glass sprayed against his face and right shoulder and across his lap. He swiveled his head to look to the right, where the window glass had been, and then at the back seat. He saw the hole in the upholstery of the left rear door, where the bullet had gone.

He stomped on the gas pedal to propel the car forward abruptly, and then adjusted his trajectory to avoid the exit from the lot, which he was sure the shooter must be adjusting his aim to cover. The rifle had to be somewhere to his right, so he kept to a course that wouldn't bring him straight at it or away from it, either of which would make him an easy target. His struggled for a definite sense of where the shooter was, but he only had time to guess. The bullet had hit the right window and ended up below the level of the left rear window, so the shooter had to be higher and to the right of where the car had been parked.

He was on a beach parking lot, where the only places higher within reasonable range were the roofs of the food stands, the rental building, and the restrooms. The bullet had arrived a fraction of a second before he heard the shot, and sound traveled at 1,100 feet per second, so the rifle could be as close as a hundred yards.

Duncan drove hard for the narrow strip of concrete where the beach met the grass and made the turn, trying to reach the cover of the first food stand. This time, before he heard the sharp "bang" he saw the muzzle flash. The bullet went high and hit somewhere behind his car. He sped up because he knew that the next one was coming very soon, and the sniper would adjust his aim to lead Duncan's speeding car.

Duncan reached the side of the food shack just as he heard the next shot, and stopped. He got out and stepped quickly to the trunk of his car. He lifted the false floor and took out the AR15 style rifle with the night scope attached, and two twenty-round magazines. He inserted the first one, pulled back the charging lever to cycle a round into the chamber as he stepped to the corner of the shack and lowered himself to his belly.

He pulled himself forward a few inches until he could look up the beach with his right eye. He couldn't see the shooter, so he set his rifle on the ground and pushed it around the corner with the barrel pointed in the direction of the muzzle flash. He lifted the rifle, nestled the buttstock against his shoulder, and steadied it against the food stand's corner.

He stared into the night scope and aimed it toward the place where the flash had been. Through the four-power scope he recognized the ridgeline of the peaked roof of the restroom building. The shooter must have been lying on his belly on the far side of the roof, resting his rifle on the peak. Duncan couldn't see the man, and he didn't want to be visible at the corner of the food stand unmoving for a long time. He moved his sight along the top of the distant roof very slowly. He still saw nothing, so he switched the night vision scope from four to ten power and tried again.

The roof looked as though it was only a few feet away. He moved his aim along the top again in the opposite direction, and he could hardly believe what he saw. Protruding above the peak of the roof was what appeared to be about three inches of rifle barrel. It seemed likely the shooter had set it there and not yet noticed that it was too high. Duncan studied the glowing green image in his scope, imagining the man's body lying on the roof. He could hardly have let go of the rifle on a peaked roof without fearing it would slide down, so he must still be lying there on his belly waiting an interval to pop up to aim his next shot. Ninety percent of people in the United States were right-handed, so the odds were nine to one that he was holding the rifle there with his right hand, waiting to bring it to his right shoulder.

Duncan stared through the night vision scope at the rifle barrel, moved out from his corner a little so he could rest his left elbow on the ground, and aimed at the spot just below the peak of the distant building's roof and to the right of the tip of the man's rifle. He used his imagination to create a picture of the man's position, and fired at it. His shot hit the composition roof shingle about a foot below the peak and a foot to the right of the rifle barrel. He couldn't know whether, after the bullet pierced the shingle, tarpaper, and plywood on the near slope of the roof, it could still pierce the same layers on the far slope. He had fired below the level where the thick ridge beam had to be, and that gave him some chance.

He saw that the rifle barrel had slid out of sight, but he couldn't be sure what it meant. Maybe he had correctly placed his shot to pierce the roof and the man's head or chest. But maybe he had only informed the man that he was not the only one with a rifle at the beach tonight.

Duncan pulled himself back from the corner of the shack and got into his car, set the rifle on the passenger seat with its barrel sticking out his broken window, and drove along the backs of the other food shacks, the bike shop, and the rentals, moving as quickly as he could in the light of the rising moon. He looked ahead to see if the man was alive and moving into a new position to ambush him, and to his right as he crossed each space between buildings. Duncan knew that if the man was there, his best tactic was to flash past before the man had time to aim, so he kept the gas pedal down.

When he reached the restroom building, he sped past it about a hundred feet, keeping his head low in case the man was waiting, ready to fire. He looked in his rearview mirror and stepped on the brake pedal to throw the red glow of the brake lights to be sure he was seeing what he thought, then stopped completely and sat still. Caught in the red light was a man in dark clothes lying at the foot of the building. There was a rifle lying beside him.

Duncan still couldn't be sure. He had hit the spot on the roof he had intended to, but had his shot penetrated everything and killed the man? The sniper had certainly heard the shot, but even if the bullet had hit him, would it still have had enough energy to do him harm? And if he was alive, one thing the man would surely know was that Duncan would come to check on him.

Duncan kept his eyes on the mirror as he shifted his car into reverse, throwing the bright white glow of the backup lights on the man. He began to back up. After a few yards he could see the man was Caucasian with dark hair, maybe thirty-five or forty years old. As Duncan backed closer, he could see the man was still motionless, with his eyes closed and his mouth half open. He looked dead, but Duncan didn't see any blood. He knew that if he had hit him in the head, the dark hair might make it harder to see an entry wound.

He was backing up at a slow, steady rate, but that was increasingly dangerous. He decided on a test. He hit the gas pedal and moved much faster toward the man.

The man moved instantly, much faster and with more premeditation than Duncan had thought likely, and Duncan realized he'd made a terrible mistake. The man's simple ploy had brought Duncan much closer to the man, and now the man was raising his rifle.

Duncan knew he couldn't stop, shift, and speed out of rifle range before the man could aim and shoot him. All Duncan could do was press harder on the gas pedal and reach him before the man's finger squeezed the trigger.

The man was about to fire in the instant when the rear bumper of Duncan's car hit him and propelled him off his feet and backward, throwing him into the brick wall at the side of the restroom building.

Duncan put the car in park and picked up his rifle, rolled out the open door with it, and aimed at the man. In the nightscope image he could see that this time there was blood, but what held his attention was the angle of the man's head as he lay on the ground. The neck had to be broken. Duncan stood, walked to the body, and saw the face looked undamaged. He tried to recognize the man, but failed. He used his phone to take his picture. Then he patted the man's pockets to find his wallet. He took a picture of his driver's license. He went to look at the rifle, which had ended up in the sand. He turned it over so he could see the serial number on the lower receiver, took a picture, then left it as it was, got into his car, and drove.

23

Duncan needed to get far from Foster Beach before the repeated rifle fire brought police in numbers. He had to be beyond the perimeter they would establish as soon as they saw one warm body and tire tracks in the sand. When he was a couple of miles south of the beach, the opposite direction from his hotel, he stopped on a dark street and swept the little pieces of shattered safety glass out of the car and then pulled the rest of the ruined glass out after them, so the passenger side of the car simply looked as though the window was rolled down. He opened the driver's side window a bit too, so the two sides seemed to go together. It was a little too cool out on this April evening, but there were plenty of drivers with one or more windows open, many of them smokers who were trying to let the smoke out.

He restarted his car and began to drive. He headed away from the lake. After a few minutes he began to turn north or west for a few blocks every time he was stopped at an intersection. He knew this part of Chicago so well that he didn't have to think about the directions he took. As he drove, he kept replaying the ambush in his memory. Who was the man with the rifle? Was he working for the Chicago organization above Russell? The place where this organization needed violence wasn't Chicago, it was the string of small towns in Indiana.

There was another thought that kept insisting that he acknowledge it. A few minutes before the attack, he and Ellen had both been sitting in cars with their engines off. He had gotten out of his to carry the cooler to Ellen's and put it in her trunk. He had also stood for a few seconds next to her window to talk. That was a time when the sniper could have chosen his target, or taken them both. Instead, he had waited until Ellen was safely driving up Lake Shore Drive, at least a quarter mile away and gaining speed. Then the man had fired. The target, and the only target, had been Duncan.

Weeks ago, he had warned Ellen that somebody had turned up to follow him after he'd talked to her on the phone. Today he had noticed she'd said some things on the phone that could be interpreted as damaging, which he'd taken to mean that her phones had been swept and protected. Maybe her phone had not been tapped. Maybe all that happened was that somebody had learned the number that had called the extension dedicated to this case, and then used Duncan's phone's GPS to track him.

It was also possible there could be somebody in the US Attorney's office who had been working for the other side. It would be a lot easier to get something like that from inside a phone system than to tap a Justice Department line. That sort of thing didn't happen often, but it happened. His train of thought finally went to the idea he had been avoiding.

Was it possible that Ellen, not only the US Attorney for this district, but his ex-wife, had turned on him and tried to have him murdered? She was a brilliant attorney and prosecutor, but he happened to know that US Attorneys made about $142,000, brilliant or not. For a successful civilian lawyer that figure was laughable. For a person like Ellen it wasn't much different from the one-dollar token salaries that rich politicians took. Had she been tempted to get involved in protecting an organized crime ring because it was only at the seed stage and she thought she could shape it and control it? And if she had, was that what had made her pick her fool of an ex-husband to investigate it? She might have thought that even if he found something that implicated her, he would never pass it on. She might even have thought he'd destroy any evidence that led to her.

Maybe in the old days she hadn't just felt she was wasting her time being married to him. Maybe she had felt contempt for him, even shame that she was his wife. Over time the contempt could have turned into hatred. Or maybe he had just assembled enough information to scare her, and she'd felt there was no alternative to accepting all of the information, and then having him killed so she could burn it.

If Ellen was what had caused the latest attacks on him, then he had just handed her everything she'd need to keep quiet. It would be the perfect time to kill him—but only for her.

No. It just didn't feel true. He had learned early in his career to grit his teeth whenever he'd heard an investigator dismiss a person as a suspect because the theory didn't feel right. Half the time he would find himself going back later to make the person a suspect again. This time, he acknowledged, he was doing the same thing. But still, it didn't feel right.

He turned onto Michigan Avenue, arrived at his hotel, and then drove into the underground parking garage and searched for a space beside one of the walls. When he spotted one, he backed into it to keep the broken window close to the wall. He got out and walked briskly to the elevator. As he rode it upward, he glanced at his watch. It was already 10:46. The meeting with Ellen had started at 9:15, and had not taken more than fifteen minutes, and fighting off the ambush had taken even less time. He realized he must have been too preoccupied to feel time passing while he had been driving.

Duncan picked up the hotel phone, dialed nine for an outside line, and called the number of the US Attorney's office and the five-digit number. He said, "I ran into a sniper tonight who nearly got me. I don't know if he wanted you too, so be alert and extra careful." He hung up, then used a damp washcloth to wipe every surface he might have touched, put his laptop in his suitcase, held the doorknob with the washcloth, and took the elevator to the lobby.

He roused the desk clerk so he could pay his bill—or Mr. Carlson's—and get back down to his car. He had completed his investigation, he had delivered his murder book to the US Attorney personally, and he had done the best he could to warn the woman who had once been his wife that her life might be in danger. And he had made it through the evening without having his heart stopped. He started his car, eased it away from the wall of the underground garage, and then up the ramp to the street. Why did he feel as though this wasn't finished?

24

Duncan drove to Rockford and rented a room in a hotel that seemed to be a relic of some distant era when the block it was on might have had other ornate structures. Now it looked like a birthday cake among boxes. The room was clean and the bed comfortable, and it featured windows on two sides, one of them overlooking the parking lot and the other the street. Early in the morning he drove to a Toyota dealer with a large service department that went to work on replacing his car window. He waited until the car was ready, then drove it to his apartment.

Whenever he'd left Chicago on a case and returned, he had a ritual he followed. He used a cell phone to dial the code that let him run the three security camera memories at Fast Forward simultaneously to see if anyone had been inside. This time, when he set the three images going, they ran for a minute or two, and then he saw a man enter. He stopped the images and then watched at normal speed. He noted the date. It was the day after he had watched the Clark brothers getting arrested for trying to burn Renee Parkman's house.

The man who entered was wearing a surgical mask covering nearly all of his face. He went to the camera in the corner above the doorway, climbed up on a chair, and sprayed the dome that protected the lens with can of spray paint. He noticed the next camera, which was above the hall leading to the bathroom and bedroom, and painted the dome of that one too. This was obviously not his first break-in. Two of the three cameras had stopped recording the interior of Duncan's apartment, and now just showed a cloudy whiteness, but Duncan still had hope. The intruder had become confident that he knew what Duncan's cameras looked like and the areas where he placed them, and went off looking for more. He passed through on his way to the bedroom, then headed for the kitchen. Finally, he came back into the living room office and went to work searching the desk and the filing cabinets. He looked at a couple of the notebooks on the long shelf—the murder books Duncan had made for other cases—and then gave in to the discomfort of the itchy mask, pulled it off, and kept looking.

The pinhole camera that Duncan had placed inside the electric clock caught the action clearly. The man was hard to place at first, but Duncan knew he had seen him before. He let the recording run, and then the man looked hard at the clock. The expression was intense and disapproving. Duncan recognized the face. It was the man he had seen at the Riverbend restaurant in Indiana weeks ago, standing in the waiting area and glaring at the owner, Mona Durand. Duncan watched until the man left.

Duncan didn't go inside the apartment. Instead, he parked his car in the garage space of the building, took out his suitcase, and repacked it with the things he believed he might need, and then called an Uber driver to take him to Midway Airport. When he got there, he went to the car rental area, rented a Subaru SUV, and drove it to a hotel in Elmhurst, and checked in with the credit card for the tonsorial supply company. Duncan looked in his suitcase and found the cell phone he had been using the night he had broken into Darren Spanszic's apartment and been attacked by Charles Dennison. He used the phone's memory to find the number of Dennison's phone and dialed. After a few seconds he heard him answer, "Yeah?" his voice raspy, as though he'd been asleep.

"This is Harry Duncan. How are you?"

"Not so hot."

"Why not?"

"That night, after you messed me up, and the guys arrived to get me off the sidewalk and out of there, they wanted to know all about what happened. I told them as much as I figured I could, which was too much, because they pushed me out of the car to save the upholstery and then shot me twice. So thanks for that too."

"How did you survive?"

"The two dumb bastards saw all the blood and the holes in my shirt, and figured they'd save the third bullet instead of putting it in my head. I also don't think they knew much about the neighborhood, because after the noise of the shots a lot of lights came on in apartments, and they seemed surprised. That made them take off."

"Are you in a safe place now?"

"I don't think a safe place for me exists right now. They decided I must have ratted them out or I'd be in jail. It's not likely to be much longer before somebody decides that my body should have been found by now, and it should have been mentioned in a paper or on TV."

"I'm assuming you're in a hospital. Do any of your former friends know anything that would tie you to that one in particular?"

"No. I was in the hospital, but that hospital was St. Laura Mother of Mercy. It's like the closest one to the place where they shot me. If I hadn't been shot, I could have walked there. I knew they'd figure it out. After my official visit from two cops, I decided an early checkout was a good idea."

"Where are you now?"

"Why should I tell you?"

"I'm willing to get you out of sight into a safe place if you're willing to answer questions about the guys who turned on you and the rest of it."

"I recruited a lot of the guys for that outfit, you know?"

"I do."

"Including the two that shoved me out of that car with a broken collarbone and shot me."

Duncan reminded himself to stay away from the obvious truth that Dennison had caused his own problems. He just said, "It always seems like some guys can hardly wait to betray you. I'm offering you the chance to give some back to them. Just talk to me. Since they think you already agreed to be a witness, what have you got to lose?"

Dennison paused, and Duncan knew he should give him time to think. Finally, Dennison said, "I'll talk to you."

"Are you at your apartment?"

"Hell no. They know the place. I'm in Spanszic's apartment. They knew it wasn't too far from where they picked me up, but they never got here, and for the moment I'm pretty sure they still think I'm dead anyway."

"I'll be there a little after midnight. I'll be driving a dark blue Subaru. Can you walk?"

"Not far and not fast, but I'll manage. And bring some food. Spanszic's canned stuff is almost gone."

"I'll be there tonight. That's all I can promise." Duncan ended the call.

Russell's Chicago office was the one place where he really felt comfortable. The two lower floors were like protective shells. The first floor looked like the real estate office it had been when he had actually been in the business of selling houses and condominiums for people and pretending to find houses and condominiums for other people. He seldom showed any customer a place unless he was handling both sides of the transaction and getting two commissions on each sale.

Since then, he had moved into the next step up, which was to be a developer. He didn't need the showroom look that the ground floor had, with its big counter for two receptionists and the cubicles and glass offices for salespeople and its display cases full of posters of beautiful houses, many of them not for sale. As he had moved out of the real estate market, he had gotten rid of his employees one by one.

The second-floor office was more private, and he'd found over time that he didn't even need a secretary to do what he needed to do as a developer. It was really a matter of finding pieces of land or wreckable buildings for little money, all of which was borrowed, often with the collateral of other property that he didn't own. The secret was getting in and getting out and paying loans before anybody looked at securing the collateral. Now he had stopped even that. He still used the second-floor office for his new business, and lived above it on the third floor.

His work had come to the attention of Grow. That was what they, formerly known as the Mr. Food Corporation, called themselves now, since one-word meaningless names had become popular among big corporations like Alphabet and Meta. The money for Russell got to be bigger, but the risks grew too. He had paid to strengthen the first-floor perimeter—new remote electronic locks designed for jewelry stores, smaller, bullet-proof windows, an elevator that he could control, so when he didn't want anybody above the first floor he could raise the elevator and leave it on an upper floor where he was.

He'd had to add muscle to work for Grow. This was not an unfamiliar part of business to Russell. When he had graduated from real estate sales to development he had hired a security company to watch the properties he controlled. They did nothing to discourage lumber thieves and metal scavengers that sapped his profits. He learned quickly that what he needed weren't better and more expensive patrols. He needed thieves and violent thugs. He hired a couple of men through a charitable program to rehabilitate convicts coming out of prison, and they recruited a few suitable friends for him.

That was how he had found Mullins. He had been in prison five years for a violent home invasion robbery, and prison had given him a career as the perfect second-in-command. He had learned a great deal about the world and its creatures, and he used it. He had hired six men and sent them in pairs to vulnerable spots each night to wait for thieves. Within a month a few thieves had been badly beaten, and two others had disappeared.

Russell was sure that the interest Grow had in him had come from this period. They had kept him in mind until they had a use for him.

But now there was trouble. Russell had summoned Mullins from the Ash River project to Chicago to help solve the mess, but it hadn't helped. He heard the intercom outside the street entrance downstairs, looked at the monitor, and saw him. He buzzed Mullins through the door and locked it behind him. Mullins walked across the uninhabited front office and pressed the elevator button for the second floor. Russell turned on the elevator and let it obey the summons to go down, open for him, and bring him up.

When Mullins stepped out of the elevator Russell was sitting behind the big desk directly across from the doors, so when the doors parted, Russell was the first sight to meet his eyes. Mullins stepped out of the elevator without letting his expression change, but Russell noticed that as he took his second step his eyes snapped to the right and then the left before returning to Russell. He had been looking to see if Russell's disappointment in him had produced men with guns.

As Mullins approached, Russell pointed to a simple chair in front of the desk. Mullins sat down and waited. Russell said, "Where is Charlie Dennison?"

"I was told he's dead."

"Have you seen his body?"

"No."

"So what are you going to do?"

"Find out and kill him if he needs it."

"Find him how?"

"If he is alive, Duncan has him. We'll kill them both."

25

The third time Duncan drove past Spanszic's apartment it was just after midnight. As he pulled up in front, the door swung open and Dennison's head poked out, turned in both directions, and then withdrew for a moment before he put a foot out onto the top step, and then another. When he saw how slowly Dennison moved, Duncan helped him get into the car, then got back into the driver's seat, and pulled the car back out and into motion.

Duncan accelerated, looking from side to side and in the mirrors. "Just sit still and relax, Charles."

"Charlie, for Christ's sake," Dennison said.

"Maybe it would be better to call you Mickey Rafferty. What name did you use in the hospital?"

"I didn't have his ID anymore, so I said my name was Robert Johnson, since there are probably eleven million of them. On the way in I ditched my wallet and said it was stolen by the muggers who shot me."

"You were interviewed by the Chicago police?"

"I'd checked in with two gunshot wounds. What do you think?"

"Did you tell them anything that was true?"

"I stayed way clear of that. I'm a poor sad bastard who came to the big city to apply for jobs, got lost, and found myself on the wrong kind of street, and two men beat me up, took my trip money, and then shot me."

"Do you know the names of the ones who shot you?"

"Those two were Bill Musgrave and Randy Stokes. I recruited them. The fact that they're stupid saved my life."

Dennison tried to turn his face toward Duncan, but couldn't, and twisting seemed to cause him pain. "Where are you taking me?"

Duncan said, "I'm hoping to get you to the federal building. I have to call first to be sure they'll take us right away so we're not left sitting in a public lobby or something."

"Did I say that I wanted to go to the federal building?"

"When I said I was willing to take you someplace where you would be safe you said you would be willing to tell what you know about the little mafia you were helping pull together."

"I didn't say I'd tell it to the Justice Department."

"Who, then?"

"You. Nobody said Justice Department. If I tell them anything they'll charge me with it. Then they'll make me tell them everything I know about anyone anywhere, and if I can't prove it, they'll say I lied and didn't live up to my deal, and convict me of that too. They'll lock me in a prison where everybody is willing to accept a hundred bucks and a carton of cigarettes to take me off the count."

Duncan said, "I know the US Attorney in Chicago, and I guarantee that if you cooperate, I can get you a fair and reasonable deal."

"Why should I believe that?"

"Have I lied to you about anything else?"

"How do I know? I've been getting bounced around in this rolling coffin without any way of knowing anything."

"After you tried to kill me on the street that night, did I tell you I'd be back in touch?"

"Yes, but you knew that I knew you would. Every cop or private detective who gets something on you thinks he's entitled to do that."

"When I promised that I'd come and get you tonight was I telling the truth?"

"I'm not anywhere safe yet."

"Are you out of the hospital and out of jail and out of Spanszic's empty apartment?"

"All right, yes. And you also said you'd bring me food. Where is it?"

"Most of it is in the cargo compartment, but there's a burrito in the console." Duncan opened the lid between them and Dennison reached in and extracted a fast-food bag. He opened it and smiled. "What about a drink?"

"There's a milkshake in the drink holder on my side if you want it. There's a six-pack of Coke on the floor in front of you."

"Give me the shake." He took it, sucked on the straw for a few seconds, and began to eat the burrito. He kept at it for the next ten minutes, drank the rest of the milkshake, sat back in his seat, burped loudly, and then said, "I feel a lot better now." He was silent for a few seconds, then added, "About the food, anyway. I don't like the federal building idea."

"Who do you think will be more likely to be able to keep you alive—me, or thirty-five thousand FBI agents?"

"I don't see even one thousand. I see one guy persuading me to go to jail."

"So you don't want to go to the Justice Department?" Duncan said. "We'll stay at my motel. I'll call the US Attorney's office when they open in the morning in front of you, on speaker, so you can hear every word."

"I'll listen. That's all I'll say right now." He closed his eyes and lay back. He seemed not to be dozing, but to have switched off, like a machine.

Duncan drove to the small, old-fashioned motel where he had rented a room. It was essential to calm as many of Dennison's misgivings as he could before he tried to get him to talk. He woke Dennison without saying much.

When they were both inside the room and the door locked, Duncan turned on the light. Dennison said, "Now I'm supposed to sleep on a couch in my condition while you take the bed. Is that it?"

Duncan said, "There's no couch made in America that isn't more comfortable than a gurney or the back seat of a car, and this one's practically new."

Dennison fretted for a few more minutes as he tried sitting on the couch, then lying down, and then he seemed to run out of energy again and lapse into sleep. Duncan put the keys to the Subaru in the pocket of his pants, and placed the heavy armchair in front of the door on the chance that Dennison would wake up feeling ambitious and try to hot-wire the car.

In the morning, after the two of them had taken their turns in the shower, dressed, and eaten some of the coffee cakes, muffins, and protein bars Duncan had bought at a nearby supermarket before heading for Spanszic's apartment, Duncan took out his cell phone. He said to Dennison, "I'll call the US Attorney now, before the press of business starts to pile up." He dialed the number of the Justice Department office and hit the speaker icon. "You have reached the US Attorney's Office. If you know the extension of the party you would like to speak with, please dial it now." Duncan dialed the five-digit extension.

A recorded voice said, "We're sorry, but the extension you have dialed is no longer in service."

Duncan said to Dennison, "Of course. They change the extensions all the time. It's a security thing." He looked away from Dennison at the wall. He had ended his investigation, and so they had closed the dedicated line.

He stood. "It occurs to me that maybe the signal we're getting here just isn't as strong as it should be. I'll try outside." He stepped outside the motel room and redialed the main number. "US Attorney's Office. How can I help you?"

"I need to speak with the US Attorney directly. I've been using an extension, but the recording says it's no longer in service, so there's been a mistake."

"Can you tell me the extension?"

"90586."

There was a three-second delay. "I'm afraid that's correct," she said. "The extension has been removed from service."

"I need to speak with her personally, please. My name is Harry Duncan."

"Is she expecting your call?"

"No, but it's urgent and she'll take it."

"May I ask the subject of your call?"

"It's a criminal matter, and it's confidential for the moment. If you can just tell her my name, Harry Duncan, she'll know what it's about and take the call."

"I'm sorry, sir, but I'm not authorized to do that."

"Then can you please transfer me to someone else who is authorized to do that?"

"I'm sorry, sir." Now she was irritated, and engaging in a politeness contest with him.

"I apologize if I sound impatient," he said. "I understand your situation. But please, if you could just write my name and phone number on a piece of paper and hand it to anyone from her office when you see them, you might be saving someone's life. My name is Harry Duncan, and the number is," he paused to read it aloud from the screen of the burner phone.

"Yes, sir," she said. "I've got it. Now I have a number of other calls lined up holding for me to answer, so I'll have to go." And she was gone.

He put away the phone and reentered the room. Dennison looked at him and said, "Now you're going to tell me that you got through to the US Attorney himself, and it's all worked out and taken care of. You only let it slip your mind that you said I would be able to hear it all."

"I'm afraid not. I didn't get to talk to the US Attorney. And he's a she."

"Jesus," Dennison said. "I've got to have that too?"

"I guess so. She's at least as good as any other US Attorney, so we'll all be fine. She'll call me when she gets the message I left, I'm sure."

He plugged his phone charger into the only unused outlet, which was the lower one for the lamp, half-obscured by the bed, set the phone on the nightstand, and checked to be sure the ringer was at its loudest setting. He thought about simply driving Dennison to the federal building without making a prior arrangement, but there were too many reasons not to. The members of the criminal start-up would know that the place in Chicago where there was jurisdiction over crimes ordered here in Illinois to be carried out in Indiana was the Justice Department. If they knew by now that he had Dennison, they would be waiting around the federal building to stop Duncan from delivering him. If Duncan got to speak to Ellen, maybe she would arrange to have the FBI pick Dennison up.

He was afraid after hearing the receptionist that Ellen must have given orders that she wasn't to be disturbed. It would be like her to go through all the material he had given her before she ordered anybody to act. It could easily take enough time for Dennison and Duncan to be found and killed before she did anything. He kept catching himself glancing at the phone to see if its screen lit up with her call without his hearing it.

He didn't want to sit like this waiting for the time to pass. The only thing he could do right now was to try to get at what Charlie Dennison knew. If there was a chance that he wouldn't live to get interviewed by the FBI, let alone say it in court, he couldn't let the information in his head get obliterated. He had to make a recording.

He had to try to get as much recorded as could. Dennison knew the way the business worked, he knew the names and personalities, and he hated them. There wasn't going to be any better witness than he was.

Duncan went to his suitcase and took out his laptop, set it on the round table near the window, opened it up, and set it to record what was about to happen. He went to the nightstand and took the motel's Bible out of the drawer and set it on the table.

"Dennison said, "What are you doing?"

Duncan said, "Living up to our deal. I'm the one you wanted to talk to, so we're starting it now. I'm going to ask you to do a deposition. I'm not a lawyer, so I'm not the best one to do it, but I'll do my best to get the technicalities right. Come and sit in this chair."

Dennison got up from the couch and walked to the chair.

Duncan looked at the tiny camera along the top of the computer screen. "It is April twenty-sixth, at ten-nineteen a.m. My name is Harold James Duncan. Please state your name for the record."

"Charles Dennison. Now you're going to read me my rights?"

"No. You're not in police custody. If you're free to go, you don't get the Miranda warning."

"Humor me. I don't want to leave them any excuse to call bullshit to what I say."

"You have the right to remain silent. You have the right to have an attorney present during questioning. Anything you say can and will be used against you in a court of law. Do you understand these rights?"

"Yes."

"Do you wish to speak anyway?"

"Yes I do."

"Do you swear to tell the truth, the whole truth and nothing but the truth, so help you God?"

Dennison put his left hand on the Bible and raised his right hand. "I do."

"When did you first become aware that a group was being formed to move into the Ash River region of Indiana for criminal purposes?"

"I know exactly, because it was the day I got out of prison last year. There was a man waiting beside a car across the street. It was last August, the twelfth. They let that day's group out at once, but I could see he had his eye on me. I figured he was some kind of cop who was going to give me bad news, like they were picking me up to take me somewhere else to ask questions about something else I'd done, or maybe try to get me to rat somebody out. I walked straight toward him, staring him in the face, starting to relish the chance to tell him to fuck off. When I got there, he said, "Would you like a job?""

"Who was that man?"

"His name is Gerald Russell."

For the next three hours, Dennison answered questions. No matter what Duncan asked him, he made an attempt to answer it. The only times he stopped were to use the bathroom or accept a glass of water. At the end of the three hours, he said, "I need to rest for a while," so they stopped. He hobbled to the couch, covered himself with the blanket, and slept for three hours, as though to make up the same energy he'd used. Duncan kept his phone plugged in, waiting for the call from Ellen. He checked the ringer volume again to be sure he hadn't failed to hear it, but it had been at the highest level already, and the phone said there had been no missed calls. After a couple of hours Duncan wondered if Ellen had simply told her people to have the dedicated extension reconnected, so he called it again, but he got the same result.

When Dennison woke up, he drank a glass of water, then another, and then sat down where the computer's camera was on him, and began to talk. It was as though he was finishing a sentence and had just stopped to take a breath. He told Duncan about the division of the group of recruits into seven crews of five men each. Above them was an underboss named Mullins, who had been hired before anyone else, and above him was Russell. Above Russell was an entity Dennison had never met. When anyone referred to the entity, it was just by its location, Chicago. Russell might say "Chicago isn't going to like this," or "I'll have to clear this with Chicago." Sometimes it had sounded to Dennison as though the entity must be a group of backers who functioned as a committee, like the "Commission" that had kept the Italian Mafia organized, and other times it sounded to Dennison as though it was a single man who had a great deal of power that had existed before the founding of the new group—maybe a connection to a bigger and older criminal force who could be counted on to reward the faithful and destroy the disloyal.

"Tell me about Mullins," Duncan said. "Does he know what 'Chicago' is?"

"I'm pretty sure he must, but if so, he never told me."

"Where did he come from?"

"He's from Indiana, and he's the one who seems to know the most about the small towns up and down the river. Maybe Russell is from there too. I don't know. I never heard of him before I met him."

The interrogation went on for another three hours before Dennison took another break. When he returned, Duncan began to ask about the criminal enterprise. "What do you know about the business end of things? They seem to be devoting all of their efforts to extortion—selling protection."

"That's right. It's the best way to get started. The idea was to get as many businesses as they could right away. Once the stores and restaurants and bars and repair shops and things were paying some of their income to Russell, there would be no overhead. It would be like collecting rent. Protection is also something where you get to show off all the muscle you have on your side. You're hoping that at least some of the owners will tell you no, or maybe do something they think will get rid of you. Then it's your turn. You beat the shit out of a couple of people, maybe wreck their building, sabotage their cars and delivery trucks, break some bones. All you have to do is hurt a few bad enough to make them scared, and they'll make everybody else scared. After that, time is on your side.

"You can sign up a couple of businesses a day. You show them how easy life is for the businesses that pay, and show them how terrible the losses can be if they're not paying you for protection. You can take your time, but you don't. It's best to start with a few established businesses that everybody knows and thinks will never cave in. When they do, the others start to feel powerless." He went on about the method. He wasn't sure about the names of the businesses now paying extortion, but he remembered being told there were some in every town along the Ash River.

"Where is this going?" Duncan said. "What's the next step?"

"Get fat from the protection business, adding more places that are paying. Next they'll start raising the rates. When it gets to be too much for the ones who pay, they'll start taking shares in businesses as silent partners. Now that they've got a little money to throw around, they'll try to build some leverage with the local cops in these little towns so they'll have immunity. Then they can get into other ways to make money—like drugs and hookers—the sorts of things where you just wait and collect a percentage. But you need police cooperation."

The conversation went on for a long time before Dennison was finished. When he had fallen asleep again, Duncan took the entire recording of his deposition and sent it to the email address of the office of the US Attorney. After that he added an email message telling Ellen that another attempt had been made to kill him, and that the informant on the tape had been shot twice and needed protection. He repeated the number of the phone he had been using. He waited for a half hour, and then lay on the bed and fell asleep.

The cell phone rang. Duncan's eyes opened and he saw the phone's screen. It lit the deep darkness of the room like a night-light. He lunged from the bed to the phone and thumbed the "Accept" circle. "Hello?"

"Mr. Duncan?"

"This is Duncan." He was confused, his mind dulled by hours of sleep. Why would Ellen call him Mr. Duncan? But was it Ellen? Maybe she was an assistant, or maybe a federal officer making the call on a secure line before connecting the US Attorney at her home. Assistants often started to sound like their bosses.

"I just got your message. We need to get this man Dennison to the Justice Department right away. We'll pick the case up from there, as you requested. We needed an informant and now we'll have one. It's great work."

Duncan's mind suddenly saw several things at once. The voice on the line was not Ellen. It was incredibly close. Jeanette must have watched video recordings of a speech at some civic event or an interview or something. She had listened carefully and rehearsed it. Her voice was clear and businesslike, the way

Ellen's probably was in public or in court. There was only one thing she didn't seem to know. Ellen was once his wife. Without that, no mimic's performance could be anything but ridiculous.

"Will there be somebody at the door to let him in tonight, or do we wait for business hours?"

"No. There will be three FBI agents sent to transport him, and I'll meet him later. Are you still at the Nitelite Hotel?"

"It's a motel. But yes."

"I'll talk to you again tomorrow after I've talked with him."

"All right," said Duncan. "Thank you."

The phone went dead. Duncan reached for the lamp beside the bed and switched it on.

Dennison groaned and pulled his blankets up over his eyes. "What is it?"

"The US Attorney called, but it wasn't her. She knows where we are, and she says she's sending FBI agents to pick you up."

"How does she know where we are?"

"I left the US Attorney's office my phone number. I also sent it again with the interview I emailed. If you have the number, you can locate the phone. We've got to get up and out of here before the fake FBI agents get here."

Dennison said, "Why didn't you say you had moved to the Hilton?"

"Asking for our location was a test. She knew where my phone is, and I was on it. If I lied, she would know I wasn't fooled. Sit yourself up on the couch and get ready to move. You can go back to sleep in the car."

In five minutes they were ready and on their feet. Duncan took one last look around, stared at the phone in his hand, then went to "Settings," told it to clear its memory, and opened one of the drawers of the desk and put the phone inside, sliding it to the very back. Then he stepped to the door. "I'd better go out first and bring the car up close."

He took his suitcase and stepped out. He moved quickly, staying in the shadow of the roof overhang along the walkway beside the room doors so the light from the motel's sign didn't make him an easy target. He put the suitcase in the cargo bay, got into the driver's seat, started the engine, and moved the car to the door of the room he had rented. He opened the door, held Dennison's arm tightly to support him, got him into the rear seat, and stepped around the back of the car to slip inside quickly.

In a moment they were gliding across the lot and onto the road. Duncan's head turned in both directions to look for enemies on the road and his eyes flicked up to the rearview mirror as he accelerated away from the motel. He looked at the clock on the car's dashboard. "Almost two o'clock. I don't see the car yet."

"What car?" Dennison said.

"They knew where we were. Why not have somebody there to follow us before she called?"

"Didn't she say she wanted to get me to the federal building? If there's an ambush, wouldn't it be there?"

"I don't think so. I think that's just to make us think we're safe. I think they wanted to get us at the motel. Now that we're away from there, they'll want to intercept us on the way, before we're at a place that's staffed by real federal agents. The follow car should be behind us, to cut off an escape. Maybe more than one."

Dennison said, "Do you give lessons, or what?"

"I used to stop cars for a living."

"I forgot. Sometimes you seem almost human," Dennison said. "I'm going back to sleep. I assume if there's gunfire it will wake me up."

"You won't miss a thing."

Duncan drove south away from the federal building, took Interstate 80 east, and then Interstate 65 south.

As soon as he took the exit onto 65, Dennison said, "This is familiar ground. Are we going where I think we're going?"

"We're on the interstate because it's fast and flat, and I'll see it if somebody tries to catch up and cut us off. It was also the opposite direction from where a woman who wants to kill us said we were going to go."

"In about three hours we'll be in Kentucky," Dennison said. "Maybe sooner, at the speed you're going."

"Driving fast is a way to spot anybody who's trying hard to catch up," Duncan said. "You should go to sleep for now. I don't know what's happening tomorrow, but I'm guessing it won't be restful."

26

Dennison eased himself down to lie on the back seat, and soon he was asleep. Duncan drove on. He kept his speed up, staying about ten miles an hour above the speed limit, and looking into the mirrors frequently to be sure no car was trying to keep up. It was almost five A.M. when he came down the road beside the Ash River and turned up the driveway in front of Renee Parkman's house. He got out of the car. There was just enough light now so he could see the big scar on the front lawn where the two Clark brothers had set fire to the third brother's car.

He pulled up the garage door, then backed the Subaru in. He collected a few things from the trunk and then opened Dennison's door to wake him.

Dennison looked at him with startled eyes, then closed them, leaned back, stretched, and sat up.

"It's five o'clock," Duncan said. "We should get inside before the light starts to come back."

Duncan helped Dennison up and out of the car, and walked him to the front door. Duncan took out the lock pick and tension wrench from his wallet, and then looked more closely at the lock. "This isn't it."

"Isn't what?"

"The lock. There was a regular old Schlage lock. Somebody changed the locks on the house."

"I wonder who," Dennison said. "Let's get out of here."

Duncan said, "Sit in the car. I'll be back in a couple of minutes." He walked around the house looking in windows and examining doors and latches. Finally, he came to the wooden door set at a thirty-degree angle that covered the entrance to concrete stairs leading down to the basement. It was still locked there by the big padlock he'd seen when he'd been here before. The key was probably somewhere in Renee's kitchen, but he'd never seen it. He opened his pocketknife and slid the blade into the narrow crack between the underside of the door and the concrete below it, and found the hinges at the inner side of the door. He used the blade to poke the end of the pin that held the first hinge, pushed it about an eighth of inch, and then slid the blade in to find the upper end of the pin that was wider to keep it from sliding downward. He pried the pin up and out. Then he repeated the process with the second hinge.

He lifted the door from the hinge side, went down the steps, and then used his pick and tension wrench to open the vertical inner door. He had been sure the men in the gang had not been familiar enough with the features of old rural houses to realize that changing the basement lock was necessary. Maybe they didn't even know that door was there, since they seemed to move around mostly at night. And men who believed they were part of an overwhelming force got careless and lazy.

He was inside now, standing in the basement of the dark house. He remained perfectly still for about a minute and heard nothing. It was a cool night, but the house was warm inside. He could hear the oil furnace running. He hoped it was because Renee had missed the thermostat when she'd walked walked around turning off before he'd helped her leave town.

He climbed the wooden stairs upward and stopped in the kitchen to listen again, then went to the front door and opened it from the inside so Dennison could enter. He held his finger to his lips to keep him quiet, and then climbed to the second floor to be sure there was nobody asleep in the house. When he came back down, he said, "Nobody's here."

"If we're smart, neither are we," Dennison said. "What the hell made you think this town was a safe place for either of us?"

"They're not expecting us," Duncan said. "And there are more people here who hate them than there are who hate us."

"What are we going to do now—wake all three of them up?"

"I'd like to get some sleep, and for the moment, I think we'd better stay out of sight." He relocked the door and started to climb the stairs. He stopped halfway up. "I hope you won't do anything foolish, like getting in touch with your friends while we're asleep."

"Not me," Dennison said. "When people who know me try to kill me, I take it as a sign that there's little to look forward to in the relationship." He paused. "I hope you're not expecting me to climb up those steps."

"There's a small bedroom down the hall by the kitchen. The back stairs are right there, and the door next to them takes you to the basement."

"All right," Dennison said.

When Duncan reached the upstairs bedroom, he closed and locked the door. He stood by the window and looked up and down the street for a few minutes, and then realized he couldn't sleep in the room. It offered him no way to protect Dennison. As long as he had Dennison and he was alive, he was winning.

He went back down the stairs, checked to be sure Dennison was in the small downstairs bedroom and asleep, and then went to the couch in the living room and used his jacket as a blanket. In a short time he was asleep. Hours later his eyes opened.

There was the sound of a car bumping up over the edge of the pavement onto the driveway. Maybe it was just turning around. He waited for the sound of the car bumping as it backed off, but it didn't come. Instead, there was the growl of the engine working slightly harder as an impatient driver pulled in, keeping up his speed on the incline. The car stopped.

Duncan hurried to the room where Dennison was, shook him awake, and pulled him to a sitting position. Duncan whispered, "Charlie, listen. Somebody is coming to the front door. We've got to get you down the basement stairs."

Dennison stood, and Duncan helped him to the bedroom door, then helped him to the stairs to the basement. Duncan went first and backed down the stairs with one hand gripping Dennison's and the other on the railing so he could keep Dennison from falling. When Duncan had gotten Dennison to the bottom of the stairs, he sat him down on a lower step, climbed back up and closed the door to the kitchen. He stayed there and listened.

It was two men. One clomped upstairs, and the other stayed on the ground floor. Duncan kept his ear close to the door.

There was the sound of heavy footsteps coming toward them on the hardwood floor of the hallway, so Duncan put his hand on his pistol. He waited until he heard the footsteps reach the room where Dennison had been sleeping. Then they stopped.

Duncan waited for two minutes to see if the man noticed any-thing different—that the bedcovers had only been hastily pulled up, that the bed felt warm, or anything else seemed wrong to him. The springs creaked as the man flopped onto the bed, and within another few minutes there was the sound of snoring.

Duncan went down the stairs slowly and quietly. He whis-pered, "I'll be back in a few minutes. Don't make any noise."

Duncan opened the door that led up the concrete steps where he had entered the house, pushed the wooden door on an angle at the surface level upward far enough to climb out, then low-ered the door again. He walked along the side of the house, not touching the outer wall and watching to be sure he didn't step on or kick anything on the ground that might make a noise. When he got to the corner of the house, he looked around it and saw that the men had left their car in front of the house's entrance, not in front of the garage. He turned and went back to the cellar door. This time when he opened it, he left it open and went back down into the basement.

"They didn't block the garage. Let's go."

He pulled Dennison to his feet and then went up the concrete steps slowly, supporting Dennison at each step. When they were up on the grass Duncan closed the cellar door and led Dennison around the house to the garage. When they were there, he very slowly lifted the garage door to keep the rollers from making noise on their track. The two stepped inside, and Duncan helped Dennison into the back seat again.

He started the Subaru. When the car cleared the garage door he got out and lowered the door as quietly as he could, then eased the car forward, barely pressing the gas pedal, then let the car coast down the driveway and turned right onto River Road.

Dennison said, "Where are we going?"

"I'm not sure. There are hotels within a few miles, but I don't know which ones have your friends staying at them. You said there were over thirty of them, and they must be sleeping somewhere. We need a place where we can be invisible for a few days at least. The night Renee Parkman closed down the bar, she stayed with a friend of hers. I'll think of her name in a minute." A moment later he said, "Madeleine Foster. I'm setting a course to her house."

Dennison said, "Will she take me in too?"

"I don't know if she'll take either of us. I know if you tell her who you really are, she won't," Duncan said. "Tell her you're a friend who got stuck here because you were visiting me when you were injured in a car accident."

He parked the car on the quiet street where he had left his car the night when Renee Parkman closed The Elbow Room, and they got out and walked through the large empty lot that brought them up to the back door of Madeleine Foster's house. Duncan walked around the house and looked up and down the street and then up and down the cross streets to detect any signs of danger, and then returned to the back of the house. "I don't see any cars parked near here, and I don't think they'd walk any distance to keep a low profile."

Duncan rang the doorbell and waited. He counted to twenty-five and then rang it again. Above them a light came on in a window, and then the window was pushed upward and Madeleine stuck her head out to look down at them. "Oh my God," she said. "What are you doing here?"

"Can I talk to you for a minute, Madeleine?"

"I'll be right down."

They heard her footsteps coming quickly, and then the door opened and Madeleine, wearing a fuzzy robe over pajamas, appeared at the threshold. "Come in, come in," she said, looked out past them as though she was afraid there were other people coming, then stepped back to let them pass, and forward to shut and lock the door. "I figured they'd gotten you," she said. "You just disappeared one day, and when you didn't come back everybody started to think you were dead."

He looked over Madeleine's shoulder. "What are those boxes?"

"That's some kitchen stuff. If it fits in my car, I'll take it. If not, I'll probably put it on somebody's porch to keep those bastards from getting it."

"What? Why?" Duncan said. "Are you moving or something?"

"Yes," Madeleine said. "They want me out tomorrow. If I'm not, they said four of them will move in with me."

"The crooks are taking your house?"

"Buying it. They're too smart to just throw me out. They came to me with a set of papers already made out, including the price, which is about a fifth of what it's worth, but it's still a lot of money. They had the cashier's check too."

"And you had to sign?"

"Had to? I don't know what they would have done if I didn't. Maybe scare me until I signed, or maybe nothing. But I think I'm being the smart one. I don't think the job I had working at the bar is coming back, and there's not much else I can do here. The creeps are moving in and taking over, so everything is going to turn to shit. This way I'm still healthy and unhurt. I still have my car and whatever clothes and stuff will fit in it, and the cashier's check for forty thousand is already in my bank account. In six months do you think I'll be able to sell my house for more? I don't. If I don't want to be here if those creeps are, nobody else will either."

"I'm sorry," Duncan said. "I was hoping you could let us stay for a few days."

Madeleine said, "I would have. I'll still do whatever I can. I just can't stay. I feel terrible."

Duncan said. "Don't. None of this is your fault, and you didn't do anything wrong. All we need is a chance to sleep where we won't be noticed for a few hours before we go. Did they say when they were coming to move in?"

"They said in the afternoon, so I guess this is still my house until noon. I've got just about everything packed already, and I was going to load the last things into the car and leave whenever I woke up, but that was before you showed up. I'll stay and make us breakfast before I go."

Duncan said, "That would be great."

"There's the couch in the living room, and there's a spare bedroom upstairs across from mine. Will those work?"

Duncan said, "That's great. Thank you." He added, "How is Renee doing?"

Madeleine looked surprised. "Why ask me?"

"You're her good friend, but you didn't ask me about her, so I guessed you've been in touch with her since we both left."

Madeleine looked at Duncan for a moment. "I have. She came back weeks ago. She said she'd been going out of her mind hiding in Denver and wondering what was happening here. She knew those guys were looking for her, but we both figured she'd be safe here for a while. When I decided to sell the house and leave, she left first."

"Did she say why she didn't call me?"

"She said a lot of different things, and I hadn't even asked. My guess is that she was kind of attracted to you, but it wasn't the right time or place, so she didn't want to be involved, much less dependent on you."

"I'll be honest with you," Duncan said. "I'm trying to pull together an argument to get this town some law enforcement help. At some point, I'll need to get in touch with her. I want her as a witness, not a girlfriend."

Madeleine hesitated for a moment, then went into the kitchen and came back with a slip of paper from a pad and handed it to him. "This is her new cell number. If she doesn't get in touch with you by the time you need her, this is the way."

"Thanks, Madeleine."

"Okay," Madeleine said. "I'll see you in the morning." They waited while she went back up to her room.

Duncan turned to Dennison. "You okay with the couch?"

"It's looking better every second." He began walking stiffly toward it. His six-inch shuffling steps seemed so laborious that Duncan took his arm and helped him there, then lowered him onto the couch. Dennison said, "Turn off the kitchen light before some of my loyal friends see it, and then you can get lost so I can sleep."

Duncan turned off the light and headed for the stairs. As he climbed, he thought about Ellen and the Justice Department. Had she received the video recording of him interviewing Dennison? Had she even finished reading the murder book? As he took each step upward, he pictured possible events taking place, producing in him different predictions of the future.

He imagined her persuading an FBI Special Agent in Charge to raid Russell's office in Chicago, or to get his colleagues in the Indianapolis office to raid the gang's haunts in Parkman's Elbow, or maybe making a pitch to the Attorney General's office in Washington to get them to order everyone to move in on both places. Then he imagined her in a home office in the big house on the north side she probably had, going over all of the excessive information he'd assembled because she'd demanded it and making copious notes about the steps she would be ready to take in a month or two.

When they had been in law school together, he had secretly felt frustrated at the slow, methodical pace she set when she was working, making lines and lines of notes he felt were unnecessary, creating delays by missing the obvious shortcuts, so it was difficult for him to even discuss cases with her because it took so much time that he felt strangled.

He pushed Ellen out of his mind, back into the shadowy corner where he had shut his memories of the marriage. If she was still that way, he and Dennison were probably going to die. He reached the spare room upstairs and lay on the bed fully clothed, then closed his eyes and invited sleep to take him.

The sounds began outside, near the front of the house. First it was the hum of a car coming slowly up the quiet street, the faint swish of tires on pavement, and the thumping beat of a radio. He'd been in this area before, and the residential neighborhood around Madeleine's house hadn't had any traffic after around nine o'clock. Madeleine had probably come in most nights after 2:00 A.M. because she'd worked at The Elbow Room, but her garage was at the back of the lot behind her house, and she would have driven up the curved driveway into the garage and got out there. Most of the time she would have been alone, so there was only one car door to close.

This car had music playing, heavy bass, and a couple of windows were open, so the voices of the men inside were audible. Like most of the inebriated, whatever they said was loud and intended to make the others laugh. The music stopped, and in an instant Duncan was up and at the window. He looked, pivoted, and ran to the stairway. He clutched both railings and vaulted down the stairs four at a time.

When he reached the ground floor he moved to the couch in the dark and reached out to wake Dennison, but Dennison wasn't there. His whisper came from the direction of the dining room. "I'm over here."

"I think it's the guys who are taking the house," Duncan whispered. He could see the shape of Dennison crouching by the dining room doorway. "What is that—a knife?"

"I found it in the box she packed full of kitchen stuff. It's the best I could do. If you want to lend me a gun, I'm pretty sure I can drop all of them faster than they can drag theirs out of their jeans."

"You're done as a witness if you've killed people."

"I'm done as anything if they kill me."

Four car doors slammed, and the shuffling of drunken footsteps and the muttering of voices moved up the front walk toward the house.

Duncan said, "Get in the front closet. If I come for you, I'll knock on the door. If somebody just swings it open stab him." He helped Dennison into the empty closet and closed the door.

He quickly climbed the stairs and slipped into the guest bedroom. He went across the hall to Madeleine's bedroom, whispered, "It's me—Duncan," and pushed the door inward.

"Madeleine?"

"I'm here," she whispered. "Behind the bed."

He said, "We've got to get all of us out of here. Think about the best way."

He went to the window and pushed the curtain aside to look down. There were three men on the front steps, and a fourth at the door. That one rang the doorbell, rang it again, and then knocked hard. "Madeleine," the man called. "We're here to kiss you goodbye before you leave."

"Better than that, Madeleine," another one added. "We'll give you a night to remember us by," another one called.

The third said, "Open up and let us in. This is your lucky night."

Madeleine was shaking. "I don't know. I can't think."

The sounds coming from below changed. There was an impact, the boom of a foot stomp-kicking the front door, then another one. A man's voice called, "The wolf pack is at the door. We'll huff and we'll puff and we'll blow the house down." That brought laughter from the others.

Duncan moved to the window beside the bed, where Madeleine was pulling herself up. As soon as she was standing, he looked down and saw something on the floor. It was cylindrical, a rolled-up object, and he could see wooden slats and plastic. "What's this? Is it a rope ladder?"

"Yes," she said. "It's for a fire. This is an old house, and—"

He picked it up and unrolled it a foot or two to examine it. There were two hook-shaped pieces of steel intended to attach it to a windowsill and extend outward a few inches, so the two ropes would be held away from the siding of the house. He went to the window that looked out on the garage and the back lawn. One of the four men had separated from the others, and he was sitting on the steps at the back door.

"There's one guy down there waiting for you to sneak out the back."

He returned to the guest room and stepped to the window that looked out on the side of the house away from the driveway. There was no door on that side, and nobody waiting. He slid the window open and fitted the two hooks over the windowsill, then hurried back to Madeleine's bedroom.

They heard a third kick against the front door. "Open the door, bitch!"

He said, "We're about out of time. Madeleine, get the things you really need into a purse with a shoulder strap, fast. If it won't fit in the purse, you don't need it."

While Madeleine pushed things into her purse, Duncan whispered, "As soon as you reach the ground, run into the field behind the house and get to the Subaru parked on the next street. Here are the keys. Don't leave without us unless they head for your car or you hear gunfire."

She nodded. "Got it."

"Okay," he said, "Come on."

He hurried her to the window and fed the rope ladder out carefully to keep it from swinging against the house. "Go."

"I'm scared."

"Me too. That's why we're running." He laced his fingers together and bent down. "Here's your first step."

She stepped on his hands and he hoisted her to the windowsill. He held her around the waist. "Now turn around to face me and put your feet on the first strep. Good. Step down. Keep your eyes on the wall and keep moving down until your feet touch grass."

He waited, then leaned out the window. She was nearly down. As soon as she turned to run, he turned away.

As he did, he heard more sounds from downstairs. There was another stomp-kick, the crack of wood breaking, and the door flying open to hit the wall. Heavy footsteps thumped on the hardwood floor of the entryway. Duncan stepped to Madeleine's bedroom door, locked it so they'd assume that was where she was, came back to the guest room window, and looked down.

He sat on the windowsill, rolled to face the window, tugged the curtains across the window and then pulled the window down to the sill, so the two hooks were barely visible from inside the room. He went down the rope ladder to the grass as quickly as he could, and then hurried around to the front corner of the house, looked to be sure all four of the men had gone inside, and ran to the kicked-open front door. As he reached the doorway, he heard the footsteps of the men going up the stairs to the second floor. He stepped in, knocked quietly on the closet door, and pulled it open.

Dennison was there with the butcher knife, which he lowered as Duncan stepped aside. He heard one of the men upstairs kick the locked bedroom door. "Come on."

Duncan took Dennison's arm to pull him out, then closed the closet door again, and guided him out the front door. They went around the house where the rope ladder hung. Dennison looked at it as they passed, but said nothing.

They made it to the empty lot. Dennison seemed exhausted and in pain, gasping whenever his foot slipped or he had to step over a root, but he never spoke. Duncan was aware that Dennison's actions were probably just a lifelong criminal's need to seem tough, because any other pose was dangerous, but for the moment he was grateful for anything that gave them an edge.

He kept Dennison moving and kept him from falling, and soon their route intersected with the path. They emerged from the lot into the backyard of a house and walked beside it to the street. For a second, Duncan felt alarm as he saw that the car wasn't in its parking spot, but he heard an engine start and then Madeleine pulled the Subaru up beside them so they could get into the back seat, and then drove on.

The night was quiet and appeared to be empty of people, but they knew now that it wasn't. There seemed to be men—malicious men with ugly intentions—billeted in homes in different parts of the town, wide awake even at this hour looking for victims.

The three people in the car were silent for a minute, and then another minute before the silence became an irritant. "We've got to get out of town, obviously," Duncan said.

"To where?" Madeleine said.

Duncan said, "Is there somebody in any nearby town who will hide you?"

"I'm trying to think of someone. All my friends seem to have left already. A lot of businesses are closing around here."

"Pull over somewhere and we'll switch places. I'll try to get up the river road before they call ahead and get some of their friends to block it."

"What's up the river road?" Dennison said.

"Places where there aren't any more of those jerks trying to find us."

He drove northward, away from the residential neighborhood where Madeleine's house was, looking in the mirrors often. "We need to stay out of sight for a few hours."

"What good is hiding?" Madeleine said. "It just gives them more time to find us. You know what they were going to do to me. Now that it's been said, do you think they're going to forget it?"

Duncan said, "They were pretty drunk. Before too long at least a couple of them are going to pass out, and then the other two will feel like they're too small a group to do anything to anybody that involves effort and risk."

He knew that wouldn't satisfy Madeleine, but it made her fall silent for the moment. He drove on, intending to put as many miles of road behind them as possible. He reached the outskirts of the town and then saw a pair of cars far ahead, one stopped on the right shoulder of the road and the other stopped on the left shoulder. He turned off his headlights, coasted to a near-stop, and performed a U-turn. He drove slowly back the way he had come until the next curve so he wouldn't have to apply his brakes and make the brake lights come on. He took the first road away from the river, switched on his headlights again, and drove faster.

For the next two hours he parked in a lot behind a fast-food restaurant in a town called Bainbridge and let the others sleep until the sun was fully up. As soon as the first cars were passing on the road, Madeleine and Dennison began to stir. Madeleine opened her eyes and sat up, then pulled down the sun visor to look in the mirror behind it. She began to adjust her hair with her fingers, then reached into her purse for a hairbrush, and noticed him. "Have you been awake all this time?"

"I wanted to know as soon as they found us," he said.

"Thank you," she said.

"I didn't mind. It gave me time to think."

"Good for you." She brushed her hair and then put on lipstick. "Do you think that restaurant is open?"

"They're not."

"I would really like to find a place with a bathroom."

Duncan started the car and pulled the car out of the lot and drove until they came to a small town with an open gas station and a strip mall that had a diner at one end. "Your choice," he said.

"I'll try the diner. Will you go in with me?"

"Sure." He turned around in his seat. "Charlie," he said. "Are you awake?"

He sat up. "Sort of." He looked around and saw the diner. "I knew I smelled food."

"Let's get some breakfast."

The three went into the diner, where there were a few customers, most of them elderly, but they could see empty tables. The waitress said, "Sit where you want," and then brought them menus. They ordered breakfast, and Madeleine disappeared into the ladies' room and came back with fresh makeup and perfect hair. She said, "I've got to get out of this place."

"We haven't even tried the food yet," Dennison said.

"I don't mean here. I mean the town. If I had my car I'd be gone already."

When they had finished eating, Duncan paid in cash and they got back into the car. He drove to the exit from the lot. "Do you still have your car keys?"

"Yeah. A lot of good they'll do me."

"By now the guys who came to your house are sleeping somewhere, maybe in your house. It's probably the perfect time to get your car." He drove back toward the town of Parkman's Elbow.

She said, "You could be risking your life."

Dennison said, "You could be risking my life."

Duncan shrugged. "I'll try not to lose either one."

He drove the Subaru back to the quiet street near Madeleine's house where he had parked before. "Stay here. Where is your car now? Is it in the garage?"

"It was. They could have driven it somewhere and sold it by now."

"You still have the keys. That means they don't. They could hot-wire it, but I don't think they will have done that already."

She handed him the keys. He looked at them, removed the single car key, and handed the rest back. "Does the garage have an electric opener or anything?"

"No. I just lift it open."

He got out of the car, walked to the field, and followed the path toward Madeleine's house. This early in the morning the weeds were wet and the path was damp. The air still had a slight feel of fog. He listened for the sounds of people as he came closer to the house. As he approached the garage, he saw the kitchen door open. He put his back to the side wall of the garage and froze. All four of the men Duncan had seen last night came out and hurried down the driveway toward the street. The first out told the others, "He said to get over there right away and see what she's doing."

Duncan hesitated, not sure what to do. He waited until he saw their car pull away past Madeleine's driveway, opened the garage door, got into Madeleine's car, pulled it out onto the driveway, and backed into the street. He drove quickly to the quiet side street where the Subaru was parked, expecting that the four men would be there. They weren't. Either they hadn't been talking about Madeleine, and there was another "she," or they didn't know where Madeleine was, and they'd started looking again. He pulled up in Madeleine's car, got out, and left the motor running.

Madeleine got out of the Subaru and ran up to him. She threw her arms around him and said, "Thank you, thank you, thank you, Duncan. I'll never forget it."

"No trouble at all. I hope you're happier where you're going."

She got into her car and said, "I'm happier already. Thanks again." She let the car drift ahead, then gave it more gas, accelerating as she went. He saw her window slide up and close as she sped away from the central part of the town beside the river and headed for the interstate highway.

Duncan got into the driver's seat of the Subaru, pulled away from the curb, and turned back into town.

"I hope you made a wrong turn," Dennison said. "Maybe out of habit."

"Not this time," Duncan said. "It's still early, and I want to get a quick look around."

He drove into the center of the town, and looked around for the dark blue Ford that had carried the four men from Madeleine's house. They had clearly been ordered to find someone who was referred to as "she," but was apparently not Madeleine. The only person he could think of as likely was Renee Parkman. He drove along Main Street without seeing the car, moving from block to block at a speed that was slower than normal for him. He was just about to head for the river road to get to Renee's house, and beyond it, The Elbow Room, when he saw the dark blue Ford. It was parked on the street near Rhonda's, one of the restaurants he had visited in the first days after he'd come to town.

He wasn't sure whether these men had ever seen his rented Subaru, so he turned the first corner he saw to avoid driving past their car, pulled the Subaru into a parking space, stepped off the street into the narrow alley behind the commercial buildings, and went into Rhonda's through the back entrance. He went past the kitchen and the servers' station and into the dining area and then stepped aside and paused.

Sitting alone at a small table near the front of the restaurant was Ellen Leicester. He rapidly scanned the rest of the tables, but saw nobody he could identify as among the four men at Madeleine Foster's house. There were a couple of families with young children, a table of three women, an elderly couple.

He went up to Ellen's table and said, "Good morning."

She looked up. "You're still here?"

He said, "May I sit down?"

"I guess so. Sure," she said. "I thought you would be back in Chicago."

"I was, but things have changed." He let his eyes move to sweep the room. "You didn't return my calls or I would have explained it before."

She was eating an omelet made of egg whites and spinach, and she took another bite. "Have you had breakfast yet?"

"Yes. The reason I came in was that there are four members of the group outside doing surveillance on a woman. When I got here, I was surprised to see the woman was you."

She looked at him and raised an eyebrow. It was an expression that came back to him from fifteen years ago. He'd always hated it. He wondered if she knew.

He leaned forward and spoke in a quiet voice. "I'm not manipulating you or trying to scare you, but you've already caught somebody's eye. You need to stay closer to your FBI people."

"Thank you for the advice." She took another bite, chewed, and swallowed it. She took a sip of her coffee and then sat back. "Anything else?"

"Have you read the case files and reports I sent you?"

"Yes. The main points directly, and the rest the way these things get read in busy places. I had executive summaries from assistants and deputies for a lot of it. Ten examples of a crime might help us later, but right now, no. Don't worry. You more than earned your pay."

"I know. Right now, I'm concerned about you. At this moment you're in real danger. If you don't have people very close by to escort you out of it, I'll do it."

The eyebrow rose again, and this time the suspicion of a smirk came with it. He remembered that too. "That's very sweet of you," she said. "Gentlemanly. You've always been that way, and I always appreciated it. This is going to surprise you, but I didn't come with an entourage of steely-eyed men in dark suits. I was trying to be unobtrusive, and just take a look around for myself before I recommend anything official. I suppose that's out now, since you seem to have become a local character."

"Maybe, but these four haven't seen me yet. Will you accept my help getting out of here?"

She sighed. "I suppose I'll have to." She smiled at the wait-ress, who was across the room bringing coffee cups and a pot on a tray to another table, and made a very small pantomime of signing a check.

Duncan glanced at the front window, and then at the hallway to the back door. He waited while the waitress brought the check and resisted the urge to put cash down and drag Ellen out, not because it would irritate her, but because it would draw atten-tion to them when he needed to make their exit as unnoticeable as possible. She took an incredible length of time digging in her purse for her wallet and then searching her wallet for the right credit card. He said very quietly, "I have Charles Dennison here with me."

She looked up. "Who's that?"

"Nobody watched the recording?" Then he said, "We don't have time to talk about it now. We need to get moving."

He kept the front window of the restaurant at the edge of his vision so his eye would pick up motion, while seeming to pay attention to Ellen. He was intensely aware of time passing, and aware that Ellen was dragging this out to torment him for the offense of showing up during her breakfast and risking her anonymity.

The waitress was bringing back her card and the receipt to sign. He began to feel calmer. As she signed, he saw two of the men from the blue Ford come from across the street and head toward the door of Rhonda's. Duncan stood, walked to the front door to look out, and while he was there, turned the small thumb-lock handle to lock the door, then returned to Ellen's table and pulled her chair back in what he hoped would look like a polite gesture but was really forcing her to leave. There was a sudden furious hammering on the glass of the front door, and when Ellen stood, she turned her head to see the two angry men trying hard to get in and the waitress stepping toward the door to see if it had somehow gotten locked. Ellen walked quickly to catch up with Duncan as he headed into the back hallway.

Duncan walked to the back door, which was a windowless metal security door. He looked for a peephole, but there was none, so he stood beside it and opened it cautiously only a half-inch. Instantly a man hurled himself against it so it swung inward fast. Duncan stuck his foot out to trip him as he came in with it, and gave him a push to increase his momentum into the bare wall. The second man Duncan had been expecting stayed outside, taking a step backward and reaching behind him for a weapon. He was too slow, because Duncan was already charging. Duncan collided with him while both the man's hands were still behind him. As the man toppled backward, Duncan sped his fall with a right chop to the neck. When the man hit the ground there was the pop of a pistol shot.

Ellen was out the door when Duncan looked for her, and he grabbed her hand and pulled her up the alley and around the last building to the car. He pushed her into the back seat, got into the driver's seat, and drove.

Dennison looked at her and said, "Another one?"

Duncan said, "Charles Dennison, this is Ellen Leicester, the US Attorney. Charlie is the one who recruited the men who are taking over the towns around here. He probably recruited the four men who just tried to get us. Now they all know he's ratting on them, so they want to kill him."

"You had an informant and didn't tell me?" She seemed incredulous.

"I sent you a report, called you about him, left messages, and sent you a copy of a deposition he and I made."

Dennison said, "Hey, I'm right here. Am I invisible?"

"When did you send this stuff?" she said.

"Let's see. The last time I called you was two days ago. The woman who phones and impersonates people for the organization certainly had seen it, because she called me about it pretending to be you, and saying she was sending FBI agents to protect Charlie. So about two days."

Ellen paused for a second, then said, "Hold it. You're saying that somebody in my office has been intercepting my communications?"

"At least your phone system, which I told you weeks ago on a message to the dedicated line."

"I didn't get that either," she said. "Is it possible somebody in the office is a mole? I wonder if that's how these people knew I was coming. But it doesn't seem likely a small operation like this has the—"

"I'll let you think about that," he said. He looked in the rearview mirror. "Right now I'm trying to get us someplace where we can stop looking behind us."

"My hotel is out. My office made the reservation."

"Is there anything in your hotel room you can't live without?"

"No. I would never bring any sensitive papers or my laptop or anything on this kind of trip. Do you think I'm stupid?"

"This isn't a conversation I want to have," he said. "I was just asking if you could leave your suitcase until this gets cleared up."

Dennison said, "So what place isn't out?"

"I'll let you know when we get there and it turns out to be safe."

Duncan took the series of turns he had taken a few hours ago to get to the parking lot of the fast-food restaurant in a town thirty miles away where they had waited for dawn. Duncan had remembered a motel, and he stopped and rented a pair of rooms. He said to Ellen, "Dennison and I will take one room to get some sleep. He's recovering from gunshot wounds, and I was up all night. In the other one you can watch television or use your cell phone or whatever. Just don't call anybody in your office, even if you can trust them. You can't trust the phone line." He handed her a key, watched her go inside, heard the dead bolt, and then said to Dennison, "There are twin beds. Wake me up if anything seems to be happening."

Duncan fell asleep in a minute or two.

27

The car pulled into the parking lot of the Riverbank Restaurant, and Renee Parkman let it glide to a stop by the main entrance. There were no cars in the front lot. She drifted forward around the sprawling building to the back, but there were no vehicles there either. She had hoped to find her friend alone, or at least nearly alone, after the restaurant had been closed and cleaned. She supposed her own sense of timing was distorted after all her years of working in a bar. The Riverbank had been closed and locked hours ago.

Renee drove to a neighborhood nearby, where the houses were large and set back from the street on plots of at least an acre each, all sharing a long, low hill. This was where the old families of Riverbank had lived. Families then were big, about a dozen kids, grandma and grandpa, and a maid and a cook. Most families were half a generation off the farm, so a lot of them still kept a cow or two, a giant vegetable garden, and horses to pull the carriage. It took her a few minutes to find the right one. When she had, she stopped the car at the curb, took out her cell phone, and selected the number.

In a moment there was a voice, whispering. "Hello?" In the extreme silence, the whisper seemed loud.

"Hi, Mona, it's Renee."

"What time is it?"

Renee looked at her phone screen. "About midnight. I'm really sorry, but this is an emergency. I'm parked on the street outside. Can I pull up the driveway and talk?"

"Better not. Stay there. I'll come down." The phone went dead.

Renee pushed the red oval to make her screen go dark. It was better that she was coming out. It meant she was already committed. Renee looked out the car window at the large house and grounds. The old barn and stable were long gone, but the big property would almost certainly still have a place to park the car where it wouldn't be seen.

Renee sat still and waited. Then she saw the front door open and the small female figure come down the steps from the porch and trot down the driveway to push the front gate open about a foot to slip out. Renee slid her window down as Mona came around the front of the car.

Mona's face looked distraught as she passed in front of the windshield. She came to the driver's side and Renee saw her face more clearly and got out to join her. They hugged, and stayed huddled beside the car.

Mona said, "Everybody thinks you're dead."

"I'm not, at least not yet, but I'm in a bind. After they kidnapped me and trashed The Elbow Room, Harry Duncan took me out of town. I went to Denver. Duncan was investigating them, and they've tried to kill him at least twice, but I don't think they got him. I came back a few days ago because I couldn't stay away while they destroy everything. I stayed with my head waitress Madeleine Foster, but then they wanted her to sell her house to them. She gave up. She wanted to sell by then. But they shouldn't be long now."

"Who shouldn't be long?"

"The FBI. They'll come in and arrest the men who have been doing this stuff."

"Who told you that?" Mona said.

"It doesn't matter. Mona, I need a favor. I came at night so nobody would see me. I need a place to lay low for a few days, and then I'll be gone. Can you help me?"

Mona looked anxious, and turned her head to look back up at her house. She didn't seem to see what she was looking for, so she looked again at Renee. "You're putting me in a terrible situation."

"Why? What do you mean?" Renee asked. "I promise I won't be any trouble. I just want to stay out of sight until the FBI gets their show on the road. The last thing I want to do is draw attention to your house."

"No," Mona said. She seemed to be fighting back tears. "Don't you see? I thought they had taken you away and killed you. It's not just Parkman's Elbow. It's all the little towns around here, including Riverbank. When you and a bunch of other people disappeared, it proved that holding out was a sure way to end up dead."

"You don't have to tell me this right now," Renee said. "We can talk after we're out of sight. Can I pull the car up behind your house?"

"You're not listening, Renee. I gave in too. I got so scared that I couldn't do anything, or say no to anything. I can't hide you in my house because somebody is already in there. In my bed. His name is Tim Mullins, and he's kind of a leader of the gang. Like a foreman, or underboss or something. He went to Riverbank High School with me before his family moved away. Being with him seemed to be the only way to keep myself and my parents safe from the others. He told me he didn't know what had happened to you, but he was pretty sure you must be dead. I'm so sorry."

Renee had already taken a step back from her. "I'm sorry too. I don't blame you for doing whatever you had to do. I'll get out of here now. I'm just hoping I didn't get you into trouble with him. I'm so sorry." She turned and stepped back to the car door, opened it, and sat in the driver's seat.

She watched Mona take two steps backward, turn and walk to the gate, slip inside, drag it closed again, then pivot to hurry up toward the house.

Renee kept the headlights off and pulled the car away from the curb slowly to keep the engine purring quietly. After a minute, she pulled the car to a stop, wiped her eyes, and sat up straight to drive.

Maybe this disappointment was so painful because it had not been her first of the day. She had arrived at her cousin Elliot Barrett's house and there had been a giant moving van parked in front. She could see men coming out of the house carrying a heavy dark wood sideboard that she'd remembered from when she and Elliot had both been children. When she walked up toward the house Elliot had spotted her.

She said, "Elliot, you're moving?"

He said, "Yes. I expect I'll be gone in another hour or so. I'm surprised to see you. I thought you were already gone."

"I just left town for a while, to catch my breath after I closed The Elbow Room. Where are you moving to?"

"Nebraska. Omaha."

"I'm sorry to see you go. Can you give me your new address?"

"Really?" he said. "I wouldn't have thought you'd be interested. You didn't seem to notice over the years when things went bad for me—and this year, when the insurance company folded and killed my career, I thought you might have gotten in touch, maybe offered me a job, at least. My mother was as much a Parkman as your father. As the oldest male descendant, the bar could just as easily have been mine. But it doesn't matter, since nobody has it now."

"I'm sorry, Elliot. I heard the insurance company had closed. I thought you already had a better job somewhere. If you had called me—"

"I did find one, and I'm on my way to it. So if you'll excuse me, I've got to try and get there before the van does."

After that he had turned away and walked into his house. She'd had an urge to run after him, but what she would have said to change things didn't come to her. A few hours later she drove to see Mona Durand in Riverbank, and now she was searching her memory for the next place to try.

28

I t was still dark when Duncan drove away from the motel where he and Dennison and Ellen Leicester had slept. He said to Ellen, "Before I do this, I want to be sure we agree. I think what we should do now is get you and Charlie out of Indiana and back to the federal building in Chicago, where you'll both be safe."

"I don't agree," she said.

"What don't you agree with?"

"That we'll be safe in Chicago. You've convinced me that somebody in my own office, or somebody who has a way of tapping the phones in my office, is working for the other side. Somebody there had to have been part of the attempt to kill you at the beach, right?"

"Failed attempt."

"Against you. If they try to kill me, they'll succeed."

Duncan thought for a moment. "How about the US Attorney's office in the Southern District of Indiana?"

"That sounds better. This is probably going to end up being their case, or some parts of it will, anyway. Their building is on Market Street in Indianapolis."

Duncan said, "Charlie? What do you think? Have you ever heard anything to indicate they had a connection in the federal building in Indianapolis or anything like that?"

"No. And if they did, I wouldn't be the one they'd tell."

Duncan said, "Good enough. That's where we'll go." He took out his phone and handed it to Ellen. "You might want to use this phone when you call to let them know you're coming."

She turned on the phone and looked at the display, then began to type rapidly with her thumbs, stopping now and then to select some option with her forefinger. Finally, she said, "Good morning. This is Ellen Leicester, the US Attorney for the Northern District of Illinois. I would like to speak with the FBI office, please." There was a short delay, and she repeated her name and title and added, "I'm on my way to the Indianapolis Federal Building, and I'm bringing with me a witness in a criminal matter who needs to be protected. We're coming by car from Ash County, so you can predict an ETA better than I can."

She listened for a minute or two, and then said, "Yes. That will be fine, thank you. Goodbye." She handed back Duncan's phone.

He headed in the direction of Highway 37, which would take them through Bloomington to Indianapolis. As he waited to take the left turn into the highway entrance, he saw two cars, one on either side of the on-ramp, each with two men visible inside. Both had their warning signals blinking, and neither had anyone out trying to change a tire or looking under a raised hood. The oncoming traffic passed and he began the turn, but extended it into a U-turn and drove back the way he had come, accelerating.

"What are you doing?" Ellen said.

"I didn't like the look of that," he said.

"Why?" she said. "People have car trouble all the time, and maybe the second one stopped to help the first one." She paused. "Are you sure you're not just feeling a little anxious because of your fight outside the restaurant yesterday?"

Duncan's jaw tightened. "I could be wrong. If I am, worst thing is we'll pick up the interstate a few miles east and get to Indianapolis at about the same time. If I'm right, they'll be pulling back out of the on-ramp and coming after us."

There was a distant blare of car horns, and then a "bang!" that was clearly the sound of two cars colliding. Duncan looked at Ellen. She was staring out the window, as though she had heard nothing. After a moment, he said, "Well?"

She turned as the road made a curve and glanced at the pavement behind them. It was clear. "What?"

"The sound you heard was one of the cars getting hit trying to back out and come after us."

"You think so?" she said. "More likely trying to back off the on-ramp because it had car trouble and couldn't go on the freeway. I hope nobody got hurt."

"I hope one car stopped to help the other, so they don't catch up with us."

"I won't tell you what I hope," Dennison said.

"Thank you," Duncan said. "You can go back to sleep."

Duncan sped up, weaving his way around the slower cars ahead. He had to force himself to ignore Ellen's attempts to get him into an argument, and think only about keeping them ahead of danger. He drove hard for Interstate 65. It was much farther to the east than the few miles he had called it to Ellen, but what he'd said was essentially accurate—Route 50 tended slightly northward, so the spot where it met 65 was closer to Indianapolis than where they were now.

He drove the way he had driven as a police officer, staying to the left and keeping his speed up so high that the drivers of the cars ahead began to see him coming and move out of his path. As he passed each one, he sped up so the time spent beside each vehicle was very short, leaving little time for mistakes resulting in contact. Duncan's police experience made him identify the spots ahead where he would have waited for speeders or fugitives, so he slowed down, merged into the traffic flow until he was past those places, and sped up again.

When Duncan approached the junction of Route 50 and Interstate 65, he made the transition and headed north for Indianapolis.

Ellen had been silent for a long time, but now she looked up, pretending to be pleasantly surprised. "Good," she said. "You're not sensing any enemies lurking on any of the on-ramps or anything?"

"Not so far."

"Sure you don't want to check the shoulders for unfriendly tire tracks?"

"Ellen, you know these people are real." He dropped his voice to low volume and added, "Since you had a whole night alone to watch Charlie's deposition you also know why they'll do anything to kill him before he can testify against them."

"I'm sorry," she said. "I do know. And I know that even after fifteen years, just having me around probably gets on your nerves. I guess that I've just been trying to minimize the danger to preserve my sanity."

"Denying reality might not work for that," he said.

"I suppose not," she said. "In fact, I know it doesn't."

Duncan suspected this had been an oblique way of saying her decision to marry him had been denying reality, but then decided it probably wasn't, and if it was, he was going to ignore it.

Duncan saw red taillights ahead suddenly brighten, and then all of the vehicles on the interstate slowed in increments, from seventy miles an hour to forty, then twenty, and soon the flow of traffic stopped as though it had been dammed, and became a wall ahead of them.

The sudden stop seemed to waken Dennison, and he sat up. "What the hell is this?"

"It's probably an accident ahead," Duncan said. "We'll have to wait while they sort out the traffic." He shifted the car into park.

"How do you know?" Ellen said.

"It's unusual to have an interstate stop completely this quickly if it's something else. There weren't any signs saying there was construction, and no cones or anything to remove lanes. It just happened. Most likely the state police ran a traffic break so a crew could get a wreck or two out of the way."

Dennison lay back down. Duncan rubbed his eyes, leaned his head back on the headrest, and kept his eyes closed. Ellen said, "You've been driving a long time. Can I rub your neck and shoulders while we wait?"

"No, thanks," he said.

"You used to like it in the old days."

"I mostly liked the things that came after."

She said, "Wow. You couldn't skip the chance to take a kind gesture and use it to humiliate me?"

"You didn't have anything to be humiliated about."

"But I do now?"

"I'm sorry. I don't know you now. I've seen you twice in the past fifteen years. I don't have any basis for an opinion or a right to one. I think we both just want to get through this alive and go on doing what we were doing. Right?"

"Of course. Sorry I overstepped."

"It's okay."

He looked ahead at the long line of cars. There seemed to be men walking between the lanes. He estimated they were at least a quarter mile ahead. He could see five of them, and they were all walking south toward Duncan's rented Subaru. He could see that none of them were wearing uniforms. They appeared to be in blue jeans and two wore windbreakers. A couple wore baseball caps. Sometimes plainclothes cops dressed that way, but he'd never seen them assigned to traffic duty.

Duncan said, "Charlie." He waited. "Dennison!"

Dennison sat up. "What do you want?"

"Take a look ahead. There are guys walking toward us looking in all the cars."

"That's weird. But it seems more like your kind of thing than mine. Like cops looking for somebody."

"Cops sometimes stop traffic, but if they're looking for somebody, they usually divert cars off the first exit and look into them one at a time."

"So kick them out of the police union."

"Don't go back to sleep," Duncan said. "Keep looking at them as they get closer and tell me if you know any of them."

Minutes passed with Dennison leaning on the front seat and staring through the windshield. The five men walking between cars would sometimes stop and speak to the driver of a car, and then walk along the car looking at anyone in the back seats. Once one of them had a driver pop open his trunk, looked inside, and then pushed it shut again.

"Oh shit," Dennison said. "Larson and Kirk."

"You know them?" Ellen said.

"I hired them," he said. "The big one in the center is Larson. The smaller one on the right is Kirk. I'm not seeing a way out of this for me. This car's a rental, right? The two of you could just step out and sneak off the highway. I can't outrun one healthy man with these holes in me, let alone five. But I can buy you some time."

"No," said Duncan. "We'll do it another way."

He shifted the car into reverse and looked in the television display on the dashboard. He only moved backward about three feet before the man in the car behind him honked his horn, but he had gotten far enough, because he knew the driver in front wouldn't feel any impulse to back up. He pulled forward and swung out of line onto the shoulder of the road, shifted into reverse, and began to back up along the empty shoulder.

He used the dashboard display and sped up, going faster and faster so after a few seconds he was simply driving in reverse. Then he realized he'd set off an unintended effect. The drivers who hadn't seen his maneuver seemed to misinterpret the blaring horn as a protest against the roadblock. Other horns sounded, and then variations were added—rapid series of short beeps, longer and more insistent notes, and finally, specialty horns that sounded like bars of music. It grew louder as more cars stuck farther back in traffic lanes joined in, and soon the trend caught up with Duncan and outpaced him as he moved farther back in traffic.

"What are you doing?' Ellen said.

"What I can."

"Driving backward on an interstate? They wanted us to do something desperate to show ourselves, and now you've done it."

"They stopped the traffic. If they've spotted us, they'll have to run a distance—maybe a quarter mile—to get back to their own cars and let the traffic move before they can come after us."

Duncan was focused on maintaining as much speed as possible as he backed the car along on the shoulder of the highway. At last, he saw the stretch he remembered seeing when he'd passed it the first time. The shoulder was much wider there than it had been on the rest of the interstate. He pulled onto it, turned the car so he could back it up in an arc, stop, and swing it forward, back up in a sharper arc, and go forward. Now he was driving along the shoulder facing against the other cars. He could drive forward much faster than he could back up, and he took advantage of it. He was going at least sixty miles an hour on the shoulder now, heading south for another place he remembered passing on the way north.

He knew he had to reached it before any other risk-taker got the idea of driving forward on the shoulder and causing a collision. It was a spot where the northbound lanes and southbound lanes were separated by a wide field of grass with a grove of trees near the middle. He had noticed the single narrow stripe of asphalt bisecting it, and recognized it as a feature he had used a few times when he was a cop. They were built for maintenance vehicles, but the state police who patrolled the highways often used it so they could reach the boundary of a patrol area and turn around to come back toward their station on the lanes flowing in that direction. This one came close to the grove of trees, so it had probably also served them as a hiding spot to wait for speeders.

He saw it, slowed down enough to turn onto the narrow stripe without losing control, drove across to the southbound side, watched for an opening in the traffic, turned into the left lane, and accelerated.

"That was something," Dennison said. "Did it work?"

"I don't know. It's kind of a minute-to-minute thing." He took a long look into the rearview mirror to see if anyone had followed him from the northbound side, and then they were so far past it that he couldn't see that part of the landscape anymore.

The only ominous sign was that the northbound lanes he had left were no longer jammed. The traffic was flowing now, which meant that their pursuers had reached their cars, cleared the way, and driven north. They had created a stretch of highway, probably miles long, where the road ahead of them was empty. They could be driving to the next exit at a hundred miles an hour so they could come back after Duncan on the southbound side.

Duncan said, "This isn't going to work much longer. They seem to have at least a couple cars on every route to Indianapolis, and they're keeping each other informed by phone."

"At least we're not backing up or driving head-on against traffic," Ellen said. "Thank you for that."

"I think we've got to get some help," he said to Ellen. "Can you call the Indianapolis office and get the FBI to come to us?"

"Where are we going to meet them?" she asked.

"Wherever they want that isn't Indianapolis," Duncan said. "The opposition knows that's where we want to go. Use my burner phone again."

He heard the part of the call when she said who she was and what she wanted, but then she was silent, listening. After a minute passed, she said to Duncan, "I'm being transferred to the right office." She seemed to land in the new office, and she repeated her request. She listened, then said, "No, you have it wrong. The man is a witness, not a suspect. And I'm not an agent, I'm the US Attorney for the Northern District of Illinois. I explained it to the man I spoke with before, Special Agent Angelides. He can explain it. I just need to have agents meet me somewhere, because the suspects have been trying to kill the witness, and are doing everything they can to keep us from reaching Indianapolis. He is?" she said. "When did his watch end?" She rolled her eyes. "And he didn't write anything down or tell you that I was coming?" The answer she heard did not please her. "Yes. Originally, I was intending to drive there. But the reason I called was to change my request. I'm in danger, and the witness is in danger and unable to get there in the normal way. I need to transfer the witness to the FBI to keep him safe. You don't? It doesn't have to be twenty agents. How many can you spare?"

The call went on for more minutes, but Duncan knew it was already over. He stopped listening and concentrated on driving as fast as he could to the south so the five men he knew were behind him couldn't get ahead and ambush him at an exit or assemble enough comrades by phone to do it for them.

They knew he had come to Interstate 65 by Route 50, so he avoided any reception being prepared for him there, went past 50, and kept going south at high speed. By the time he reached Ash River country he had decided where he was going to go. He had been driving since before dawn, and the sun was already going down. He was nearly at his destination by the time Ellen gave up. She handed him his phone and sat staring out the side window of the car.

"Don't worry," he said, "We can try again for Indianapolis as soon as we're rested, or try for Chicago next."

In another half hour he stopped in the lot of a supermarket. He said to Ellen, "Come in with me," and went inside with her while Dennison waited in the car. She said, "Harry, what are we doing?" He said to her, "Getting supplies. Look for things that will keep us fed even if we can't cook or refrigerate them—bottled water, fruit, nuts, baked goods, canned tuna and canned meat, beans. Nothing frozen. You get the idea."

"I'm sure you're still great at this sort of thing, but I'm not going camping with you."

"It's not exactly that," he said. "If you don't feel like doing this, you can wait in the car, but I could use your help."

He pushed the shopping cart while she helped him select some supplies. They put the groceries into the back of the Subaru and drove on.

After a few minutes he pulled to the side of the road, took out his phone, and used the map app to see a rendition of the area. He pulled the car back on the road. A few miles later he took the first in a series of turns, each bringing them a bit nearer to the Ash River. The sun went down, and clouds began to sweep above them to darken the land prematurely. One of the turns took them to a section of River Road. The first traffic sign they passed read "Speed Limit 35" in black letters on a reflective white surface and the second was a yellow diamond shape with a snaking black shape and the words, "Winding Road." The next told them they were at a town line.

"Groomsburg," said Ellen. "Wasn't that the place where they were hiding the woman they kidnapped?"

"Right," he said. "We just have to be sure the birds have moved on. If they have, so have the ornithologists."

"Are you two talking in code?" Dennison said.

"No," Duncan said. "We'll be there in a minute or two."

Duncan drove at the speed limit until the road straightened and began to cut across the peninsula, and he passed a sign that said, "Veterans' Memorial Park." A hundred feet farther, he turned onto the entrance road and stopped. "Wait here while I check," he said. He got out of the car, ducked under the chain strung across the entrance that said "CLOSED," and walked toward the river. He listened for the squawks of cranes as he went, but heard none. As he passed through the wooded area, he felt surer that the cranes were gone. When he reached the park building, there were no lights on inside. He tried the doors, and they were all locked. He turned on his phone, pressed it against the highest pane of a window, and tried to detect any sign of current occupants or their gear, but saw none. There was a room with office furniture in it, but nothing on the desks. The scientists had cleared out.

To make sure, he completed a circle of the building looking for tire tracks or ruts, but no vehicle had been there since the last rainstorm, so he headed back toward the road. When he saw there was a baseball field, he went to look more closely. He trotted along the inside of the fence and found what he was hoping for, a place not far from the backstop where there was a permanent bolt near the ground to close a gate in the fence. It would keep people out, but it was easy to open from the inside. He slid the bolt, pushed open the gate, and saw in front of it a second driveway that wasn't blocked by a chain or stanchions. He pushed the gate closed, held it there with a rock, and returned to the Subaru.

"I found a way in," he said. He drove to the baseball field entrance, pulled the gate open, drove in, closed it, and slid the bolt in. He steered to a narrow gravel strip that went behind a set of bleachers to the entrance he had used to walk in. He turned and drove to the building above the shore, and parked behind it, where the car wouldn't be seen from across the river.

As they all climbed out, Ellen said, "I'm beginning to see why we stopped for supplies."

"I suspected it might help us stay out of sight for long enough for things to calm down."

"In case I don't get to thank you later, I'll say it now. Thank you."

"I'll accept that, but if you think of it again later, feel free to repeat yourself."

They set the grocery bags near the door to the office, and Duncan went back to the car and opened his suitcase to get his burglary tools. The door was double-locked. The doorknob lock was the easy sort that he knew he could open with one of his bump keys, but there was also a deadbolt, and both locks had to be defeated before he could open the door. He began with the deadbolt, kneeling in front of it, working with the pick and tension wrench to line up the pins until he could slide the bolt over, and then inserting his bump key into the doorknob lock and turning it as far as he could to maximize the tension while he bumped his shoulder against the door. The door swung open to let Ellen and Dennison inside.

Duncan turned on his phone's flashlight app and surveyed the building. It was small and plain, and mostly made of painted cinderblock. There were two sparsely furnished offices and a larger common space with a few chairs and a table. He held his light high while Ellen and Charlie got settled at the table and Ellen turned on her own phone's light.

He began exploring. Propped up on two sawhorses in the common room was a white twelve-foot aluminum boat that looked like a small Boston Whaler. There were a pair of oars on the seats and two circular lifesavers attached to coiled ropes in it. There were red letters along the side that said "Lifeguard." Attached to another sawhorse a few feet away was a small Evinrude outboard motor.

There were only two windows in the building, both on the side that faced the river. He wondered why, and walked along the back wall until he reached what looked like the door to a closet. He opened the door and saw that behind it was a utility space and storeroom, with a mop and wheeled bucket for washing floors, a shelf full of cleaning supplies, about a bale of paper products, a deep metal sink with a faucet, and a water heater. He also saw the main water pipe with a valve for turning off the water, and the circuit box for the electricity. He opened it and saw the handle of the main power switch.

He also saw that hanging on a nail was a large key ring that only held two keys that looked like house keys. He took it and walked back out to the office where Dennison and Ellen were sitting.

Ellen said, "There's a microwave and a little refrigerator and a space heater in that other office, or cubicle, or whatever it is. But the power isn't on."

"I found the box and the main power switch," Duncan said.

"But you didn't turn it on?"

"Not yet. I also found these two keys." He held them up to the glow of his phone. "I'm guessing at least one of them goes to the restrooms."

"Great," Ellen said. "I was about to go for a walk in the woods."

"I already did," Dennison said.

"I haven't turned the water on yet either," Duncan said.

Ellen said, "Can we go from the scouting stage to the implementation stage now?"

"Sure," he said. He handed her the key ring and returned to the utility room. He turned on the water valve, and then the electricity, then heard Ellen yell, "Turn it off!" He disconnected the main power switch and came back out.

She said, "A bunch of the lights went on. I think when they closed down the building somebody just cut the power instead of turning each one off."

"How bright was it?"

"Bright. I should have thought of that before I asked you to do it. I'm sorry."

He shrugged. "We caught it right away, and there probably wasn't anybody across the river to notice. If there was, it probably wouldn't have been anybody from the gang. If it was, he probably wouldn't think a light going on and then off was likely to be us. There were probably lights sometimes when the bird-watchers were here."

"I'm worried too," she said. "I haven't dreamed up as many reasons as you to talk myself out of it yet, but if I do, I'll share them with you."

"Thanks. We'll just have to be alert."

"I'm going to see if I can turn off all the light switches before we try to turn the power back on."

"I'll help you. Then maybe we can use the microwave. The room it's in is windowless."

In the search for light switches they found an old electric coffee percolator that they could use to bring water to the office and heat it, a few coffee cups that they could microwave food in, and a box of plastic knives, forks, and spoons. It took Ellen and Duncan a short time to make a simple dinner out of canned soup, canned dried beef, and some cans of mixed vegetables. They and Dennison sat around the table in the windowless office with the door shut to prevent the light from escaping, and ate together.

At the end of the meal, Dennison said, "Thinking of this place was a good idea, and the dinner was practically heroic. I'll give you that. For the moment nobody seems to be close enough to actually kill us. I'm sure after the day we've just had we'll all sleep just fine. But do you have a plan?"

"It's a fair question," Duncan said. "At the moment our best move is to stay out of sight."

"So you're just going to wait."

"For tonight at least, yes. We need to get some rest, and I'd like to give the opposition a day to tire themselves out looking for us and assume we already slipped past them."

"What's after that?"

"After that, I think our best bet is to try again. I'd like to drive to the rental lot where my car is stored, return the Subaru, which they've seen, and head for Chicago. It's the best idea I have left." He waited, then said, "Anybody else have another one?"

The small, windowless room was silent.

29

erald Russell arrived in front of Renee Parkman's house in the black Cadillac SUV in the middle of the night. The driver was Banks, the same man who had gotten Russell away ahead of everyone else the night of the attack on The Elbow Room. Russell said to him, "Pull up the driveway and wait there."

When the car stopped at the top of the drive, Russell slid out of the back seat, left the door open, and climbed the stairs to the porch of the Parkman house quickly, his long legs taking them three at a time. Jeanette scrambled out after him, stopped to swing the car door shut, and caught up with him after he had reached the top, as he pounded on the door. One of the curtains in the front window moved aside, then fell back in place, and a few seconds later the light came on and the door opened inward.

Russell brushed in past Williamson, the man beside the door, who was busy returning his pistol to the inner pocket of his jacket.

"Is Mullins here yet?"

"Yeah. He got here about an hour ago."

"Get him."

The order was unnecessary, because Mullins heard it as he was coming around the corner into the foyer. "Right here," he said. "I've got things set up in the dining room."

Russell set off in Mullins's direction and followed closely on his heels across the living room, as though to emphasize the urgency and importance of everything that occupied his attention. They arrived in the dining room together and moved to the big table, which had been set with several kinds of drinks on a tray—beer, bottled water, coffee, and a bottle of scotch with an ice bucket and glasses. Russell ignored them. "What have you done so far?"

Mullins picked up a cell phone from the table and tapped a couple icons, then held it up so Russell could see the screen. "This is a picture that Larson took and sent me today on the interstate—no, I guess it's yesterday now. The car on the right, the blue-gray Subaru, is the car that Duncan was driving. Larson had enough foresight to take this picture of the car, including the license plate, before he got away."

"Good for him. He's not a moron."

"I remembered that when our guys killed that cop Glen Slater, they took his cell phone, which was issued to him by the police department. I pretended I was a cop, and used it to call the DMV to find out the name and address of the owner because it was used in a hit-and-run. They told me the name of a rental car company, so I called them with the same story and asked them to activate their anti-theft tracking system to tell me where the car is now."

"So where is it?"

"Groomsburg, in a municipal park by the river."

"How far is Groomsburg?"

"Maybe half an hour from here."

"Call the guys."

30

The three had tried to devise various ways to sleep in the park building—lying on the desks and the table on the theory that since they were wooden and up off the concrete floor, they would be warmer and marginally softer, using rolls of paper towels as pillows and jackets as blankets. When that failed they tried putting both feet on one chair and sitting on another. After an hour of that they all went outside, reclined the car seats, and tried again. Duncan ran the engine to make the heater work until the car was comfortable. By then Ellen and Dennison had dozed off, so he turned off the engine and let himself sleep.

It was at least two hours later when Ellen woke to the sound of other car engines. It wasn't that the cars were especially loud. There were just so many, and they all arrived in one long stream, each one pulling over to the shoulder outside the park road and idling while more cars arrived, passed them, and pulled over too. She sat up, and shook Duncan.

He heard it too. He sat up, reached above the windshield where the dome light was, switched it off so it wouldn't light up when he opened the car door, and got out. He stood still for a moment, turning his head to locate the direction of the sound. He began to walk, his body bending into a crouch as he moved into the trees beside the park road. In a moment he could see the line of cars along the straight stretch of the river road. Men were getting out of the cars now, the drivers shutting off the engines and turning off their headlights.

Duncan turned and ran back toward the car. He flung the door open and said, "They've found us. We've got to get out of here now."

"We're ready. Drive."

"We can't get the car past them. I need to take a second to get some things out of the trunk, and then I'll meet you inside. Don't turn on the lights."

Ellen helped Dennison to walk inside while Duncan went to the hatch. He took his computer, slung the strap of the case over his left shoulder, the rifle case with the two AR-15s and the loaded magazines, slung that strap over his right shoulder, then locked the car and ran around the building to the entrance, stopped and threw the keys up onto the flat roof, and stepped inside.

He hurried past the others, already talking as he stepped to the boat. "This is our way out. Ellen, I'll need you to help me while I haul it out of here and down to the river. Charlie, try to get there on your own. If you can't make it, I'll be back right away to help you." He stepped to the bow of the boat. He lifted it above the front sawhorse, pushed the sawhorse aside with his foot, and set the bow down on the concrete floor.

When he went to the stern and lifted it, Ellen pulled the second sawhorse aside. Duncan set the stern down.

Duncan dragged the boat a few feet and started it through the doorway. Then he and Ellen both pushed from the stern, and soon the boat was out the door and sitting flat on the sand. As soon as Dennison was out the door to join them, Duncan locked the door from the inside and closed it, put the rifle case and computer in the boat, then slid the life preserver tied to the bow over his head to his chest, wrapped the first six feet of the attached rope around the cleat at the bow, leaned forward, and began to drag the boat across the sand toward the river. His feet dug in and he increased his speed as he went. Ellen and Charlie followed, and soon the boat was at the edge of the shore on the wet sand that sloped down into the river.

Duncan unwrapped the rope from the cleat, then went to the stern and pushed the boat into the water. "Ellen, you take the bow seat." He held the boat steady while she climbed in and stepped to the bow. The bow sank an inch and the stern rose an inch. "Charlie, sit on the rear seat for the moment." Duncan heard men's voices and turned his head to see flashlights coming toward the beach.

He leaned forward and pushed off the wet sand with his foot. He flopped onto the middle seat, stuck one oar's Y-shaped pin into its oarlock, picked up the second oar and seated it in its oarlock, and began to row hard, moving the boat out from the shore and into the main current. The boat began to move on its own, the flow of water pushing it southward. He straightened the boat so the bow was pointed downstream, and rowed with longer, harder strokes to add to its progress.

As he rowed, trying to put as much distance as he could between the boat and the small stretch of beach they had just left, he could see the flashlight beams emerge from the park road, moving back and forth, lighting up the shore and then sweeping along the side of the park building. He saw three circular spots of light suddenly converge on the parked Subaru beside the building, heard some male voices yelling, and then saw several other flashlights bouncing as other men ran to surround the car.

He rowed harder, and the boat swung around a bend in the river. He heard a shot, then a volley of them. He could only guess that, with all the waving of flashlights, somebody had mistaken a moving shadow for the silhouette of a man. He corrected himself—for the silhouette of Harry Duncan.

He heard a noise that sounded almost like the river was boiling. He looked over his shoulder, saw nothing but the dark shine of the river and the darker strip of trees and brush beyond it, but then he realized the river had widened, and then recognized where he was. He said, "These are the shallows, where the cranes were. Ellen, if you see us heading for a rock or—" The boat made a grinding noise and stopped. They had run aground in the shallow water.

"Damn," Charlie said. "The water. It's freezing."

Duncan could see water was washing over the stern. "Move forward, quick." Dennison moved ahead, and the stern rose a little so the fast-moving water stopped sloshing in. Duncan knelt on his seat, took an oar out of its oarlock, and pushed down on the oar to lift the boat, but couldn't get it off the bar. He moved to the right and stepped over the side into the water. It came up only to his knees, but it was as cold as it had been when he'd swum to get Renee. He stepped to the bow, lifted and pulled it, and then took the life preserver and wrapped its rope around the cleat again.

With Duncan's weight out of the boat it had risen a bit, and he could tow it along in the shallows by the rope. He walked with a determined, trudging step, pulling the boat along, but mostly steering it away from the obstacles that he felt with his feet. He kept going this way for about three hundred yards before the riverbed narrowed again and deepened. He flopped into the boat near the middle, rolled, got onto the seat, and began to row again.

Ellen said, "Turn around and just steer for a while."

He did, pushing the oars instead of pulling while Ellen tugged off his wet shoes and socks, took off the fleece she'd worn over her top and used it to dry his feet, and then wrapped them up. "You didn't have to do that," he said.

"Feels good, though, doesn't it?" she said. "It's nice to have all your toes."

"Yes," he said.

The next bend in the river veered away from the road for a stretch. In a few minutes they heard the sounds of car engines, and then others joining them like a single big machine that was moving along the road. They caught moving beams of headlights as the cars took the turns of the river road.

Ellen said, "What scares me is that they're heading the same direction we are."

"You're right," Duncan said. "We didn't have much choice. The gas tank for the outboard motor was stored empty when the park closed for the winter. And if we'd had it, the noise would have told them where we were. They would have caught up with us in the cars and shot us from the road."

"What's stopping them from doing it now?"

"They must not have seen or heard us yet."

They fell silent again, and the whispering flow of the river and the rhythmic, small splash of Duncan's oars dipping in and the faint metallic squeak of the pins in the oarlocks were the only sounds. As the night went on and the air grew cooler, they passed through wisps of fog that hung over the river.

Duncan was relieved that the men had not figured that their prey might have taken a boat. The ones he knew about were all new to the towns along the river, so it wouldn't be surprising if they didn't know there would be a boat in the park building. If they had managed to pick the lock on the door or broken a window they might have gone in and seen the outboard motor clamped on the sawhorse, but apparently they hadn't. They seemed to have driven south on the assumption that since the Subaru had been abandoned they must have left on foot or had another car.

Ellen was back in the bow watching the river ahead. Suddenly she said, "I think we're near Parkman's Elbow. I remember that building with the billboard above it when I was driving into town."

"That feels like good news," Duncan said.

"Is it? Those cars were heading in this direction."

"I meant that I'd rather arrive in town while it's still dark than come sailing into town in bright sunshine."

Dennison said, "I suppose you have another of your wonderful ideas."

"A couple of them."

"God help us."

"What I think we need right now is to get to the police station. It's in the middle of town, on Main Street. There are old brick buildings behind the station, about three stories high." he said. "I'm not sure how much of that you can see from the river." He was busily putting on his wet shoes.

"I don't know," she said.

"Probably the backs of a bunch of old buildings." He pointed. "See? I can see a couple from here—some of those red-brick ones just above the water. I think the fronts might be those stores and diners behind the police station's parking lot."

He rowed hard for the short series of buildings. When the boat reached the concrete retaining wall behind the buildings, he took one last oar stroke and then stood to grasp the top of the wall to hold the boat up against it. "Okay, Ellen. You go first. Step on the middle seat and pull yourself up."

Ellen climbed up onto the concrete, rose, and took two steps from the edge.

Duncan turned to Dennison.

Dennison said, "I see you looking at me. I just don't know if I can do it."

"You can't not do it," Duncan said. "Grab my hand and step on the seat."

Dennison got up on the seat and tried to push down on the top of the concrete with both hands to get up, but seemed to be overexerting himself just to hold himself there. Duncan held the boat in place with his left hand and put the right under Dennison's bottom to push him upward. Ellen squatted and took one of Dennison's arms, stepped back, and helped drag him up until he could get one knee on land. He crawled the rest of the way up and leaned against the brick surface of the building, panting.

Duncan slipped the strap of his laptop computer case over his head, then the rifle case, took a last look into the boat to be sure he hadn't left something, then hoisted himself up onto the concrete, looked back, and watched the boat slide along the retaining wall, reach the end, and begin to drift out, drawn back into the main current by an eddy, which turned it slowly as it went downstream.

Duncan lifted Dennison to his feet and they began to walk. Dennison said, "I've been wondering when this was coming."

"What?" Duncan said.

"Here we are, just victims of a strange turn of fate, eh? Who would have thought that the safe place you promised to deliver me to would be a police station?"

"You knew from the beginning that at some point you were going to have to be in custody, because otherwise you'd be dead. Without some help right about now, we'll all be dead. We barely got you out of Chicago, and we've tried four or five hiding places since then. I'm about out of alternatives."

Dennison nodded. "That's what I thought."

"You have my blessing to consider any of your other offers."

"Very generous."

They had caught up with Ellen, who was waiting in the space between two buildings. Duncan knelt on the ground, took the Glock 17 out of the pocket of the rifle case and stuck it into the back of his belt, then slung the case over his shoulder again. "I guess this is it," he said.

Ellen looked at him. "You're not going to tell me how to do this?"

"When you get to the corner of the building walk at a good pace with your head up, as though you're there on business. Everything is normal, calm, and easy, but you're not somebody who likes to waste time. If you see any of the guys we've been running from, that's over. Sprint. Make it inside the front door as fast as you can. Charlie and I will be a few feet behind you, so don't linger and don't block the doorway."

Ellen said, "When do I start?"

"Now would be good."

Ellen walked down the narrow space between that building and the next one. After she'd gone five steps, Duncan and Dennison started after her. Dennison was weak and limping, holding onto Duncan's arm for balance. Ellen reached the corner, where she stepped into the growing light and turned left. Duncan propped Dennison up until they reached the end of the still-shadowy alley and made the turn.

What he had expected to see was wrong. Ellen was sixty feet ahead and running hard. Duncan turned his head to look for what she had seen, but detected nothing threatening—the deserted street, the row of closed and dark shops and diners long before business hours. He pivoted on his heel to see if there was someone behind him, but the sidewalk was empty and the street had a couple of cars parked at the curb, a small delivery truck, but no people. For a second, he wondered whether Ellen had seen something harmless and panicked, but she had never been that kind of person.

Duncan hurried Dennison along the sidewalk toward the double doors of the police station, and looked ahead just as Ellen arrived at the doors. She tugged on a door handle, tried the other, then tugged harder, but the doors didn't move. And then he saw her head turn to look at something, and her face was a mixture of fear and anger. He followed her gaze and saw what it was.

Three men had emerged from somewhere on the street perpendicular to Main, and they were running toward the broad lawn in front of the police station. They were still three hundred feet from Ellen, but they must have been hoping to cut her off, and now that they had seen her stopped by a locked entrance, they were running harder. Ellen rapped on one of the bulletproof doors with her knuckles, and yelled, "Open the door! Let us in!"

The men were sprinting onto Main Street, then across it, now almost to the lawn. They veered sharply to spread apart, intent on rushing her from three sides.

Duncan snatched the pistol from his belt and fired a round into the air. He shouted, "All right, you three. Stop where you are."

The men looked away from Ellen and turned toward Duncan, apparently not sure what to do, but knowing that surrender wasn't going to be the answer. They began to advance toward him, drawing pistols of their own.

Out of the corner of his eye Duncan saw a uniformed policewoman arrive at the front entrance to the station and push it open to let Ellen in. Ellen stayed a few feet from the doorway. She said something to the policewoman, who leaned out of the door and saw the three men. She touched the radio mounted on her left shoulder, drew her sidearm, and stepped out. She shouted, "You! On the lawn! Drop those guns! Do it now!"

The three began talking urgently to each other. Seeing a second armed person confronting them seemed to have made a difference. They began to step backward toward the sidewalk, trying to keep eyes on Duncan, Ellen, and the policewoman at the same time, studying each to detect an imminent intention to open fire. Duncan noticed that Dennison was almost to the station door now, and he hoped that the three men might be too distracted by their personal vulnerability—on a lawn two hundred feet from cover—to think about Dennison. He saw Ellen sidestep behind the policewoman and pull Dennison inside with her, and felt relief as he returned all of his attention to the three men.

They had reached the pavement of the street, and clearly thought they were out of pistol range. They all turned at once and ran, this time ducking beyond the first building to get out of sight.

The policewoman, Ellen, and Dennison were inside the police station. The policewoman turned the key to relock the door, but Ellen stopped her. As Duncan ran to the glass door, he heard Ellen say, "That's Harry Duncan. He's with us."

The policewoman said, "I'm not supposed to let anybody in."

Ellen said, "I'm a US Attorney. Do it. He's—oh fuck it."

She took a stride to get her leg behind the policewoman's, pushed and brought her to the floor, then whirled around and turned the key herself. Duncan stepped inside and relocked it, then pulled the key out of the lock and bent over to take the policewoman's hand and pull her to her feet. "I'm sorry," he said, and handed her the key. "Are you okay?"

The policewoman said, "I don't know anybody who is 'okay' today, and it just started. Do you?"

"Not offhand."

"You'd better come with me."

They all walked into the lobby and up to the counter. The policewoman said, "Put that gun away before anybody sees it. And let me go in first." She reached down over the counter's gate and released an unseen catch behind it, then opened the waist-tall door to go through it.

Ellen, Dennison, and Duncan followed her as she opened the door into the big open bay where all the desks were. The room was full of people, but only four were uniformed police officers. There were at least twenty children, some of them babies being held by weary-looking young mothers, others of elementary school age gathered around desks drawing pictures on the plain backs of forms, playing worn board games, or just being underfoot. A few kids were as old as fourteen or fifteen, and they were slouched in various places gazing at the displays on cell phones or just looking bored and unhappy.

Dennison said, "What the hell is this?"

"This is bad news," Duncan said.

The policewoman beckoned to them to follow and walked ahead to the smoked glass door of the only office. She gave the military knock, a single flat-handed palm on the woodwork. A male voice came from inside. "Enter."

She went inside and closed the door behind her. Ten seconds later Sergeant Griggs appeared at the door, and the policewoman walked back out into the bay. Griggs said, "Well, you're here, so talk to me."

The three came into his office and he closed the door. Duncan said, "Sergeant Griggs, this is US Attorney for the Northern District of Illinois Ellen Leicester."

Griggs looked at Ellen. "Pleased to meet you, ma'am. I wish you hadn't assaulted one of my officers to get in here."

"I'll start regretting it as soon as I calm down," Ellen said. "I had to be sure that Mr. Duncan got in."

"In the end she might have been doing him a favor to keep him out."

"What do you mean?" she said.

"You must have seen all the people crammed into the building. They're our families and they're here because, right now, keeping them with us is the only way we have of knowing they're safe. Officer Poole was just doing what we're all doing. Her husband Ron is here with her three kids."

Duncan said, "When we went through, I saw a lot of kids and a few parents. I didn't see a lot of cops."

Griggs shrugged. "We've had some retirements—the chief and the lieutenant with a month between them. They were both scheduled in advance, but we also had half a dozen resignations, most of them since Glen Slater was murdered. Can't blame them either, really, but it leaves us with a total force of fourteen to cover three shifts. That's why you only see four of us now. It's the night shifts that need the extra man."

They heard the military thump at the office door again. "Enter," he called.

The person who came in was a middle-aged woman with an intense set of eyes behind a pair of round glasses who seemed to be a civilian employee. "There's a man on the 911 line who insists he has to talk to you right away, Sergeant Griggs. He said he was trying to do you a big life and death favor."

"And you believed him?" Griggs said.

"I don't know," she said. "But I wasn't the one to decide."

Griggs picked up the telephone receiver and looked down at the button on the dial that was blinking.

He looked up at the others. "Can you give me a minute?"

Duncan, Ellen, and Dennison went out. The woman came out after them, closed the door, then stood in front of it with her arms folded across her chest. The three stood and endured her attention for a minute before she said, "You're seeing us at a bad time."

"We're not at our best right now either," Ellen said.

The door swung open behind her and she stepped aside. Griggs came out looking serious. "I take it that this is Charlie Dennison?"

"That's right," Dennison said.

"I was about to get to the rest of the introductions," Duncan said.

"Come back in."

They walked past Griggs into the office, but he leaned out and called, "Damon." In a moment a male cop about thirty years old came from across the bay and paused in the doorway. "This gentleman is Charles Dennison," Griggs said. "No need to book him or take his prints or anything. He's not under arrest. But he needs you to lock him up in the solitary cell. Then come back."

Duncan said, "He's recovering from two bullet wounds, and he's a crucial witness."

Damon glanced at Griggs, who shrugged and said, "If he says so. And make sure to give him a couple bottles of water and whatever snacks the kids haven't eaten."

Dennison said to the room in general, "Just don't forget I'm in there."

"I won't," Griggs said. He turned to the lady from the emergency line as soon as the door closed. "Write it down and put it someplace where it will be found, will you?"

"I will." She walked off.

Griggs said, "The phone call came from a guy who says he's the leader of the gang. I guess he agrees with you that Dennison is important. He says that he's giving me an hour to send Dennison outside. Obviously, that isn't something to ask a cop to do."

Duncan said, "No, it isn't. Look, I didn't know that you would have the families here, or I wouldn't have brought him. We lost the car we had, so we came down the river in a borrowed lifeguard boat, and this seemed like a better idea than it was."

"It would have been fine, except some of those guys recognized him. Let's forget that stuff. I've got to catch up with Officer Damon and—" The door opened and Damon entered. "Good.

Damon, come with me. This guy on the phone says he's got the station surrounded. Let's see if he's lying."

As soon as they were gone Ellen turned to Duncan. "Thank you for saving my life, maybe twice in twenty-four hours. But we did this, you and me. We brought our troubles to share with a bunch of civilians and children who never signed up for this, and don't even know what it is yet."

"I think they gave Griggs an hour because that's how long they think it will take to gather their men and isolate the building. It might give me time to do something."

"I'll go with you," she said.

"No."

"I'm still your boss."

"No, you're not." He walked deeper into the station toward the rear of the building.

She hurried after him and grasped his arm.

"Please."

"This is going to be dangerous, and it isn't even likely to work."

"It will be less dangerous if I can watch your back, and I'll do anything else you ask. Just don't leave me here to do nothing while people get hurt because of us."

"Come on then," he said. They hurried past the two inter-rogation rooms, a storeroom, restrooms, a locker room. Finally, they passed a door that led to the cell block. Duncan knew the cops assigned to other shifts were probably occupying bunks in some of the cells trying to get some sleep. When they reached the plain steel-clad back door to the department's parking lot, they found that there was a key in the lock, so any cop could unlock it. He said, "We're going to need somebody to relock the door once we're out."

"I'll get someone to do it," Ellen said. She turned and trotted back up the hall to the open bay, and a minute later she was back with a boy of about twelve.

Duncan turned the key to unlock the door, opened it a crack, and looked out. He closed it again. "It's pretty much what we thought. It's clear for the moment, but it won't be. Last chance to stay. Once he locks it, we won't be able to come back."

"I'm going."

They stepped out the door and ducked down low to run between the parked personal vehicles of the families inside the station. They never stopped moving. When they reached the end of the last aisle, they moved along the five-foot brick wall that separated the lot from the street until they reached a closed dumpster. They climbed on top of it, crawled to the wall, and went over it.

As they crossed the street there was a sound of car engines. It was the same sound that they'd heard during the night at the Groomsburg park, this time about twenty vehicles coming up Main Street at once. Duncan and Ellen moved up the parallel street and looked in that direction from behind the hedge of the first house. The first ten cars pulled up to the curb in front of the police station's lawn and then adjusted their positions so they were only about a yard apart. They had formed a semicircular wall of shiny steel that wrapped halfway around the building.

Cars were still arriving. Four parked at the street corners, so each had a view of two sides of the building. Two more cars blocked the exits from the parking lot for personal vehicles and the lot for police cruisers. "I guess we just made it out," Ellen said. "What will they do now?"

"We can't stay to find out." Duncan began to hurry along the street away from the police station, and Ellen caught up.

"You know, don't you?"

"They'll bluff and threaten and try to get Griggs to give them Dennison. I'm pretty sure Griggs won't consider it. I hope he takes up a lot of time before they realize it's not going to happen."

"Then what?"

"Even they probably don't know it yet, but then they'll stop bluffing. They'll have to. Dennison knows all about every one of those guys, and everything they've done, and he's got every reason to hate them for shooting him. If they can kill him, the threat is over. They'll attack the station and try to go in and get him."

"What are we going to do?"

Instead of answering, he took his phone out of his pocket, pressed a number, and waited while the phone indicated it was ringing. There was a voice and he said, Hi, Renee. This is Harry Duncan."

"What do you want?"

"You're in the area, right? Madeleine told me you'd been here."

There was silence for a moment. "I can't believe she told you. She promised—"

"The reason I'm calling is that the police station in your town is being surrounded right now by the gang of crooks because the cops are protecting a witness who can send them all to prison. I have the US Attorney with me. But I need your help."

"Let me talk to her."

"What? Why?"

"To see if you're lying."

"Hold on." He held out the phone to Ellen. "She wants to talk to you."

Ellen took the phone. "This is Ellen Leicester." She listened and said, "Yes, really. I hired him to come here, and now I'm here too. I wanted to get a look at the place on my own, maybe verify a few facts before any arrests. It was a mistake." She listened for a moment. "Here. She wants you."

Duncan took the phone. Renee said, "Okay, I believe you."

Duncan said, "The situation is deteriorating, and it didn't have far to go. I think you can help. Where are you?" He listened. "How long will it take you to get here? All right. We're on Constitution two blocks north of Main."

"Can I meet you someplace?" she said.

"There's a sporting goods store in town, right?"

"Yes. McCloskey's. It's on Jefferson, between Third and Fourth."

"Do you know the owner?"

"In this town, it's like asking if one little piggy knows the next little piggy. Of course I know him."

"Good, because that's where we need to start. We'll meet you there." He ended the call.

Duncan and Ellen moved along side streets, favoring the ones with lots of trees and bushes, cutting through empty lots and between buildings. "Why did you call her?" she asked.

"I'm going to need to persuade a lot of people to do something risky. She's a local person and people trust her. I'm an outsider. If I ask, they'll listen politely, shut their doors, and lock them."

She said, "Did she say Jefferson and Third?"

"Yes, Jefferson between Third and Fourth. But we'll stay off those streets for now, because they're both heavily traveled, and those guys probably don't know any shortcuts yet. Take the second turn up ahead on the right."

In about ten more minutes they were walking on a quiet street under sycamore trees, and they could see the sign that said "McCloskey's Sports" over the store's green awning across Third Street. "We'd better hold until we see her."

They stood for a few minutes, and then the first car arrived. It was an old Chevrolet driven by a man with white hair. He drove into the lot, got out, and unlocked the door to the store. He disappeared, and then the lights came on.

Five minutes later, Renee Parkman drove up and parked beside his car.

Duncan said, "Well, let's see what we can do."

They walked around to the side of the store where Renee was getting out of a white pickup. She looked at them and Duncan said, "Renee Parkman, this is Ellen Leicester, the US Attorney for the Northern District of Illinois."

"I figured," Renee said. "Are you sorry you came yet?"

"Not yet," she said.

"You will be."

They walked to the front of the store and stepped inside. It was surprisingly large, a rectangular space with double glass doors. Inside they saw a variety of equipment that pertained to dozens of sports, and the clothes, shoes, and headgear worn to participate, all arranged in sections so a customer could walk right to it and feel fully outfitted. The arrangement of cases and shelves in the store limited the walking space so when a customer came in, he had a sensation that it was a place of possibilities opening. When the customer was leaving, he came to the same spot, where it was a narrowing. There was only a counter with a cash register, and the space to the right of it bordered by a railing so a shopper who wasn't buying had to pass close by.

Renee stepped ahead and called to the man at the register, "Hey Larry."

Larry was at least seventy, with a head covered with white hair that had probably been blond at first, a worn sunburned face, and a smile that showed a set of porcelain white dentures that probably gave some of his youngest customers night-mares. "Hey, Renee," he said. "I thought you had left town."

"I'm back now," she said. "This is Harry Duncan."

"Is he a new boyfriend?"

"Not in his wildest dreams. And this is Ellen Leicester, the US Attorney who's trying to help us get rid of the trash."

"What can I do to help?" McCloskey said.

"We wanted to take a look at your firearms," Duncan said.

"I figured." He was already on his way to a wide wooden counter in front of a wall of long guns. They were all butt-down, muzzle up in a single rack with a thick chain strung through their trigger guards.

Duncan said, "Mind if I go behind your counter?"

"No, if you promise you won't hurt yourself and sue me."

Duncan walked along slowly, looking at each weapon, and then said, "We'll take them."

"What do you mean? One each for the three of you?"

Duncan said, "I make it five hunting rifles and twelve versions of an AR-15 in .223. We'll take all seventeen rifles."

McCloskey half-turned to look at Renee, but saw nothing in her serious expression to dispel his confusion. "What the hell?"

She said, "You know that we—our town—have a problem. Those new guys who showed up a while ago are all criminals. They're busy surrounding the police station right now. They want the cops to give them a man Duncan brought in as an informant and witness against them."

"Jesus. You mean like a lynching?"

"The style is different, but the result will be the same," Duncan said. "They'll put him in a car and nobody will ever see him again. They outnumber the cops by far, and the cops have their families with them in the station with no safe way to get them out."

"You're talking about taking my whole stock of rifles."

Duncan took out his wallet and removed a card. "Here. You can charge them to this Visa."

McCloskey looked at it, frowning.

"Go ahead, Larry," Renee said. "You know I'm good for it if his card isn't."

"Don't close it out yet," Duncan said. "We'll need two boxes of ammo for each of the five hunting rifles and as much .223 as you've got in the store."

For the next fifteen minutes they loaded Renee's pickup with rifles and ammunition, leaving the long narrow boxes that came with the rifles. When the transaction was finished, Duncan said, "Thank you, Larry."

"Wait," McCloskey said. "I'm going too. I've got to close the store and lock up."

Renee said, "You might want to take one of the rifles back."

"No," he said. "Even I know enough to keep a loaded one out of the rack. A dealer who sells somebody all his guns is liable to lose the guns and the money too. You want me to follow you, or meet you at the station?"

"We'll meet you on Prospect Street just above Main," said Renee. "When, Duncan?"

"Make it either nine o'clock or the moment you hear a shot fired, whichever is first."

"Got it," Larry said. "You mind if I invite a few friends?"

"Not at all," Duncan said. "Tell them we're bringing the guns and ammo."

Larry snorted and shook his head. "The friends I was thinking of will bring their own."

Duncan shook Larry's hand, and then Renee hugged Larry. "I know you're tough as hell, but don't be too proud to duck."

"I won't. You either."

Duncan, Renee, and Ellen got into the pickup and set off. Renee said, "I'm getting the idea the guns aren't for us. Who do you think we should start with?"

"You know people here better than I do. How about the people who worked at The Elbow Room?"

"I'd say Vic MacDonough. He was in the army a million years ago. Should I call him?"

"Where does he live?"

"Right near here. The next right, then the first left."

She reached the spot and said, "That's his house up there. The white one with the shiny black trim." She got out and ran up the porch steps and rang the doorbell. In a moment Mac-Donough opened the door. He was wearing old khaki pants, a blue work shirt, and a sweat-bleached baseball cap, all with white paint spatter on them. Behind him was a folding ladder with a paint pan and roller. He smiled. "Renee."

"Hey, Vic. Sorry to interrupt the painting."

He stepped out on the porch and closed the door behind him. "It's a favor. I dearly love the woman, but since I'm not working for you, I'm doing double shifts for her. You look serious. What's up?"

"You remember Duncan, right?"

"Sure. We've all been worried about how you two were doing. Somebody started a rumor you were dead."

"Duncan found an informant who was willing to be a witness, and brought him back here, so he's in the police station."

"Protective custody," Duncan said. "But he's been spotted, and right now the whole gang is gathering—or maybe gathered by now—outside the station. They want him, and I think in a few hours they're going to try and get him."

Renee said, "I think if we let them know the few on-duty cops aren't all there is to stop them, they might back off."

"How do we let them know that they have more to worry about than a few cops?"

"The back of the truck is full of guns," Duncan said.

"Who else have you talked to?"

"Larry at McCloskey's Sporting Goods," Renee said. "He's calling some friends."

"Jesus. I didn't think this day could get much worse."

Duncan said, "If you don't want to do this, we'll understand. It's a last resort. I think they won't make their move until after they've given the police time to sweat. Right now we're going to see the rest of the people from the bar. We've got an AR-15 rifle and a couple of boxes of ammo for each."

"Can you give me three rifles? I'll make calls to some people I trust who didn't happen to work at the bar."

Duncan went to the car and carried the weapons and ammunition up to the front door, and MacDonough held it open for him. "Just set them on the rug over here."

When they reappeared on the porch, Renee said, "Nine o'clock unless you hear shots."

"Got it," he said.

They went back to the car and headed to the next stops. First there was Mick, the tall, curly-haired bartender who had been on duty the evening when the three Clark brothers had come to The Elbow Room to demand extortion payments, then to Rice and Stallings, the two waiters, then Dennis Flaherty, the head chef. He took six rifles—two for his cooks, two for the busboy and the dishwasher, and two for himself and a friend. Patsy and Tanya Moss, the two early evening bartenders, were next. They each accepted an AR-15, and their boyfriends both volunteered to come and bring their own rifles, pistols, and ammunition.

As Duncan pulled away from Tanya Moss's house, he said, "It's seven o'clock, and we've got six rifles left."

"There's still Glen Slater's family. There are a lot of Slaters, and a lot of cousins who aren't named Slater. Some of the older ones used to be cops."

"Point me to the closest one."

They made it to the homes of several people Duncan remembered from Glen Slater's funeral. Most of them had their own weapons, and all volunteered to call others to let them know what was happening. When Duncan, Renee, and Ellen had finished making their rounds, the only weapons they had left were his two Glock pistols, and Renee's father's old .38 revolver. Duncan had left his rifle case in the police station, and there wasn't likely to be a chance to retrieve it.

Renee drove her rented pickup to the shady residential street near the police station where they had told everyone to meet. As they moved slowly up the block, people in the parked cars nodded to them or waved a hand to acknowledge them.

"I can't believe it," she said. "There must be fifty people here already."

"Drive to the nearest supermarket," Duncan said.

"What for?"

"Bottled water. We're likely to be in a standoff, maybe for hours. I've noticed that when you're scared, your mouth gets dry."

"Scared?" Ellen said. "I think this is the first time I ever heard you admit fear existed."

"Fear is natural and useful," Duncan said. "The trick is to use it to make you focus and think fast, not let it paralyze you. It will help these people. And the water will give us an excuse to talk to them."

Renee said, "How long have you two known each other?"

"A long time," Ellen said.

Renee turned around in a driveway and drove back away from the police station, and in ten minutes she was pulling into the parking lot of a store. A few minutes later they were pushing carts full of cases of bottled water out of the store and loading them into the back of the pickup. When they had bought the store's supply, Renee drove them back to Prospect Street.

Ellen got into the driver's seat to move the truck ahead slowly while Duncan and Renee walked from car to car carrying cases of water. At each car they gave out water and Duncan told them what to do.

"Wait here. This may take a while. If we drive out onto Main Street in the white pickup, it's on. Follow us to the police station. Park on the left side, across the street from the gang cars. Get out on the left side, keep the car between you and the street, and aim your rifle. Pick a target and aim. That's all. If anybody opens fire, you won't have to waste time deciding."

After Renee had heard his instructions a couple times, she began to repeat them to the occupants of the next few cars. Each time Duncan or Renee ran through a case of water, they would take another out of the back of the truck and move on to the next car.

When they had reached the front of the line of cars, Ellen parked the truck. Duncan walked to the end of the street and stood behind the tall hedge of the corner house to observe the siege of the police station. The cars that had parked along the sidewalk in front were still there, and Duncan could see the heads of the men occupying the seats. All of their attention seemed to be directed toward the front of the station. His eyes followed the direction their heads were turned and studied the front windows of the station, the front entrance, and the lawn and shrubbery to see if any of the attackers were out of their cars and moving up yet, but so far, those open spaces were clear.

He called 911 and when a woman's voice said, "911. What's the location of your emergency?" he recognized the woman as the one who had insisted Sergeant Griggs take the call from the man who had called himself the gang's leader. Duncan said, "This is Harry Duncan. Can you connect me with Griggs?"

"I'll try." There was silence, and Duncan didn't know if she reached Griggs or not. "I'm sorry, he's on another call."

"Then connect me to any cop. If you have to, drag one into the call center. This is urgent."

There was a pause that seemed interminable, but then he heard, "This is Officer Damon."

"This is Harry Duncan. I need to know what the suspects are saying to Griggs."

"They said they'd let our families walk out of here if Dennison came out first. Sergeant Griggs turned that down. They asked him what he would take to get Dennison and he said they could keep thinking."

"Maybe that will get them to waste some time. What's going on now?"

"What's been going on all day. He's been on the phone on and off with the departments of the other towns up and down the river trying to get them to come and help us. He's also called the state police and the FBI. Everybody says they're coming, nobody says when, and so far, they haven't shown up."

"Your town isn't going to abandon you. They're already gathered, waiting."

"Really?"

"Yes. Tell Griggs what I said. And make sure that if you hear a shot, you get the families to stay down on the floor."

"Of course," Damon said, then realized he was on a dead call. He handed the headset back to Ruth Cosgrove and went out to the open bay and called, "Listen up! Can everybody hear me?" He had a loud voice and a commanding presence. "Everything is fine, but it doesn't hurt to know what to do if something happens. Anybody here know what to do if there's a big loud noise, like firecrackers?"

About twenty young hands shot up, so Damon gestured in the direction of one boy, and about five others answered at once, "Down on the floor." "Lock the doors and get down." "Crawl under a desk and stay there."

One of the mothers sitting nearby said to Damon, "My husband gave active shooter drills at school this year."

He nodded. "Those are all good answers. Did everybody hear them?"

There was general agreement that they had. "I'm impressed. Thank you for your attention." He turned and walked toward Sergeant Griggs's office.

Gerald Russell sat in the back seat of the Lexus. He craned his neck to get a clearer look at the police building around the back of Gil Banks's head. He was tall, so it wasn't difficult. He had become accustomed to having Banks the getaway driver as his chauffeur. It seemed to him to project the image of power and importance that would keep the other men respectful and obedient.

As he looked at the line of cars that stretched along the front of the station his eyes passed across Jeanette at his side, then returned and settled on her. She was good for the same purpose, really. She was an asset that everyone could understand. She had a striking appearance, with the bright copper-colored hair, the big blue eyes, and the nicely rounded little body. In a normal, egalitarian world, a woman like her wouldn't go near a man like Gerald Russell. She would probably cross a street to avoid him and get closer to some man who would appeal to her sexually. But here she was, a mistress who would do anything to keep from losing his favor. The men were as capable of seeing that as he was. She was the proof that he was a leader who could take anything he wanted and keep it.

He said, "There can't be more than the few cops and Harry Duncan. It's time to make the call to Duncan. He's trapped in there. If we get him confused and demoralized, he'll spread it, and maybe it will get to some of the cops. Do it and put it on speaker."

She took the cell phone out of her purse, looked at the list of calls she had made, and touched one. She listened for a few seconds until she heard him say, "Duncan."

"Mr. Duncan," she said. "You're finally answering my calls."

She sounded angry, and her voice seemed to Russell exactly like the voice of the US Attorney in the recorded speech online that Jeanette had played over and over while she was learning to imitate it. He was delighted.

Duncan said, "I've been waiting for you to call. Are you saying you already called?"

"Of course I called. And I texted and I emailed. You were supposed to meet me at the FBI office in Indianapolis today at two with your star witness. Where were you?"

"I've been a lot of places. I started trying to reach you in Chicago, had to leave there to save my witness, and I've been trying keep him out of sight since then."

"Well, I wish you had spent some of that effort checking your phone. I had the US Attorney for the Indiana Southern District close to committing to taking on the investigation. He had the special agent in charge and his two assistants sitting in his office. We were in there for two hours, until I finally ran out of excuses why you could be that late without even calling to explain anything to anybody. You couldn't get a flight, your witness didn't have current ID, you drove and had car trouble, your cell phone wasn't working. I finally had to take the blame for the mess you caused, apologize, and just leave a copy of your report with them. If they even bother to read all that, getting them to begin their investigation will take months."

Duncan said, "I don't know how this happened. But they can't delay this any longer. These people are violent. I gave you a list of the people they've killed."

"I told my colleagues that much. You know what the FBI special agent in charge said? 'Maybe they killed Duncan too.' The others laughed."

"What about your office? Can't you send help on an emergency basis?"

"No. We can't. I've already heard from the Attorney General's office that the Illinois office can't just butt in."

"I don't know what to say."

Russell heard it and wished he could hear it again to savor it. The despair and hopelessness in Duncan's voice sounded complete. He felt a sudden wave of affection for Jeanette. She was an artist. He ran his finger across his throat to tell her to cut the call.

She nodded, and said, "Say goodbye. You've left the people there defenseless." She pressed the red oval to end the call and looked at Russell.

"Brava," he said. "That was perfect."

"Thank you." She lifted her face to receive a kiss on her cheek, and then put the phone back in the outer pocket of her purse to keep it away from her hypodermic needles.

Russell took out his own cell phone and pressed a number. "Mr. Mullins," he said. "When we get inside, the primary target is Dennison. But don't forget Harry Duncan. As long as he's alive we'll keep having problems."

"Yes sir. We won't forget him," Mullins said.

"How are the preparations going?"

"We're ready."

Duncan stood beside the truck, put his phone away, and looked at Ellen. "Jeanette again, pretending to be you. She's getting better at the voice, but she doesn't seem to know you're here."

"That sounds a little bit like good news," Ellen said.

Renee said, "I wonder why she chose to do that right now."

There was a new sound of an engine coming from the direction of the police station. It was large, a throbbing sound that rose in volume, and then there was a groan that sounded as though a driver who wasn't accustomed to a clutch and gearshift was trying to get the transmission of a truck to shift into second gear.

Duncan ran across the street to the hedge of the corner house, then turned and ran back to the white pickup truck. He got in on the right side and heard engines of cars behind them on Prospect Street starting. The nearest drivers had seen him, and then the ones behind them saw their taillights go on, and the starting sound moved quickly from the front to back of the line and around the corner. He said to Ellen, "It's time to go. Pull forward, turn left onto Main, and drive to the left past all the parked cars. Set a pretty brisk pace so everybody can get into position before the bad guys can react."

He pulled the slide of his Glock 17 to cycle a round into the chamber, lowered the side window with his left hand, and held the pistol just below it so he could aim and fire quickly.

The truck moved forward, and as it did, fifty-six cars shifted into drive and pulled away from the curb to follow, the engines rising in volume as more and more cars accelerated.

As Ellen made the left turn onto Main Street, Duncan looked out the back window to see the long line of cars moving, and watched the first three make the turn. Then he looked forward and saw the dump truck. It was ahead of them, moving along Main Street at about twenty miles an hour. Its brake lights came on, and Ellen had to coast to keep from catching up. The dump truck's brakes stayed on, the engine grumbling, and then there was a groan as the driver downshifted. The truck turned to the right, very slowly bumped up over the curb, straddled the long sidewalk leading up the lawn to the station door, and stopped only fifteen feet off the street. Renee said, "What the hell is that for?"

Duncan said, "They're going to drive it through the front of the building." Ellen drove a bit faster, staying to the left of the gangsters' cars parked along the curb, turned right and then drove along the perpendicular street, then turned right again onto the broad asphalt rectangle of the police department's lot, past parked police cars, a couple vans for forensics people and crime scene investigators, and four plain-wrap cars, and on to the separate lot for police officers' personal vehicles and the cars of visitors, and then around to the front of the building again and stopped on the left side of the street, across from the cars of the station's attackers.

The truck was behind a car driven by one of the townspeople just arriving, because the brake lights flashed as the car pulled into place, and immediately went out as the car was shifted into park. The doors on the left side opened and the driver and three men spilled out holding long guns, and stood in a row resting their rifles on the car to aim at the men in the cars only sixty feet away across the street laying siege to the station.

Duncan and Renee got out of the truck holding their pistols, and Duncan could make out that that along the line of newly arrived cars, there were men and women steadying rifles on hoods and trunks of cars to aim at the men across the street.

The dump truck was still in place on the front lawn of the police station, the engine's low tone unchanging, proof that the driver's foot was not on the gas pedal. Criminals with pistols in their hands who had been standing on the left sides of their cars aiming at the front of the police station turned to gape over their shoulders and then scuttled around their cars to face the sight that had just materialized.

The thirty-five men who had surrounded the police station hours ago were now themselves surrounded by men and women from the town. Their numbers were hard for even Duncan to estimate, because the line of cars he had just led here had circled the police station and the gang cars outside it, and he couldn't see them all. He guessed that there were about two hundred citizens, maybe more, and all the ones he could see seemed to be aiming rifles at members of the gang.

The criminals he could see were wide-eyed, looking first at the people across the street from them, then moving their eyes along the line of cars surrounding theirs, and then glancing at each other and making hurried, muttered consultations about their predicament. About half of them hurried around their cars to get shelter from the rifles, and others got into the cars, aware that a car door wouldn't stop a rifle bullet, but not sure which side of the car left them most vulnerable.

What worried Duncan now was the dump truck. It was still there, still idling. If the driver didn't stall it with his terrible clutch and shifter work, he could get it up to a speed that would easily obliterate the locked safety glass doors and much of the brick wall that held them, and probably smash through into the open bay where the officers and their families were.

Duncan's phone rang and interrupted his cogitations. "What?" he said into it.

The voice sounded angry. "What do you think you're doing, Duncan? Inciting an armed mob is illegal and disgusting." It actually sounded like Ellen.

He said, "Jeanette, hand the phone to Russell."

"I don't know who that is."

"All right." He hit the end call symbol and it went dead.

The phone rang again about two seconds later. "Mr. Duncan."

"Russell. What do you want?"

"Do you see the truck on the police station lawn?"

"It's kind of hard to miss," Duncan said.

"You know what it's there for, don't you? Any minute I can have it driven through the front of the building. Within five minutes after that, the men who follow it in will have Dennison, and all the cops and most of their families will be dead. Or you could just get Sergeant Griggs to release him to you now."

"Not possible."

"I'm trying to negotiate with you to avoid needless casualties. So what's your idea for how resolve this?"

"You and your friends put any weapons you have on the front lawn of the police station, back away from them, and lie down on the double yellow line that runs up the middle of Main Street."

"Now you're being ridiculous. What are your real terms?"

"You wouldn't have called me if you weren't aware that there are three hundred people surrounding you and your men." Duncan was sure Russell couldn't have counted, so the exaggeration felt safe. "We've got you outnumbered ten to one, and everyone is aiming a rifle right now that will put a round through one of your men. You could be alone in about three seconds. You'll have to decide for yourself, but to me it looks like a surrender or die situation."

"I'll tell you what. My friends and I have made more money than we ever expected here. It's enough. I can just tell them it's time to leave. They'll get back in their cars and we'll all drive out of your lives."

"It's too late for that. People have been killed."

In the car seat beside Russell, Jeanette watched him tap Banks on the shoulder and point away from the police station, and then saw Banks nod his head, start his engine, and swing out away from the curb. Banks accelerated rapidly as the car moved away from the others. Russell said into the phone, "If you insist on sticking to stupid demands, you'll be responsible for lots of deaths." He turned and looked out the rear window of the car. He could see the scene at the station diminishing into the distance. The last image he could see was the dump truck on the lawn.

He said, "Think it over and then call back," and pressed the icon and ended the call. He tossed the phone on Jeanette's lap and took out his own phone. "It's time to get inside, guys. Stay behind the truck until you're in the building, and then get Dennison." He called Joe Trilby, the man in the truck's cab. "Trilby. This is Russell. Make sure you build enough speed to break through the front wall. Go now. I repeat, go now!" He ended the call and put away his phone. "God, I hope the first one they kill is Harry Duncan." Jeanette, who had listened to his end of the telephone call, wisely sat up straight and still, stared out the window at the diminishing image in the side mirror, and kept her mouth shut and her teeth clenched. She knew he was likely to hit her soon, and she hoped it might keep the blow from breaking her jaw.

Duncan had never been able to see where Russell was, so he didn't see him leave, either. What he saw when he looked up from the dead phone was the dump truck. The engine growled as it moved forward on the lawn. Its headlights went on and threw two overlapping circles of light on the glass doors in front and the bricks around them, as though they were a laser sight. The truck's engine whined and the driver shifted into second gear, accelerated, and then to third, and accelerated. About a dozen men who had been crouching behind the parked cars ran up the concrete walkway after it, pistols in hand, using the truck for cover and preparing to follow it into the building.

After another second, the front door of the station opened and a cop that Duncan recognized as Damon appeared with a rifle at his shoulder and knelt. He fired three rapid shots that Duncan could tell hit the windshield of the truck, then spun and dived away from the entrance.

The truck seemed to falter and lose all intention like a creature with a severed head, not accelerating now, but drifting off the concrete walk to the right on the broad, empty lawn. Its weight made its tires sink deeper into the damp lawn as the upward incline sapped its momentum, and created deep ruts. The twelve men who had been following in the expectation that the truck would crash through the front of the building saw in a moment that following the truck on its mad, altered course across the police department's lawn left them in the open. They stopped running, threw down their guns, held up their empty hands, and knelt on the ground. Behind them, the dump truck coasted onward for a few more seconds while the resistance turned its front wheels even more sharply to the right, and then hit the station in a slow, glancing blow, scraped the brick facade for a few feet, and then stopped.

Duncan ran to the car parked ahead of Renee's truck and yelled, "Block the intersections with cars. Get some cars into every intersection. Everybody else aim at a criminal you can hit, and stand by. Do not shoot anybody."

Duncan watched as the gang members on the right side of the street tried to understand what they were seeing. The quickest of them hurried into their cars and pulled away from the curb to escape, but by then each of the streets had several cars parked at odd angles blocking the intersection, so they screeched to a halt. Some began to back up to try another way, but saw that cars driven by their comrades had pulled up behind them and stopped, making it impossible to move.

The gang members could see there was no way to move a car, and that being immobile with four or five people pointing rifles at each of them at close range was a situation that would be fatal any second. Their car windows slid down, they tossed their pistols on the pavement, and got out.

Several of the men who had run to get into their cars could see that the streets were now impassable, and bumped their cars up over the curb to drive across the police station lawn to make it around the building to escape on foot, but as they turned at the corner of the building, they met cars coming the other way driven by men with the same idea. The most astute stopped, got out of their cars, tossed their guns down, and looked for someone to accept their surrender before some nervous civilian fired a round that set off a barrage of shots from their neighbors. Others hesitated, but as they saw their friends giving up and the numbers of holdouts shrinking quickly, they resigned themselves to defeat.

Officer Damon was joined outside the station by eight heavily armed uniformed officers, some of whom looked at first as though they were skeptical that the sudden capitulation wasn't a trick. They evaluated the strange, complicated scene, and then began putting the men, whom they now referred to as "suspects," on the ground and using zip ties on their wrists and ankles, gathering weapons, and then moving on to others. The largest group were the ones who had been trapped in the blocked cars and were now lying on Main Street under the hard eyes of townspeople with rifles. The more the numbers of uncaptured gangsters diminished, the more grossly overmatched they were, and the pace of surrenders increased. The police went to work moving them onto the lawn so they could be watched over by only a few police officers.

Within ten minutes, there were thirty-five men on the front lawn. The last one was a man in handcuffs conducted to the place by Officer Damon.

Sergeant Griggs said, "Is that the guy from the truck? I thought he must be dead."

"He's a lucky man. I didn't hit him, but when I shot out the windshield, he ducked and lay down across the passenger seat, and couldn't steer or reach the pedals. Just now I happened to see him crawling out of the cab to sneak off."

A few minutes later, as the police officers were busy searching prisoners for hidden weapons, Duncan went into the station and walked to the back of the building, where the cells were. Duncan said to the officer there to guard the cell block, "Can you let me see Mr. Dennison, please?"

The officer walked with him to the cell in the back that had a solid steel door and opened it. Dennison was sitting on his bunk, and looked up. Duncan said, "I don't know if anybody told you yet, but it's over. Your former friends are all handcuffed on the front lawn."

"You're saying this was a safe place?" Dennison said.

"I think we still have a deal. Do we?"

"I'll testify to everything I told you, and if I remember anything else about them, I'll swear to that too."

"And I'll remember to tell the authorities you can't be in a facility with any of them, even for a second. I'll see you again before too long."

Dennison lay back on his bunk and put his feet up. "A year or so will be soon enough."

31

The next morning at six, as the sun was about to rise over the town, a convoy of vehicles belonging to the Indiana state police and the police forces of the towns of Riverbend and Groomsburg burst out of the nearly opaque morning fog along the Ash River, turned at the Main Street sign, and sped through the town of Parkman's Elbow up to the corner of Prospect Street before they were blocked by several cars parked at odd angles in the intersection.

The convoy came to a stop and approximately one hundred police officers wearing a variety of uniforms—the state police their distinctive black campaign hats, black shirts, and blue pants, the Groomsburg police khaki shirts and green pants, and the Riverbend SWAT Team olive drab battle dress with heavy duty body armor and helmets—threw open their car doors, streamed from their vehicles holding their weapons, and stormed toward the police station.

The front door of the station opened and Sergeant Griggs came out and stood there while the wave of armed officers washed up on the lawn and stopped about thirty feet from them. Griggs called out to the police on the lawn, "Officers, I'm Sergeant Griggs. Seeing you show up like this to help us is really heartening to me. Thank you for making the effort and having the bravery it takes to go toward the fight. However, we found that we and the people of the town had to act before you got here, so that part was already over last night."

The cops on the lawn looked at each other with a mixture of relief, puzzlement, and confusion, and began to holster sidearms and lower rifles. A few of them looked amused.

Griggs called out, "But we do need your help with the next part of it. Inside the station we have thirty-six suspects in handcuffs and zip ties who all are going to be charged with felonies ranging from possession of a concealed weapon by a convicted felon to homicide. We don't have the space or personnel here to accommodate them, and will appreciate your cooperation with that. You can sort out among yourselves who can take prisoners where, and how many. Just tell us who you're taking and where he's going to be. And please take care to treat them humanely and respect all their constitutional rights. Trust me when I say that these are not people you want having any charges dropped or convictions reversed. Thank you very much." He turned and went back into the station, followed at a distance by ranking officers commanding the various visiting forces.

It was later that day that the team of six FBI agents arrived in the town of Parkman's Elbow. They were three women and three men, and they were not the kind of agents that wore dark suits, nor the kind of agents with khaki pants and windbreakers with big yellow letters that said "FBI." They were wearing the sort of civilian clothes intended to make them look like the local residents. The third interview they had was with Harry

Duncan. The senior agent, a middle-aged man named Schuler, took Duncan aside before they were to start the interview in the police conference room.

He said, "I'm sorry for keeping you waiting for help. Your messages weren't getting through to us. Apparently one of the US Attorney's clerical staff was working with the other side. The woman has been arrested and will be held without bail until all the conspirators are in custody."

Duncan said, "Is she cooperating with the investigation?"

"I don't know yet. Probably she doesn't either. Would you like to get started?"

Duncan said. "There's a lot to tell."

"Yes, we've read your murder book and seen the evidence pictures and videos. We've been at it for weeks, since the morning after you submitted it. The Bureau had no idea things were breaking this fast. We were expecting to come down here to begin an undercover investigation. We rented three houses so we would look like three couples establishing a branch of an insurance company based in Indianapolis."

"So how can I help you?" Duncan asked.

"We just need to ask a few questions to clarify the information you submitted and determine what steps have to be taken first. We're particularly interested in what you can tell us about the ones we don't have yet, Gerald Russell and Jeanette Walrath."

"You haven't picked them up?" Duncan said.

"Don't worry. You gave us the address, complete with a phone video of them going into the building. The Chicago office has them under twenty-four-hour surveillance. They're not going anywhere. Today we just need to be sure to get the charges right for the warrant."

Jeanette was lying on the big couch in the living quarters above Russell's office. She had been thinking about what she had seen at the police station in Parkman's Elbow. She had spent a couple of months congratulating herself on making the leap from Paul Rankin, who was dead, to Russell, who was not only alive, but was the leader that all those men had looked up to. He was much richer than Paul Rankin had been, and had been in the process of taking over a whole part of Indiana.

The past few weeks hadn't been too bad from day to day either. He had spent lots of money on her and taken her to nice places. He was very selfish and expected her to have sex with him whenever the idea floated into his mind, but that same selfishness meant he didn't spend much time at it, trying to get her excited about it or anything. It was very quick—a few minutes, usually—and she'd found it easy to make it reach its conclusion more quickly by faking responses.

But for the past three days she had been getting more and more worried. He had saved her from some unthinkable punishment that had been contemplated by the mysterious collection of scary people above him in the hierarchy. She had known that whatever it was, it would have been terrible, and she was expected not only to suffer it, but to humiliate herself, present herself to receive it, maybe even suggest it. She had to acknowledge Russell had prevented that. She wasn't eternally grateful, because she wasn't really capable of holding an emotion like that after conditions changed and it was no longer what she needed. She already had what she'd needed then, and wasn't sure what she needed now.

The upper level of the organization was terrifying. She had first gotten involved with the group because the three Clark brothers had made a mess of their attempt to sell protection to the businesses along the Ash River. She and Rankin had been hired to kill them. To Jeanette the lesson was that in this organization, people who made mistakes got executed.

What worried her now was that Russell had just made an enormous mistake. Russell had tried to neutralize Charlie Dennison, who was ratting out the rest of the group, and blown it. Not only was Dennison still alive, he was undoubtedly still talking to the police. That meant he was trading their freedom for a lesser charge for himself. The group of high-level bosses that Russell referred to as "Chicago" must be aware that all the foot soldiers of the group were in jail cells in Indiana right now, waiting to be charged and tried. All the progress that had been made was lost.

She had noticed a few things over the past couple days since they had returned from Indiana. She had taken the elevator downstairs one morning to get Russell's mail for him. Everything outside had looked pretty much the way it always had, but in the second when she had opened the door to check the mailbox, several people—a man sitting in a car that had signs on his window for both Lyft and Uber, a woman pushing a stroller, and the mailman—all glanced in her direction, and then looked away and kept doing what they were doing. She had checked the mail and seen that it hadn't come, even though the mailman was already across the street walking away. She didn't go out and try to catch his attention because she was wearing a nightgown that was practically transparent and a peignoir of the same material. She had stepped back, closed the door, and locked it with the bolt. On her way upstairs she had looked at her reflection in the mirrored side of the elevator. The fact that people had looked wasn't surprising, but the two men, at least, shouldn't have looked away. After a few minutes upstairs she had persuaded herself that she was just being jumpy. They weren't a crew of killers getting ready to take Russell out. Would one of them be a woman pushing a stroller? That was just silly. She noticed the black purse she'd carried with her in Parkman's Elbow, picked it up, and put it behind a throw pillow on the couch so Russell wouldn't see it. He hated it when she left her things lying around.

She reached for the remote control and turned on the big television set on the wall. As always, it lit up the brand name under it, and she pressed the button beside it so the cable box would come on. That one showed a blue light. The screen was dark and silent for a few seconds, and then the picture came on of a woman sitting in a newsroom set, her face wreathed in blond hair and her eyes fixed and serious. She spoke, and her voice was loud as a shout. "The Indianapolis office of the Indiana State Police gave a statement—" Jeanette turned it off because that was faster than lowering the volume, and she didn't want to remind Russell of her presence. Whether his attention would be hatred or affection, she didn't want it.

But here he was. He looked awful coming into the room—not just his normal appearance, which she always tried hard to resist thinking of as "spidery," because of his long arms and legs, his curved spine arching forward over her, and the intent, inhuman way his eyes stared down at her—but because he looked disheveled and exhausted, about fifteen years older. Even his usual arrogance and coldness were better than this.

She couldn't ignore him, so she chose friendliness, which for her had to be seductive because they had never been friends.

Her voice went soft and warm. "Good morning, Lover." She patted the couch. "Come be with me." She slid her body against the back to make room, and he stepped to the couch and sat. She reached up to his neck and began to massage the back of it, moving outward a little to his narrow shoulders and down his bony shoulder blades. She could feel his muscles relaxing a little, his back stretching with the movement of her hands. She kept working at it, not letting her fingers rest. Her efforts seemed to be pleasing to him. She thought hard, and then decided this was her chance to talk. She moved her body up against him for a moment. "May I speak?"

He shrugged.

"Do we have anything to worry about?"

"What do you mean?"

"The bosses—the ones your guys just call 'Chicago.' Will they blame what happened on us?"

He snorted, and his shoulders moved up and down. He was laughing. Was he laughing at her?

"Why is that funny?"

"I had assumed that you knew better than that, or had at least figured it out by now. You've been with me every minute since the beginning of April. Have you ever seen these people visit the state of Indiana? Jesus Christ. How stupid can you be?"

She realized she had stopped rubbing his muscles. She thought she knew, but she had to be sure. "What are you saying?"

He turned to look at her over his shoulder, his mouth open in a grin that looked like he was a corpse, his thin lips retracted and his long yellow teeth protruding from the gums. "They're not bosses. They're backers. Investors. If I weren't around, they could do nothing. I gave them a big image so all the morons who worked for me would be afraid to ignore my orders or try to take over. There would always be an invisible power ready to punish them."

She sat still. It was as though her hands were no longer following her will. She was reliving the past few months, not to verify or disprove what he'd said. He was the biggest liar, but she knew this was true. Instead, she was reliving, one after another, the most humiliating moments. She had endured anything he felt like doing to her and now she was surprised at how completely used to it she had become. She was one of the morons he was talking about, probably the biggest moron of all.

He said, "Keep going. That felt good."

Her hands seemed to know before she did. They began to work at his shoulder blades again, pressing softly, and then gradually harder. Next the right hand took over, massaging his right shoulder blade while the left felt for the purse behind the pillow and opened the latch, and then the right hand was replaced by the left and slipped into the purse and came out with one of the needles and left it on her lap. Both hands now worked together for a while. Massages were partly about expectation, making the client want the hands to reach some neglected part of his body, to think each time the hands came close it was happening, but then it didn't and he wanted it more.

Her left hand stopped and the right worked on his back, finding each muscle that was stiff and making its swirling palpating way to the next. The hands had done this minutes ago, so he felt the familiarity and symmetry when the left hand took over and the right stopped. This time Jeanette's right hand went to her lap and lifted the needle to her mouth so she could close her teeth on the plastic cap and bare the steel. The right hand lowered the needle to the spot just at the back of Russell's belt where her left hand was massaging, working the muscle just above the left buttock. The left hand kept working on it as the needle slowly penetrated the muscle and the thumb began to press the plunger.

Russell lurched forward off the couch to his feet and whirled to face Jeanette. His eyes were wild and his teeth bared. "What the hell are you?"

Jeanette was trying to hide the needle, but he obviously knew what he'd felt. He took a step toward her and she began to scream. His long arm shot out behind the pillow and snatched the open purse, spilling needles onto the floor as he hurled it across the room. Jeanette's screams grew louder, her incredibly strong voice crying, "Aah! Aaah! AAAH!," as he came toward her.

"Shut up, Jeanette," he yelled, but he could barely hear his own voice. He could see she still had the needle she had started to use on him, so didn't charge right at her. He took one quick step to get behind the couch and flipped it over so she landed on the floor with the heavy couch on top of her. He stamped on her right hand, then flopped on top of the couch to hold her down while he snatched the needle, jabbed it into her neck, and injected the contents into her, then flung the needle across the room.

"What was in the needle, Jeanette?" he said. "Is it heroin? Fentanyl? Whatever it is, it's all yours now. I only got a little." She didn't answer. She was lying still. He reached under the couch, pulled up on the backrest, and flipped it back over onto its feet, leaving her lying facedown on the floor. There were needles around the room, but none of them near her, so he knelt and turned her over. She looked as though she was asleep—a deep, peaceful sleep.

He stood up again, his mind crowded with impressions. She had tried to kill him. Hadn't he made it clear enough that there were no bosses coming after them? Could she have misunderstood? They would have gotten through this. He was a respectable businessman, and Dennison and everybody else who might testify against him was a convict, a lowlife who would be easy to take apart in court.

There was an odd noise. It was a heavy "Bump! Bump! Bump!" and it seemed to be coming from downstairs. He went to the window and looked down at the street. All he could see was that there seemed to be several cars out there that weren't moving. The noise got louder, and then he heard something metallic crash against something else. He went to the desktop computer on the kitchen counter and clicked on the security camera page. The screen was divided into six sections, each the image picked up on one camera.

The camera focused down on the front door showed that the door was wide open, and men wearing body armor were streaming inside with guns drawn. The camera aimed at the elevator showed a man with a very short beard holding a leather identification folder up to the camera and shouting something, but he didn't turn on the sound. He knew who they were.

He turned away and saw Jeanette lying faceup where he had left her. That expression, so peaceful and free of fear or pain, was so odd that he was drawn to it. He couldn't go to prison. After what had happened, all the men he had hired would get long sentences, and now, so would he. Lawyers couldn't make Jeanette disappear. He stepped close, picked up a fresh needle from the floor, sat on the couch, and looked down at her, thinking how pretty she looked as he pulled off the plastic cover and stuck the needle into his arm.

32

Duncan spent a morning retrieving his black car from the lot where he had paid to store it, went to pick up his computer and rifle carrying case from the Parkman's Elbow Police Department, and stowed them under the floor of the car's trunk, and then his phone rang.

"Hello?"

"Hello, Harry. This is Ellen. I'm on a brand-new phone. We need to talk in person before either of us leaves. Where are you?"

"I'm at the police station."

"Too crowded. Can we meet someplace else?"

"Do you have a car?"

"Yes."

"Can you find The Elbow Room? It's deserted."

"I looked it over the first day I came here. I can be there in about ten minutes."

Duncan was in the parking lot of The Elbow Room leaning against his car and looking across the road at the Ash River when she drove up and parked beside him. She got out of her car and stood in front of him.

"What's on your mind?" he said.

"The news hasn't been released yet, but Gerald Russell and Jeanette Walrath are dead. It looks to the FBI arrest team that came for them at his Chicago place that they both had been injected with something. They were still warm, so the team called in an ambulance and the EMTs gave them Narcan, but it didn't do anything. They apparently went through all the other things they try, but by then both were dead."

"Damn. I assume nobody had a chance to ask questions. How far has the search of the building gone?"

"They've been at it for a few hours, but if they've found anything it hasn't been enough to rate a phone call. They'll start searching computers and phones within a day or two, so you never know. What are you hoping we'll find?"

"It wasn't enough. You understand what I mean?"

"That was what I was saying to you all along," she said. "Not enough evidence, not enough background. Get me more. And you did."

"I didn't mean that," he said. "The whole thing looked like the founding days of an old-fashioned crime organization. It was set up that way. But it had to be something more than that—something bigger. There just isn't enough money around here to make all the effort and risk worth it."

"What are you thinking?" she said. "Financial crimes? Dark web stuff?"

"I don't know," he said. "There was just too much that didn't fit the old patterns. The proportions were wrong. They were killing people they could have made pay them for decades. They were scaring people to death, and then buying them out, complete with sales documents and cashier's checks."

"Gerald Russell's cover was that he was a real estate guy—not a fake one, a real one with licenses and permits and an actual business with sales in both states."

"He started buying months ago, but never tried to sell anything he bought," Duncan said. "As I said, I just don't know, Ell."

She stared at him. "Nobody has called me that since—you know."

"Sorry. I wasn't thinking."

"Yes you were," she said. "Just not about that. I didn't mind. I guess in the past few days we both got comfortable again because we weren't thinking about the old times."

"Maybe."

"Well, I've got to get moving, since this part of the investigation is in my legitimate district. I just felt it was better for you to hear it from me right away." She handed him a three-by-five card where she had written a phone number and an address. "This is my new number. It's safe to call if you figure this out. When you have your next phone number you can text it to me. I wanted to keep you out of court, but—"

"I understand. I'll make sure you can reach me when the time comes."

"And thank you. It didn't escape my notice that you saved my life several times in just the past two days. I didn't know what to say—to say that would mean anything to you at this point—so I'm saying that. And I won't be calling you again to get you to risk your life. I apologize for what you've been through. From here on what has to be done is part of my job." She smiled. "Take care of yourself."

"You too," he said. She was standing there, not moving. What was she expecting—that he would kiss her goodbye? He didn't move, just waited.

She got into her car and drove up River Road to the north. He watched the car all the way up the road until it disappeared at the first curve and then waited to see it reappear for a second at the next loop, and then it was gone.

Duncan got into his car and sat still for a moment. She was right about getting new phones. He had used several disposable ones with different numbers during this case. He would need to sort them out and preserve the ones with important information on them. If nothing else, they would support the veracity of the notes he had put in his murder book and what he would say in his testimony.

He started the car and headed for Interstate 65. He would go north to Gary and then take the short stretch on 80 into Chicago to reach his office. He glanced at the dashboard clock and estimated that the trip, about two hundred fifty miles, would get him there around six P.M. That wasn't bad. The heavy traffic would be streaming out of Chicago at that hour.

Duncan's early career had made him an expert, tireless driver, and he let the sameness and simplicity of it relax him. He made it into Chicago at five-forty and was parked in the converted basement garage under his office building and climbing the old steel and terrazzo staircase to the third floor by six-fifteen. When he reached the door of his condominium he pulled out his pistol, stood to the side, and knocked, waited and knocked again, and then flung the door open and went in low.

As he knew it would be, his condominium office was a mess from the search Mullins had carried out that he had seen on security video. It occurred to him as he was putting it back in order that the video could serve as a guide to which parts of his office had been disturbed and which had not, so he used it, and finished quickly.

He walked to the small grocery store three blocks from his building and bought groceries. Using his legs felt good after all the driving. He bought a small rotisserie chicken for his dinner, but all the way home he was smelling it, so when he got there he didn't want it anymore. He put it in the refrigerator and made himself some oatmeal and ate it while he checked his laptop for that day's email.

When he was finally ready to sleep, it was with the door deadbolted and a filing cabinet pushed across it. He sometimes had a few days of residual restless watchfulness after violent cases, but they always went away. As he was pushing the cabinet into place he thought of Ellen. At least he didn't have anybody like her around to explain it to and have to justify it.

33

He woke at five A.M. from a dream in which he was paralyzed—maybe strapped down in a moving ambulance—and the red-haired woman was looming over him with a needle. It seemed curious to him because he knew she was dead. If he was anxious about anything it should be something that was at least possible.

When he had made himself a breakfast made possible by his trip to the grocery store, he began the task of putting a charged battery into each phone he had used, cataloguing the information it contained, and then removing the battery again.

While he was doing it, he ran across the phone he had used to speak with the ornithologist at Cornell University. He made a note of the number, and when he had finished his inventory, he dialed it. A man answered and Duncan asked to speak to Dr. Magnuson. The man said she was not in the lab on Wednesday afternoons because that was when she held her graduate seminars.

Duncan called again the next morning, and then at noon, and again in mid afternoon. Finally he heard her say, "Magnuson."

He said, "Hello, Dr. Magnuson. I don't know if you remember me, but my name is Harry Duncan."

"Of course I remember you," she said. "In fact, you seem to have become sort of a local celebrity in Indiana. Not here yet, but I'm sure your fame is growing as we speak."

"What do you mean?"

"I got a call right afterward from the police there to thank me for helping you to save a woman's life, and the officer had high praise for you. A few days later I got a call from Renee Parkman for the same reason. She said you had just spirited her away from the people who had been after her and sent her to California. I wondered if I was going to hear from you again."

Duncan noted that Renee was still being careful. She had gone to Colorado, not California. "I'm sorry I wasn't able to really thank you enough. Most people don't understand the special kind of courage it takes to trust a stranger who asks for help. I know that when you told me where the sandhill cranes were, it could have risked your reputation and standing, and maybe your career."

"Thank you for saying that," she said. "But I'm afraid I'm more of a trust-but-verify sort of person. After Sergeant Griggs called, I looked up the number of the police station in Parkman's Elbow, Indiana to be sure that it matched the number on Caller ID."

"I'm glad to hear it. I guess verifying information is part of what scientists do. It's a good habit for all of us. You know, after you told me about the cranes, I only went close enough to hear them, but never saw them. Have you found out anything about what the researchers learned when they were observing them?"

She sighed. "I'm afraid the news on that isn't so good. I heard that several of the cranes seemed to show signs of illness during their time in Indiana, and when the flock moved on, a couple of them had died. They're being studied very closely by the team, and researchers in several places are working on various things to learn what was wrong. The last I heard, the strongest theory was that it was the illness that caused them to stop in an unusual spot in the first place."

Duncan said, "That's sad. What do you think happened?"

"I don't have enough information for a hypothesis. There are highly contagious bird flus that mutate, environmental factors that an animal might encounter in a new environment, you name it. One of the leaders of the project is a friend of mine. I'll give you his number. You can ask him for an update, if you're curious."

"I think I'll do that," he said. "What should I say?"

"Just tell him I gave you his number. I told him about you, so he'll probably be curious about you too. His name is Steven Saskin. Professor Steven Saskin. He's at Indiana University."

For Duncan finding out more about the sandhill cranes was simply a step in closing out his murder book. The scientists and the cranes had been about four hundred yards away the night he swam to take Renee Parkman back from the kidnappers. But they had been there for nearly a month, probably seen the boat arrive or seen it anchored in midstream. The scientists at once had no connection with the crime wave in the towns along the Ash River and were potential informants and witnesses. He waited a day before he called Steven Saskin.

"Professor Saskin?" he said, "My name is Harry Duncan."

"Mr. Duncan," the man said. "Ann Magnuson told me you might call."

"I didn't want to bother you, but your work set off my curiosity. Is this a bad time to talk? I'm free most of the time right now, and—"

"It's a perfect time," Saskin said. "And Ann told me about the kidnapping and everything. You're a hero, and I never miss a chance to talk to one of those. If you have any questions for me, I'll be happy to answer."

"Well, if you don't mind," Duncan said. "When did you and your team arrive at the river?"

"April second through sixth. The cranes were noticed on the second, and because I was the closest, I drove down right away to see if it really was a breakaway flock of sandhills, and to figure out how to get close enough to study them. Fortunately, there was an ideal set-up—a building with water and power in a public park that was barely used in early April, and could be closed to the public for a month. I explained to the mayor and the police chief of Groomsburg what was happening, and they gave me their complete cooperation. It took four days for the rest of the team to arrive, but I had camera and sound equipment going early on the third."

"How many of you were there?"

"Four of us—Jacqueline Sperlock and Will Morris from Cornell—both of them postdocs of Ann Magnuson's—Leon Meister from the University of Groningen in the Netherlands, and myself."

"And you were all there continuously?"

"Most of the time. Every few days somebody would make a trip out for supplies, but that was all."

"Do you remember if there was anything that struck you as out of the ordinary while you were there?"

"Human activity?" he said. "No. If I had been told that while I was asleep you were rescuing a woman less than a quarter mile away, I wouldn't have believed it. Of course, by then, we were aware that some of the birds were in some kind of distress, so that took practically all of our attention."

"Yes, Dr. Magnuson mentioned that. It must have been a real worry. Have you found out what it was?"

"We know a possible part of what it was. Since the beginning of wildlife science, part of every ornithologist's specialty has been figuring out what was killing some species or other. If it isn't songbirds dying from DDT, or ospreys laying eggs with shells that break, it's condors feeding on deer carcasses and ingesting lead bullets.

"We saw that some of the cranes would sit down instead of standing up, wading, or flying. They seemed weak, as though they were fighting a viral infection. Most of the cranes seemed to recover, but not all. At the end of April, when they took off, there were three dead cranes. We sent each one to a different lab."

"Like an autopsy," Duncan said.

"Exactly. While we waited, we collected samples of the water from various places in the river, drilled core samples of the river bottom and the banks, tested the air for pollutants, and consulted with the city of Groomsburg to learn what pollutants might have entered the river, not only from current industrial sources, and also checked their historical records to learn what industries had been pursued in the area since it had been settled."

"What did you find out?"

"A great deal, but all of it was ambiguous. At times there had been factories and workshops and mines with particularly polluting byproducts: smelting and plating metals, industrial scale farming that produced chemical fertilizer runoffs, and so on. But at all points, including now, the river has been a habitat full of birds—not only perching birds and game birds, but also wading birds—herons and bitterns."

"I noticed that myself. But you said you might have part of the answer."

"Yes. When the analyses came back, we learned that none of the three cranes had any evidence of viral infections in their blood from any familiar kind of bird flu, and we detected none from any new strain. That was a giant relief. But the birds did share one thing. It was a very high presence of rare earths in their bodies."

"Rare earths? Really?" Duncan said. "Like they use in computers?"

"Yes."

"I thought they were all in China or someplace. But the cranes migrate huge distances, right? They could have picked them up there."

"That did occur to us, but concentrations of the minerals were also present in water samples and core samples we took. It's quite a list: cerium, scandium, lanthanum, yttrium, samarium, holmium, thulium, promethium, and on and on. The thing about rare earths is that they're not actually rare. They just don't come in big chunks or veins. They're spread all over, often too far underground to make the digging and separation practical. Up until now nobody's doing it here because people are doing it in other countries, so we don't have to."

"I always assumed it was just that we didn't have any."

"That was why one group wondered if what we were seeing was the effect of some company dumping electronic waste upstream from the park. To make a cell phone you need forty different 'rare earth' metals. So maybe a company was collecting old phones and other things—LED bulbs, wind turbines, aerospace equipment, and other high-tech junk—and quietly dumping them. It made sense, at least historically. People have been ruining rivers that way for thousands of years. But we eliminated that."

"How?"

"We consulted experts in geology departments. Not only is nobody doing it, but the main reason is that there wouldn't be any profit in it."

"So all these minerals are natural?"

"Not just those. The list from the analysis has reached seventeen so far, all present in the dead cranes, the water, and the deep core samples—there most of all. That was the clincher. The minerals aren't from some foreign strip mine. They're from the bed of the Ash River right here in the Hoosier State."

"Let me ask you this," Duncan said. "Do you know if the concentrations would make mining the rare earths worthwhile?"

"Given the increasing prevalence of the technology of cell phones and things? Sure. But it'll never happen."

"Why not?"

"The mining is very messy and destructive. It involves moving countless tons of earth, strip mining huge areas, and utterly destroying the landscape to get small, gradual accumulations of ore. Indiana isn't a state where people are likely to let a company do that."

"Thanks, Professor. I hope the rest of the cranes survive."

"We've banded a few, and we have high hopes that they'll all turn up at the other end of their return migration. We think the three casualties were on the old side and might have been especially vulnerable, and they could have also been unlucky enough to have been close together during an upwelling from under the water that brought up an especially potent dose."

"I hope you can solve it."

"I think we will. But of course, we still don't know the thing we wanted most to find out—what brought sandhill cranes here in the first place. We may never really know."

As soon as Duncan hung up, he found the number Ellen Leicester had written on a card and dialed it.

"Hello."

"Hi, Ellen. It's Harry Duncan."

"I know your voice, Harry. I'm just surprised to hear it again so soon."

"I just had a conversation that might be important to your case. Do you have a few minutes to listen to some of it?"

"If you think it's important, I do. And if I have an interruption, I'll call you back."

Duncan played the recording he had made of the call. At the end of it, he said, "What do you think?"

"This was already not just a case. It's thirty-five defendants involved in about a dozen homicides and hundreds of other felonies. Now what I think is pretty much what you think—that long before the cranes flew off course, somebody knew there was a chance to corner what's going to be a major domestic market. It would have to be someone who could afford to spend millions to make billions."

Duncan said, "We know Gerald Russell was buying the land, houses, and businesses of people who got scared enough to take very little to move on. At the time I wondered how he got enough money to do that. I kind of held the question off because it seemed like a side issue."

"And now you're thinking that it's not a side issue."

"The possibility is seeming more real. Russell was always telling his men that the real power was 'Chicago,' some remote set of bosses that he reported to. The men he recruited were all convicts recommended by other convicts from Illinois prisons. They were tough, and people with that background know tough when they see it. They knew Gerald Russell was not tough, but he didn't have to be, because behind him was 'Chicago.' "

"What do you think I should do?"

"Be patient. If there's somebody seriously trying to get control of the rare earths market, it's less likely to be a person than a corporation—maybe only the inner circle inside one. The best way to start is to seem to be looking the other way. Concentrate for the moment on what your investigators find in Gerald Russell's office, his home, and his business accounts that show any traceable sources of money."

She said, "I know this is going to sound stupid. But it's seemed to me from the beginning that this case has been harder to get started than most. I've been walking into headwinds since the start. I would try to get people in the Justice Department interested, and they would be busy with something of a higher priority, and couldn't listen. When I asked, people would dismiss it, or give me a list of other issues I ought to be working on instead. I actually wondered if they were trying to distract me. But it never occurred to me that their concern might be keeping me from stepping on some powerful toes."

"Stranger things have happened. Don't charge straight at this, or the links could mysteriously dissolve. I would try to get my hands on the personnel file of the employee who was compromising your phones. Somebody recommended her, and she also had a history of working for somebody before you. Somebody hired her to fill the slot in your office. Take a look."

"And how about you, Harry?" she said. "Your contract is over, and you've been paid for it, but now we're finding out that we missed the real story. Are you in or out?"

"I'm going to be trying a few things that private detectives do without raising anybody's eyebrows. I'll let you know what I find."

A minute later, Duncan was off the phone and packing for another trip to Ash County, Indiana. He included the usual equipment—his laptop computer, his two Glock pistols and his gun case with two AR-15 knockoff .223 rifles, and loaded ammunition magazines. In his toolbox he had his burglary tools and a fresh pack of disposable prepaid cell phones.

The drive from Chicago had become a familiar one now. He had done it several times on different routes, and was comfortable and easy on all of them. He knew the places where cops would wait for speeders, the exits and entrances that had misleading signs that might cause a driver ahead of him to suddenly change his mind, the upward stretches where a big truck might have to labor a bit, and the grades where an overloaded truck gained too much speed. For this trip he reverted to a favorite method, which was to sleep early in the evening, wake around 2:00 A.M., and leave around three. Traveling at night kept the major highways mostly clear of passenger cars. Often his only company was long-haul fourteen-wheelers, whose giant trailers lined up in the right lane and only passed each other occasionally and with adequate warning. The hour also kept his arrival at his destination less likely to be noticed.

He had to admit his first quiet arrival for his undercover assignment in Ash River country had been a disaster. Within an hour of his arrival he had been in hand-to-hand combat with his first two gangsters. The only way he'd had to keep the story from becoming local gossip was to drag them off to the state police two hours away in a citizen's arrest and come back to The Elbow Room to make a friend of Renee Parkman, something which had taxed even Duncan's capacity for disinformation and obfuscation.

Duncan was no longer under the impression that what he had accomplished so far was to solve the main problems. That part of this situation had just been the start, and now he was only trying to learn what the rest of it was. The county seat of Ash County was Riverbend, about ten miles north of Parkman's Elbow, where his face had become familiar to people. In Riverbend, the only people who had reason to even recognize him were the deceased Clark brothers and Mona, the owner of the Riverbank Restaurant. He hoped he didn't run into her, and hoped more fervently that he didn't find himself wherever the Clarks were spending eternity.

Duncan drove into the main business district looking for a diner or food business of any kind that was open at six A.M. After one circuit around the area on the most promising streets he found a doughnut shop with its lights on and people moving around behind a counter. There were three tables inside, so he parked at the curb a block away and walked to the shop slowly enough to give them time to get ready to open. When he arrived, a middle-aged Asian man he assumed was the owner was just unlocking the front door.

He ordered two of the plump cream-filled doughnuts with chocolate frosting that he saw on a tray in the display case and a large cup of coffee to keep the proportions balanced. He could see through a half-open door a woman about the man's age take a tray of crumb doughnuts out of a big oven to cool, and a much younger woman pick up a metal tray of glazed doughnuts and bring it in for the display case.

The man said, "Are you with the FBI?"

Duncan said, "Not me. I work for a living."

"Oh. We've been getting a lot of FBI in the shop lately, because of the stuff that's been going on around here."

"Well, it's not a myth that cops like doughnuts. And it's just as well to have them around for a while, I think. At least until everything gets cleared up and we know it's safe."

"I don't think the area is ever going to be the same, though," the man said. "A lot of people have already moved away. Our neighbors on both sides are gone, and three of the businesses in this block are empty."

"How did that happen?" Duncan said.

"People got scared. There were creepy guys trying to get people to pay them to leave them alone. A few people got their windows smashed, some of them or their customers beat up. And you know how it is. When a lot of people start selling out, other people get scared that if they wait too long, everybody else will be gone and their places will be worthless. In another month the town would have been a ghost town, just another bunch of bricks for archaeologists to dig up in a thousand years."

"Did you ever see any of the paperwork for those sales?"

"No," the man said. "I saw one of the cashier's checks, though. A friend of mine sold his house and some land. They weren't paying what things were worth. But maybe now they are worth only that little. I keep wondering if we'll have any regular customers coming in after the FBI people go."

Duncan said, "Do you happen to recall what the name on the cashier's check was?"

"What name do you mean?"

"A cashier's check usually says who the purchaser of the check is."

"Gerald Russell Development."

"Interesting," Duncan said. "Development." He felt his enthusiasm draining away. He had hoped that this one single step might be easy. Russell was a broker, not the principal in the purchase. Duncan had been hoping to hear a name he didn't know.

34

At seven-forty-five Duncan set off for the county office building. In his experience the offices in county seats tended to open at eight o'clock, mostly for the convenience of the people from law offices who needed to submit papers or research deeds, permits, or judgments. He liked to be in this first group, because they were used to the procedures, tended to be quick, and were mostly too smart to be rude to the clerks. Beginning around ten they were mostly replaced by random members of the public, some of whom were none of those things. When he arrived, he was only third in line at the counter, and his request was simple. He wanted to see the changes of ownership of real property in Ash County for the past two years. The clerk gave him a printed list to aid in title searches.

Duncan was amazed. There were hundreds of purchases in the past year, but few during the year before that. The most common way for land to change hands a year ago had been inheritance. Everything changed eleven months ago, when Russell Development started buying. The number of title changes filed by Russell Development had begun at twelve a year ago in

March, and grown rapidly. Duncan studied the list. Some of the purchases were businesses he had seen or even entered, restaurants where he had eaten. Others were houses on streets he had come to know. There were also farms, some of them a hundred acres or more, and some of the parcels the city had obtained over the years were much bigger than that.

He picked up certain trends immediately. Russell had begun by buying up places as close to the Ash River as possible. Duncan could also see that Russell had managed to cause some panic sales. A single house on Bancroft Street in Pine Bend had sold for a price that was barely on the low side early in the process, but then others sold in later months, each one for less. In the past month there had been ten on Bancroft, as though the owners were competing not to be the last.

In the later months there had been some mass purchases. Ash County had land it had taken over—some of it referred to as "wooded" or "unimproved"—apparently abandoned or foreclosed for unpaid taxes decades earlier. Russell Development had bought it in individual transactions, but they all had been registered in the same week. It looked to Duncan as though the county had seen the opportunity to unload it as a godsend.

Duncan's discoveries went on and on. Russell had apparently not cared what the features of the property were. He had wanted it all. The morning went by without Duncan noticing the time. He looked at the entries all the way up to May 15, the day when Gerald Russell committed suicide. And then he noticed that one of the most recent entries was different from the others. Because the words Russell Development had been on all the entries he'd examined, this one hadn't caught his eye at first.

This entry was a two-day-old notation that a court action had occurred in the State of Illinois allowing an entity called "Grow" to claim ownership of Russell Development, Gerald Russell Inc., Russell Estates, and Russell Holdings. It noted that the company had given Russell Development $985 million in loans, with all assets of the Russell-owned companies as collateral.

Duncan took photographs of the list with his telephone before he returned it to the clerk. In a moment he was outside calling the number Ellen Leicester had written on the index card.

"Harry?" she said.

"Yeah, it's me again. I found something. Have you heard of a company called 'Grow'?"

"Yes. All the big companies that want to seem young and lively have lately changed their names to something that doesn't really mean anything. Meta and Alphabet and so on. Grow used to be called Consolidated Industries. Before that it was the Mr. Food Corporation."

"That I would have recognized. I guess I don't have enough investments to keep up."

"I put my money into a blind trust when I went to work for the government. For all I know, when I retire I won't have cab fare to get home. You and I are still two people who never gave a crap about money. I live on my paychecks. I just know about that company's name changes because they break a lot of federal rules and have to keep settling and correcting. How did they come up?"

"I was looking at the real estate that Gerald Russell scared people into selling him. There's much more of it than I thought. But the big thing is that the day after Russell died, Grow filed a claim in Illinois to assert ownership of all the assets of Russell's companies. The reason is that they lent Russell almost a billion dollars, with his companies as collateral."

"Where in Illinois did they file?"

"It doesn't say."

"I'll assign somebody to find out and get us a copy of the claim."

"Make sure that whoever you assign doesn't just ask them. We've got to keep finding things out by looking the other way. Once they know you're aware of what they're doing, things will get harder."

"You're right, of course. We'll be up to our butts in company lawyers sent to smother us with a million pounds of word salads. Big companies always do that to bleed the government of time and manpower."

"There could be more than that this time. Most big companies aren't hiding involvement in murders. Once you've had a dozen or so people killed, one or two more don't add much stress."

"I'll keep my distance from it," she said. "It's a routine procedure that's done a thousand times a year. Any time a huge corporation does a billion-dollar deal, it might get referred to us for possible problems by Treasury, the SEC, any number of federal or state regulators. We're used to it, and so are the companies."

"Will you let me know if anything interesting turns up?"

"If I can," she said. "Ethics and confidentiality, you know."

"I think—" It seemed to him that the background sound was different, and he realized she had disconnected. "Forget what I think," he muttered. He determined not to resent her reassertion that their roles were different. There had to be a wall separating Justice Department prosecutors from outsiders, and even though he had done some work for the government, he was not part of it. He put his phone away and went back into the Ash County office building.

There were other things to look for. He searched the tax rolls for assessments on office buildings or other facilities that were owned by Grow. Then he checked for any under the old name, Consolidated Industries. Next he looked for business permits under either name, then for fictious business name declarations. When he reached the end of those searches, it was midafternoon, and he was hungry and had reached the degree of fatigue that made him admit that if he didn't take a break he would start missing things in the records.

He walked out of the building. After sitting for so many hours he felt like walking, so he headed for the river and found his way to the Riverbank Restaurant. As he came closer, he detected a sense of surprise in himself. So much had happened so quickly that he had unconsciously expected some visible change, but there was none. The parking lot looked as full as it was the day he had come for lunch, and he could smell food cooking as he stepped up on the wood decking on the porch to reach the doorway.

He entered and saw the elderly woman was at the lectern waiting to seat the next guest. She gave him her professional glance—acceptable sport coat and pressed shirt but no tie, respectable but casual shoes—and said, "One, sir?" He wondered if she recognized him from his first visit but found her unreadable. She conducted him to a good seat, a table for two by the window shaded by the awning where he could see the river but not be in the sun's glare, and he felt he had passed some test.

The waiter who came to him was a woman about thirty years old with her blond hair pulled back in a tight bun. She set a newly printed menu with today's date on it in front of him and then recited two dishes that must have been added after the menu went to press, and then left him alone to think about his choice.

While he was choosing, his phone vibrated with a text. He read it. "Co has 1st Deed of Trust on ea prpty & Prom Note for ea loan. Ironclad." He texted back, "Thx."

He looked out on the river. Here the course was narrow and deep, with a one-foot muddy margin along the far bank where a few gray and white killdeer strutted on four-inch stilt-legs spearing invisible prey. He felt he was looking at a scene that was already fading.

If Ellen and her people saw nothing to keep Grow from undisputed ownership of a few miles on both sides of the Ash River, then in a year or two this place would only exist in people's blurring, shifting memories. The river would be captured to flow through a culvert and the banks would be a strip mine with spiraling roads for the big trucks to haul the dirt up from below to reach some kind of factory for the latest separation and refining process.

When the waitress returned, he asked if the trout was locally caught, and when she said no, he ordered it. He waited for his lunch watching the river, but after it came, he returned his attention to the people in the restaurant. The first time he had been in this dining room he had seen a man that Charlie Dennison had later identified as Mullins. He was the one Duncan had watched on a recording breaking into his condo in Chicago. This time, he knew Mullins was in the custody of Indiana State Police in Indianapolis. It crossed his mind that all the people in the building probably thought the troubling time was over. It was likely that he was the only one here who knew it wasn't.

The group of professional criminals Russell had recruited had been nothing but a way of clearing the inhabitants of the region out of the way to prepare the ground for the arrival of the future.

He finished his lunch, looked around at the room, and noted that it was a special place—the old wood hand-fitted and then hand-polished for most of a century would not be retained in any future that was possible. After the coming destruction was over and the rare earth mines played out, there probably would be nobody left who wanted the place back, and the lavish use of prime wood would no longer be a practical investment. The original forests were long gone already, and the thinner second-growth replacements would be bulldozed soon to make way for the strip mines. He accepted the likelihood that he would never see the restaurant again.

He paid his bill, got up, stepped out on the wooden board quay by the river, and walked to the lot by the river road. He started the walk back toward the central part of Riverbend, going to his left close to the left edge of the parking lot, so he could see any cars coming toward him. He was now hoping to exhaust the county's public records today. There wasn't much incentive to spend more than one day on it if the opposition had already won.

It wasn't a shock. Duncan had spent his adult life following the activities of loathsome people after they'd already done serious damage, and then finding ways to help prosecutors prove it to juries. He had always started after the murder had been committed, the armed robbery was over, the tainted heroin had been sold to a hundred people and ten of them were dead. Detectives always arrived on the scene when the blood was already spilled and drying, and his next months would be spent struggling to make up the lost time, to catch up so that finally, the day would come when he and the perpetrator were together on the same piece of ground.

This time, the records he had seen told him that the crime had been fully conceived and its execution under way at least a year before Ellen had called him. The entity behind it was here and growing before his great grandparents decided there wasn't much in the British Isles to hold them there. He wasn't sure there would be something he—or the Justice Department—could do, but he would try. Businesses could engage in all sorts of secret moves and deceptive actions, and they could hire questionable people to help them make money without breaking any laws. But their business practices couldn't include murder. This time they had.

He walked a little faster as he thought about it. Today he would keep searching for information until the county office building closed. Maybe he would have to come back for another day, or another week, but he would be sure he had everything he could find before he gave up.

He heard a car coming across the parking lot behind him. The sound was low, mostly the small pieces of gravel the tires kicked up ticking against the steel chassis and the whisper of the rubber, but then the engine grew louder, and he lost the sense of how close it was. He started to turn his head to the right to find out, and all his senses seemed to sharpen.

He dived to the left over the curb toward the mound of grass and shrubs. The driver of the car must have anticipated this would be his direction and swerved closer, hoping to tag some part of his body while he was in the air.

Duncan landed on top of a two-foot privet hedge, and instinctively pulled in his legs to bring them out of the car's reach. In an instant it was apparent that the arc of the driver's sudden swerve had extended too far. The car's left front wheel hit the curb and bounced up over it onto the landscaped strip. The driver accelerated and corrected his course to the right, but when the wheel dropped down to the parking lot the tire was flat, the left wheel was far out of alignment, and the air bag had deployed. The car was still moving, but the wheel was wobbling and in a moment the rim was scraping on the pavement, pulling the car back to the left, where it lodged against the curb.

Duncan sprang up and ran to reach the car. The man in the driver's seat had already released the clasp of his seat belt, but the inflated air bag was pressing him back against the seat. Duncan could see he had somehow gotten a knife out of his pocket and was stabbing the bag to try to deflate it, but seemed to be failing.

Duncan ran to the car, but approached cautiously, staying in the man's blind spot. When he was close enough, he could see that the man's movements had taken on a panicky quality, flailing to get out. Duncan flung the door open and said, "Leave the knife on the passenger seat and I'll get you out."

The man hesitated.

Duncan took a step forward as though looking at the front of the car. "Looks like you scraped your fuel line when you went over the curb. Do you smell gas?"

The man said, "Oh, no. Help me." He dropped the knife. The man's face was half-smothered in the air bag, so his panic seemed to be getting worse.

With the door open Duncan could see the seat adjustment controls, so he pushed the horizontal and the tilt toward the rear of the car, and the seat slid back and the backrest pulled the man away from the airbag and Duncan tugged the man out by his left arm.

It didn't escape Duncan's notice that the panic hadn't kept the man from retrieving his knife while the seat had been moving back. Duncan was ready when the man pivoted to bring the knife around toward his belly. Since Duncan was still holding on to the man's left arm, the stabbing must have seemed easy, but it also kept Duncan close enough to kick the man's legs out from under him before the man sensed it was happening.

The man hit the pavement hard, but rolled to start to push himself up, a movement that gave Duncan an instant to stomp on the man's right hand to make holding the knife too painful. The man opened his hand and Duncan kicked the knife under the car.

Duncan held him on his belly with his left arm up behind his back. "Who sent you?"

"Nobody. It was an accident. The sun got in my eyes when I made the turn. Get off me."

Duncan patted the man down, tugged out his wallet, and looked at the driver's license. "Chicago, Illinois." He set the wallet down open and took out his phone to photograph it. "Joseph Minter." The man strained to look at the wallet on the ground beside his head, and Duncan took a photograph of his face and used his free hand to search the wallet for business cards or a company ID, but didn't find any.

He stood up and said, "I know I met you on a bad day, Joe, but any day you meet somebody who does this for a living is going to be a bad day for you. You don't have the vision or the reflexes to make it as a killer. If you're willing to accept some help I can get it for you, and you could be out of this mess. You still haven't done anything that will stick to you. We can just leave this looking like a minor accident."

Joe Minter shook his head and chuckled. "You're a hard guy, and you have all the instincts, except the instinct to pay attention."

"What are you talking about?"

"You don't notice that nobody like you dies on a big case. Today you didn't get hit by a car. Tomorrow maybe you won't overdose. Another day maybe you won't step in front of a train or choke on a steak or just vanish. But people who make a career out of getting in the way don't die of old age."

"Getting in whose way?"

"Everybody's."

Duncan looked at him for a moment, then turned and walked back toward the county building. He looked over his shoulder after a hundred feet and saw Joseph Minter standing up, talking on his cell phone. Just before Duncan passed the last place in the road where he could still see the parking lot, he looked back and saw Minter on his hands and knees reaching under his disabled car to pick up his knife.

35

Duncan went past the county office building and walked to his car. He searched it thoroughly, including the engine compartment, underside, and trunk, but didn't find the transponder he had expected.

He drove toward the south this time, and checked into a hotel in Scottsburg that was small enough so he could sit in the bar and watch the lobby at the same time. He had never been to Scottsburg before and couldn't think of anything that connected the town with the case, but it made him feel better that he didn't see anybody come in who might have worried him—a man without a wife or girlfriend, a pair of men checking in with little or no luggage, anybody whose eyes betrayed curiosity about him. He went to his room, locked the lock, bolt, and chain, and then set a wastebasket far enough in front of the door so it would make a noise if the door swung open into it. He slept deeply until his phone rang at nine in the morning.

"Yes?"

He heard Ellen's voice. "Are you in the county office building?"

"No. A hotel."

"Scored, huh? Is she still there?"

"I'm alone. I'm positive we're on the right track now. A guy tried to run me over with his car. I had a talk with him. He implied that it was at least partly a warning. People who get in the way die mysterious deaths, the sort that don't raise any eyebrows—accidents and things. He also mentioned overdoses."

"Jeanette is dead," Ellen said. "Did he say anything to connect him with Grow?"

"No. Just that the forces we don't want to obstruct are everybody. Do you have a pen?"

"Of course I have a pen."

"His name is Joseph Minter, and he lives in Chicago." He read the address from the photo of the license. "I'm sure your people can find out who he is, and maybe how he's connected with Grow. Do you have anything new?"

"Sort of old and sort of new. You probably know there was a law passed in 1950 called the Defense Production Act. It's been resurrected a couple of times in recent years—once to help produce the Covid-19 vaccines, and once to get obstacles out of the way of mining more minerals, primarily lithium, nickel, cobalt, and a few others for battery technology. But apparently Grow has started exploring the possibility of getting it invoked to speed up what they're trying to do."

"These people never sleep."

"If you're a big corporation you can have a lot of people doing different things at once. The problem is that building a domestic source of rare earths is a pretty good fit, the kind of thing the law was made to promote."

"If they hadn't been killing people to accomplish it, I'd probably be fine with it," Duncan said. "Have you seen anything they've submitted to get government approval?"

"We haven't found anything on paper yet," she said. "There was a tip from a finance reporter. It seems their lobbyists are having one-on-one conversations with members of Congress. I think it's to see if they can line up the votes to get around environmental studies and short-circuit the permit process. Neither side of that would want anything in writing."

"All right," he said.

"What do you mean by that?"

He recognized the tone. In the old days it was the tone she used when she was getting irritated and defensive. He was too tired and frustrated to want to get trapped. "I meant they're being smart about this. Your finding out was great work, but the news is not good news."

She said, "You sound as though you don't have any confidence in me."

"I do. I just had to prevent a man from killing me with a car, and then keep him from stabbing me to death by taking his knife away. I probably sound tired."

"Wow." That expression of feigned amazement was often the way she used to begin her negative interpretations of his actions. "I remember this. Whatever I bring to the table gets pushed off and belittled to make room for the Tales of Brave Harry."

"You know that isn't what I was doing. I've learned you're a great US Attorney, and you always were a great prosecutor." He wished he hadn't said the last part, and he kept talking to bury it. "I'm sure you'll find some way to prove what's really happening. Right now, I'm going to figure out my next move to learn more on this end. Let's keep each other informed. Bye."

He pressed the red oval to end the call and put the phone in his pocket. He felt it vibrating a moment later, looked at the screen, and saw she wasn't ready to let him go. He considered answering, then thought better of it and turned off the phone.

He had no desire to listen to her parting shot right now, and he didn't owe her that. Before she had left him fifteen years ago had been the time to talk about his failings. Now there was no point. He had meant it when he'd said she was great at her work, but that was the only sphere he was willing to inhabit with her. He was sure he had as many flaws as ever, but they had ceased to be problems of hers the moment fifteen years ago when she had left the key on the kitchen table and walked out the door.

Duncan kept mulling over the things he knew in order to find the spaces that lay between them. He knew all about the thirty-five professional criminals Russell had recruited and set loose on the Ash River region. He knew a great deal about Russell and nearly as much about Russell's girlfriend Jeanette Walrath. It was all in the murder book.

He now knew what had motivated the whole enterprise, the discovery of concentrated deposits of rare earth minerals around and under the Ash River by Grow, a company that was big enough and rich enough to mine, separate, refine, and exploit the minerals. It would be an enterprise that had not been accomplished yet anywhere in the country.

There had been two much smaller companies trying to do it out west, but at least one of them was already out of business, and the other had not had the size, people, or money that Grow had. Once Grow bought the small company or killed it, they would have a domestic monopoly on a commodity necessary to make a piece of technology that virtually every person in the world carried every day.

Duncan knew, and Ellen could prove, that Grow had funded Russell's violent scheme to depopulate and acquire a large part of the Ash River region. Part of the company's claim to owning the land now that Russell was dead had been to prove to a court that they had lent him nearly a billion dollars to buy out the old owners, and to show that they held the first deed of trust, on every piece of land.

Their claim, made hastily right after Russell's death, had also proven other things. It had proven that Grow knew before Russell bought anything that the land was going to be worth billions of dollars. Grow knew that Russell's company had no other significant assets or agreements to offset their claim to own all Russell's company's assets.

There were a few things missing. The only one he needed was proof that someone, some specific human being or set of human beings, dealt with Gerald Russell directly and was aware of the scheme to scare people out of the towns along the Ash River, even if it meant murdering a few to increase the fear and speed up the exodus. If Duncan found that, he would have everything. A few years ago, the Supreme Court had stupidly ruled that a corporation had to be treated as a person, but that didn't mean a corporation could be put in prison. He had to find the human being who had caused these crimes.

He needed a name.

36

Duncan spent the next two days reviewing the version of his murder book that he had put on the laptop and sent to Ellen's office before the arrests. He read over the reports he had written on events, interviews, and observations. Occasionally he would stop and look at videos and still photographs he had taken to refresh his memory or confirm details.

He was well into the second day when his thoughts drifted to Ellen. He wondered what she and her people had found out in the past seventy-two hours. She hadn't seen any need to get in touch with him, probably because that request had been the last words he'd said to her. As he was running through his memory of the conversation, hearing her voice in his mind, something came back to him from an even earlier conversation.

When he had called her to tell her what he had just learned from Professor Saskin the ornithologist, she had made a comment about how complex this case had already become. She had said something about prosecuting thirty-five defendants in a dozen murders and hundreds of other felonies.

He had no choice. He picked up his phone and called her again.

"At your service, Harry," she said. "Maybe you can make it short and sweet, though. I've got work to do."

"I will. A couple days ago, you mentioned the figure 'thirty-five defendants.' Did you mean about thirty-five, or exactly thirty-five?"

He heard her laugh. It was a particular laugh, and as he pictured her, he knew she was looking down at her desk and shaking her head. "You've known me for seventeen years," she said. "Which do you think it was?"

"The reason I called was that I think it was probably an exact number."

"Good for you," she said.

"I don't want to waste your time, but do you have on hand the names?"

"You want me to read you the list of defendants? We got them from your murder book, Harry. After that, it was just verifying."

"They're all in custody, right?"

"Yes. Some local or state, some federal. The bail amounts are in the millions. Grow could bail them all out with petty cash, but that would be like a guilty plea."

"Do you have it, though?"

"I do now. Ready?" She began to read the names, and Duncan wrote a numbered list at the same time. When she came to the end she said, "Well? That's thirty-five."

"We missed one."

"Who?"

"The driver. Russell had a driver. When I was hiding in the kitchen cupboard in Paul Rankin's condominium, Jeanette

Walrath came in with a man to make drinks. She asked who wanted what, and the man said, "Gil is driving, so just water for him."

"That doesn't prove anything."

"Right now, proving is not what I'm doing. I'm trying to figure this out. Russell's driver was really good at it. I saw him driving away from The Elbow Room in a Lexus the night it closed. At that time I didn't know who Russell was, and I assumed the driver was just one of a smart pair of thugs who left before they got arrested. After my visit to Paul Rankin's condo, I followed the black Escalade to Russell's office, saw Russell and Jeanette get out, and saw another man take the Escalade to the lot next door to park it. That had to be Gil. At the end of the evening when the cops rounded up the men who had laid siege to the police station, he was already driving Russell and Jeanette to Chicago."

Ellen was silent for a few seconds. Then she said, "And the team that was at the Russell building to serve the warrant didn't find anybody except Russell and Jeanette there, both dead. No driver."

"I need some access."

"To what?" she said.

"First, I need to talk to Charlie Dennison, and see if he knows what Gil's last name is, or anything else about him. He may have recruited him."

"Give me an hour. I'll call you when I've got it set up."

Duncan spent the next hour at his desktop computer looking at phone videos and stills he had taken during the times when he'd been in proximity to members of the criminal organization. Most of them were too dark to see anything much even when he tried to lighten them, and all were taken from too far away to show a face, no matter how much he stretched them.

The call came on the hour.

There were no greetings. It was just Ellen's voice. "Can you be at the Metropolitan Correctional Center on Van Buren Street in an hour?"

"Sure."

"An FBI agent named Ron Keller will be waiting for you. Let me know what you get."

"Okay. Thanks."

Duncan was there ten minutes early. As he walked into the foyer he spotted the agent waiting while he stepped to the metal detectors, emptied his pockets into a plastic tray on the conveyer, walked through the arch, and stood still while the guard ran the electronic wand over his clothes.

As he stepped to the end, the agent waited while the guard examined his belongings, put them in a bag and labeled them with his name, then set them in a cabinet.

Duncan turned and the FBI agent said, "Mr. Duncan? Come with me."

They didn't speak on the walk to their destination, which was down a hallway, through a set of bars, and up to a plain door. "Right in here," the agent said, then opened the door for him to enter.

It was a standard room of the sort that was probably used for conferences between inmates and their lawyers. The chairs were better than the ones in interrogation rooms. Duncan chose one that gave him a view of the door. The agent took out a small, plain pad and a sharpened pencil and set them in front of Duncan, and then said, "I'll stand by outside. All you have to do when you finish is open the door."

"Thanks," Duncan said. He wondered how much Agent Keller knew about him, but he clearly wasn't used to doing this kind of thing. Duncan realized that Ellen would have said very little, and that what she'd said hardly mattered anyway.

The door opened and Charlie Dennison came in while a guard held the door. He was wearing a prison jumpsuit, white socks, and sandals. He looked rested, walked a little better, and was standing up straighter.

He sat down across from Duncan, and the guard stepped outside.

"Hello, Charlie," Duncan said. "Are you making out all right?"

"So far nobody's killed me. Accomplishing that is a little lonely, but it's enough for now. My lawyer tells me if I'm a good boy I won't regret it."

"Good advice."

"You didn't come here to ask after my health. What do you want to know?"

"Russell's driver. His first name is Gil. What's his last name?"

"This is a little embarrassing. I don't know."

"You didn't recruit him?"

"No. I didn't know him before this mess, and the times when I saw him, he was kind of separate."

"How?"

"He wasn't talkative, or anything. He didn't hang out with anybody much. He would show up with Russell in the car, and if Russell got out to talk to somebody or something, he would stay with the car. If he got out, he'd be cleaning the windshield or checking the air in the tires or looking at his phone. He's big on looking at his phone. The only person he talked to that I could see was Russell, and all he said to him was 'Yes sir.'"

"Did you notice anything distinctive about him—looks, accent, tattoos, that kind of thing?"

"Nothing that strikes me. He's about five nine, kind of slim, short brown hair and brown eyes. He isn't the kind of guy who's big and crazy-eyed or anything, so in that crowd he wasn't the one you watch. It was just that you saw Russell one time and he was driving himself, and then the next time you saw him this guy was driving him. No explanation or introduction. That wasn't how Russell did things. And I didn't see him often. I guess I noticed the driver probably in February or March, but he might have been hired much earlier and I didn't know."

"This is a disappointment. Is there anybody else who might know more, like where he's from or who hired him?"

"Tim Mullins. He could even be the one who hired him, come to think of it. He was the guy in charge of most of the routine stuff, day to day."

"Okay," Duncan said. "If you think of Gil's last name, or anything else, tell a guard you need to talk to the US Attorney."

"I will," Dennison said.

Duncan stood and walked to the door. "Good luck, Charlie."

"Same to you."

As soon as Duncan had retrieved his belongings near the building exit, he heard his name. The FBI agent was trotting up the hall toward him. "Wait," he said. "He's got something else to say."

Duncan handed the bag back to the guard and turned back to follow the agent back to the room. The agent opened the door, and Dennison was sitting there smiling. "Banks."

"What about banks?"

"It came back to me. It's his name, Gilbert Banks. He's the driver."

37

"**G**ive me twenty-four hours," Duncan said. "When that time is up, or before, I'll give you his name and location."

"What are you saying?" Ellen said. "You know that's not something I have the right to do—give a private operator permission to go out and do his own criminal investigation in a federal criminal case."

"I didn't ask for permission. I told you what I'm going to do. You're in the clear."

"What if you get killed?"

"I've got a computer and two phones programmed to send you emails when the time comes, if I'm alive or not."

"You know I didn't mean that, Harry."

"I know you didn't. You can be my mildly sad widow. Nobody else has emerged to take that job away from you. Look, Ell. We know we're not going to change each other's minds on this. Just sit tight and I'll get back to you."

Duncan hung up. He took both of his pistols and an extra loaded magazine, a few plastic ties, and checked to be sure he had his lock pick, tension wrench, and bump keys. He had already cleaned the lens covers of his security cameras, but he checked the display on his computer screen for clarity, and looked at the new keyhole camera he had added to the kitchen spice rack.

He left the condominium locked, and went down to his car in the underground garage. He came down the staircase and opened the steel door to the parking area an inch to be sure he was alone, then gave his car an extra thorough inspection to detect transponders, and this time, to spot any wires that had not been in the car when he'd bought it. There didn't have to be any devices. A car had many things about it that could be made to spark, and a cup of gasoline could have the explosive power of eleven sticks of dynamite. Grow was aware of him, and a company that size probably had thousands of engineers, thousands of electricians, and thousands of workers who maintained, drove, and repaired their fleets of cars and trucks.

Duncan was feeling a controlled excitement. He had learned the name, found the address, and was now on his way to find the man everybody had forgotten. In the desperate struggle to get the men with guns in their hands subdued, nobody had even given a thought to the driver. Duncan didn't know for sure, but he had a strong hunch about Gil Banks.

Duncan reached the address in midafternoon. It was in Back of the Yards, not far to the east of Midway Airport. He knew the area pretty well from his time working in the Chicago police department. Its name had come from the fact that it had been the site of the Union Stock Yards, and ran to the railroad tracks. Gilbert Banks was a driver, and that meant he needed space and flexibility for cars. Parking wasn't hard to get here, and most of the single houses in the area had garages. Gilbert Banks's house had one.

It looked as though this one had started as a single one, but the asphalt driveway had widened around the back, and an addition had been built to expand the garage by two more spaces. He probably worked on cars here.

Duncan knew that whatever else happened, it would be wise not to allow himself to get into a street chase with a professional driver. Duncan was good, but Banks was probably as good, and maybe better. Duncan knew these streets pretty well, but not like a man who lived here.

Duncan had not seen Gilbert Banks, only found his address online. There were photographs labeled with that name, which told him only that there were several of them in different parts of the country. He had picked this one on the basis of geography and probable age. This man was twenty-eight. Everything he was doing was built on probability rather than certainty. None of the Gil Bankses had a criminal record.

Duncan waited and watched the neighborhood in a loose surveillance. As he drove by the house the first time, he took a phone picture of it to show the cars parked nearby in case one belonged to Banks, the front of the house to show the positions of curtains, whether anything like a coiled hose was on the lawn, and then drove around the block to take a shot that included the back of the house. Then he kept going. For the next fifteen minutes he drove around the area to get a sense of the rest of the neighborhood, the fast streets that Banks could use to get away quickly, the commercial buildings and parking lots, the seldom-traveled streets where somebody like Duncan could lurk, watch, and wait.

Next he went to a small diner a mile away and sat at a booth beside a window where he could keep an eye on his car. He didn't know much about Banks. He did know that if he had been part of a criminal organization and he'd seen almost all the other members disarmed, handcuffed, and taken away by the police, he would be very watchful for a while, trying to detect whatever might be coming for him.

Duncan spent a few minutes searching the State of Illinois records to see if Banks was the owner of any cars. There were two. He had a black Cadillac CT5-V. Duncan noted the license number. He looked up a description of the CT5-V. The car wasn't too surprising for a man in Banks's profession. The car had a 668 horsepower engine and special technology to aid steering and handling, but looked like any high-end sedan. He also had a new blue Honda Accord, which was a good car, and not a bad choice for a driver who didn't want to be noticed. Russell must have paid him well, and he'd used some of it for two new cars.

Duncan drove past Banks's house again at dusk, and didn't detect any changes. This time he left his car in the street outside the diner and walked the rest of the way. It was fully dark when he arrived at the house, and there were no lights on in the house. He had always been extremely patient when he was investigating, but this time he couldn't afford to wait. This was an area of single-family one-story homes, so most people had good jobs. The neighbors all seemed to be off at work, and Duncan wanted to be inside before they returned.

He was over the back fence in seconds, went to the rear of the house, and looked in every window to detect an alarm panel, a window sticker, or anything that might be alarm wiring. Then he knelt at the back door, and used his lock picking kit to unlock it. When he was inside, he sat in the kitchen listening until his eyes grew accustomed to the faint light, and it felt safe to move.

First, he verified that there were no alarm panels he hadn't seen. Next he looked in the refrigerator and found fresh food, so Banks wasn't back in Indiana. He found the bedroom, discovered that the bed had been slept in, but not made.

Duncan went out the back door again and tried to find a window to look in and see if either of the cars was in the garage, but he couldn't find any glass surface anywhere. He could tell by sighting along the wall that there had once been a door on the yard side of the garage, but the door had been taken out, the space boarded over and painted, so nobody could break in.

Duncan went back inside and searched the house. He was looking for firearms, but apparently Banks hadn't thought of a gun as his best way to get through trouble, and so far, he had been right. Duncan looked for computers, address books, bank and credit card records, but he saw nothing of any interest. Gil Banks had a checkbook for a checking account at Chicago National, but the entries were for his electric bill, credit card bill, and phone bill. Duncan searched Banks's desk and took a picture of it so the FBI could get a record of the calls. The best thing Duncan found was a comfortable chair in the living room, so he sat in it, and waited.

After less than an hour, the living room window on the front corner lit up with headlights passing across it, and Duncan got up. He walked to the kitchen and watched Banks pull up to the garage, get out to open the padlock, and lift the garage door. Duncan saw he had been driving the black Cadillac. The Honda was already in the other side. Duncan stepped back and waited in the living room while Banks locked his garage and came in the kitchen door.

As Banks turned on the kitchen light switch and came up the short hall through the arched entrance to the living room, Duncan was taking a few deep, silent breaths to steady himself. Duncan fell into step behind Banks, wrapped his left forearm tightly across Banks's neck, and said, "Hi, Gil. I'm Harry Duncan. There's nothing to be afraid of. I don't want to hurt you."

Banks tried to struggle, but Duncan had been prepared for that. He concentrated on keeping his arm tight, pressing his left hip to Banks's back to avoid a counterattack, and riding through the bucking and attempts at headbutting. The struggle went on for about a minute in silence. Duncan let Banks tire himself out trying and failing to hurt Duncan, then to throw or shake him off, then to use his legs to run Duncan into a wall or over a piece of furniture. Duncan held on, tightening his grip whenever Banks's struggles made more of his neck accessible, shifting his own weight onto Banks. Then there was the first false surrender, when Banks rasped, "Okay, okay," and stopped trying to pry Duncan's forearm off his neck.

Duncan had been waiting for this. He loosened his grip, and instantly Banks made a quick move to spin around to face him. Duncan let him lurch forward, grasping his arm and pulling it up behind his back. He guided Banks to the floor onto his stomach and straddled him. He produced one of his plastic ties, dragged Banks's other arm behind him, and bound the two wrists together.

Duncan got up and sat on the easy chair, watching Banks lying on his stomach with his face in the carpet, panting to catch his breath. Duncan said, "I understand your being scared, Gil, but I'm not here to harm you. I just want to talk."

Banks lay there panting, but said nothing.

Duncan said, "You were there for the stupid attack on the police station, so I guess you know about that. You got Russell and Jeanette back here to Chicago. I don't know how much you heard since then, so I'll assume you've just stayed out of sight a few days and know nothing. Russell and Jeanette are both dead. They either got together and stuck each other with two of Jeanette's needles, or one stuck the other and then realized the FBI was breaking in the door and decided to avoid prison. I don't know. Did you know?"

"I don't care."

"Neither do I, really," Duncan said. "But that leaves you."

"What about me?"

"I want to know some things. The Justice Department does too. I got to you first. You're in a tricky position. They could charge you with speeding and give you a stern warning, or they could charge you with being part of a conspiracy to commit multiple murders."

"Let them."

"You should rethink that. The Justice Department has an unbelievable record for convictions. Part of it is that they're thorough. In group crimes they interrogate everybody. Lying to them is a crime that they prosecute. And they have very wide latitude. They've arrested thirty-five men so far. They're all convicts, so they know how the game works better than you do. The man who is the first to tell the truth and give testimony about the others wins big. He gets off pretty close to free, and the others all take their turns, the smart ones racing to cooperate before the others, and to give more information than the others can offer. Do you think none of them is going to throw you in to sweeten his chance of a deal?"

"You're wasting your time."

"I know Tim Mullins hired you."

"Who told you that?"

"Did he know you from before, or did he just ask around to find a good driver?"

"It doesn't matter."

"I wondered how well you know him. He's in jail right now, and there's nothing he can do to protect you. But he seems to me to be about the smartest one, so he might be talking already. I would be."

"I didn't do anything but drive Russell's cars." As Banks said it, Duncan could see he was beginning to think about Mullins.

"That's all I know about you. The Justice Department knows the same. They could take another way of looking at that. Were you present for any murders, like the two at The Elbow Room the night it closed for good? And they'll ask that, and if you called the police, as you're supposed to. Did you ever carry a gun anywhere at any time? You have to be careful to tell the truth, even about small things."

"What do you want from me? Just to scare me?"

"I'm trying to scare you smart, to tell you how to save yourself. To be honest, I don't think you're anything but a driver. I'd rather see you be the big winner in this than any of those guys who couldn't wait to murder some old shopkeeper. I've got a lot of things I'd like to forget in this life, and I don't want one more."

"You really think I can get off easy?"

"I think the Justice Department guys would rather give you a chance than set free one they know instinctively is guilty. I know I can make at least one of them see it that way."

"What do you want to know?"

"Mullins hired you. Why?"

"I met him one time here in Chicago a couple of years ago. A guy we both knew introduced us. We spent a long time talking about cars, and then I took him for a little ride to show off the car I had then. Maybe he already knew I was a pro driver, or maybe he asked about me later. I forgot about him, but I guess he didn't forget me. He called me like a year later."

"What exactly did he say the job was?"

"Look, you won't regret it if you take these plastic things off my wrists and let me sit. I'll answer your questions."

"Okay. But if you make it necessary, I'll have to defend myself, and you won't like it." Duncan stood, took out his pocketknife, sliced the ties off, and put the knife away before Banks sat up, rubbing his wrists.

"Why did he hire you?"

"He didn't trust Mr. Russell," Banks said. "He thought he was doing things that Mullins didn't know about. He didn't feel like he was being let in on things that were going on."

"What did he want you to do?"

"Make Mr. Russell get used to me, learn to trust me, and take me for granted, like the car and I were just parts of one machine. You said Mullins was smart. You don't know how smart. It was exactly like he said. I took Mr. Russell everywhere. He would call my phone at all hours of the day or night and say, 'Pick me up,' or sometimes just, 'Back door of the office,' and I'd pull up there."

"And you were supposed to keep Mullins informed?"

"Where he went, who he saw, everything. But I didn't just tell him. I took pictures, videos. Stuff like that."

"How?"

"I always had my phone with me. It was usually plugged into the car outlet to stay charged. I would have it on all the time. Mullins gave me a pinhole camera that connected with it, and it was rigged to attach to the phone, or sometimes to a second phone that would be in the console—not hidden, just there. It was just like the other one, so if Mr. Russell saw it he would think it was the other one. As time went on, we got better at it. We rigged the cars—the Lexus and the big SUV—so whatever went on would get recorded. You just have to drill a small hole and fit it. The wires were under the upholstery."

"What happened to the recordings?"

"I forwarded them to Tim Mullins."

"Did you keep a copy?"

He looked uncomfortable. "No. I didn't feel I should do that."

"Damn," Duncan said. "If only you had, I know we could get you off. You know, you were just trying to gather evidence, because you were afraid if you didn't have it, the police wouldn't believe you. Hell, that was what I was doing."

Banks was staring at the carpet. After a few seconds he looked up. "I kept some of them."

Duncan could sense it was coming. He decided he had to try. "Did Mr. Russell ever meet with anybody from Grow?"

"What do you mean?"

"The big company. Their office is right up near the Art Institute."

"Oh, you mean Todd Storrings. Mr. Russell met with him a lot. A couple times they met outside the Art Institute. They would act like they didn't know each other."

"Then what?"

"They would kind of pass by each other. Then I'd take Mr. Russell somewhere and park, and Mr. Storrings would be somewhere on a nearby street. I would swoop in and he'd get into the car, and we'd be off again. When we were sure nobody had followed or anything, Mr. Russell would tell me to take a break. I would leave, and he'd call me when he was ready to go."

"This is really important. Do you still have any recordings from any of those meetings?"

"All of them."

"Can you show me any of them?"

"I guess so."

Two hours later, Duncan dialed the number of Ellen Leicester's cell phone.

She answered, and her voice didn't sound sleepy. "Duncan?"

"Good guess. You sound pretty alert."

"I just got your email, with Gilbert Banks's address. How the hell am I supposed to sleep after that? Did you talk to him?"

"Oh yes."

"Has he got anything worthwhile?"

"Yes. And now I've got it too."

38

The video showed Todd Storrings, a man about sixty years old wearing a well-tailored gray suit, white shirt, and a dark blue tie with a subdued pattern of tiny red diamonds, and Gerald Russell, sitting in the back seat of the big black SUV. The tint on the side windows was very dark, so it would have been impossible for anyone outside to tell there was anyone in there, let alone who they were. Russell said, "Thank you very much for coming through on short notice, Mr. Storrings."

Storrings, whose demeanor conveyed a calm confidence, said, "You said you needed it right away for the buyouts."

"I do. I know the transfers will be instant, but it will take a few days for the checks to clear. I don't want somebody to see the death in the papers, realize all that farmland must be for sale, and outbid us."

Storrings smiled. "Particularly when it's a death the company paid you for?" He reached into the inner pocket of his suit coat and pulled out an envelope, but he held on to it and used it to emphasize what he said next, his face turning stony. "You need to time these things better. Remember, every single one of these transactions is going to be audited and looked at from every direction, beginning in time for the next quarterly report. None of them will ever go away, and none of them is legally confidential. If every time Grow transfers funds to the Russell Company it's right around the date when the owner of a property is killed or disappears, we've got a problem. Grow doesn't have any problem for long. Am I being too vague?"

"No, sir," Russell said. "I understand."

"Good. You'll notice that this time there are more checks drawn on more banks than usual. Pay attention to the dates, some of which are in the future. That's so we won't have to respond to any more emergency cash calls. Keep up the pace, but keep things strictly controlled. Grow has operations in every state and fifty-six countries. We use vendors and contractors just like you in all of them. Don't be the one who keeps coming up."

Storrings tossed the envelope on Russell's lap, turned to look through the tinted windows, then forward toward the windshield, then got out of the car and slammed the door.

Duncan stopped the video. "I think that's my favorite one." He closed his laptop and picked it up from her desk.

Ellen looked at him. "I can hardly believe it. Can you send it to me right away?"

"I already sent you all of them. This one I just sent separately in case you wanted to use it to help get you the warrants for Grow. And before I forget, the driver, Gil Banks, needs to be considered for leniency."

"That's another tough one. It's hard to argue this isn't proof he knew they were committing murder."

"An argument could be made that it proves he had reason to fear for his life if he went to the authorities. And you're going to need his testimony, just like Charlie Dennison's."

"I'll have him investigated. If he really didn't carry a gun, and didn't commit acts of violence, I'll have him canonized."

"Amen." Duncan stood and stepped to the door of her inner office.

"Are you leaving?" Ellen said.

"Yeah. I think it's time to get some sleep."

"I'll probably do the same as soon as I pass off all the work to my staff. Thanks for the evidence, Harry."

"You're welcome." He went out and closed the door behind him.

39

It was three years later when Harry Duncan decided to pay attention to the insistent ring of the cell phone he kept plugged in on the bottom shelf of the wall-size bookcase to the left of his desk. Since he had moved to California he had given up trying to store the murder books that recorded his cases on open shelves. Every time the ground shook a little, he didn't like having to pick them up off the floor. He had run a wire from one side of the bookcase to the other across each shelf so all the notebooks stayed where they were.

He picked up the phone and touched the green oval.

"Harry?"

"Yes?" he said.

"The last verdict came in on the last defendant from Grow. Guilty on all charges, including conspiracy to commit murder."

"Hi, Ellen. Congratulations. Who was this one?"

"His name is Stanley Sanders. He was vice president in charge of the legal division."

"They sure had a lot of vice presidents."

"This is the seventh one we convicted."

"Great."

"It's over, Harry. We're going to have an unofficial celebration tonight, all of the people who worked on the cases—the prosecutors, the investigators, the technicians, everyone."

"Good for you. Have you heard anything about the Ash River project? That was what it was all about, right?"

"I guess so. That we can't control. The Grow company is out of it, of course. Everybody who was anywhere near it has either gone to prison or been fired. But projects like that don't die. Once they found the mineral deposits in Indiana nobody was going to forget they were there. I've seen reports that said some giant tech companies are banding together to form a new corporation and buy the land and start mining. It seems to have strong support in Congress."

"I figured. Have a good time at the party. Get a sober FBI agent to drive you home."

"I wish you could come."

"That's okay. It's a long flight just to get a hangover when I can get one here. But thanks for letting me know, Ell. Have fun." He pressed the red oval to end the call and unplugged the phone.

As he walked back to the bedroom, his girlfriend said, "Who was that?"

"A client from about three years ago. A courtesy call, just letting me know the trial for the case turned out right. I'll tell you about it later."

"That was nice." She looked at him, and her deep green eyes widened and moved from his face down to his feet. Her head tilted a little, so the long red-brown hair hung like a curtain to her right shoulder. "Is that what you're wearing to dinner?"